Front Cover Design by Alice.

Alice is a partially-sighted 14 year old schoolgirl from Birmingham, diagnosed with autism. Despite these difficulties, Alice's big love in life is art and illustration. Alice has to overcome obstacles on a day-to-day basis that most of us take for granted. This includes creative opportunity, hence I offered her the chance to design the cover of this book, and from there have seen the significant amount of effort she's dedicated to this. On my side, I feel very honoured, privileged and thoroughly pleased with the end-result of her efforts. Alice, you're awesome :-), I know your family, friends and teachers will be very proud of you, as I have been, and that you can use this to get top grades and get into college when the time comes. Sidney :-)

ABOUT THE AUTHOR

Sidney Topham was born in 1969, grew up in Lincolnshire, attended Huddersfield University, and has been a lot of things, but mainly a youth worker in and around Sheffield for 25 years. His previous literary work consists of some very descriptive song lyrics in the early 1990s which he then gave away to some unbelievably awful recording artists, and some reviews, which might still be on the internet somewhere, of various late 90s/early 00s House, R&B and Trance nights across the North of England, successfully traded each time for a few drinks and a box of spicy chicken.

Acknowledgements....

For the help, patience and occasional bollockings they've given me, I'd like to offer much love, fistbumps, and sincere thanks to....Pagey for letting me make endless cups of tea whilst typing this, Bella for the grammar corrections, my football consultant Dan, Joan for coping with the swearing, Janet for coping with the football, Alice, Rachel my favourite childhood superhero, Samantha Arnold Buckingham, David, Claire for the regular supply of background goosebump trance, Lauren, Jean, Lesley, Roy, Gemma, Nicky, Kelly, every English teacher I ever had, especially the one who let me keep my badboy rep by publicly giving me detentions and letters to parents whilst privately enclosing my work with an A+ within the same sealed envelope, and finally to the one person who gave me the original idea and wishes to stay anonymous, but the original conversation went a little like this....

(Setting...A grim, bare waiting room in an emergency housing office in a large northern city)

"You know if anyone could be arsed, they could seriously write a book about all my shit."

"So have a go yourself then. It'll keep you occupied for a bit. "

"It'd be shit if I did it."

"You never know til you give it a pop."

"Why don't you have a go?"

"People would twig it were about you. I'd get in bother."

"So mash it up a bit. You've never been short of a lyric or two?"
"I only use those lyrics when I have to."

"If you never used them, I'd be inside. Maybe even worse than that. Remember that reference you did for me for court that time? The judge even said when he gave my homework out that if it weren't for that comprehensive and eloquent reference from you, I'd have got custodial."

"Like I said, I use those lyrics only when I've no other choice."

"That's a pity, fella. You've obviously not spotted people hanging on your every word when you're in full flow."

"No, not at all, pal. You're thinking of someone else."

And from there, I opened my eyes. I noticed. You weren't far wrong. So I've had a go. You're in here somewhere. Mashed up like you suggested. You'll spot it. Enjoy, fella. :-)

number, I'd choose the knackered old brick every time. Showered, properly, then tried doing something with my hair so it didn't look so 1983, but failed. There's always that one lad in 6th form who's thinning on top before he even sits his exams. Most people see his premature hair loss as a tragedy. If that ends up being me I so won't care.

Made my own breakfast unaided. I made porridge. It's easy. You just pour it into a bowl, add milk, microwave it for 2 minutes, then mix in whatever you fancy, Haribos, M&Ms, whatever. I sat on the bus so self-satisfied at my achievements, all the way with just a continuation of my porridge-induced daydream. I came round when I realised my phone will end up somewhere wet if other kids spot it. Even if I flashed an Iphone around, some arsehole would be flushing it down the toilet. If I was seen with this brick, it would be just one more excuse to delve into me, and the phone would still end up in the toilet. I lose either way, so I'd rather cost my Mum a tenner than £300 for the headache of it all.

Anyway, once I'm at the school gates I finally have a word with myself. I check no-one dodgy's walking towards me, get my phone out and type *"Hello, I'm free later today. Message me when you are and I'll meet you. Edward :-)"*. I check it twice for spelling and grammar, and, once sent, check twice that I've just sent it to Shelly and not Grandma. Bloody hell was it that difficult? Hardly worth the headache I've carried since yesterday afternoon. I look down the street one final time before I re-enter my personal torture chamber. I used to watch in awe when some of the year 11s and year 10s, girls mainly, walked in with lattes and frappe's. It convinced me that they were really mature and civilised, and maybe that "I'm so adult" look was something I could relate to. I see straight through it now. It's bullshit. Another tool to project affluence, used the same way as trainers or bags or phones to determine the top and bottom of the food chain in school. The kids who walk in sipping an iced latte see this as just like walking in in Versace. That delusion of wannabee adulthood's gone. I know better now.

Today's become one of those days where I've got places to be and people to see, so weirdly, I could do without education interfering with this too much and would actually welcome some form of harrassment as soon as possible. The first person to even stick their tongue out at me will be my excuse to walk through the ugly grey gates and meet my friend. Friend!! I walk the long way to registration due to the higher likelihood of getting abuse yelled at me from the year 8 rooms and the sports courts, and once in, stare at the worst kids in the class. Corey Hendricks's crew are the worst of the worst here, in my lessons at least. I catch their conversation. COD and GTA. That's mild for them. I already know which one of them goes loopy from cheap drugs laced with multiple chemicals, which one of them loses their shit from sugary drinks, who their top 5 kids they want to beat up is, and who their top 5 lasses that they want to "do" is, along with the sequence of sexual acts they'd "do" them. They're nothing new. There's another group of goons exactly like them in Moor Vale and if I walked into any other school round here, I'd find an exact copy of them in every year group.

Much as I detest them, today they can be useful to me. Come on, come at me, have a go, give me my chance to walk out of here. Two of them just look over at me and laugh, one of them nudges Cory and he clearly can't be arsed, looking over fleetingly before returning to whatever he was talking about. Bloody hell even the bullies here are crap. Back in the old days you could rely on them to break your nose as soon as they saw you look at them for too long. Nowadays, you can't rely on them to do their job properly at all.

Nothing happened in registration, so I hoped philosophy would be good for an argument that might go too far. We studied 1950s America, all that Alabama stuff where black kids got abused by stupid white people for the unforgiveable sin of wanting to get educated, and Rosa Parks

i) Animal Farm.

I can read. I can write. I can add together any numbers you give me, subtract them, divide them, multiply them, giving the answer in English, French, German and fucking Gaelic if you wish, so if anyone fancies explaining to me what the point is in turning up to this bullshit, then by all means, have a fucking go. Like, what do people really think I've been doing in Aunt Bernie's stinking trailer since age 10, and what exactly do they think they can tell me any better? I can put together 50 bacon butties before I even go to school, balance the till, even fix the generator if it packs up, and school thinks I'm behind? Maths, food tech and engineering all at once. School make you do all this separately. How backwards is that?

Anyways, it's not like I have much choice right now. Aunt Bernie parked her stinking van out on a site near the motorway just where Dad and my brothers are bulldozing some old ironworks down and telling everyone they're turning it into some massive shopping place that'll have a big shiny glass dome sticking out of it and 300 shops in it. Harrods, Selfridges, all them poncy places that charge £100 for a handbag, will open up in Attercliffe. They're talking shite. I mean, who's ever going to go shopping in Attercliffe? It's grim. There's nowt there worth stealing let alone buying. Nowt but burnt out warehouses and scrappies. Everything looks like it's been bombed. I've argued 'til I'm blue in the face that only a fool would ever try to buy a £100 handbag which some scally will rob off them before they even get to the bus stop. I try and tell Dad to get real and just accept that the old steel mill he's flattening will probably just be another Kwik-Save, but he's convinced that once he's flattened the whole site, it's gonna be a giant shopping mall, with some space age bubble train getting built to shuttle all the shoppers into the city centre and beyond. Everyone else agrees with him, saying they've heard the same. I could ask them what drugs they've been smoking, but they're beyond smoking anything at this rate. They're injecting straight into the intravenous.

So, not only do I refuse to buy into their nonsense, I miss out on twenty easy quid each morning making greasy butties and transforming the dishwater into hot tea. Parked next to Bernadette's stinky van each morning is a rusty pickup van that Uncle Stan's filling up with all the scrap metal lying around the rubble (there's fucking tons of it!), then running over to Ronnie Hessle's scrappies in Rotherham and weighing it all in. So while he waits for the walls to crash down, he butters the breadcakes instead of me. Everyone's making a fortune out of this except me. My bit of the deal is I get dropped off at Ronnie Hessle's house to go and feed his horses, muck them out, and sweep the stable yard ready for his spoilt precious little dollybird daughter to have a ride out on at the weekend if she can be arsed, then walk a mile to school freezing, hungry, filthy, and minging of horse shit. For all that £10 wages will get me at the end of the week, I've no time to go home and get cleaned up, so here I am walking through the gates with gunge all over my trainers. Apparently they're not proper uniform, but if anyone in this place thinks I'm gonna clean horses out in a regulation pair of dollies and white socks, they can think that one over a bit more.

Dad can hurry up and finish bulldozing as soon as possible, as far as I'm concerned. School's for all the other docile penguins my age who need telling what colour shirt to wear each morning. It's not for me, full stop. Somehow, the kids here think I'm not normal. Normal to me means lifeless, dull, with fuck all interesting worth talking about, so why they ever think I'd wanna be owt like them, I don't know. The classrooms are cold, the corridors stink, and the teachers seriously care about fuck all, unless you do summat proper unforgiveable like wear the wrong socks, then they go ballistic. I've been here every day for the last 6 weeks, been sat outside the heads office twice, and they've tried giving me detentions a couple of times, but I've not gone. When I've seen to the horses, I need to get straight home and get tea started off, even more so while Mum's out at work. If school think I'll give an honest income up to stay there longer than anyone else, then they're injecting mind-bending shit, too.

I'm 10 minutes late. If anyone has a go, I'll remind the fuckers to be grateful I've turned in. I'm stressed so I'm nipping to the offie first. The world's biggest makeover still couldn't make me look 18, but I've already chatted soft lad behind the counter up, fluttered my lashes and buttered him up for 10 Bennies. Funny how when I'm not at school I never need to smoke? School moved my lessons about last week. I had some drama with some daft cow from the year above. The usual, summat went missing from her bag, so she decided the gypo kid nicked it. I'm not even a gypo, but it's not like anyone ever listens. Dad taught me to use my fists properly when I were proper young, so that one day I'd not need to rely on any bloke to look out for me. I could probably go bare-knuckling myself, but Dad reckons I've got more brain about me than me brothers, so it's not happening. Anyway, this gobby bitch, Marnie or someone, shoved me just the once, and seconds later she were picking herself up off the floor and dusting herself down while everyone else stared at her. I thought that'd be it, done with, move the fuck on, but the kids here are so sly, so sneaky, I could never trust any of them, ever, and, as expected, her mates grassed me up, saying I'd picked on her, so school swat me out of my lessons into new ones.

It's supposed to keep me out of trouble, but I can't see that happening. English with the boffins, Art with the boffins, Maths with the divvies, Food Tech with the kids who are shit at essays but quite useful with their hands and then back with the divvies for History and Science. P.E's Friday afternoon if they can travel far enough to find me first. Like most things here, registration's pointless, so I skipped it. Straight to English. Whatever boffin chat was going on in there turned to silence instantly when I opened the door. Everybody gazed down at their boffy books, their boffy shoes, anywhere they could to avoid eye contact. Whatever it is, I'm not playing. I scan the class, not for a fight, but just for somewhere to sit down, like you do when you get on the bus.

I go to the nearest spare desk, and, politely but assertively, ask the lass next to it "Is this seat free?"

"No, it's Angela's." Smarmy smile back - she's deffo lying, no doubt.

I walk across the room to the next vacant desk. "Anyone sitting here?"

"Yeah, there will be in a minute. He's just gone to the loo."

I don't believe them either. I've no time for bullshitters. I'm going to need to be the teacher here. I scan the two remaining desks. Some tiny lass, her head in some book doodling flowers on the cover. Then a big lad, looks like a rugby player, and a sunbed addict by the state of his orange skin, with one of them quiffy haircuts like that ponce from Wham, not George Michael, the other one who does nowt. He holds eye contact and stretches his leg across the vacant chair next to him. I spot his giant bag, Head bag or whatever it's called, next to it. If he tries lying to me that anyone's sat there, he's the one I'll make a cunt of in front of everyone, just so they understand.

I start politely, "This one taken?"

"Yeah, it's Alex's." replies the orange cunt with more confidence than his haircut deserves.

"Who's Alex?" I press, not taking the quiffy ponce out of my gaze.

"My mate," he answers back.

"Well, he's not sat here right now is he?"

"Yeah, he'll not be long." I catch the smirk, the look to the others in the class for acclaim. He thinks he's bossing this. He's gonna get such a massive surprise in a minute, I fucking promise.

"Well, where's he gonna sit?"

"Here. Where else?" He's lying again. I trust the kids here as far as I can throw them. Which I might.

"He's not even in school is he?" I press again.

"What's it to you? Where've you been anyway? You smell like shit." He looks around for acclaim again, and gets smarmy grins from a couple of lads near him in response.

I'm bored of this. I'm cold, hungry, knackered, and I've no patience for quentins like him. In an instant, I kick the back right leg off his chair, snapping it clean off. He lands on the floor like a sack of potatoes. I grab his bag, it feels like it's got fucking plumbing rods in it, and swat it high across the room.

"MOVE!" I yell, not taking my gaze off him. *Wham!* wanabee looks up at me standing over him, like he just saw a ghost. "NOW!"

"CAITLIN MCALLISTER! WHAT'S GOING ON OVER THERE?!"

Teacher's in.

I turn to face the teacher. Hands on hips, head to one side, I sigh, "The usual," I reply.

"Caity, we can't keep having this."

I stare the teacher down. 5 seconds. Like it's the gunfight at the OK Corral.

"If I have to sort this kinda crap out just to get a chuffin' seat, what chance have I got of getting through't day without getting expelled, eh?"

The teacher stops, stares at me. Same bunny in the headlights expression that Andrew Ridgeley on the floor here had a minute ago.

The silence breaks.

"You can sit here if you want to...." came a timid voice.

Who the fuck squeaked that out? I look over. Little mousy girl from earlier, the one that was doodling little flowers. Straight brown hair creeping down her forehead and over her eyes. No make up, no stench of hairspray. Quite plain looking, except for a shoulder bag as big as herself with a *Smiths* logo and a hundred little flowery badges and patches and stickers. She's the most harmless looking girl I've ever seen. She looks like a librarian or summat, but I'm still taking no chances.

I walk over to the seat to the left of her. My left fist stays clenched, just in case she's on a wind-up, too.

"Thanks." I whisper. I check the chair has 4 legs firmly attached, then run my hand over the base for chewing gum and superglue, finding none. She stays silent. From the corner of my right eye, I check where her hands and legs are. I'm on alert. I keep my fist clenched, but she stays still. If it did come to anything, I could blow on her and she'd crumble. She stays focused straight ahead, like she's actually listening to the teacher.

"Right, everyone. Animal Farm. Start from page 32. Darren, you read out."

As if I even have that book. It sounds proper easy though. I mucked horses out this morning. I probably know more about both animals and farms than the teacher - and the writer.

Penny, if the inside of her pencil case is true, opens her book, and then, with no-one even having to tell her, moves the opened book centrally between me and her. I put my finger on the bottom left corner of the book as she puts her finger on the right hand bottom corner. She looks over, maybe fearful that I'll swat her across the room too. I return the look. She introduces herself in a whisper, "I'm Penny." I nod with my reply, "Caitlin." Gradually, the tightness of my left fist eases bit by bit until, once we make it to page 40, it totally relaxes.

----

1. Shitflickers.

New shoes, new hair, new term. The shoes are nowt to write a book about, just the usual school shitflickers. No escape, sadly. I did try to dodge the haircut with the 'you should check out the state of everyone else' argument, but Mum gave me that look that referees usually give me if I decide to fall over anywhere near the penalty box and not do it properly. This is one of the rare occasions where the big sister Shelly, a proper dickhead and my rival sibling most of the time, becomes useful. With issues such as hair and clothes, I can trust her implicitly. If I'm spotted walking round looking ridiculous, it rebounds on her, so she sent pictures of some K-pop pretty-boy to her mate Fyza, second year trainee hairdresser. If Shelly lets her loose on her own hair then it's gonna be legit, plus it's a second year. I'd never risk a first year unless I fancied having to wear beanies 24-7 like Archie, so I was only too happy to become a mutually free-of-charge K-pop guinea pig. I finish the job meself via the bathroom mirror. Tiny little bit of gel, only a touch, the outermost tips of my fingers dipping into the pot and nowt more, then phone out, best Cristiano pout, and upload. School selfie. There's still a bit of tan left from my Spain trip, just enough for everyone to spot it's natural and I've not been doing that chavvy essexy sunbed thing. Made it the profile picture. It's not good enough for the wallpaper. Whilst I'm the most creative player in Sevenhill City's Under-15s, the action shot of me in full flow stays as wallpaper. If Beyonce and Rihanna entered this bathroom right now and took a selfie with me, it still wouldn't make it.

Mum and Dad are both away to work already, so I have to feed myself. I'm on a 'sportsman's diet', so Rice Krispies, Sausage Muffins and Wotsits are banned. The club handbook lists everything I'm allowed to do, everything I'm not, and everything where "caution should be exercised". I'll not share the full details as most of its boring, but ice skating and bungee-jumping can wait a bit, anyway. I hit 13 goals from midfield last season, against some decent sides too, then 5 more in this big tournament in Spain during the holidays too, a tap in and a sweaty scramble against Utrecht, 2 worldies against Valencia, then curled a free kick into the top corner against Gothenburg. If you're hitting worldies in against Valencia, you don't tend to miss donuts that much, in all honesty.

I open the fridge door with utmost care. I once opened the door and the eggs fell out of their little compartment and smashed all over the floor. It were deffo an accident but I still got bollocked. Even now, the shelf they're in wobbles too much for my peace of mind, so I always take this door in second gear tops. There's nowt in here that goes well on toast, which is about the optimum limit of my cooking skills. Everything's just occasional shit like Thai curry paste, pak choi, which is basically lettuce that's been to the gym and done a few press ups, then a million other items that are useless in a morning. Hidden behind some other stuff that I don't even know what it is, I spot cheese, not grated, but fuck it, it'll do. The cheese graters in the washing up bowl, itself filled to the brim with cold water that's got some orange greasy gunge floating about on top. The proper cheese cutting knifes in there too, the one with the white handle thingy, so I just pull a normal one out the drawer. I managed to cut 4 or 5 decent lumps out of the cheese block and plonked it on the bread. It looks a bit mad, big lumps everywhere. I could have done with putting more on, so it drips goo down the edges, but never mind.

Phone check. 3 likes already. A lass from set 3 who likes everything I post, then Aunt Bernie, my Mum's aunt actually but she's OK, then a random lass in Year 9 who I'm not sure I've ever spoken to. Another little red box to click open. Sam Blake.

Tickets for Sat?

Easy reply. *Will find out later, msg me tonite*

I don't put anything like as much online as other people. Odd photo, not much else. Sometimes your friends are actually your frenemies, and you never quite know who gets to see your stuff. My feet do the talking way better than my fingers ever could. Shelly's on my friends list. Mum made her add me. Mum's not. She comments on everything, and I mean EVERYTHING. Social networking with her is a step too far. For that reason, I've no Twatter, and if I was any good at photos, I'd stick to Insta and bin Facebook. Kept scrolling, school photos everywhere, even the ugly kids, even the kids that never turn up to school. Eva from my year has put sunny holiday photos on. Swimsuit pics, too. Knowing what some of the lads in our year are like, that's either brave or stupid. I don't mind her that much, so I'll say brave. Click. Like. On the whole album, mind, cos if I just liked the swimsuit shots it'd be a bit wrong.

Bloody hell!! Cheese on toast cooks quicker than I thought. I can't see fuck all for smoke. Door open, windows open, noisy fan thing on. Not sorting it. Best find the smoke alarm before that goes off. I can just reach the ceiling if I leap high enough. Two jumps. Not made it. Swat my shoe at it. Made a reyt noise. Think I've smashed it. Job done though. Shelly's now awake and swearing her head off at me from upstairs, and the house is still filling with smoke, so either by sibling violence or inhaling smoke, I'm going to die. Oh yeah, dickhead, maybe try turning the cooker off? How did I screw that one up? I've done way more difficult recipes in food tech and got them bang on. If Gordon Ramsay were here right now, he'd be full-on in me face yelling 'USELESS TWAT!!' at the very top end of his vocal range. If Delia Smith was here, she'd be yelling 'useless twat' at me too.

I screw my eyes up to gaze through the smoke, and all that's visible, and edible, are bananas. I'm not struck on them. It's the feel of them I'm not keen on, but the nutrition lady who comes into the academy says they're like a magical food, full of instant energy and riboflavin and potassium, so, though I'm not entirely sure what those things even are, I force them down on her say-so. Mental checklist. Bananas, lunch. Not with it, me, why didn't I just eat summat from my pack-up on the way to school? Try again. Bananas, lunch, phone, bag. Oh yeah, shoes. Shitflickers. As if walking round the city centre with a Clarks bag while Shelly deliberately carries a Footlocker bag to take the piss wasn't painful enough, these ugly monstrosities are gonna hammer today, on a training night too. Apparently I've grown a size, which is great for new footy boots, but shite for school shoes. I've started the new season with Puma Agueros, purple, bedded them in instantly and they're like slippers already. Slippers that can destroy a man. As soon as a pair of shitflickers eventually become comfortable, it means they're knackered. I know that every other kid in every other school has to wear them by law, but they're still wanker's shoes.

I spotted Archie lounging outside the Co-Op. He's permanently got a beanie on, not because he's been to a first year hairdresser, but because he's far more ginger than society deems acceptable. I'd not even arranged to meet up with him, just pure telepathy. He should ring City up and trial as left-back, we'd be dynamite with that kind of understanding. Weekends and holidays, we do nowt together, maybe I bump into him if Mum sends me to the shop and we'll chill for a bit, but I've never thought to call round for him. Even though we've like, NEVER fallen out, he's just a functional mate. All of my school mates are functional mates. They all serve a purpose in a certain part of my life. With Archie, its walking to and from school and nowt else. Anyway, though I've not seen him for weeks, from the Co-Op all the way to the school gates, non-stop bantz from exactly where we left off 6 weeks ago.

"Joe, I'd like to just say well done to your hair for finally being open about its sexuality. I've suspected for years, but I'm cool with it, and I'll always remain friends with you regardless."

"Thanks fella, I'd compliment you back, but unfortunately your beanie precludes this. The suns out if you'd not noticed. I don't suppose you've still got that dead rat on top of your head at all?"

"Only till't weekend. Ah'v booked in wi't stylist, and gi' her a new design for her try on me. I got the idea when your Mum were naked in me bedroom last week."

"I already tried to do the same thing based on your Mum. But she's bald downstairs. Upstairs too. Them wispy wavy curls she books in for at't salon each Friday? Sorry mate, she's bluffing. Collar matches the cuffs, but not how you think."

Silence. Think I won..."Damn I've missed this."

"Don't tell your boyfriend, but I actually missed this walk this summer. Been anywhere?"

"Aye. Just to Spain. You?" UNDERSTATED!! I have just been to Spain. For a giant whopping international tournament. Villarreal and Valencia were there, Benfica, teams from Sweden, Holland, Germany, France, all over the world. I curled a ball in from the left against Valencia, yep, Valencia, which looped, touched nowt on the way, then dipped under the crossbar just at the right time. Additionally, I got buddies with 2 drop dead gorgeous Dutch lasses who are now on my friends list, even though I've no idea what to chat about with either of them. They even sunbathed topless and never even looked bothered. No-one likes a bighead though, we always get told to cut out the trumpet-blowing, so I'll be modest.

"Scotland to me Dad's for a bit. Miles from anywhere. That were about it"

He's there every school holiday, so I weren't really listening. The bus stop's rammed so one must be due soon. A couple of women in office clothes had cigs on the go, and the smoke always seems to float my way, so I walked down to where Alicia May were stood. I used to sit on her table all the way through primary, but I have nowt to do with her now. Nowt personal, I get on with her OK, just got different mates and lives and that.

"Hey, Joe, u see that Mr Bean kid stood over there wi' his Mum, d'ya reckon he's coming to ours?"

Actually, it's his Mum I recognise. She's mates with my Mum, sort of. Not a prosecco-guzzling party mate, or a shoulder to cry on mate, or even one of those mates that me Mum only ever meets in some coffee place, but the sort of Mum mates that stop and talk drivel for 25 years at a time in the middle of Morrisons, blocking the aisle and preventing any access whatsoever to fabric conditioner or dog food or whatever. Mum once said she had a lad my age, but I weren't really listening. I don't remember seeing him before, but with that comedy coat he's got on, I doubt I could have forgotten him, really.

"No idea." I can't see his uniform under that comedy coat he had on anyway, but as long as he's not on his way to the same place as me, I don't care.

Not many new faces on the bus, a few year 7s in brand new everything, some looking terrified, others looking proper cocky like they're still running the show like they did in year 6. Aside from that, just the lad that Alicia were banging on about, with his Mum. Everyone else bombed upstairs, so I put myself downstairs where the timid kids sits, in sight of the driver in case anyone tries to bully them. I get funny looks when I sit there, but I like the change of scenery, and listening in on the other kids conversations. They're way different conversations from the ones I have, about things I've never cared for, Dr Who, Fortnite, Love Island, or some indie band or boy band that sounds exactly like any other indie band or boy band. Then there's the daft gossip, like who's got excluded, who's got ebola, who's got a blue waffle, all that drama. I never join in, just listen to see if I'm missing out on anything amazing away from my own life. Mostly, I'm not.

The bus takes about 20 minutes. There's a tram too, which drops off at the bottom of this road with a reyt big hill to go up, and a pokey shop to go past where the owner's either dodgy or needs to go to Specsavers, always getting took to court for selling vodka to year 8s. Even today, there's a mass of kids in school uniform stood outside under a cloud of fag smoke, giving the owner away to the coppers clear as. The bus goes a longer way round some estate, but drops off near enough outside the gates. As the bus pulled up, one of the brand new Year 7's tried to go down the steps from upstairs a second too early, unaware of just how shite the brakes on these buses are. When the driver jammed his brakes on, the whole vehicle jerked suddenly and the kid landed on some office lady. The year 7s with him laughed uncontrollably, giggling and cackling like all the little kids do when they're nervous or when they've overdone it with the cheap sweets. The lady gives him a pretty annoyed look. This is where I step in.

"I don't think he meant to land on you. He's just daft. I know his Dad so I'll mek sure he knows so he can give him a proper beating".

The kid looks up at me, eyes full of fear. Maybe I overdid it just there, like what if his Dad really is one of those wankers who batters his kids every time his horses don't win. I still made him wait for me when he got off. Like any year 7 shiting it on their first day, he did, while the other year 7s he thought were his buddies scattered and left him to it.

"Listen fella, this in't year 6 anymore. This school's a gret big jungle of a place. There's lions and tigers and snakes all over, and you're just a tiny little ant in it. Owt you do in year 7 that stands you out won't go well. You may just be an ant but trust me, all them lions and grizzly bears and snakes will still find time to make a mess of you. This means learning straight away how to get off a bus properly. I've got your back wi' this one, but next time you land on't floor like a twat, I might not give a shit."

"OK sorry" he squeaks, timidly, now totally abandoned by his mates to the wolves, lions and snakes, nervously half-expecting a battering from me or maybe his bruiser of a Dad or whoever.

"Walk in wi' us. Only this time, though. Good job I've no fucking idea who your Dad is, eh?" I lightly push his left shoulder. This kid's shitting it already. Time to calm it. "Where've you gotta be?"

"Room E3, do you know where it is please?"

I note the 'please'. Polite, respectful. "Yes, fella. In fact me and Archie are going that way, so we'll show you, won't we Archie?"

Archie turns his freckled, bean-shaped head towards me "WTF?"

Alicia chips in "Joey! I never thought I'd see you flushing year 7s heads down the toilets"

I was a year 7 once. I had it easy. Shelly were in year 10. She could out-drink, out-smoke and out-fight any of the lads, and they knew. Also, thanks to football, I bombed straight into a friendship group full of kids who'd played against me before, remembered me, and wanted me on their team every break time. No-one was flushing my head anywhere, so, now I'm the year 10, I'm actually about to do summat quite kind. I'm just not telling anyone yet. Anyway, past reception, where big coat boy is sat with his friend of my Mum Mum looking well out of place. I remember her name now, Penny I think. Turned left into English block, parting a sea of year 7s bouncing off the walls. Cherry Tango and Fizzbombs for breakfast at a guess. I asked the wee boy, brand new uniform, shoes, hair, everything, "What's your name pal?"

"Charlie, why?"

The swarm of hypo year 7s stop still and fall silent as we approach. "Which one's your class, Charlie?"

"7SB"

"This second one, then"

Walked amongst the flock of brand new coats and bags and shiny shoes and stopped. "Reyt, Charlie, see you later pal, if you're up for doing owt after school then inbox us, ok?"

Two minutes ago Charlie looked like dead man walking. His last steps to his class were full on struts, proper Fresh Prince swag. I clocked what looked like the year 7 badass with a meet-me-at-McDonalds twatcut, tramlines on the sides, and gave him a big fuck-off deathglare, which he returned with the same tewwified wabbit look that Charlie had 10 minutes ago.

Archie grabs my shoulder and remonstrates. "What the fuck were that lot all in aid of?"

I explain, "You remember your first day here? I bet it were proper eventful, what wi' you being kinda Scottish and freckled and ginger and all that?"

"I don't remember any day here that fondly. I do remember meeting a full-on fool at the bus stop that, 3 years later, I can't get fucking rid of!"

"Well that kid looked like he got pushed when't bus pulled up, probably chosen for a full year of grief, so I just decided if he walked in like he were one of our boys, no-one would bother."

"Why would you even give a toss? It's not like anyone's ever gonna pick you out, you being't school Beckham 'n all that?"

"I were thinking about it earlier. Shelly were in year 10 when I started here. That's me now. I don't need to look out for anyone, apart from you maybe, being a rare vulnerable ginger species at risk of being hunted to extinction. I just fancied doing what she did back then, just so she can't go all preacher-man on me. I needed a witness. You'd do."

"Strawberry blonde actually. Last time I saw Shelly she were on't tram to town wi' some other lasses wi' a dainty little black cocktail dress and glittery shoes on, all of them giggly as fuck off a bottle of Malibu that one of 'em sneaked out o't house and they were offering me and Welshy in on crafty colas. Can you do that in 3 years time, too?"

"Too right!" I beamed right back. "I've already got your Mum's special underwear to start the whole outfit off, she gave it me to say thanks fo …."

Archie was off. Him to his class, me to mine. The form tutor arrived before me, as usual. I should know his name, but he doesn't teach me so I CBA to find out. He didn't look up but just handed me a sheet of paper as I strolled in. Timetable. I found my seat without looking. Left side as you go in, by the wall, two from the back, no blind spots. I see everything. The tables are in twos, 1 boy, 1 girl, where possible, since year 8. Apparently everyone behaves better that way. I don't get how, but as I don't really misbehave, I don't care that much. I don't know Sophia that well, but I know her well enough to realise I could be sat next to someone way worse, like Shironda or Beth, so I've made a point of not falling out with her. She advised me quite clearly in year 8 that she detests football with a passion, doesn't care who I play for, what position I play, what tricks I've got or whether I win or not. She's made it clear that whenever I get presented some shitty award in assembly, it's a sympathy prize to make up for me being hideously ugly and useless at anything of merit. However, as she has to sit next to someone, and I don't smell as rank as most of the other lads, she'd allow me the chance to become someone she could cope with first thing each morning, and that would be to never breathe a word to her about the stupidly repugnant sport that I actually live for. I'll never let this on to her ever, but I quite liked it when she said this. Despite football running my whole life right now, which I don't mind that much, if truth be told I like that very much indeed, I get surrounded by a whole endless pile of bullshit about it. Every second person's an expert, even if they've never kicked a ball before, and just like alcohol, powders, weed and every other losers drug, football is capable of turning the most sensible of adults to moronic idiots within seconds. There's distant aunts and mates of my parents who think I'll captain England one day, and don't get that I have as much chance of this as David Sadler from year 11, 19 stone with specially made elasticated school trousers, has of winning the London marathon. So, I let Sophia talk to me about whatever. She has let on that her Dad and big brother have season tickets somewhere (again, she absolutely doesn't care where, and closely examines me to see if I do, like it's a test) and her brother plays FIFA all day and most of the night instead of working or getting educated, and at least 5 times each evening he'll swear his head off at his X-Box at the very top of his vocal range, swat his controller across the room, then suffer spicerat-like withdrawal symptoms once he's actually broken it and can't play it until its fixed.

I know loads of kids just as sad as that. This Saturday I've got Leeds United away. On the same Monday morning that I come to school boasting of beating them, on the pitch, 11 v 11, hundreds of sad gamers will talk about having done exactly the same via their no-mates virtual world where they probably spent £20 or so on virtual players. I guess if this is what she gets at home, I'm probably the last person she wants to sit near. I've barely got a clue what she's into, who she knocks around with or what she does when she's not sat in registrations. It's like she's been put on this earth to keep me company for 20 minutes then disappear again til the next day. She never looks interested in much. In fact, she never shows her feelings or even facial expressions, to the extent that I'm not sure she has any. Weirdly, though this is just another friendship of convenience, I'm slightly attracted to her. She's not beautiful, or as others may say, "proper fit", but she carries all this expressionless, don't give a shit about anything or anyone with such coolness that if I ever tried to copy it I'd fail. I could happily chill next to that all day long. I can find everything out about most girls in minutes, if I could ever be arsed. That sounds creepy, but what I mean is there's loads of girls that'll do owt to get my attention, not just me, but most of my immediate mates too, on account of them being mates with me of course. I like the fact that this girl doesn't care that I sit next to her, and each morning the reception I get is as welcoming and enthusiastic as I'd get if I went on one of them tube trains in London and tried saying "hello" to whoever were stood next to me. I've worked out that she cares about as much about school as I do, but, thanks to her very endearing mysteriousness, I've no idea why. I know my reasons. I'm just going through the motions. Sevenhill City say that in order for me to continue chasing my dream, and every other kids dream, I have to maintain good attendance, achievement and behaviour in school. Therefore, I turn up, don't mess about, and do my homework, usually basic as shit, but done.

I scan the class. Shironda is showing this techy lad called Joel her new nails. He looks like he has no escape and would rather be dead than listening to all that toss. I half-glance at Sophia's, they're proper bitten down and are about as glamorous as mine, like they're just fingernails, who cares? Again, I've no idea why, but a lass with that attitude weirdly interests me more than some dolly who spends £30 on them every weekend and clogs Instagram with the end-result. Elsewhere, you can see the girls and lads sat together but chatting separately from each other, most obviously Cory Hendricks's badboy crew, who've managed to position themselves in the back corner next to each other whilst staying 2 to a desk.

Oh yeah, stuff trying to be a shite psychoanalyst, I should maybe have a look at my timetable. I picked my options last term. I had no choice over English or Maths, and Science is another one they force you to do, but I managed to dodge the GCSE and do the BTEC with the slower kids, not like proper slow, just the kids that won't be off to Uni, but won't be doing foundation learning either. Plus, no exam. Swung it.

PE picked me, easy grade A in the bag. I can't even make my own breakfast, but the seating plan in Food Tech last year put me next to Millie Frost, whos' straight-ten fit. She told me once that her favourite food is cherry crumble. I immediately learned that recipe off by heart. Some kids choose their options based on daft shit like whether it'll be useful to them in the future, or whether they can pass it easily. Not me. As long as I'm sat with anyone who's either proper bant or proper fit, then that'll do nicely. I struggle with languages, but I decided to do for when Barcelona try to sign me. You hear their fans chanting "Barker! Barker! Baaaarrrrkker!!" at every home game. That's who they want their next signing to be. Unfortunately, school don't offer Spanish so I picked German and they put me in French. I were thinking more about Bayern, Dortmund and also Katie Eastgate who does ice-dancing and her Mum's German so she'll deffo be studying it. The teacher told my folks I'd cope better with French, probably because Katie Eastgate wouldn't be there and I might concentrate a bit. People get all precious about Germans, but I've been there, to this city near Bayer Leverkusen called Cologne. We went on a big long boat ride where Mum got drunk and kept shouting "Castle number 41!!", "Castle number 42!!" Even though she were being proper embarrassing, everyone were bang on friendly to us. I was happy to dump both history and geography, I've tried both and they're grim, and I'm doing Philosophy instead. I've no idea what it is, but Shelly got a B in it and I've already got her old homework stashed away, so that one's in the bag with minimal effort needed

I'm in set 2, which means I'm one of those kids who learns reyt easy and should pass everything, but not as well as boff class. They're predicted 'A's. We should breeze 'C's, 'B's if we can be arsed, maybe an A here and there. The big difference between us and the boffin class is banter. We're all good for a chat, but boff class banter's shite. They're like sponges, absorbing everything in and spilling nowt out. Some of them do philosophy with us. We did a taster class before we broke up for summer. The teacher gave us a subject to talk about – life after death. Our class bossed the whole chat, even if some of it were proper daft, while the boffins were like statues. I remember Shironda spouting out "everyone comes back to life, it's just your body that's the shell, but that spirit thing that mex ya do everything ya do just teks over a new shell, and it cud be owt, like a daffodil, an iguana, whatever", then Welshy dissing her with "Nah that's shite, that. No iguanas, no bunnies, the light goes out and dun't come back on". Then everyone else from our class just flew in and I worked out that Philosophy might just be a GCSE in banter, minus the swearing and pointless insults. If everyone savages each other and the teacher's well into every single moment of it, this could be the best choice I ever made. I must previously have spent a maximum of two minutes of my life even thinking about life after death, those 2 minutes being at my grandad's funeral when I were 4, and stopped thinking about it as soon as some random Aunt gave me some Haribo Bears.

I don't get the boffs. How do you sit in silence, take in what everyone else says, then write 20 pages parroting someone else's ideas and getting A's while the person that gifted them their ideas gets a C+ instead? I don't get what's grade A about that. At least with the banter class, the school day passes quicker, and I'd even guess that's how we learn all our stuff. Hardly anyone in my class chose drama, but when there's a play or a presentation going on, it's always my class they beg or bribe to take part. Shironda, still banging on about her fucking nails even now, got offered a KFC to stand and mime in the school choir at a presentation evening, so it looked like there were more than just the usual 3 billies who ever turn up to it. Even though turning the first offer down is a golden rule of business, there'd also been a bullshit rumour that Shironda had it away wi' some spotty boy racer in the back of his Nova in exchange for a KFC, so she naturally had good reasons to turn the offer down. She suggested that a £20 Nando's voucher may tempt her to consider a minor backstage role. Her negotiating skills looked bang on, as she sealed the deal amicably with a £15 Pizza Hut voucher, valid only on weekday daytimes before 2pm, but with 6 week holidays just round the corner, a reasonable payment for her talents all the same.

I'd actually be cool in set 3. I do Science with them. Science does nowt for me. The teachers know this, so they've sat me bang in the middle of the room, away from the windows so that I can't daydream the time away. What they forgot is that the kids they put me with all spring to life at the opportunity to take a dead rat to bits or make stuff explode, and I'm perfectly happy to sit back and let them do the work. I'm rambling. Kanye West with a gram of coke up his nose rambles less than me. My timetable. P.E on Monday afternoons will kill me. I'm footballing four days per week so school can get ready for a call from City requesting I play table tennis all winter. School team trains on Mondays and plays matches whenever I'm available. I never train. They simply ring City up, ask permission for me to play then fix a date. Double food tech on

Mondays should be good. Friday afternoon's double English, which could be worse. I don't really like school, but as I said earlier, it's a means to an end.

This was the second most important bit of the day. The most important was, without any doubt, the lunchtime ritual. I wasn't mates with anyone here before year 7, but they'd played against me before and recognised me, and we palled up from there. Some of the kids here take the break time kickabouts and the school team very seriously indeed. I don't, higher level and all that, but it's a good place to practice my moves. If I can pull tricks off in shitflickers, I'll breeze them in Puma Agueros. I did the same trick twice on one of them, Marcus I think. I start to go into a 360, so the opponent moves to try and block me, but I change direction part way into the move and I'm away. He bought it each time. I did another party piece at the end. Haydn tried to prank me by ringing my fone just as someone passed the ball out to me, hoping I'll not be able to do 2 things at once. So, I answered, did the false-360 again, took off, slowed down towards Alfie, dropped me shoulder, sped past him, pretended to lay off to Pawel but waited for someone else to try sliding in, then left them on the floor with a dragback and placed it low between the keeper and his left post, all the time whilst on the phone asking Haydn if he'd missed owt and did he want me to do it again? Tomorrow I'll do exactly the same but throw a selfie in there too. If you're as talented as me, the possibilities are endless, even with shitflickers on.

----

2. Changing My Landscape

6:30 alarm. Reluctantly, I opened my left eye, then, once the mundanity appearing before it fully registered, my right. Usually, I'd remain motionless within my quilt until it hit 6:35, then, 5 minutes later, I'd be like "OK, give it til 6.43, and I'll definitely get up then". I'd continue this nonsense til about 6.48, 6.50, maybe even 6.55, but today's a bit different.

School number three. New blazer, new stripy tie, feet still aching from 6 hours of shopping. Burned so much time checking out rulers and lunchboxes that the trainers got bought last. Not that I care about casual footwear, but trainers are one of those stupid possessions that determine whether you get picked on or respected. You can be the most obnoxious arsehole in the whole school or hopeless at everything in P.E, which I am, but if you show up in Adidas original classic stuff, then you're straight into the A Team, as there's this unwritten rule that says you're somehow a much more superior person in every way than anyone who doesn't wear them. Even the discount Adidas beats everything else. Nike comes second, followed by Converse and Vans. Without them, you could kick a football like Cristiano, slam dunk like Kobe, sprint like Usain and still be last picked, first kicked. At Moor Vale I thought I'd be OK with Slazenger. Every player at Wimbledon wears it, but in school, even the kids that played tennis wore Adidas or Nike while pointing at me. Before then, I saw all the boxing champs, thought Lonsdale would be fine, but in reality might as well have trampled dog shit all the way to P.E instead. I don't get it at all. The whole point of sport, to me, is to stop you getting fat and bloated. I'm not fat, so what's the point? Being fashionable is daft. Expensively daft in some cases. The point of clothing is to keep you warm in winter, not too sweaty in summer and also to ensure that no-one gets a sneaky peek at your genitals. Most of all, this is all achievable without hassling your folks to waste their month's salary on whatever has a little label on the side. So when Mum voluntarily wastes her salary on clothing me, I'm simply responding to my ethics when I act bored and suggest going home. She's doing the job of both Mum and Dad, on a part-time wage topped up with child benefit, so I'm doing her a favour here by not scamming her for £80 trainers, but however much I try to show that I'm openly rejecting the year 10 peer pressure nonsense, she doesn't notice.

All through year 9, I'd wake up absolutely dreading the day ahead. In fact, on most days I didn't bother. When everyone found out what was really going on, and how I'd been injuring myself, I just gave up on attending altogether. Today, I guess I have hope, and with hope, comes a reason to get out of bed. There's a lot of people with no hope right now. I stepped over hundreds of them yesterday, sat on the pavement under sleeping bags with discarded coffee cups out begging for loose change. We live in ideological austerity times. I've read up what that means, and it's not good. I still can't say I know politics that well yet, but I still know way more than most adults who actually vote. I know that when the Prime Minister's a Tory, everyone gets poorer except for the richest and greediest. Those with no money, no home, no job and nothing you'd think they could lose, still lose, be it hope or dignity or self-esteem. I saw that for myself yesterday. There's always that chance it might be us sat one day, shaking an empty cup whilst being deathglared by passers-by carrying a £3 coffee and a £6 sandwich that they could easily have gotten cheaper and had enough left to maybe chuck 50p at someone who's breakfast probably came out of a bin. I could go on, and morph into one of those rebel types that love nothing more than being shouty all over Twitter or throwing bricks at riot police, but what I'm rambling on about here isn't meant to be political ideology. Like I said, I'm still working all that out. What I mean is that today, in a lot of ways, is the first day in ages where I have hope, and maybe even dignity and self-esteem. So, I get out of bed in quite a reasonable mood, totally forgetting I had a boner.

I've no explanation how I got that. I don't go on rude websites anymore, not since they slowed my laptop down to snail speed, and I can remember vividly what I dreamed about. I dreamed about being sat painting at an easel, in the city centre, the bit with the narrow cobbly street and little interesting geek-shops in old buildings with flower beds in hanging baskets along each side. I've had that dream before. I have a book that tells me what all my dreams are about. It says that as long as I'm not in Paris or New York or Venice or somewhere classy like that (well not yet anyway), then the book says that sub-consciously I want to change my landscape in a positive way, which is exactly what I'm doing today. Changing my landscape. It explains that my conscious and subconscious are both well in tune with each other, but doesn't really explain the boner that well. I get loads of them, often when I don't want them. I pull two pairs of underwear out of my drawer and stick both on, as insurance against anything popping up unexpectedly today.

I hear the downstairs kitchen noises, pots clanking, TV blasting out whatever inane shit Lara's got on, so my path to the bathroom is clear. Big. Solid. Dump. I could go into immense hyperdetail, but I won't. I did need to spray around some air freshener of Mums, Chanel something or other, afterwards, and open the window. Decided to shower. If I can avoid getting the 'smelly kid' label that'd be a bonus. Got the added bonus, of having hair that looked normal, if only for the next 10 minutes before it goes off in its own freaky freestyle again. My hair's that totally impossible sort that barbers hate. It's thick, wiry, looks wrong if you grow it, and even when it's short it looks equally wrong. There's a very short list of what could actually improve it, of which baldness is probably the most viable. I took a long look at the special soap Mum thinks I should use, then looked in the mirror, caught the spots on my shoulder and the ones I've got on my face and decided there was no point. There's a belter on my forehead that I should really name, it's a very sizeable living organism in its own right. I dab a bit of water on it and baptise it Gerald. The one consolation is that by viewing myself in the mirror, I got rid of the unwanted boner. My physical attractiveness knows no bounds here, seriously.

Got dressed. Experimented with rolling my shirt sleeves up. Rolled up makes some people look cool, but not me. It just makes me look older than I am, not in a cool 18 or 21 way, or even a sophisticated late 20s, early 30s way, but just old, in an Antiques Roadshow kind of way. More importantly there's still the scars on my arms that people who don't know me will spot, and ask multiple awkward questions that I won't want to answer, so that decided it. Went downstairs, sleeves down, cuffs buttoned.

Mum's made me a cup of tea with one sugar in it. As soon as she leaves the room, I'm adding a couple more spoonfuls in. I'm too intelligent to do that flag-waving crap, but a cup of tea is one of the best things Britain has ever invented, alongside maybe the Lancaster Bomber, Harry Potter, James Bond, the internet, free healthcare and hanging on long enough against Hitler until the rest of the world could get to us and kick both his backside and his one remaining freely dangling testicle. Without sugar, they're foul. The sweeter the better. Cups of tea, that is, not Hitler's testicles. To counter this, I put some bread in the toaster, buttered it once it popped up then spread marmite on. There's no sugar in that, so Mum should be happy that I left the Coco-Pops alone. I'm a scruff with them. I let them stew in the milk, like tea bags stew in hot water, then when they're all soggy, mix in Haribos, M&Ms, whatever sweets are lying about. Mum gets really annoyed by it, but she's fussing too much today.

"Are you excited today, son?"

If I was going to Disneyland or the Rio Carnival this morning, then I might be, but I'm going to school. In theory, I'm going from one mundane suburb of town to another one. I went there yesterday. "No. I'm not excited. Not at all."

"Nervous?" she asks, this time not quite so animated.

I could be sarcastic but Mum's put serious effort into changing my school, and in theory, in her opinion, ensuring I don't try and kill myself again in the near future, thus, arguably, saving my life, so I'll refrain. "It's a big place and I don't know anyone, but I'm getting older so I've got to be grown-up about it. I'll not let anyone see I'm nervous, don't worry."

Mum senses a rare opportunity to practice her counselling therapies, learned over night classes she did years ago. I remember only because Grandma would babysit us and send us to bed an hour earlier than Mum would, so we were glad when she finally got a job and packed the night school up. I don't want psychoanalysis for breakfast, however. "There's nothing wrong with being nervous, it's a natural human emotion. Being nervous just shows you're human." She's got that position where she leans against the kitchen top at 30 degrees, balances herself with one hand and holds her stupidly oversized coffee cup close to her chest with the other, slightly tilting her head to one side. "I quite liked the way the head stopped and spoke to the students when she was showing us round, and I liked how the teachers ate in the same lunch hall as the pupils. The receptionist seemed nice, too"

"Mum, you're probably the only person in the world who rates a school on how friendly the receptionist is. You really should work for Ofsted. They need you."

"OK then, I didn't see any pupils being unruly."

It's too early for this, "Mum, they knew we were coming so they gagged and wrapped all the naughty ones in duct tape and shut them all in a store cupboard til we'd gone. Have you anymore inspirational advice for me today?"

Lara shouts out across the room, "Yes, try not to be a nobhead, maybe?"

"Lara!!" screeched Mum across the room.

Lara has a slightly vested interest in my change of schools. She's told Mum that she's heard the science and drama facilities are amazing, and if I settle, she'd consider changing schools too, total bullshit which Mum has totally fallen for. What Lara really meant is that the boys at St Kevin's are infinitely fitter than the sweaty GTA-addicted trogaladytes that she currently shares her weekdays with. Additionally, you have to pass Maccy D's and a poncy coffee place to get there. She's not considered even momentarily that she actually has friends where she is, and, thanks to an afternoon's copying and pasting that got an award for a history project, the teachers all look out for her so she doesn't get the stick that I did, and generally gets left alone. She's luckier than me in many ways. She didn't get the wiry hair, her skin's not as ravaged by acne, but like half of year 8, she does have a mouth full of braces that wouldn't look out of place on the eventual losing side in a James Bond film. She was even named after a superhero, from a computer game my Dad played. I say nothing, just fix my gaze at her. I've seen proper tough guys, and girls, do this gaze in movies on the telly, and if it works for them, then it's worth a try.

"What *ARE* you staring at?" she replies. I might need to work on that stare. She utters something that sounds like "weirdo", but the TV and the washing machine mean I can't quite make it out. I let it go, for now. It's time to go.

"Do you want me to walk to the bus stop with you?" Mum suddenly makes things worse.

Lara's head immediately jerks upwards from her phone, just in case I answer 'yes', which she will then tweet out globally, and I might as well change schools yet again before I've even started my first day. Mum may as well hold my hand, spitwash my face and tearfully wave a big snotty hanky as the bus carries me through the foggy hinterland until we become dots fading into the landscape.

"No, thanks. I'll get the tram then drop into Maccy D's for a sausage muffin and a chocolate milkshake to settle my nerves. Or maybe a hazelnut macchiato from that coffee place. I've not decided yet."

Lara looks up from her phone again, briefly. Yes Lara, Maccy D's or poncy coffee for breakfast, every day if I fancy it, 5 days a week for 2 years. I don't like burgers or poncy coffee that much, there's other stuff I prefer, but if the thought of me dropping in there every day annoys you intensely enough, then I'll gladly bring the empty wrappers home and ask how long you had to wait outside the Co-Op cos they only let 2 school kids in at a time, and if you got served before everything sold out except the Werther's Originals.

Talking of things from the distant past, this coat needs replacing. It's warm, but it's no longer good for either school or this decade. I should look for the new waterproof, but CBA. It had to go through the wash every day last year. It's had chewing gum pressed in it, all manner of bodily fluids projected onto it, food rubbed into it. If I ever hung it up in the cloak room, I'd return to find it on the floor with footmarks all over it at the end of a good day, half flushed in a well-used toilet on a bad one. It always washes well though and it's very durable. Marks and Spencers may be the trusted option of dull people everywhere, but I'll give it some credit. Nothing I've ever had from there has ever fallen apart quickly. Like me, my coat's one of life's survivors.

My bag's empty at present. It's actually a satchel, looks like its leather and just like my coat, it's had a battering, but it's one of those items that looks better once it's been bedded in. I expect to be using it when I embark on my glorious career. I've seen loads of adults using them, arty types, techy types, uni students, all that lot. It's a wise investment, though it doesn't really fit in with the carriers of choice of other kids in school. I've not a lot to carry in it, just pens, rulers, schoolbooks, as expected, but there's small pockets all over it. I don't use them yet, except for the tiny flap that's designed for business cards but today a Penguin biscuit fits in it perfectly.

It's a bit windy, but I'm warm from walking, so I unbutton a little and look at the sky. I spot a plane going west. The wind's blowing from the west, which means there's a very severe storm somewhere, not here, maybe at sea somewhere, or on one of those Scottish Islands where you can only land a plane when it's not windy. You can see the plane using all of its metal albatross strength because even that high up, the vapour trails are really thick and it's only got two engines. I've sat on Flighttracker before, we're on a direct flightpath going west, all planes from Europe and further east going to Dublin. There's a few that go to Liverpool, too, but if you were the pilot and could choose to fly to Liverpool or fly 35000 feet over it, you'd stay up high wouldn't you? I've never been to Liverpool, it's just something I heard my Dad say when I was small, and as I don't have many memories of him, it's one of the few things I remember him saying. Hopefully I'll see him before I'm an adult, as I've got a very long list of questions ready to fire at him. I've asked questions. I've had some answers, but each answer sets me off with five more brand new questions, so I end up letting it all go in order not to mess my head up. Some of the answers sound a bit suspect, like I'm only getting told so much cos I'm 14. The amazing all-encompassing power of Google has already put my mind at ease that I'm not the product of a terrorist, a paedophile or a serial killer. There's no evidence whatsoever to suggest he's whacked anyone, killed anyone, nor am I aware of him running off with another woman, or another man, or a donkey for that matter. Intermittently, anything between a week and two months after our birthdays, me or Lara will get a card, maybe even a present, through the letterbox. They used to come with his name on and a letter. The last time I had anything like that through, back in April, a month after my actual birthday, I got a 'Diary Of A Wimpy Kid' books and a remote control car. Last year Lara got a doll, as if she was still 5. It's like he forgot how old we were, and still minds of us as small infants in his head. That is, if it's him. It may be someone sending them on his behalf, like the phantom grandparents we never see, who knows? Anyway, he's very much a mystery Dad. He could even be trying to dodge Liverpool in that plane up there. He was into his planes. He was in the RAF for a while, not for long though, and when I was small and he lived with us there was a grand gold-framed painting of a Spitfire above the mantelpiece. Nowadays it's wrapped in a bin liner, buried under a load of outgrown clothes and other jumble under my bed, out of sight.

Suddenly, my path forwards is halted very abruptly. "Oops, sorry". No answer back. Probably because it was a lamp-post that I'd just slammed into and apologised to. Two schoolkids spot me. If they're going to the same place as me then I already have problems. I've been out of the house for a full 2 minutes.

15 schoolkids are waiting for the bus, none for the tram. They may know something I don't, but I'm not taking the risk with anyone who saw that lamppost try to kill me just now, so I'm getting the tram. If it's full of adults it's probably more civilised. The tram network has 25 trams on it, and usually 20 of them run at any one time. There's usually one getting taken to pieces and rebuilt when it gets too rattly, another one sat giving bits to any others that break down, and 3 parked spare in case another one breaks down. I found all this out from a lad I got talking to online once, who, despite living in Devon, knew the exact workings and functions of the entire tram system as if it was the only thing that existed here. I always get put with these guys. There's those who can't drive but can label every piece of a car engine, name every type of car and what colour they come in. There's the guys who can tell you 1926 World Cup Winners, or Rotherham's shirt sponsors, but have no idea how to kick a football properly. There was a lad in my last school who was an expert on porn stars. He could name them all, where they were from, what stuff they did in their films, whether their hair colour or their tits were natural or artificial and who, if they ever asked you round for tea, you'd give the vegetables a miss. In the real world, of course, he'd never ever seen a naked female in real life but could still reel all that off. I think Social Services ended up involved. He never made it to the end of the school year, no idea why.

So why do I get lumped in with these weirdos? Easy. Social stigmatism. Society classifies, pigeon-holes and places me into a compartment based on its perception of things I like. I watch Big Bang Theory, Doctor Who, and Time Team. My favourite manga's are Attack On Titan and Ouran Host Club, the latter being, in fairness, weird and perverted, not in a good way, but, like everything Japanese it's so messed up that I'm curious about it. I like Marvels too, though not as much as the mangas, and I also read Terry Pratchett, JK Rowling, anything with Doctor Who in it, but, being realistic, I'll happily read anything you put in front of me. There are some exceptions, like Heat magazine or those cheesy romance novels that Grandma's got in her house sometimes. I keep an eye open on Ebay for old Ipods and first edition Marvels and mangas when I spot any. I make money on these already, only a little bit, not enough yet to pay me through university or take me on the round the world trip I visualise when I'm trying to get to sleep. I play Minecraft, Skyrim and League Of Legends. None of this stuff will ever be 'cool' and I'll never be 'cool'. I am available, as ever, for Bollywood movies, Milan catwalks and auditions for the next James Bond, but I'm also very realistic. It won't happen. They're simply not in the correct compartment that modern society has placed me into. One day I'll decide to sell the Ipods and comics, and trade them in for a top of the range car, a white or electric blue shiny Audi at the bare minimum. I'll also be living in Italy, or possibly the Dalmatian Islands, or wherever I feel like it at the time, but until then, and probably beyond, I'm not one of the popular kids and never will be. Changing schools won't change that. Plastic surgery won't change that. Lottery wins won't change that, nor will changing homes, parents or hairstyles. If I could rap like Snoop, dance like Michael Jackson or fight like Jackie Chan, it'd be overlooked and I'll still be lumped in with the socially inadequate kids. I could show up to school in Versace and still look a geek. Things might get a bit better maybe in 6th form, or at uni where I'll team up with other geeks and research all kinds of cool amazing geek shit. Geek chic is what I'm aiming for, think Elijah Wood or that Jarvis Cocker chap who pops up in the local paper every now and then, but even that won't happen for years yet.

The trams rammed. It's going to be a fight to get off. Loads of school kids, most of them look like they're going to the same place as me. Sat opposite me are 2 younger girls, probably Lara's age, silky scarves on and sipping lattes, like 'hey look how grown up we are!" It's comical, but I kinda empathise with it. They use lattes as the same aspiration to adulthood as my techy satchel, and classier than an ecig and a can of Monster could ever be. I think that's how teenagers should be, striving for adulthood. Once you know who Santa really is, and watching Frozen doesn't give you the feels anymore, then it's time to move on.

The next time the tram leaks its human contents across a platform, I'm part of it. I tentatively enter my new landscape through the big grey gates. I go to turn my phone off and there's 2 messages, which is about as many as I normally get in a month. Mum..."good luck, Mum xx", Lara... "I meant it, don't be a twat!" Mrs Frogson, my new head of year, was waiting for me in reception already. She's a tall thin lady, with one of those Mum haircuts that you know was once long and jazzy, but now shortish and manageable. It's been dyed red-meets-purple, Sharon Osborne-meets-Barney-the-dinosaur.

"We've had your details through from Moor Vale, nice to see you made top sets there", she said, smiling. I think teachers secretly prefer clever kids, as they remind them of themselves back in their youth. "We've tried our best to accommodate your wishes where possible. Top set Maths and Science should be fine, and will set 2 be OK for English while we assess how you get on?" Well, without being awkward I'm not in a position to argue too much. She continued, "We can't offer history and geography together, it has to be one or the other, so I've put you in history, but changing that can be easy enough if necessary." I'll think that one over for a couple of days. "We've just put you down for one PE lesson per week" Now you're talking!! "You've got French, Food Technology and IT. Any of these can be changed, Food Tech to Woodwork, IT to Graphics, French to German, but you'll need to let us know before the end of the month. We don't do GCSE R.E so we've put you in Philosophy instead. The pupils in your tutor group are mainly sensible, but some are a bit talkative and lively sometimes." She pauses, long enough for me to suspect she may be lying. "Mostly sensible, though."

If there were any faults to pick with that, I couldn't see the point. I was more concerned about my stomach turning now that I'm through the doors and into the building. Shit just got real. I really have changed school. Again. It should get easier but it doesn't. My stomach was in so many knots that I didn't so much walk through the form room door as slide in sideways. My main priority was to not vomit, faint, or do an involuntary poo. I felt like an unwelcome invader. Mrs Frogson's tone changed and she pointed me to a seat. "Edward, this is Shabana, Shabana, this is Edward". My new neighbour glanced at me, raised an eyebrow and then gazed into space. Mrs Frogson addressed the class. "Morning everyone. If we can ensure that Edward settles in easily and peacefully I'd be very grateful. Joel." she beckons to a chunky looking lad sat in the middle of the room, "Edward's in your lessons this morning, so can you show him where he needs to be please?" The lad concerned looked at me as a passing stranger would, and did the same eyebrow thing that Shabana just did.

The bell went. Joel stayed at his desk, waited for everyone else to go, not looking too impressed about it. As I waited, one of the lads from the back of the class whispered "Nice satchel chap". Not sure if he was being sarcastic or not, and was about to say thank you when the girl stood in front of him turned to him and said "No way! It's gotta be the coat. Where do you even buy them?!" Might not have even been me she was on about. But only I had anything that looked like a satchel.

Mrs Frogson said these were the talkative kids. In Joel's case, he spoke twice, once to grunt "not that way pal", and once to grunt "in here." A charmer, radiant with joy and enthusiasm for life. Every now and then, kids in the corridor would giggle after they walked past. I did overhear someone say to their friend "did you see the state of that fucking coat?" Was that about me? If other kids are noticing the state of it, then its condition may be much worse than I thought it was. I'll see if Mum can give me the money to go and sort a new one on Saturday.

Into French. A girl, mixed ethnicity of some sort, multi coloured fingernails, leaning on the 2 back legs of her chair, shouted over "There's a free seat just there, mate" pointing over to the near side wall.

I sat down, bag next to me, inside from the corridor so no one could kick it, and waited for the lesson. I could feel muffled laughs going on, like I was being set up for something.

"Do you like pink lemonade, mate?" some lad sat in the back corner asked. Whatever I'm being set up for, I thought pink lemonade might be part of the plot. Answer this carefully. I was about to say "No sorry", before the lad continued, "You sure? Me mum keeps sending me to school wi' it. I've already told her, like, look at me bitch, do I look like I drink anything pink?"

"As if you've ever called your Mum a bitch?" another kid chipped in

"You look at me, you think Jack Daniels for breakfast, vodka for lunch. On their todds. You just don't look at me and think pink pop...."

Suddenly, from totally another direction, "What the fuck?" A lad walks towards me. I clocked him on the bus yesterday, possibly one of the posers that Lara's mates fancy. "Who said you could sit there?"

Slightly longer than I predicted, but this is deff where I've been set up. "That girl sat there said the chair was free?"

The lad was neither angry, nor friendly, he just seemed tired of the entire communication. "I sit there. She's having a laugh. Fucks sake, Shironda!"

Silence descends. For all I know I might have been set up to get into a fight on my first day. The lad beckons me to move. A bit self-assured, bit of an exaggerated swaggy walk, but if it came to it that I'd need to get my fists out, he looks a bit lightweight for all that. "OK, no problems, I didn't know". He just shakes his head and offers the Shironda girl a one finger salute. I carry my coat and bag and stand by the door. Other seats are free, but I'm not risking them. I really am a stranger in a strange hostile land.

My discomfort ended with the teacher's arrival, 5 minutes late, stinking of cigarettes. I chose a spare seat based on who wasn't deathglaring me, in this case at the front next to a gingery haired girl who was sat texting through the whole of that wrong chair episode and barely noticed me invading the space next to her. I could answer every question in this lesson if I wanted, but I decided it wasn't wise. Science was with the boffs class, and was way quieter, so quiet it was like none of the kids in there even know each other. We got told we'd be solving a murder, CSI style this term, and would need to work in groups, which sounds cool even if all it achieves is getting all these kids to talk. I came out of science knowing the names of no-one at all, and the teacher barely gave any clues, having addressed nobody by either first name, surname or nickname. Double English after that. Got given a book, "To Kill A Mockingbird" to start reading. Apparently it's a classic. I'll decide that, thanks. If I sit on the sofa at home and reach chapter 3 without falling asleep then it's readable. If I sit on the sofa at home and don't get off it until the book is finished, then it's a classic.

I kept getting asked what was in my satchel. I told one person that asked that it had a bomb in, and another that I'd filled it with green jelly. One girl in year 11 shouted "Wow, you're dead fit!" and I knew it was aimed at me because no other boy was in hearing distance. I looked around, but there were 4 girls together, all laughing at each other, and I couldn't tell which one had said it, but I think they need to have a closer look at me, particularly that massive pus-filled spot on my forehead.

Even though I wasn't hungry and didn't want anything, I went into Maccy D's on the way home purely to piss Lara off. I could have wound Mum up too and stopped at Cafe Bella. I've heard her before..."ooh their caramel frappes are to die for!"...but that's an alien concept to me. It just tastes like coffee to me, and besides, I had £1.54 to my name. That poncy stuff Mum said she would die for costs twice as much, so Maccy D's chocolate milkshake it is. They make my jaw ache and they take ages to drink, which suited my needs as it lasted long enough to still be half full when I got through the front door.

"Good day, love?" Mum looked up from her pride and joy of a garden.

Before I could answer, Lara shouted through "Anyone slapped you about yet?"

She's probably triggered cos I've been to Maccy D's and she hasn't, but she's not reacting. The only way I'll get any reaction is if I tip what's left of this chocolate sludge over my head in the middle of the living room, or her head too maybe. MTV was tragically having a Robbie Williams afternoon. Mum must have put that on. No-one's ever going to like anyone that their Mum may have thrown their knickers at 20 years ago. To my knowledge, Mum hasn't done that, but a girl called Lauren in my old class at Moor Vale found out that her Mum used to camp outside Gary Barlow's house when she was 16, and when the police moved her on, her and her mates then camped outside Gary Barlow's Mum's house instead until the police moved them on again. The lass needed trauma counselling, but Lara resolved everything simply by knocking the volume off.

I've never fancied throwing my underwear at Robbie Williams either, so, in the privacy of my room, I logged on. The sun was shining weakly onto my wardrobe, on top of which the cat was basking, stretched out, belly up, not moving until sunset, as did I. I put timelapse videos on and drifted from vegetables rotting, skyscrapers crumbling down, giant ships crashing. YouTube's the site where I just drift. Imagine going swimming in the sea at Cleethorpes beach, then the undertide takes you away while you're doggy-paddling, and you get out of the sea and you're in SkegVegas instead. That's me on here. From the ships crashing, to a Chinese Army parade, then onto Japanese cartoons, I drifted blissfully through the evening unaware of the passing hours, content. No-one assaulted me, wrecked my stuff or projected snot at me today. I'll go again tomorrow.

----

3. The Alphas In The Hatchery

One day, Mum will send me to the Co-Op to fetch milk, and I'll confidently reply "I'm busy, tek yersen there!" It'll happen, but decades from now. I've just managed to get taller than her, but she could still floor me in seconds. Half her family were bare-knucklers, but if I ever needed to fight my way out of a problem, I'd be useless. Shelly hit black belt karate in primary school, so only a suicidal or stupid person would piss on her strawberries either. Other kids do say that they'd never mess with me, or, if I'm telling the truth here, what other kids actually say to me is "If Shelly Barker weren't your big sister I'd punch your teeth out!"

I've never seen Mum in action, but I've heard stories. One of the stories is about how she was in some disco called Roxys, dancing round her handbag in a dainty party dress and stilettos, when some creepy bloke tried to grope her mates arse on the dancefloor, so she knocked both him then his mate to the floor instantly, with just her bare fists. Looking at her though, you'd not imagine it, well I wouldn't. I just know her as Mum, so when people say she's the first person you'd want alongside if someone had beef with you, it's a totally alien concept to me. When she were my age she worked in her Aunt's caravan next to the motorway flogging bacon butties. Nowadays she deliberately parks her ambulance in the same spot she once fried eggs in, then once some truck driver loses control and creates carnage, steams in with flashy blue light and sirens. Shelly's one of them brutally honest people that doesn't give many compliments out. I scored a worldly against Arsenal once, one that only Messi, Pele, or myself could pull off, and her words were "That's nice. Well done. Shut up". She's never one for pretty adjectives, but if Shelly does say she's proud of you, you know you've done summat seriously impressive in life. Mum becoming an ambulance driver was one of those rare moments. I'm proud too, in that she's got the skills to brutally injure a man, but also save the same man's life afterwards. However, she proper takes the piss sometimes. She says that if she's on duty when I'm at football, she'll park up in the academy car park, and joke that if I smash my legs she'll get to be the lucky driver that rushes me to intensive care. She even says how proud that would make her. Today though, she's a star. I've walked in, there's food ready, she's ignored the bombsite I created this morning, and my gear's laid out neatly, smelling like the full bottle of fabric conditioner's been swat in it. The t-shirt, plain black with a gold trim, costs £25 in the club shop. I don't know who's daft enough to pay that amount of ££ for polyester, but plenty of mugs seem to. I get mine free with my initials already on, along with the tracksuit, hoody, shorts, socks, waterproof and initialed waterbottle. I'm guessing £250 in the club shop for that lot. All I have to spend on are boots, pads, skins and a pair of black woolly gloves, them cheap ones that market stalls sell for a quid. We only see the shirts on match days. We have to 'earn' those.

The training ground is 20 minutes away if Mum drives, 40 minutes if it's Dad, and 100 years by public transport. Today, Mum drops off in rush hour traffic. Expect drama and some very strong language. When Mum's at work, the siren and blue whirly light means everyone shifts out of the way for her. Her pokey Fiat Punto has neither a siren nor a blue flashy light, so she defaults back to the street-fighting legend that the old people describe. Thug life all the way. Though I'm fixed on my phone, I know exactly when we're at a junction as Mum's got her window down yelling "dickhead!", "dopey twat!" and other pleasantries at total strangers.

Red boxes...Oh yeah, forgot about that. "Keisha Craig, and Talia Vasek posted on your photo" ... Opened comments. "*Cute!*" twice. When a lass says "cute", though, don't get too excited. It doesn't mean they even fancy you. It merely means they'd like to ruffle your hair or maybe poke their finger in your cheek like they do to Archie sometimes on account of his dimples, and nowt more.

Another red box. Sam Blake again, asking if I've got Saturday's match tickets. He gets first dibs on any tickets I get. He pays immediately, in cash. I get given two tickets every home league game, then cup games if it's some League Two donkey side. I'd rather have the ££ in the Junior Saver towards whatever cool shit I can't tap me folks for, so I'd auction them to the highest bidder. Sam won every time. As well as being a full on badass who no-one annoys, he has money. He works in a sweaty roid gym and boxes at amateur level. Looking at his nose and cheekbones, he doesn't lose many. He could simply bully me remorselessly for the tickets, but, to my benefit, he's a massive Cityite. Massive in every sense. I did a match with him and a few others once, Brighton at home on a Tuesday night in January. Kids for a quid. Brighton had 200 fans tops, but he were as near as he could be to the away end, staring them out, then making a bee-line for the away end exit at full time. If I weren't signed for his beloved team, I doubt he'd even care who I was, but, as he's a mindless thug where football's concerned, there's parts of my life where he's handy to have around, and parts of his life that I keep a wise distance from.

I walk in as a load of 7 year olds are just finishing their session, sat fiddling with their socks or bootlaces or looking round everywhere but at the UEFA qualified coach who's trying to point out stuff that their parents and their grassroots coaches wouldn't have a clue about. Concentration's gone, as is mine, til I hear a shout from behind me.

"Bloody hell Joe, them boots look shite!"

Brodie Fowler. Formidably big, formidably ugly, and, despite being one-footed and the slowest player in the squad, team captain. His left's fit for a sidefoot pass and nowt else, which makes me curious how he got this far. There's a rumour, especially when he has a bad game, that his Mum booked herself and the Head of Academy Recruitment into a Travelodge to seal the deal. I can't see it cos his Mum looks like a horse on the best of days. Personally, I'm fine if he plays behind me, crunching into the opposition, softening them up so that I can do the game winning stuff. If we played Barcelona, he'd be last on the team-sheet, but when we get a local grudge match, the coaches pick Brodie first then fit everyone else around him. Some say he's deffo the best choice for captain. I'm not sure. I can see him being one of them proper arrogant wanker players if he makes it. The type who'd get one of the youth team washing their Audi before offering the same fella's girlfriend a ride out in it, or poncing about in casinos blinged up in designer tat and letting every average joe know who they are.

As regards boots, Brodie wears black Nike or Adidas. Always black, always studs, always black laces. He views my purple Agueros in an entirely opposite way to me. What I see as tools of a beautiful but deadly craft, weapons that can humiliate any opposing full back or goalkeeper, crafted to support my ankles and metatarsals whilst at the same time tuning my instep into a finely tuned missile launcher, he just looks at them, looks at me deadpan, looks back down at them and says "gay". Not appropriate, I know. In matches, he always looks for the opposition player in the brightest boots and decides that's the kid he's sending home with rearranged ankle bone composition. When he was young, Brodie would shove you out of the way for everything, corners, free kicks, the lot. He'd banana everything high and wide, and he eventually listened to the very vocal coach yelling at him at the top of his voice from the sidelines to "get central" or "drop 10". Brad (from the right) and moi-self (central and from the left) have those duties. If I'm taking, the plan is to loop it over the keeper with plenty chasing it in. I don't put enough force in them to blast in, not like Ben or Hassan can, but I'm on target 9 out of 10. The keeper might get one hand to it, but rarely two, so the pressure falls on the keeper, not me. If he's sensible, he's pushing it over the bar for a corner, otherwise he's dropping it for one of the big lads to get on. They know what's coming, so they've got a split-second start on the defence, which is usually enough.

"You up for Leeds, then?" I enquire.

Brodie's face beams a massive toothy grin as his pointy finger draws an invisible line across his neck. Everyone has that one fixture that gets the blood up, the one game where the flair players like me dream of slaloming around centre backs then curling one in the top corner, slow motion, goalkeeper flying at full stretch but still not reaching it. The more aggression-dependent types like Brodie imagine crashing into 50-50s, cracking bones, drawing blood. Some of us count the days down for Leeds, others count down for United, Wednesday, maybe even Barnsley, while a couple of the out of town lads save it for Derby and Forest. For Brodie, it's every fixture. Brodie would relish singing "Fields of Athenry" in the East Stand at Ibrox whilst dressed in green hoops, loving every second, then the weekend after, waving a union jack from the middle of the Green Brigade at Parkhead for the exact same buzz. He has the same lunatic side on match days that Sam Blake has. To him, every single other player, in every other team, is a disgusting bastard that he wants nothing more than to destroy. Even Accrington Stanley.

When the floodlights are on, you can see the training ground from the top of the hill as you enter town. I was 7 when I first went in. I were proper wonderstruck by it, though once there it were freezing and the pitch looked way bigger than it already is. It was still amazing. Everything's amazing when you're 7, though. The cat when it jumps 20 times its height, the funny noises Dads car makes if you don't put your seat belt on, chocolate fountains, I used to proper buzz over stuff like that. Then I got older and none of that shit's special any more. If I were a grassroots player coming here on trial, I'd love it now just like I did then, eyes wide open, speechless, like I were walking into Disneyland on fireworks night. I barely think about it now, which I guess is proper sad.

Benny starts. "Reyt, last week I weren't struck by't work rate off the ball. When we lost the ball, it stayed lost. If the effort's not made to win it back, then what'll happen?"

We always look at Brodie to answer, what with him having the prestigious role of captain and chief gobshite, "We need to mek sure we don't lose the ball in't first place." He glares over at Hassan Fawaz, menacingly. Last week I sent Hassan free, 1 on 1 with the keeper, with Brodie going like an express train to the edge of the box, unmarked, onside, in space. Despite the dome echoing to the sound of Brodie yelling "Square it!!" Hassan decided to try and trick the keeper with a half-hearted step-over which got read easily and the chance got wasted.

"What about when we don't even have the ball in't first place?" asks Stevie

I chip in "Press the opposition, even when't keeper rolls out, get at the defenders, gi' 'em no thinking time, get a mistake out of 'em."

I immediately regretted speaking. "Then I wanna see you practice what you're saying right now. Some twinkletoes wannabee Brazilian's no use to anyone if he's standing on't touchline most o't game wi' his hands on his hips, hoping for someone else to do all't graft."

I've learnt over time not to argue with the coaches. No matter how good my point may be, being labelled a smart arse means you'll last as long here as you would in the infantry. The discipline here's a little bit army-like, and in reality I'm deffo the type that would question the sergeant major if I thought he were wrong, but I'd get the same letter that the other 10000 kids receive before they disappear never to be seen again.

Our squad are sort of my main mates, or more realistically, mates til someone sends them home with a letter in a white envelope and they forever become strangers. We've just got the one keeper, Oscar. He trialed as a striker and didn't do much. I thought he'd be gone, but they got rid of both the keepers we had, who seemed decent enough to me, and put him in nets. He doesn't take the footy too seriously, there's nowt about it on his pages. His main pictures of a burning candle. I guess that's for his Mum. I'd never ask this but if he could pick between his Mum still being alive, or signing for Barcelona, he'd deffo pick Mum.

My main mates here are Ben and Brad. We trialed together, signed together, and if either of them got released I'd be proper distraught. We've had sleepovers, mainly at Ben's house as he's got a hot tub and an X-Box with all the attachments, whereas if he stays at mine all I can offer are idiot sisters. Brad plays like me, but I can con the ref way better, otherwise there's nowt between us apart from I'm better looking, obviously.

Sam was happy to be the best player in his grassroots team with his school mates, but his Mum told all the other parents that City were so desperate to sign him that they bought her a black

Frontera to stop him signing for United instead, who only offered her a new kitchen. My Mum detests her and calls her "up-herself bullshitting sixpence millionaire", amongst other things. Mo Wahid lives on his proper rough estate. Me and Ben have called for him and kicked about on this dog-rough concrete pitch he hangs about on, broken glass and cans scattered all over. His sisters say he'd spend the entire day kicking about there and they had to drag him home kicking and yelling just to get him fed. City ran a community thing there with some PCSOs. As soon as they saw him bossing kids twice his size they got the police to hand him a trumped-up ASBO to ban him from playing there, then signed him to play with us. He still hangs about there, but I'm not a grass.

Anything I can do with a size 1, 2, 3, 4 or size 5 ball, Tyler Dolan can do with a cola bottle, a plant pot and a beer can. He can win a game by his self. Unfortunately he knows it. When we were in Spain, he got offered a game with the 16s, big-step up, proper faith in your abilities and that, and he replied that he'd only play if Real or Barca were there, otherwise he were off to the beach. He got a proper roasting for that off the coaches, and his Dad too. That's where Brodie comes in handy. Brodie's clobbered him before when he's got too cocky. He's also one of those kids who got saved by football. If he weren't here, he'd deffo be running deliveries or twoccing cars out of Meadowhall lower level on his weekends.

Hassan Fawaz was once the best player here. He can score from anywhere. All through a game, he has this look where he's just standing, looking useless, then within a split-second, he's away, and one-on-one with the keeper. When he were 8 everyone wanted him, Man United, Everton, all the glam clubs. I looked at him like I look at Tyler now, but something changed in the last few months or so. He didn't go to Spain with us, no idea why as it were all paid for aside from a bit of pocket money. The ability's there as he hit a worldy in against Bradford a few weeks ago, but in other games you see his body language and the look on his face and get the buzz off him that his heart's not in this.

I don't know the other lads here so well. I avoid Danny Flanagan, though. He's fast, nippy, can spend all game laying unremarkable but sensible simple passes, and then, just once, send a long diagonal over that changes the game. I have a moral duty, if he sends them my way, to get onto it and do summat useful, or I feel obliged to clean his boots with my toothbrush afterwards as a means of apologising for spunking away the product of this kid's talent. He's got aggression, but it's more of a bad attitude really. He loves giving out insults on the sly, hoping his opponents will snap. I wonder how he never gets the shit kicked out of him as he's 3 stone wet through. He'll ask lads twice his size who their Mum sucked off to get them signed, always when the coaches are on the other side of the pitch and the ref's miles away. We don't join in, but we don't stop him either, as he wins his mind-game every single time. He's got legend written all over him, especially as he doesn't even care about football. He tells us all, in a way that suggests he's trying to headfuck us too, is that he wants to be an RAF fighter pilot, and he only plays for us cos it'll look good when he applies to them.

I notice a new lad. There's always a trialist. Looks a bit Spanish, maybe Portuguesio, quite big, a bit on the chunky side. We always look at each one, then each other, and wonder who's place he'll take if he's any good. Half of us got signed this way, and when we signed, someone else got the white envelope. That's how these clubs operate. For each one that comes in, another goes, and you're never sure who it'll be.

We get split into two lines of 7. The new kid's about 5th in his line, so I push in to about second in mine, just in case he's the next Neymar or summat. Sam in front of me has no ball, so he runs to the goal line, and waits for his opponent to set off. The opponent's got 2 tiny goals to go at, but can't shoot until he crosses the line, then as soon as the ball's gone the attacker has to switch to defensive mode. 15 minutes of this, then its "switching play". You start off 1 on 2, and you've got to get a long pass across the pitch for your team mate, who's allowed 1 touch then he has to get his shot off. Brodie uses the exercise to let the new kid know who he is, captain gobshite, team nutter, whatever. As soon as the new lad becomes his team mate, it's not even a pass he sends over, but a shot, waist high, hard, impossible to bring down. The lad raises a foot but the ball bounces off him and trickles away insignificantly. Brodie runs back and whispers "even Kyle McCullum could kill that".

Kyle McCullum, a defender with the technical skills of an attacking mid, well-liked across the entire team, who rejected the chance to travel abroad as a track and field athlete, opting instead to pursue the needle-in-a-haystack chance of being one of the lucky 2 or 3 of us who might make City's first team one day, all achieved without his Mum ever considering offering to get naked in a Travelodge with anyone, overhears. "What?"

I predict drama. Brodie continues. "Any of us can kill that ball dead. If you can't, you're in trouble".

I chip in."So you can do it wi' your left, yeah?"

I get the look of impending violent death in return. The drill ends. Territorial game for twenty minutes, which leads into a training game. The new lad's fast and can handle a bit of pushing and shoving. I'm guessing here, but Hassan Fawaz needs to get his shit together if he likes it here as much as I do.

Training ends. Didn't notice Dad watching, but he's here waiting. It should be the coaches whose approval I look for, but they say very little, so I always look for feedback from Dad. Dad says little in the ground. He says that in the time I've been playing football he's seen parents square up to each other, square up to coaches, yell abuse at coaches, their own kids, opposition kids, as in child abuse, get kicked out by security, all manner of parent weirdness. He's selective who he chats to. He'll chat to Ben and Brad's folks, maybe Oscar's Dad, Hassan's Mum, but to everyone else he'll politely say hello then stand as far as possible away from them. He says that parents, not just in football but anywhere where kids perform, like dance, drama, whatever, are a total fucking nightmare and he wants away from all their shit.

He saves the footy chat for the ride home. He's played before, albeit in medieval times with tiny shorts, curly mullets, curly taches, Liverpool winning the double, Chelsea and Man City getting relegated, proper comedy shit that just doesn't happen in the real world. He didn't play pro, just non-league in front of whoever was out walking their dog at the time. He were on Wednesday's books for a bit when he were a kid, so he's been where I am, so even though he's not got the UEFA Level 4 that my coaches have, he still understands way more and talks infinitely less shite than your average fanboy. Dad fumbles in his jacket pocket and pulls out 2 match tickets. One adult, one child. "You were so intense on't pitch I knew you'd forget. You gonna flog 'em?"

"£10 each. Sam Blake. He pays on time plus all the usual side-benefits." I reply.

"Last time I saw him he were hanging around't some pub wi some reyt goons chanting fan tunes. It din't need a detective to suss that City were at home, even though there were plenty of detectives hanging around wi' hafe an eye on him. They don't know you yet. Don't get to that level."

"He's fine in school. They give him this card to sit outside o't lesson if he gets stressed, but he dun't need it. Everyone remembers what he's capable of if he loses it, so no-one winds him, not even't teachers."

Dad doesn't respond, eyes on the road and all that. Unlike my thug of a Mum, Dad obeys the speed limit and slows for orange lights, Theres a reason. He were a train driver once, til one day someone stepped in front of him, suicided themselves, and proper messed his head up so now he just does summat in an office. That conversation's off the agenda forever though. I pull my phone out. Battery on 29%. Red box. Sam. I bet the lads ears were burning. Message sent. *"On Kop nr front, £20 both, ££ by breaktime"*. He'll deffo be prompt, so I can chill. Start scrolling. Memes of Mr Bean being shared, whatever that's about. I twig when someone comments about how they laughed their tits off when I walked into French and the new geeky kid with the saddo coat and bag was in my seat. At least I've just rumbled that they told him to sit there, just to wind me up. That new kids going to get wrecked. If he actually sees any of these comments he'll never come to school again, surely. Some of the comments on here sound like bullying, which automatically makes it no business of mine. One bad phone call from school will permanently stop me playing football at a high level ever again. Not worth it. I'm not grassing, but I'm still keeping my distance from this kid anyways.

So, I scroll on, and spot *"Chloe Evison is in a relationship with Jamie Heppenstall"*. I check Jamie Heppenstall's page. No mention of any lass. Neither Facebook, Instagram, nor Snapchat. Only she's DTR'd. Some lass I don't know has said *"ooh, you DTR'D, congrats bbe xx"*, then some lad has put *"so its tru then?"*, and Archie's asked *"its official?"*, to which Chloe's replied *"yes! so happy! love my bae! X"*.

I interpret this love story much differently, as I'm sure Archie does too. We got told Jamie and Chloe were outside Popeye's Pizza Shack waiting for cheesy chips, they'd both been with a bundle of other people where all manner of substances had gone round, vodka, weed, powders, no idea what, but if it's powders they'd not know what it were anyways. They were sat monged out together waiting for monged-out stoner munchies, and one thing led to another ending up with him fingerblasting under the tables outside, in public. It could so easily be one of those rumours that goes round that you bat away as the bullshit invention of some malicious kid who either fancied him or hated her, or even fancied her and hated him, but the rumour's been out there since the weekend. I keep my eye on the post and return to it once I've showered, stuck my gear in the wash and found a comfy bit of sofa to watch the back-end of the Champions League on. It's only Arsenal. I know they're the British team but this is a Champions League match and their stadiums like a library. Home to PSV. I'd cheer PSV on out of those two. Dutch footy > English footy. In fact I watch football in this order. Spanish > German > Dutch > English> Italian >everything else. Back to the phone. As I expected, Chloe's status just went viral, the tipping point of which came from Archie. *"Jamie if u wanted fishy batter u shudda gone chippy insted fam"*. Then half a million *"OMG's"* and *"eeeeewwwws"*. I bet my £20 off Sam that Jamie will come out of this a hero, and Chloe's going to be topic of conversation for months. Even though my refusal to get involved in the impending online drama and, once I'd read everything, continued to scroll down for the full savagery, confirms that I may well be a horrible person just by ignoring a mere child being flamed online, school will be interesting tomorrow. Maybe that new geeky kid won't be noticed so much.

----

4. Day Two.

I should be waking up fresh and looking forward to this, but I'm not sure I'm really happy about anything. I delay getting out of bed for a few minutes. Through my childhood, this quilt has sheltered me from monsters, thunderstorms, has transformed into a pirate ship, a space capsule and a jungle tent, but more recently it's been my safest refuge from bullying toe-rags. I think about yesterday, as well as I can when I'm half-awake. I'm on my third secondary school in four years. I didn't get spat at or kicked on the shins, but also didn't get the feeling that changing school is going to make life any more fabulous. I'm like a piece of a jigsaw that fell out of its original box a long time ago, and people cluelessly keep trying to slot the piece that is me into every other available jigsaw lying around to see if it'll fit, hopelessly failing each time of course. I agree with the suggestion that one day, probably when I'm an adult, I'll fit in somewhere, but believing that took a lot of persuasion.

The scars on my arms are fading, but I'll still get odd looks if I go out in a t-shirt. My knuckles aren't so bad now either. If anyone asks, I'll say I had a holiday job chopping logs or on a building site and got my knuckles all misshapen that way. I have to explain a lot of things to adults, in the adult way that they always insist on kids talking to them in, but I couldn't explain my head away today. At other times, I'm calm, sometimes euphoric, for no reason at all, then other times feel flat as a witches tits. I don't get it one bit, but I just go with it.

If someone could explain it all, it'd help. Mum thinks she has answers, not because she's a self-appointed know-all, but I can tell she thinks that as my only useful parent she'd be failing me if she didn't have an answer. The contrived advice she ends up dutifully forcing onto me is never practical or sensible. She needs to learn that for every negative feeling that exists, there isn't always a remedy for it sat on the shelves at Holland and Barratt, or any kind of natural therapy, like going for a woodland walk and listening to birdsong, or playing mood music and pretending to be a windmill or some other yoghurt-weaving tosh. When some complete grunter of a Year 11 has just snotted over your coat, and you've got 6 hours of being able to smell nothing but the decayed remnants of his nose-lining, then pretending to be walking along an empty beach at sunset to the sound of mellow fucking panpipes doesn't quite solve the issue. I don't know if Mum ever even got any grief when she was my age. She doesn't say much about her past. Lara gets no grief. She has it easier than me. Everyone notices me and I don't want them to. Lara would love to be noticed, but it's sad to say no-one notices her, nor her friends. They just slide under the radar whether they want to or not. I can hear Mum and Lara arguing downstairs, which will hardly entice me from this comfort blanket of a comfortable blanket. I don't understand girls either, but I think a lot of boys have similar difficulties understanding them. Learning about girls is like a dog trying to understand a cat. I should have a head start by living with two, but I'm still no wiser.

7.16. Whoa. Deep in thought. Deeply late. I live in my own head too much. Mum and Lara are so embroiled in whatever their argument is that they've forgotten to yell at me to get up. I drag myself out. Usual regime, big shit, big shower, wash my face with this special organic soap that Mum buys for me because she thinks it won't irritate my spots. She maybe needs to take a closer look at the state of my face, then return back to the shop and demand a refund on the £10 she paid for a tiny pot of that crap.

Mirrors should have a warning label on them. They do the same thing for my self-esteem as the front cover of one of those men's magazines, not the ones that always have a half-naked bimbo on the cover, but the fitness ones that always feature some ripped, tanned, toned bloke on, pecs out, abs out, hair slicked back, moodily looking sideways. My hair's impossible to do anything with. The bushiness leans backwards, upwards and leftwards all at once. Thinning it out doesn't work, layering it is just comedy at my expense, and even sticking products in it does nothing. Growing it has potential, but I'd have to wait for it to go through a big afro phase, like Michael Jackson when he was a kid. I can't sing or dance so forget that, though I could emulate him by setting my hair on fire and seeing if that improves things.

I once believed I had acne because I was dirty or scruffy, but I shower and change my clothes daily. Sometimes, when I've been harassed, I don't just shower but scrub myself so vigorously that my skin goes bright red and sores and grazes appear, not too far away from blood coming out. Strangely though, when I've done that, I get this relaxed and mellow feeling, like someone's just taken you at your unhappiest and wrapped you in cotton wool for a bit until you feel ready to face life again. Then I noticed people my age that actually do smell, like totally totally stink, like a plague of rats live in their armpits, and they have no acne at all. I once thought there was a competition where you get all these changes, like hair sprouting all over, voice dropping, all that stuff, as quickly as poss. That way, by age sixteen I'd look old enough to drive and drink vodka while everyone else would have more face perforations than a used tea bag and be incapable of walking in a straight line without falling over. I was kidding myself. I can't imagine any girl wanting to kiss me for decades yet. If I was a girl I wouldn't want to kiss me either. Gerald's grown so large now that Mum might need to get her tax credits reassessed for another dependent in the house.

I spray some of that Chanel toilet spray around. It says "Eau de toilette" on it so I spray a load into the loo too. One last look. I'm not a fat bloater, but I'm also no Olympic athlete. Not flabby, but not ripped either. I should start running or doing a sport, if I can ever find one that's not mind-numbingly tedious.

I make it downstairs. Lara and Mum both now silent. Mum's already made me a cup of tea and some cereal. The tea's halfway cold and the cereal looks like toilet paper that's been sat in the toilet unflushed.

Mum spits out a new topic. "Edward, love, could you help me with the groceries tonight?"

A question where 'no' and 'yes' aren't respected equally. Only one acceptable answer exists. "I'll probably have loads of homework", I seek a third way.

"OK, we can go later when you've got it finished."

Sod that. Mum can burn an hour scrutinising the ingredients on one single yoghurt pot. Everyone's annoying. In my desperate rush I grab the duffelcoat again, my bag and I'm gone. The number 14 bus pulls in rammed top to bottom with schoolkids. I let it pass, and get the next one based on a higher adult:kid ratio, find an empty seat and grab the free paper that gets left on every seat each morning.

I don't get why anyone would choose to read a newspaper. Who seriously wants to know any more than they already do about David Cameron (front page), Boris Johnson (page 2), Donald Trump (page 3), Katie Hopkins (page 4). The editor of this paper is probably calling many urgent high-level meetings to try to solve the baffling dilemma of why nobody under the age of 60 reads this bullshit. I skip past pages 5 to 8 and reach the world news. Page 9, Vladimir Putin, page 10 some religious fruitcake, don't know which type, could be Muslim nutter, could be Christian nutter. They're just opposite sides on the same coin aren't they? I hate sport, but the back page is getting more appealing by the second. I reach Page 11, Justin Bieber, Simon Cowell and the Kardashian woman who got a million dollars to get her arse out. My mind's made up.

The sports page depresses me less for the simple reason that I've no idea who any of these people are. Someone I'm blissfully indifferent to is about to sign for Chelsea for the same money that could buy medicine, food, education, clothing and shelter for every child in Ethiopia, twice. Someone I'll probably never speak to won a tennis match, narrowly beating someone who may be sat on this sodpot of a bus right now and I just wouldn't know. A big ugly total stranger will soon have a fight with another big ugly stranger and both of them, winner and loser, will get enough money to buy a fleet of Ferraris, as well as whatever plastic surgery's needed afterwards. They're both hideously ugly already and haven't even thrown a punch at each other yet. The plastic surgeon would be most successful in removing their faces totally and replacing them with something different, like a fantastic pair of watermelon sized breasts with eye sockets where the nipples should be, and relocating their nose onto the back of their left hand and their mouth onto the back of their right. They'd look amazing.

Why am I so indifferent to sport? Well, I could find a way to complete World of Warcraft in its entirety quicker than a golf or cricket match. To watch me do so would be equally riveting. Football turns sensible people to morons, and morons to full-on cockwombles who pick their friends based on who they cheer for, which to me is like choosing friendships based on which breakfast cereal they pour milk on each morning. No matter how hard advertising wankers try to persuade me with expensive marketing, football is not a religion and never will be. I say with certainty that the Pope, the Chief Imam, the Dalai Lama, Buddha and that Hindu God with six arms would agree with me, or at least empathise as I doubt any of them would be good footballers, except for the Hindu God who'd be a very handy goalkeeper. Handy. Damn, I'm sharp this morning. Actually, I was never last picked for cricket. I'd get picked first to go to the very end of the pitch and wait for the long balls, miles from anyone. No balls ever came my way, which suited me as I'd have left them where they landed and cracked back on with whatever I was doing at the time. Boxing's pointless, unless you're the guy who's happy to have his face destroyed in exchange for never needing to get out of bed for work again and a selection of Ferraris.

When my generation are adults, newspapers will vanish, followed by TV soon after. You only ever see old people reading newspapers, and even then, not all of them, just the ones whose brains have been so poisoned by them that they'll insist that anyone poorer than them is evil yet anyone richer than them is wonderful. I've seen so many people get brain-poisoning like this, I decide in the interests of self-preservation to immediately toss the paper away onto the floor.

Even with a very loud invisible robot man yelling out the name of every stop, a big readable electronic strip in the vestibule, and the fact that I've done this journey hundreds of times, I'm still checking the network map on the wall to check I'm going the right way, just in case it's all a big lie. I think Crystal Peaks would be a wicked name for a stripper. I've never seen a stripper. I'd panic that Mum or Lara might walk in on me. To be fair I'm not overly keen on rude sites. I'm not exactly an expert on this, but what's on the porno sites doesn't really look like sex to me, if you get what I mean. None of the people look like they're into each other that much, and the bits I've seen look more like rampant explicit hate than rampant explicit love. Of course, I like looking at naked ladies, but normal ladies, just naked. That's natural, isn't it?

I'll tell Lara otherwise, but I walked straight by Maccy D's and everywhere else. My stomach's turning exactly as it did at the same time yesterday. This time, no sitting in reception, no welcome from a smiley teacher, just find my way to where that tutorial is and find a free chair. I pass the Year 7 classrooms. I don't expect any of them to speak. They're all as new as I am, so should be equally, if not more, scared of everything than me. A single voice, accompanied by muffled sniggers, asks, "Excuse me mate. What do you keep in that funny bag? Is it like secret files or summat?"

I'm lost here…."Eh? Yeah, sort of"

I shrug my shoulders, then another voice, different girl. The group is growing. "So what's in that bag then?" she presses.

A smaller lad, next to her. "I think you might be a terrorist or summat proper undercover, dressed like a twat but really you're gonna let an Isis bomb off packed full of ebola."

I'm struggling, "What?"

Another lad, "Nah, he's a gangster. Proper one, no chavvy postcode shit, but yardies or them Italians who shoot you then cut your cock off and plant it in your mouth. Do us a favour and do a job on Mr White. Needs eliminating he does."

"I'll see what I can do. I'd need to organise it properly", I turn to go.

Just as I think everything's calming, another girl, hair scraped so far back it must make her face hurt, asks, with no expression of friendliness or joviality, "So what's in that bag that you can't swat in a normal bag like normal people do, you fucking weirdo?"

What's normal anyway? This won't get any better will it? I walk to my room, then inside, still feeling like an intruder. The lad that showed me to French yesterday looks over at me, waits till I half acknowledge then immediately looks away like I don't exist. The girl I've been sat next to sees me and pretends to study her timetable, no response, no eye contact, not even one of those grunts that the thick kids do. I follow her lead, pull my timetable out, and study it for longer than I really should.

"What's wi' satchel then chap?" a voice calls from the back.

I look round. I've no smart answer. If I had, he doesn't look like he'd understand it. "It's just a bag." I reply.

"What about t' coat then, were it your Grandads?"

Maybe they'll shut up if I just be honest. "My Grandad's dead. Like I said, it's just a coat, it's not that important to me. Does it really matter to you?"

The girl across from him, separate cheesy patterns on each fingernail, turns to the lad and says "So now you know. Any more idiot questions or are you gonna gi' yersen a tea break?"

The lad turns to her. "Fancy him, do you?"

The girl puts her hand up to his face, whatever-mode.

He turns back to me. "What do you reckon pal? She's single!"

His smaller mate with some kind of zigzag carved into the sides of his head and one of those pot noodles haircuts on top joins in, "I'd get on it now, pal, while it's still Thursday. She'll be airtight with the whole boxing club by Friday."

The arsehole squad laugh. No-one else does. I play naive. "Why are you telling me this?"

As I say this, another lad, the lad whose seat I got put in yesterday, walks in, acknowledging no-one, though somehow everyone pauses as he enters. I've no idea why everyone does this. He doesn't look much of a hardcase. The girl sat next to him barely acknowledges him, apart from shifting her seat sideways a bit.

"Hey, Joe, guess what you 'n't new kid have in common?"

Joe briefly glances at me, expressionless, looks back at the gobshite boy and replies. "Nowt probably."

"Neither of you to have been wi' Shironda yet"

The boy Joe immediately extends an extended middle finger towards gobshite boy.

Shironda, I know her name now, furiously throws something at him, but misses. "Just FUCK OFF!!" She clearly dislikes him intensely.

Another lad who's so far laughed at everything this lad says, continues, "Satchel boy's way ahead of you, she can't tek her eyes off him. Tha'll be on sloppies. Everyone's had a blowie off her minimum. Except you and dweeby-boy here. Google it.""

Shironda turns, shoulders trembling with rage "FUCK OFF!! I HATE YOU SO MUCH!"

I see a chance to win respect. I'd have rather practiced my deathglare a bit more before using it, but needs must. I glare at him. He stares back, head cocked to one side, tongue hanging out over his bottom lip, like kids do when they tease learning difficulties people. I stay focused. "Do you always talk about lasses like that?"

A girl who looks like she's a mate of Shironda's chips in "It's OK mate, we laugh about him too, every time he snapchats his maggot." She does a little wiggly gesture with her smallest finger.

"So you've got sexual frustrations then? So why are you projecting it onto her?"

Everyone's heads turn from me to gobshite boy. I keep my gaze on the end of his nose. I've no idea if he's violent or not, but at the same time, for all he knows, I could be Jackie Chan. He's up from his chair regardless, walking towards me. I should have got out of my chair too, but I thought of that too late, and he's leaning over my desk, going face to face with me. I can see every repulsive detail in his face, the black dots in the pores of his nose, plaquey stuff puttied between his teeth, a single hair growing out of a mole on his cheek. His breath is rank. Could be cigarettes, could be faeces. I'm really not sure. I maintain my gaze. "Your point is?"

"I dunno. I'm all confused" he pretend whimpers, clearly on a wind-up, then yells "MANZ GOT A FUCKIN' DEATH WISH!"

"LET IT FUCKING GO COREY YOU STUPID STUPID BRAINDEAD STUPID TWAT!" the Shironda lass steps in, sounding like she's either backing me up or peacemaking.

The teacher's in view. Corey walks back to his desk, making sure to shoulder barge me hard as he passes. "Later mate." he whispers very quietly as me walks back. If I could live that 5 seconds again I'd have stood up and answered him, but I always think of the smart moves after the event, unfortunately.

Without even looking up, the teacher calls out register names. I face the class so I can see who answers to each name. "Ali?!" – next to me, head down, "Ashley?!" – some miserable lad sat across the room, "Bradley?!" lass next to the grumpy lad who's chair I was sat in, the one who apparently hasn't been intimate with Shironda. Once everyone's been called, the teacher warns of smoking patrols going ahead all day, and he doesn't expect any of his form to be caught out, and if we get caught, he'll make sure our parents get told its crystal meth we got caught with.

At break time I walk straight to the food tech rooms, my next lesson, and loiter there so I can avoid the whole Piccadilly-Circus-at-rush-hour-nonsense that kicks off in every corridor in every school when the bell goes. Two girls around my age are sitting outside, I don't know if they're in my class, and when I ask "Are you in this lesson next?" they look at each other, one of them opens her eyes really big and wide and they giggle stupidly for a full minute before I ask them the same thing again.

I don't see the joke. I've had grief from Year 7s already, grief from that Corey lad, and now them. "I was asking a simple question, what was so hilarious about that?"

All that got was "You're fucking weird, you are!" and more giggling as they walked off arm in arm into the distance. They don't even know me but they still decided to be obnoxious. Day 2, and I already hate this place as much as everywhere else I've been.

Due to some lad called Jamie being in my lesson, who's done something a bit dodgy with a lass from our year, his presence takes the attention away from me. As soon as he's through the door, everyone's at him. Attention stays off me until lunchtime, when I think I've got 45 minutes of nice peaceful solitude in the I.T room. For 10 minutes, I have. Then, by surprise, one boy in this group of younger boys that are playing some online game, yells over to me, "So what you got in that funny bag thing?"

I listen to them guess at guns, ebola, cocaine, egg sandwiches cut into squares, a bomb, all the bread from the reduced shelf, midget porn, a dead baby, kittens. When they guess "kittens" I then agree, and say "Yes, every time someone annoys me I kill one."

One of them stares at me for 5 seconds longer than he needs to, looks at his mate and slyly does the 'wanker' gesture. I see it. Another group of people I've done nothing to offend. This school is no better than the last two. A quarter of me wants to slash my arms, a quarter of me wants to repeatedly ram these boys' skulls into each other's until they fuse and they become Siamese twins, a quarter of me wants to smash whatever's next to me, in this case the very antiquated PC I'm sat at, and the remaining quarter of me simply wants to find somewhere quiet and peaceful. The teacher dude notices the 'wanker' sign, steps in, stands over them, renders them silent and unresponsive to anything away from the screen in front of them. I forget them and keep my eyes on the screen in front of me. I go on NASA website where you can see every satellite that's orbiting over earth and where it is. I've been on NASA's website before. I can log onto this in the morning, and, without noticing, could still be on at midnight, having totally lost myself in amazing geek shit. Right now though, I'm just passing time, and would rather just be at home.

I was so focused on getting home I forgot about actually getting home safely. I thought I'd be safe from aggravation as soon as I departed through the big gates at 3.30. I was naive.

"Remember me you fuck-faced twat?"

Corey.

A bent arm suddenly clasps itself around my neck from behind. Corey pushes me onto the benches, leans over me. "I WEREN'T FUCKING KIDDING WHEN I SAID SEE YOU LATER! DON'T EVER, **EVER** BACKCHAT ME!!!!! IN FACT DON'T EVEN LOOK AT ME! YOU SEE ME COMING? YOU PUT YOUR HEAD DOWN AND SAY FUCK-ALL!!!! JUST IN CASE MANZ IN A BAD MOOD! FREAK!!"

I still can't speak. Within nanoseconds his fist has kinda prevented that anyway. Twice. I feel one hitting the side of my face, near my ear, but he's not got me cleanly. It's muffled, like getting hit by a brick that's wrapped in a velvet pillow. The second one connects with my left jaw. I can feel that. I try to push him back, but he has my arm and pushes, more like swings, me into one of his knuckle-dragging mates, who pushes me into the road. An oncoming car slams its brakes on, sounds the hooter, but Corey stands and sarcastically waves the car on. The car stays stationary long enough my assailants to split their separate ways. I didn't notice it happening, but my bag's been kicked quite a way down the street. A crowd of kids saw it all and split too. Not one of them stepped in. Not a single fucking one. I feel phlegm dripping from my hair onto the back of my neck, like a spider's crawling down it, and it's into my shirt and, by the time I can get anywhere to do anything about it, half way down my spine.

I feel like crying, but realise that, from a Year 10 on his first week, this won't be a good look. It worked in Year 7, but not anymore. I decide to lock myself in the toilets at the first place I can. Maccy D's disabled loo. I check the mirror. I've no friends anyway but at least this enemy on the wall can't punch me. I drop some squirty soap onto a paper towel, wet it and rub it in, leaving a mark darker than the rest of my coat, but at least it's soap and not lung butter. I check my jaw, dab a towel on, then change my mind as I don't want it to swell up. I open the door to see that no-one's waiting, then lock myself in the cubicle til all the tears are out.

The tears are more anger than pain. I don't want to be violent or confrontational, but it's like everyone else will keep making every effort to make sure I have every kind of angry energy that exists. No-one's going to give me a chance. Even if I did go somewhere where I could fit in, there'd always be one odious wanker who'd make sure I didn't. I cast back to everything I've had to deal with today. I've made a point of offending nobody, but I still got venom all day long. I don't even know how to fight, not properly. I've had no Dad, no big brother, no best mate to show me. I really should have done karate or kickboxing when I was younger. I don't want to go back to how I felt 6 months ago, not now all those scars are fading, but I know I'm going to get a few more punches from knuckledragging idiots like today. There's always the chance that if I don't give in, I may swing a lucky punch one day, and then maybe it'd stop. Even then, there's too many possible negative outcomes, like if I did knock that Corey lad over, 10 other bullies would appear and make things 10 times worse. I decide there's no point me spending any more time locked in a public toilet and I want to get home, away from all of it. I collect myself. I just need a walk in fresh air for 5 minutes or so then no-one will see I've been crying. One last dab of a wet cloth on my face to wash away the tear streams, though my eyes are now piggy red, and I decide to walk straight out, head down, towards the door.

I fail immediately. The table-wiper lady stops and asks me if I'm OK. This must be why she clears the tables and doesn't fry the burgers, because she's good at checking people are OK. I hope they pay her properly for her kindness and she's not a zero-hours slave at the bottom of the food chain. The content of her character deserves better, and if she's wiping tables in McDonalds at her age she probably has things way worse than me maybe.

I pass Shironda at the bus stop with up-himself Joe and some other lad who must be the biggest lad in school, stubble everywhere, probably covering up acne that might be worse than mine. They're on my platform, so I decide to keep walking at least to the next stop.

Shironda shouts over, "K chap?"

I don't want to be seen like this, and she's partly responsible for me taking a beating. If I hadn't stepped in for her and just concentrated on myself I might have avoided this. Joe and the giant lad look over briefly and then look away, no words, no expression. I've got no love for any of these people, and to talk to them would only make me more angry, even though I was expecting backchat from them and it's not happened. I don't think they're asking if I'm OK because they have any respect for me. I think it's because they hate the Corey lad and his chavvy mates much more than they hate me.

If anyone else shouted out to me or even walked past me on my way home, it didn't register. It went by in a blur. I got in. Lara's in her room out of the way and I don't know where Mum is, so I hit the shower straight away. As soon as the warm water hits me I'm in the zone. I scrub at my arms til they glow the same pink as tandoori chicken, the same on my shoulders, frenziedly, the pain I'm giving myself feeling like a relief. I scrub my face, rub my nose so hard I hear it squeak, then rub my eyes so hard that my eyelids squeak too. I get soap in them, but the pain barrier I've reached means I barely notice. I move onto my chest until it glows as pink as my arms then tense my stomach muscles so I can go even harder. I continue over my whole body. Some bits, like my back and feet, aren't in the best place for me to scrub like I can do elsewhere, so I don't really leave any marks on them. Once I feel like I've taken some of the pain out of me, I turn the water off. I would sit and chill for 5, but I forgot to lock the bathroom door, so I get dressed and sit, thinking of nothing at all, just feeling totally blank, until I hear movement from Lara's room. I stick my school trousers back on and go down to fetch my laptop and go back into my room so I can avoid any of Lara's nonsense, or Mums come to that. My jaw looks fine, he must have punched a bit that doesn't break or swell up. Mum still spots something as soon as she gets in, however.

"Oh no! What happened?" she runs over, crouches down in front of where I'm sat.

"Take a guess." I don't fancy giving a full explanation. I want to escape my day, not relive it.

"I'm ringing school."

"NO. MUM. LEAVE IT! I've only been there 2 days, I don't want the fuss."

"They assured us of your safety. I'm ringing." She pulls out her mobile.

"JUST LEAVE IT MUM." I'm shouting, but shaking too. There's tears again.

Mum doesn't accept that ringing school after 4pm is useless. Even the reception staff bunk off early if they get the chance, but she parks herself on one of the plastic chairs outside and redials several times. I remember the day she bought that table and chair set. £14.99 from Aldi aisle of wonder. Only once she'd paid for them did she remember her car was in a park-and-ride in a different part of town. Responsibility for hauling those things across the car park through the rest of the retail park place, across the main road, past the bus station – they wouldn't fit on the bus so we had to keep walking – past a football pitch, and onto the tram stop, then a similar exhibition of an expedition home, fell to me. I watch her sit there pressing redial for 20 minutes. Eventually, she gives up, gets out of her seat and checks on her flowerbeds.

"Not answering, what's up with these places?" Then, the conversation changes immediately. "Have you seen the buds poking through on these campanulas?"

I can't differentiate between a campanula and a daisy. My interest in the plant world is inversely proportionate to Mum's. In school holidays, the most likely place Mum takes us is some nature walk, where she'll stop every 30 seconds to inspect a plant, a shrub, probably weeds too, and tell us what they are. On a bad day she'll point at animal shit to tell us there's a fox or a giraffe or a rhinoceros, most usually a fox, knocking about. Even if we're skint and things like TV channels and biscuits get rationed, the garden still gets maintained. When I say maintained, big chunks of it just grow wild. There's a bit at the side that's just brambles, weeds, and something that she proudly boasts was once a weed but is now a tree. It's the garden equivalent of my hair at 6.30 in the morning.

"They'll all burst out into an ocean of blue across the rockery soon. It'll make a lovely sight."

Sadly, the only people who ever see the splendour of Mum's suburban fauna are me (don't care), Lara (never noticed her care), and Grandma when she calls over each Sunday.

"Yes Mum. Have I still got to go get the groceries?"

"Last time I shopped, you complained that I'd got the wrong stuff, so you can make sure I get it right. Cuppa tea then we'll go." Mum replies.

I estimate at 45 minutes max. I need longer. I'm still in my unhappy zone. I go on Tumblr, find poem I like called "Love Is For The Sad", which I share on my page. I'll probably never spend any time on any of the sites I save. It's like I'm collecting them. In a stupid way though. There's two types of people who collect things, those with some obsessive or aspergers thing going on, who can identify fruit labels or plane numbers from 1000 feet, and those who collect as a speculative way of trying to become a millionaire. I'd rather be in that category. When I've successfully traded my Marvel Comics and Ipod Classic, I'll trade for whatever until I turn all that jumble into a million pounds worth of diamonds. Then I'll be free from any of this venom I get now.

Time flies online. Mum's asking when I'll be ready. We already have food, so I'm really not up to going.

"Can I get my maths done first?"

"Ok, have you got anything else to do?"

I lie again. "French." And once more, "And Philosophy."

"Well, do your maths, then take a break and came back to the rest when we've been."

She bought it, kind of. I get the maths books out. If she walks in, I'll look like I'd been honest.

I pull the pencil case out too.

I pull my compass from it, put the laptop aside and gently press my pointy finger at its point.

With a very slight increase of pressure, I make a tiny red hole.

A little harder.

I need to relax a bit.

A glance over to the door. Firmly shut. I roll my left sleeve to my elbow. A second glance at the door for peace of mind. I open the maths book, then turn away from it.

5. Doing It All

Shelly beat me to the bathroom, so it's breakfast first, bathroom second. Neither the fridge nor the cupboard has owt in that I trust myself with, but fuck it, let's see if I can cock toast up. It's that granary stuff with the crunchy seedy things in, unsliced, but it looks like real bread. That white sliced crap makes this minging doughy mixture at the back of my mouth. I've made bread before, with my Gran when I was a kid, so I know what the good stuff looks like. However, have you ever tried cutting this stuff properly? My first effort proper disintegrates, but the birds won't care what it looks like so I swat all the bits a good distance down the garden so they can feed on it before next doors cat feeds on them. I try again, then realise what I've cut is never going to fit in the toaster. Across the garden again, javelin style. Third go. Kept its shape, but there's a big hole in the middle and it's nowt but a crust. The birds'll be loving me today. I just wasted half a loaf. I'll get grief for this. Whatever attempt number 4 looks like, I'll stick with it and make do. I hold the loaf at its arse end, gently, and take the knife to the other end. Nowt happens. This knife's shite. I fish another knife out, smaller handle but with a groovier blade, grab the half-loaf by its arse again and slice slowly. Eventually I do 2 slices and they still won't fit in the chuffing toaster. I'm wasting no more time. I've not even logged on anything yet, so I ram both pieces in and force the handle down. Nothing happens at first, so I wisely decide to plug the toaster into the wall. As soon as I unlock my phone, smoke appears, only a little bit, but after yesterday's cheesy disaster, I keep an eye out. 30 seconds later the smoke's getting thicker and darker so I hit the popper thing. Not much pops up, so I pull what I can out with my fingers. I think about ramming a fork in there, but I've played Dumb Ways To Die, so I think it over in a bit more depth and see the safe, sensible way forward. Both pieces are half raw, half burnt, but it's that or nowt. I stick the knife in the butter, but its rock hard. No way that'll spread, so I abandon it til I'm done in the bathroom.

Shelly's still in there.

I shout, "Hurry up I've got to get to school!"

No response, but she's blasting her tunes out in there. I bang on the door.

She freaks. "FUCK OFF!"

If she were doing her make up, she'd just say "five mins". Why do women never admit to doing big fat brown monster shites? I hate that pretend thing they do to try convincing everyone that they excrete nothing but tulip essence. Trust me I know this, I've lived with females all my life so far, they're no different to dudes in that area. I mean, Dad basically shites toxic waste out, but at least with him he warns everyone, like "if anyone's needin't bathroom, go now or regret it later." The big difference is that Dad doesn't hide the fact and doesn't care if he stinks the bathroom out, whilst Shelly sprays every single scent she owns, all that raspberry and rosehip nonsense she either stupidly pays daft money for or more sensibly shoplifts, and pretends she walked in after someone else. She wants people to think she's so pristine and lovely that it's physically impossible that she could possibly produce a big fat brown poo at least once a day. Still, this is the best opportunity I'll get today to trigger her.

"IT'LL FUCKIN HUM IN THERE ONCE YOU'VE DONE!! STUFF IT I'LL WASH IN'T KITCHEN SINK!!"

"FUCK OFF YOU SMARTARSE LITTLE TWAT! JUST GO TO SCHOOL SMELLY. EVERYONE THERE KNOWS YOU SMELL RANK ANYWAYS!! IT'LL MEK NO DIFFERENCE AT ALL!!"

Ha ha she bit. Now to get out of here before she batters me. I've got clothes, I showered when I got in from training last nite, so I'll cope. Mega spray round of Lynx. My mouth's like a tramps armpit and I've no chuddy. Shelly has never been known in her lifetime to share a single piece of hers unless she's already spat it out. I take my gel downstairs and check my hair in the reflection in the microwave door. It's been worse. I try again to butter my toast. Ripped through it. It's now just a crust with a buttery hole in it. Fuck it, I can't even make toast. Gordon, Delia, and even that Mary Berry from Bake-Off would savage me if they saw this. A life of raw carrots and takeaways beckons.

Archie's outside the Co-Op. I've not been online, but I know the today's gonna be immense, mainly at Jamie and Chloe's expense, or even the new kid with the geek satchel thing. I don't know the new kid, so my target's Jamie. Archie initiates, "Ready for't drama then, Joe?"

"Jamie or't new kid?"

Archie answers, "Can't wait to get through't gates, me."

"Is it true, though? Jamie n't pizza shop an' all that?"

Archie looks at me like I've grown an extra head. "As if I were there? Do you think owt like that woulda gone off if random dude Archie from their Maths class were anywhere near?" He adds, with a chavvy voice, "Arreyt Archeh, herp ya dernt meynd us flickin' each udda off an dat while ya gerrin ya food fam?"

Archie's on form today. I were feeling tired, but its amazing how a bit of scandal can open my senses up on a crisp September morning. I'm ready. "What's your verdict? I think Jamie'll try blaming that mamba stuff he dabbles wi', but I reckon if the opportunity were there he'd gladly tek it, no drugs, no drink, no nothing. Surprised at her though."

"Why d'ya say that? If the opportunity were there 'n all that..." Archie's not on my level yet.

Actually, I don't know why I'd say that. I'm 14 and never had a girlfriend, well not as far as DTR-ing or getting it on in the bedroom. There was a disaster of a night at the funfair with a lass when I was in year 8, a disaster as I didn't go on any fast rides cos I had United at home that weekend and she got pissed off with it. I'll actually go so far as to say I know zero, as do most people my age, but unlike any of them, and unlike my sister when she does a shit, I admit to it. I waited to cross the road before answering. This subject isn't one to shout loudly over traffic. "If it were a lass I proper liked and wanted to get somewhere with, like dating and that, I'd be disappointed."

"Eh?" Archie looks at me like I'm still half-asleep.

I check mentally what I just said. Yeah, I got the words out right. I continue, "Self-respect ya div. Like, if she'll go that far wi this dude, and most importantly, if you think about it long enough, which Jamie Heppenstall clearly hasn't done, if she does it all on a first date wi you, she could've done it all wi every other lad who's took her out."

"Get stuffed! I bet once you'd got her to do whatever you could get her to, you'd bin her off and never talk to her again."

I feel aggrieved at the 'get stuffed' bit there. I'm pretty sure my track record of copping off with absolutely nobody from school is compelling evidence of my wholesomely angelic character here. "No, I'd act same as you wi' any lass that I wanted to go out with. If I tried owt on on't first date, and she'd made it clear there'd be no bedroom action, I might feel a bit pissed off for a bit, but I'd get over it quick enough and respect her for it. Then if it were't same on't second date, I'd respect her a bit more. Then if it kept happening, I'd not just respect it, but I'd know that all the bedroom business were getting saved, and this might sound proper mad, and there's no fucking way I'd ever admit this, but I'd adore her for it, and if she'd dated anyone before me, I'd deffo not care about any of that."

"Aye right, fella, of course", Archie interjects, clearly thinking I'm full of shit.

"But any lass that gladly does it all on day one, to me, in't someone I'd want to know for long. I'd be nightmaring about that blue waffle shit, specially that STD that meks your downstairs look like a pepperoni pizza and booking straight in wi't Johnny nurse to get checked over. If she were fit then't temptation would be there but you'd soon change your number, shut your pages, and pray nowt gets itchy, plus there's that age of consent paedo thing that'd be quite nice to avoid if possible."

"Chloe's deffo a slapper. You just nailed that. But why give her the grief? Why not Jamie?"

"She'll get no grief off me. Whose idea do ya think it were? I doubt she whispered to him 'if you really loved me, Jamie, you'd tek me for pizza then fingerblast me outside the window'. He'll have started it all. He'll probably mek an excuse up like he were off his face, but so were she probly. You'd not do owt like this sober would you? They were probably just snogging then't heat o't moment carried him away and that. There's a chance she might be so fucking naive that she'd think he'd fall in love wi her if she put everything on a plate for him straight away, but I reckon she were more likely to have been too off her face to slap him one for being creepy. She's got that in her favour." We hit the bus stop. Year 7s running round like ants everywhere. A bit young to hear this. I move down a bit. "He's got to have started it. He's capable. I think he's the dodgy one."

Archie replies, "So you wun't've done't same?"

"Erm, hello? I'm 14. So's she. I'd be the one wi't crim record. Sex paedo one an' all. Beast wing at Wakefield once the police catch on. Won't matter at all that I'm as underage as her."

Archie taps my shoulder, to clarify what I just said. "What you on about? The coppers won't do owt unless she runs and tells 'em she got pregnant or raped even. She just DTR'd so I don't see that happening, not yet anyways, but I don't reckon she's mad like that either. Social workers won't give a shit, her folks might if they find out, though. Her Dad's a big massive hairy bastard and her stepdad's no beautician either. Your life wouldn't be over, but your Champions League daydreams would be once your kneecaps got turned back to front."

"What's on Jamie's pages, has he put owt?" I ask.

"Nowt. Same photo he's had for months. I looked. Nowt on Facebook, nowt on Insta, nowt on Snapchat."

"What would you have done, if it were you who'd just been DTR'd?"

"I bet he dun't even think he's in a relationship. He's had a drunken fumble and thought nowt more of it."

"She's gonna get savaged." As soon as I said this, I peer out of the window and spot the geek kid, dragging himself and his spoddy bag along the pavement like he's climbing Everest with the flu. He's setting himself up to get battered and doesn't even realise it. "He's gonna get slaughtered too."

Archie thinks I'm on about Jamie, and carries on, not getting it. "Nah, he'll cope, he's got a reyt gob on him. She'll struggle, though."

I nod towards the window, "I meant that new kid. The Big Bang Theory geek wi't satchel."

"Don't care about him. Jamie tho, he should get savaged today. Dirty slimy sket that he is."

"Slimiest thing about him'd be his fingers, maybe?" I wiggle my fingers in Archie's face.

"Eeeewwwww!...you're deranged!"

I'm ashamed of that joke already, but this is how everyone will be talking about her. This is just the lad banter. The girls will be way more vicious, and proper relentless, once they get going. "I feel for her. She's just naive. The more I think of it, her status sounded like she thinks she's on some romantic fairytale, like in't movies, Cinderella meets Prince Charming, Juliet finds Romeo, all that shit. Then you spot her Prince Charming Romeo dude, and it's no handsome prince. It's Jamie Heppenstall, goofy hopeless stoner, ordered Domino's delivery once and tried to nick the delivery man's ped, gives a shit about nowt except who's carrying weed and how far he can ride his ped without a helmet or silencers. The Prince Charming who'd've deffo turned Cinderella down and got naked with either or even both o't ugly sisters instead for a quick easy result wi' less hassle. I'm saving it for him, not her."

We get off the bus, planning greetings for Jamie, then my phone pings. *"TICKETS. HURRY UP FFS"*

Sam Blake.

"Got to go see me old psycho mate Sam. You coming along?"

Archie looks disappointed. I could see he was well into this conversation. I bet every other kid in our year is. When Jamie and Chloe show up, it'll be like a pack of piranhas that had just located a sausage. Archie's not too keen on Sam Blake. Archie's not one of those wannabee badasses who wants everyone to think he's dangerous. That's never been his style. He suffers Sam on my behalf, but I know he sees hanging round with him as like living with a pitbull with a headache and no food. "Nah mate, not in't mood for him. Catch ya later."

I avoid eye contact with anyone in the corridors, spotting Sam further down, leaning on the tree next to the tennis court, on his todd, trying to look like he's that fat bloke out of the Sopranos. My Dad thinks Sam's a proper wrong'un, but Mum thinks he's quite a nice polite lad. He is polite to her. I mean, I'm as charming as possible to every single one of my mate's Mums. You never know if there's a KFC, a trip to Alton Towers or even just a chocolate doughnut round the corner with these people, so you stay sweet, and when any of your mates kick off with them, you go that step extra, take Mum's side, get them told, with the bonus of watching your mate squirm. Scores points. We call them pizza points. With Sam, my Mum's never seen the other side to him. He spends all his time, or more precisely the time when City don't have a fixture, in the boxing gym, for a reason. The same reason explains why he's still in regular lessons in a regular school and maintaining a regular temper.

I first saw him at primary age. I guested for a team a year above me at a tournament, to toughen me up a bit. I remember playing each wing, not seeing much of the ball, but the other kids had been told to leave corners and free-kicks to me. Not many kids do at that age. Everyone wants to be like Beckham or Ronaldo when the opportunity's there. Sam was a lousy footballer even then. Football's a beautiful game and Sam was born ugly as a pitbulls rear end, no co-ordination even then. Like most 7 year olds, he was a ball-chaser. If he had the ball, usually at the expense of someone's ankles, and it were on his one foot, his right, he just ran with it until he lost control. If he didn't have the ball, he'd just run and run and run after it, effortlessly bumping off anyone who got in the way, like a rugby player would. I watched him play in this one game, nowt more than a perpetual scrum where the biggest, baddest brat amongst them would emerge with the ball, then kick it somewhere irrelevant for everyone to chase after once more. He sent his opponent high in the air then down again clutching both ankles screaming, not kid screaming but proper full-on shit just got real screaming, like you'd see on the TV news if a bomb goes off. The kid he went two-footed into got carried off by his Dad running at top speed carrying him in his arms to the car, next stop hospital. It looked that bad. Then I saw Sam's face.

Some of my lunchtime mates talk about grassroots teams where the players go all out to snap some poor kid's tibia in half. This is why I'm officially not allowed on the local rec, though I'd skin everyone. I know Sam well enough now to realise that his facial expressions are simple enough to easily read his inner feelings. I like how he has none of the shady bullshit fake sincerity that so many other people have, his innermost thoughts are visible as soon as you clock his fat leathery face. I saw Sam's face that day and just knew that he were seconds away from tears streaming down his face and beating himself up about injuring this kid for ages afterwards, long after anyone else could remember any of it. He truly adores football, but sadly he's not built for it. He's tried rugby, shot putt, javelin, all the chunky-dude sports. I'm not sure what happened with any of them, but I know how he got into boxing. I saw that first-hand.

When I started St Kevins, Sam was in year 8, one of those obsessed scarf-wearing City fans who never missed a match and blew all his pocket money on whatever tat the club shop sold. I'd guess at the time anything he owned, his toothbrush, bus pass, even his underwear, had the club logo on. There was a group of year 10s that would drop-kick either him, or his bag about each day. Having seen him box, I don't get why he took all that grief and gave none back, but one day, in between lessons when the corridor were heaving, one of the year 10s swat him down some stairs. He landed on the rail, which broke his fall, but he still took a proper dramatic landing anyways. This lad turned to fist-bump his mates like twats like these always do when they've whacked some kid weaker than them but within seconds, Sam totally lost his shit. The build-up of months and months of being ragged about was exploding in one big fuck-off vengeance scene like in a movie, as if someone simply pressed a switch on him to send him from chill-out to beast mode in an instant. As the older lad was half-goading him in front of his sidemen, Sam properly flew into this lad, never stopped, like a rottweiler would if it were taking on a golden retriever that'd nicked its biscuits. He planted one on his bully's jaw, catching him off-balance and landing him halfway down the stairs with blood streaming out from his face or head, probably both. Proper ambulance job. Sam got suspended immediately, permanent exclusion a formality, while all the witness statement thingies got put together. I did one. It was simple for me. Even in year 7, I had privilege to say whatever I liked with no comeback. Everyone who wrote one just said that the big lad had bullied him and he fought back. He wasn't expelled, but ended up on the biggest fixed-term exclusion they could give him without expelling him. No-one crossed him ever again. For 6 months no-one got the chance, he had to spend every break in an isolation room eating his dinner on his todd. After a while they shifted him to the nurture room where all the really timid year 7s take refuge to avoid getting bullied, and made him mentor them so they got left alone. Nowadays, the corridors go slightly more silent than usual when he walks down them, and a gap always opens up in crowds to let him through with no hassle. If he wishes, he can walk to the front of the lunch queue and no-one would be suicidal enough to mind. All the proper bad lads from the engagement group, Sammy Ahmed, Bronson Pearce and the rest, are cool with him. He started using a boxing gym, and that podge he once had is now proper toned. I'd argue that the only guys fitter than footballers are boxers. I've been to his gym off-season, tried one of his workouts and couldn't move for days after. His one true love, who he devotes every weekend singing for and fighting for, is Sevenhill City FC. This is where the mutual respect kicks in. Sam gets to knock round with someone who plays for the club he adores, while I get to hang round with the kid who only a fool would mess with.

He's so wappy about City that any other club, regardless of how brilliantly they play the sport he professes to love watching, Barcelona, Real Madrid, Bayern, all the glam teams that he'll never see City play against, are all wankers. The prospect of me and him going to a game together any time soon is nil. In my world, that top boy bullshit doesn't make it to the pitch. It's traditional, I guess, to hate Wednesday and United, but a chunk of United's kids are secret Wednesdayites and vice-versa, and half of my own teammates' first love is Wednesday or United. I'm exempt as Dad has this weird ritual of supporting them both. For me, I've no great love for Coventry, based on being on the receiving end of a cheeky elbow and massive nosebleed a couple of years ago, and there's a couple of kids at Mansfield and Notts County who don't seem to like me too much, but explain this to a scarf-waving fan, and they won't get it, so I won't try.

"You got the goods, dude?" Sam asks me as if I'm selling cocaine.

"Aye. Should be a decent view from there?" Why am I saying that? This dude will spend the entire game staring out the opposition fans.

"Who've you got this weekend?"

"Away to Leeds."

"They're going down, them. They just flogged their top scorer and didn't replace him."

Typical fan. I play in their youth team. All he sees is the men's team. "They're not bad at my age. Got a lad in defence that's like a whippet. You think you've broke free and got 1 on 1 wi't keeper, then in seconds he's whipped't ball away, put you on't floor and slipped you a crafty punch in't ribs on your way down. If I can find a way past him, then I'll have done well."

"Nick us a shirt if you can?"

I really could take the piss here. "Ok what you fancying, Leeds home or Leeds away?"

Business done, money zipped in me inside pocket, and off to registration, late but not by much. I'll get a frown off the tutor and nowt else, and the banter will be flowing merrily. I walk in as Corey Hendricks's wannabee roadmenz who sit in the corner and act like they want to be some shitty Yorkshire version of the Crips or something are griefing the new boy. I don't waste time on that lot, but he is asking for it coming into school dressed like a train spotter. As soon as I walk in, they try to hassle me about Shironda, like why haven't I been with her when everyone else clearly has, according to their tedious fucking bullshit. I've no respect for them, always thought they were wankers, so I flip the middle finger and sit down. No-one's chatting at all. Instead everyone's witnessing Corey, the mouthiest of them, giving grief to Shironda while the new geeky kid, Edward, is face-to-face with him. He's clearly not dealt with them before. He's using long adult words like "projecting", and it's all over their heads, too many syllables I'd say, so they're just winding it up more. Shironda's at them too, but in more understandable English to them, like "FUCK OFF!", and to be fair, she's got a decent gob on her. One of them, Louis, hates me with a vengeance. He played grassroots with me til I was 8, and there was beef between our Dads when I left to go to City. He won't go near me at the moment, but as soon as Sam leaves school, I'll need to be ready for him.

This Edward geek knows no-one. It's open season on him. Corey's leaning over his table and Edward is just giving him this madman stare. People often misjudge these geeky kids as they're sometimes secret ninjas, proficient in some martial art that no-one's heard of. I'm actually rooting for him. He's not giving in, and for some reason he's sticking up for Shironda, no idea why as I can't see her ever reciprocating. In fact I'd expect her to be filming then uploading this lot if she wasn't involved. Only when the form tutor, whatever he's called, enters, does everyone switch to 'nothing to see here' mode.

If this teacher were smart, like some of the old crabby ones, he'd see through this bullshit, but he's either dopey or CBA with the extra work. I've no loyalty to the geek kid, but he did impress me by not caving in to Cory Hendricks. I do have a tiny amount of loyalty to Shironda. No-one here's worth me getting benched or dropped let alone released. She's got a proper mouth on her, and talks way too much about nails, shoes, Love Island, all that braindead tosh, but she's one of those kids who can make lessons less boring, so I check she's OK as we walk out. While he's dressing like a forty-five year old sex case though, I'm leaving Edward to it.

Who I study, not what I study, matters today. Jamie will be in Food Tech with me after break. Chloe Evison's nowhere. Everyone says she's sat in with Mrs Frogson with tears streaming out. Corey Hendricks and his dickhead wannabee badboyz spent break time looking for geeky Edward. They tried the library and the IT room, but he were in neither so they decided to wait til lunch break. This'll get nasty, but my focus is Jamie.

Double food-tech, or, as I've renamed it today, double Jamie. He strutted into the lesson, a gangly youth with a proper skeletal face, a bit goofy, and to be honest, strutting doesn't suit him. I were just going to rip the piss, but as I think more about it, I conclude he's a douche and needs schooling. I'm also wondering why I'm so triggered about it. Yes, it's entertaining, it's drama, but there'll always be drama in secondary school. Maybe it's my own mindset. If I got caught doing anything stupid, it'd be triple jeopardy for me. Once school dealt with it, it'd be Dad's turn, and the academy would know too. This is why my homework's always done, the police don't know me and I've never touched any of that mind-bending shit that other kids fancy getting ripped off for. So when I see Jamie facing none of the consequences that I would in his position, part of me feels aggrieved, plus I can savage him unchallenged and maintain my very enviable position.

I don't even savage Jamie directly. Four girls all sat together in front of me discuss Chloe Evison like she's dogshit. Proper nasty, like I don't think I'd talk about anyone like that. They don't welcome me interrupting their discussion, but I drop in anyways.

"So why you giving it all out to Chloe? Surely Jamie's the sleazebag, not her?"

The girls look only at each other, but the conversation spreads across the room instantly.

"WHAT?" Jamie, straight in.

"Yeah, what you on about man?" this lad Reidy who sits near him...

Here's where I boss the whole room, centre-mid. Because I can..."What I were trying to ask these were why just give Chloe the grief? Why's she copping for it 'n not you?"

I suss what one of the girls, Shola, is about to say, the exact words, but I think Chloe's suffered enough. "Jamie, were you stoned or summat?"

Shola gets her words in "He'd have to be. Minging, she is."

I shut her down "You're not exactly Beyonce yerself."

"You're not quite Ronaldo, but it doesn't stop you pretending does it?" she hisses back.

"Your Dad thinks I am." Her Dad's had a season-ticket since1951. He'd ask me for tea any time I wished. She knows it too. But back to Jamie. "So if the coppers ask, could you tell 'em you were so monged out that you din't know what you were doing?"

Jamie beams a shit-eating grin, looks at his sideman, shrugs and says "Owt happens wi MCAT."

"And was Chloe off her face?"

"Aye. What would you do when there's synthetics going around for free?"

"So what'll you do if she turns round 'n says you drugged her?"

"Eh?" Jamie looks up, eyebrows raised, first signs of looking stressed. This won't take long now.

As the whole class is now focused on me, I pause. "Last night she DTR'd. Dream fella and all that fairytale shite. Today no-one's seen her except Mrs Frogson. Dun't look good, that."

"Not my problem, I never said I were in any relationship, did I?"

"She deffo thought she were. How's she got that idea?"

"Well, she's never bin't smartest, has she? Everyone knows that."

"Including you." I pause again. He looks flustered, and I'm quite enjoying his unease. "I mean, you know she's a bit dippy, but somehow you've given her the idea she's in a relationship. Fuck knows what sweet talk you must have given her. "

"You know what MCAT's like. Owt happens. That's life." he paused and hand-signalled his mate, as if he were from New York and not Norfolk Park.

That's life?...Is it fuck?..."Like it were just a drunken fumble that went a bit too far?"

This brings one of the girls in. "As if it even matters what mindbending drugs she'd had, you'd still know if there were a hand crawling up your leg or not. If she said no, then nowt would've happened."

"Yeah she could've said no." chips in her mate Shola again. She's got it in for Chloe, it's obvious.

I'm back in "Jamie. Did she say no at all?"

"Her tongue were down me throat most o't time." Jamie breaks out a gormless chuckle. I remain deadpan, like you do in a card game when you've got shite cards but you don't want to lose your money.

"So wi' your tongue down her throat and her being smashed off her face, she couldn't have said no if she tried then?"

And with that, a few seconds silence.

"Not even a signal to stop? Tap on't knee? Poke in't ribs? Owt to tell you the light had gone from green to red?"

A few more seconds silence. And I'm no longer alone in my argument. It just got serious.

One of the other girls, Krystyna, who's usually quiet as, looks over and says, quietly, "Jamie. What have you done?"

Another girl, Ellie, chips in, "Jamie!", puts her hand over her mouth, opens her eyes wide, like primary school kids do when a classmate's just said 'fuck'.

Welshy, who I barely speak to cos he doesn't do football and I don't do bikes and death metal, is now in on it. "Jamie, do you know what happens to people like you?"

"Tha'll come outa young offenders wi' a bumhole wide enough to fit a wardrobe in!" Scott Trueman chips in, laughing his head off.

This might get out of hand. I'm the leading voice here. The free kicks and penalties are all mine. I'm doing it all..."When Chloe DTR'd last night, she musta bin proper loved up wi you. I bet her folks all saw it and thought it were sweet, like proper fairytale prince charming shit. She must've liked you for a while, fella. All these people calling her a slut or whatever, they don't know shit."

Fucking hell I've silenced the room. I look over at Shola's gang who had her labelled just minutes ago. "She's not a slapper, she's just fucking daft. No-one ever talked about her until today. She must've been well into you Jamie, and only you."

Everyone's hanging on my every word. Like I'm lining a free kick up like Beckham did with that one in the last minute against Greece that time. "She liked you so much she'd have done owt just to mek sure you'd like her. You just keep saying you were stoned. That's not even an excuse is it? It were just a fumble to you, but she thought it were summat else entirely. I bet she's proper suffering now."

Silence.

"But we were just stoned, it were fuck all!" Jamie protests, in vain.

"To you it was," I'm straight back at him. "I'm not going with that rape banter, we could argue that one and it'd get reyt messy. You don't need locking up, you just need to go find her and do summat reasonable." Miss Wilson's actually holding off from coming back into the room, like she's waiting for me to allow her. Such is my presence here, everyone hanging onto my every last word, not because I'm Nelson Mandela or any of those great thinkers, but because I'm Joey Barker, school Ronaldo, and, come to think of it, school Mandela, Shelly C's brother, Sam Blake's buddy, at the very pinnacle of the social hierarchy. I carry on. "So, we all think Chloe's a slut when all she actually did were fall in love, admittedly with a reyt pillock like Jamie here. Anyone here ever had a daft crush before?" I wonder if anyone else in here's done summat they'd not planned, just to impress someone they liked. Looking at a few faces, I'd guess yes. Maybe not new boy. He's just sat switching his head to whoever speaks, out of his depth, but listening and learning. I crack on, "Jamie, just go and sort it all out. You're not stupid man, well you are wi' all this fucking drama, but you know what I mean."

"But I was just stoned, and it really was nowt?"

Sophia never usually speaks in group dynamics, but she's sprung to life..."So if you were stoned and she proper rammed her fingers up your backdoor, false nails and all, bang on't g-spot, would that be nowt?"

"Erm... eh... what?"

Nice one Sophia you total dark horse. I've been slightly attracted to you for 3 years and never knew why. I do now. I take back charge. "Jamie, in 5 minutes you're asking if you can use the loo. When Miss Wilson lets you go, leave your cigs and e-cig here, cos I know where you'll choose to go. You're going to Mrs Frogson. If Chloe's there, you'll be kind and check she's OK. She might slap you, which you do deserve, so if she does, you just tek it like a man, but it's nowt like the slap you'll get off everyone else if you don't. Clocks ticking." Mine and his eyes meet. I continue. "You've got till end of lunch. Ideally, you and Chloe will have lunch together, away from everyone, not like you're dating, but at least like you give a shit about her. If you don't, then the rest of us get involved."

I look around the class. A room full of Ole Gunnar Solksjaers, and one Roy Keane.

Sophia's staring him out like she's gonna administer false nails up the backdoor personally. Shola and her Mac and Pandora gang have gone from gossip-bitches to wannabee superheroines very quickly. Even Welshy, the headbanger I say "Ay up" to if I see him in town and nowt more, is sat focused on Jamie, which amazes me as this is the first time I've seen his doped up stoners red eyes ever focus on anything. Suits him. I even nod at Miss Wilson. Yes Miss, you can come out of your back room and teach us now if you wish. Stuff Brodie, I should be captain.

When Miss Wilsons turns round, I sneak a quick text to Shironda, "*u up 4 clearin lunch hall out?*",

"*y?*" she replies,

"*we puttin Jamie n Chloe on a table 4 2 n lettin no 1 near*"

"*y me?*"

I send smileys " :-)*ur good at bossin dis shit :-)*".

It needed a few deathglares and nudges, and Welshy going "Jamie, ya look like yer about to wee yer pants", but 10 minutes in, Jamie put his hand up.

As soon as the lunch bell rang, Shironda and her queens were in full-on bitch mode, bustling the two of them to the front of the queue, pointing them to the cosy table for two in the corner of the dinner hall, and dealt with anyone who walked even close by them in her own businesslike manner. The scene just needed candlelight, gentle ambience, and fine wine, but hello, this is school, so a cheesy panini and a carton of strawberry milk were the closest that could be offered. Chloe looked like she wanted to slap his face proper hard. Shironda's little chubby arms directed all the traffic, and she had some proper unlikelies watching things for her. Sam Blake, two tables down, back to the wall, with another year 11, ensuring maximum privacy. To his right, a wall. To his left, a group of timid looking boffin boys from year 9, none of them likely to ever care about anything other than Minecraft or Dr Who. In front, three girls and a fat hairy slow lad from the special class, sat with learning assistants, also blissfully unaware of their neighbours. I poked my head through, Shironda spotted me quickly and yelled, "Joey, if you're coming in you're sittin' next to't door." She meant it, too, but she knows that the day I ever sit in the dinner hall is the day Bill Gates goes bankrupt.

The afternoon went peacefully, for me at least. I thought the new geek kid might be coping with idiots, but he's not. I left school with Sam, Shironda, Beth and Archie. As we crossed the road, Corey Hendricks and his mouth breathers had him pinned on a bench, leaning over him.

"Are we gonna drop in on 'em?" Shironda asks.

I reply straight away. "I've got Leeds away on Saturday. I'm risking fuck-all."

"Fuck football!" Beth snaps at me, "I heard you went beyond on Jamie this morning, if you can roast him you can demolish these, can't you?"

This is going nowhere. I've only been playing football competitively since I were 7, got within touching distance of every boys dream, further than 99% of my friends, and enemies, can only dream of. I'm risking none of that on an idiot like Corey Hendricks, or anyone stupid enough to come to school in gear that gets them slaughtered. "You'd not understand" I sighed, hoping the others would back me up. I kept walking.

Beth's got a sharp mouth. "If it's ever you getting banged out in broad daylight, I'll cross the road too, nobhead."

I'm not getting involved. I keep walking, head forward, no intention of looking back til we reach the bus stop.

"Sam, one look off you and Corey would shit himsen. What's stopping you?" Beth nags Sam now.

Sam's quite calm about this. "If I dealt wi' everyone that did me head in, I'd never get out of prison."

Archie smiles, and adds, "You'd be left alone in prison, Sam. No bother."

"It's like reacting to that Katie Hopkins on't telly. If you wanna mek Corey's day, then get yersen triggered about whatever he does. The attention's what he wants. Give him none 'n he'll hate it." Sam replies.

"Would you ignore them if they were pig fans on match days?" I smile.

"I can name all the top piggy boys, blue and red. None of them went to our school."

We watch Edward the geeky kid walking past the bus stop. He looks stressed, don't know if it's anger or tears or what. I feel for him a bit. Doesn't matter how much of a dickhead he looks, he doesn't deserve to get whacked for it. Damn I've even got Sam Blake by my side. I feel guilty as fuck.

"You alrite bud?" Beth shouts over to him.

Edward looks over briefly and nods.

"You sure you're OK?" Beth yells over.

He keeps walking. His geeky bag looks like it's been kicked about a bit. Time to come clean.

"You know summat? I'm an awful person."

"Yep!" Beth nods her head

"Corey Hendricks is the biggest wanker in our year. I've watched him and his chavvy crew whack some kid, 5 on 1, and despite being sat wi' you lot, I've done fuck all."

"What would you have done?" Beth chips in, "your footy match being so much more than life 'n death."

Sam's in. "Those dilberts would love it even more. Like I said, they'd get noticed. Joey, if you stepped in they'd go straight for your ankles or your knees to fuck them up. It's how their heads work. If they've got nowt good going on, you shouldn't either."

Everyone in school thinks Sam's a headcase. I think he's just got that tipping point thing going on in his head where he's OK for ages, then if you trigger him enough he'll lose it. This is why he's in the boxing gym all the time wrecking punchbags, so he can stay chilled for ages.

"And that, everyone, is why Sam dun't get involved in school drama."

"Oh get Eisenstein here!"

"You mean Einstein?"

"Aye, him too."

The bus shelter banter's lively, but I'm ready for home. My legs are stiff from last night. I barely say goodbye, just a "reyt, c ya later" and I'm on the next bus, hurtling away at 5 miles per hour back to the burbs. I pass Edward again, kicking the leaves as he strolls, deep in thought. I feel bad, for a moment, then remind myself that kids like him aren't my concern.

----

6. BARING ARMS

Fuck Maths. Fuck French. Fuck Philosophy. Homework could clear my mashed-up head and help me away from my miserable present, but it's not the only escape, nor is it the most interesting. Any essays I'd hand in would be trainwrecks anyway. It's just one of the officially approved wholesome and socially acceptable ways to escape my miserable life, along with study hard to go to college or uni, devote every spare moment into becoming good at something, go backpacking and not return til I've "found myself", or even just do what Mum does and nurture daisies. There's also the altogether less wholesome escapes. Smoke weed, sniff powder, sell weed, sell powder, inject smack, join a fruity Jesus cult, sit on GTA night and day, night and day until night and day become the same, turn GTA to reality and take a stolen car on a crazy spree. Everything on each list requires infinitely more effort than I have the energy for, and takes too long. I need something instantly. I'm too scared and too clueless to try drugs, but when I hit this state, the idea of escaping reality, wrapping myself in cotton wool and protecting myself from my venomous demons becomes tempting. I think I'll always be too scared and clueless, but for all the negative reviews that hard drugs get, that people wreck their lives with them. I disagree. Maybe the people who do them are blocking some overwhelming unhappiness out, or giving themselves something new to feel good about that the real world can't offer. If the big world is so grim that you'd inject rat poison in your veins to escape it, it's similar to why I cut myself. I get all that, I feel it, I identify with it, but for now, I'll try to fight that idea off for a while longer.

Razor blades would do perfectly, but I'm probably 6 months off shaving yet, so I'm holding my school compass just like the doctor holds his needles when he's about to give someone a life-saving injection, or maybe even a life-ending one. I need privacy for this. I can hear the noise of plates and crockery being put away, so if I can hear that, I can hear anything. My hands shaking a little. I'm nervous. Some say it's like the feeling you get when you want a crafty smoke and don't want to get caught, but it's a much higher level of risk than that. It's more like the feeling you get when you've got Pornhub on and you're not sure if someone's likely to walk in or not, and you really should bin the idea in case you get to experience the horror of being caught out, but you still do all the porn logistics anyway. I don't think I'd never live that down. Even if the house was totally empty, I'd need to know exactly where everyone was, including the cat, both neighbours, and their cats too. Though the logistics are comparable, this is a whole new ball game indeed.

I do sometimes get a feeling that an unhealthy porn addiction could solve a load of stress, but as the logistics are usually impossible, I decide I'd best not. Sometimes, I see things that make me interested, like the dancing ladies you see in music videos, or when I'm somewhere and I catch someone's perfume. That's the weird bit, as I'll then check out the person with the perfume and they're usually warthog-ugly, but the perfume smells good and I'm drawn to them yet repulsed at the same time. I'm drifting here but what I'm trying to say is, if watching "Latex Bimbos" in my bedroom needs preparation and logistics, planning to cut my arms to shreds requires exactly the same attention to detail. If Mum, or anyone really, were to catch me shredding my skin off, they might as well catch me in a gimp mask, balls deep in a dead sheep with a banana sticking out of my bum. The risk of humiliation is exactly the same.

Door? Check...Noise? Check...Cat? Check.

Oh yeah, towel, just in case I cut too deep. Can't be arsed to fetch one, cos I'd have to start the routine all over again. I pull a black t-shirt out of my drawer and stick it by my side.

Ready.

I study my old scars. I cover them usually, to avoid answering questions that I don't want to be asked. It's no-one else's business, and if I did explain myself, no-one would get it. It's like I went to war, and I made it home again. These are my battle wounds. I survived.

My last battle, a few months ago, landed me in outpatients at 1 AM. I'd cut across the front of my wrist, not deeply, but enough to let people know I was pissed off with the deal I was getting from life. The end-result of that got me 8 weeks off school, a whole term's homework either posted home or online, half of which didn't get done on time and the other half didn't get done at all as no-one there cared enough to send me the right log-ins. This was followed up by a referral to a pleasant but woefully useless child psychiatrist who drew some funky diagrams and then suggested I could make my miserable life so much better if I stuck elastic bands around my wrist and squeezed ice cubes. I've wondered on several occasions since then just how much money she got paid for advice like that. I eventually went back to school part-time, but it didn't work so I changed schools, too. A partial success, as I'm back on a very similar battlefield again.

The battle-wounds are quite faint now. Ten parallel lines neatly and perfectly streamlining the muscly bit below the elbow, the bit of your arm with no big veins in it. Another ten adorn my other arm but not quite so neat. I was using my left hand. Nothing came from that. It was winter so I was in long-sleeves all the time and no-one caught me. I felt really relaxed for a while, too, like I watched all the distress just bleed away from me effortlessly. This is my way of coping with life. It's not great, but it'll do for now, until I can discover a strategy infinitely less pointless than squeezing ice-cubes.

I remember how it all started. A group of mouth breathers in school were yelling out at me that they'd all gangbanged Lara, in my bedroom. They clearly hadn't, as Mum was at home on at least 3 of the days they said they did. I didn't react, and when they realised they'd not managed to upset me, they started on about my Dad, like is he dead? Is he a kiddie-fiddler? Did he take one look at me when I was a baby, realise I was as hideously ugly as my Mum was then disappeared forever? I followed schools rules and reported the bullying to my head of year. The outcome of this was the inspirational, ground-breaking and extensively-researched advice to "just ignore it, love", so I ignored the whole school and walked home, scratched like a maniac and refused to go to school til they actually phoned to see what the problem was. It took them 3 weeks. I look at those neat little lines, faint as they are now, and see pride. Another battle fought, another battle survived, another problem sorted.

I press the end of the compass gently, slowly, onto my thumb, just enough for a tiny dot of red to appear. What most people would define as blood here, I define as my mental anguish seeping out and flowing away. I wrap my other thumb and pointy finger around the bleeding thumb and squeeze. The red dot becomes a spot, grows a little more then becomes a very small stream down my thumb, before I turn my hand upside down and let it stream the other way. By now, I've squeezed so hard, that the thumb itself has gone from its regular pinky-whiteness, to pink, to crimson, to red, to burgundy, to full on purple. I'd need to apply more pressure to get it to blue, more than my other hand could do. I look around and spot a loose thread dangling from the pocket of my trousers. I pull it free and wrap it tightly round the middle of my thumb. It's not painful at all, well, it might have been if i was still 6. I remember tightening all sorts of stuff round my fingers at that age, not always because I was upset, sometimes just because I was bored. There's not loads of pain flooding out of my thumb, just a gentle trickle, but enough to know it's started departing me and my body. The thumbs not going blue, still definitely purple. I pretend my thumb is the boy who punched me and the thread is the rope, squeezing every last oxygen bubble from his neck. That works. I squeeze tighter, keeping the tension on until I see a light tinge of blue. It's not full on, just a slight hint, but it's enough.

I can't describe my feelings right now to anyone, not verbally anyway. If someone came in here and asked me why I'm feeling like this, I'd shrug my shoulders and stare at my feet. If they flew me to Dubai, sat me in the penthouse on floor 160 of the Burj, plying me with cheesy chips and champagne, I'd still have nothing to say. Endless specialists, psychiatrists, psychotherapists, counsellors, therapists, tofu-knitting hippies, professional busybodies, wonder babblers and chin-strokers with notepads and clipboards and shiny pebbles laid out on a side table, with reports and analyses and potential diagnoses and strategies, getting paid big wedges to try to analyse why I do this and drawing some diagram that apparently works out if I need sectioning under the mental health act or not. Collectively they have neither a chance nor a clue, but they get paid well regardless. Not once have any of these yoghurt weavers asked me anything like the right questions, and even if they did, they'd still be capable of doing fuck-all with the answer. However, I guess they manage to convince other people who know nothing but want to know something that they actually do know considerably more than them. Anyway, I don't need any of this to prove that I'm not batshit. I'm not about to set school on fire or walk into Meadowhall in my Granny's dressing gown with a loaded AK-47. I'm distressed, not crazy. In the absence of anyone being capable of making sense of this activity, I'm taking the sensible option of not talking about it to anyone. As I've said, no-one ever asks me the right questions anyway. The only people who would make sense of this, are other people who've done similar. Occasionally, I see other people with a few telltale scars. Much as I respect them for actually having their arms on show, I also know that 95% of them, unless you're absolutely committed to addressing the cause of the battle, not the aftermath, would rather tell you to get stuffed and mind your own business instead of openly discussing such an intimate personal activity. Now, if you want to see people who do want their heads looking at and certifying insane, look at the other 5%, the attention seekers, the Marilyn Manson fans, the ones who think scarring their arms is a fashion statement, waving their lower arms about in the same way they would had they had a fucking Henna tattoo there. They disgust me, and make life more difficult for genuinely distressed people like me.

Decision time. Do I go over the old scars or do I make new ones? Do I shit everyone up and go over the vein. Oh yeah, I don't need a doctor, or another chat with any of those suede-shoe-clad rosehip-tea drinking chin-strokers. Decision made. I turn my arm to an angle and slowly, draw an extended line, about 2 centimetres long, from where the old scar from my last battle ends. It's neat enough. It has to be neat. Or else there's no point. Scruffy scars look like you're a frantic maniac with no control. Control's part of what this is about. Cutting gives me control. Neat scars mean there's pride, like your appearance or your self-esteem. Blood rises to the surface of my skin then rests there. I've not gone very deep. I've not really needed to. This'll be enough. I'm safe enough. I carry on.

I go parallel, extending the scars I already have, the same length. There needs to be a pattern. I'll do all 10 scars. Just slightly under the surface of my skin. 3, 4 and 5 are to precision, like a true craftsman. I've a steadier hand than I thought I had. I could engrave trophies and tombstones one day. I squeeze my arm around the muscly bit, from lower down. The line of blood on the first scar isn't going anywhere. It's kinda set, so I decide I'll wait for it to scab over then I can always pick the scab off later on if I need to. There's little trickles from the more recent cuts though, so I watch the small streams appear, and turn my arm, to see if they can flow away in parallel lines to each other. They do, briefly, before merging into each other. I wipe it all away with my spare top. Its black, it'll make it into the washer without bring noticed.

I cock my ear. All I hear is the telly downstairs. I'm safe. Free from any negative emotion. I looked up this little habit online a while ago. It said there were all sorts of brain-rushes caused by the release of feel-good chemicals, that it was addictive, that I'd have to cut deeper and more often to get the same brain-rush again. Whoever wrote this total bollocks clearly made it all up. I feel only total nothingness, nothing matters, nothing hurts me, but at the same time nothing makes me feel good either. I am in a better place than I was half an hour ago, but it's not a dreamy subconscious teletubbyland full of love and cuddles. I'm relaxed. My brain's relaxed. No-one's hammering nails of stress and hate into it any more, well not at the moment anyway. I check my arms again. I'm calm. I've no need to move, or do anything, just sit, and chill, and maybe stare into space for a bit.

I have one nagging problem. I have 6 new cuts, next to 10 old ones. It doesn't look right. I need to do 4 more. I need to finish the job properly, even though I'm out of my unhappy zone now. Thank fuck I've only just scraped the skin. If I do 2 more cuts the same size as the last one, and then 2 the same size as the first 2, then it'll all look right, sort of, and still have a pattern. Or I could do the next cut a little smaller, then the one after, the same size as the last one, and finally, the last 2 as planned. Option 1 or option 2?

Option 2 means, only very slightly, I'll cut less. Mind made up. I take the compass to the exact spot, and prepare. I'll take my time, slow and steady, just enough to scratch the ski....

OH SHIT!!!!!!!...............WHO SAID YOU COULD COME IN?!

I'M NOT DOING ANYTHING!!!!!

LEAVE ME ALONE!!

GET OUT OF MY ROOM! YOU DIDN'T EVEN KNOCK!

Mum pauses and assesses the scene.

"EDWARD!! WHAT ON EARTH?"

She pounces towards me, grabbing both of my wrists and trying to turn them so she can see my suicide veins. I break free and try to curl into a ball. She re-grabs one of my wrists, as if I was even going to try slicing an artery open.

LEAVE ME ALONE!!

EDWARD!!

I might as well be balls-deep in a dead sheep. Nothing good is going to come from this.

I THOUGHT WE'D DONE WITH THIS?!

LEAVE!

ME!

ALONE!

Mum looks incredulously at me. I've no escape. I've lost control. I've lost everything. In one frenzied swipe, the t-shirt, compass, pencil case and text books fly across the room in different directions.

STOP THIS NOW AND CALM DOWN!

LEAVE ME ALONE!

I throw myself towards the wall. My shoulder takes the impact, but nothing massive. I curl up on the floor. The tension's back. It's too much.

I break into those big massive sobs where you can't control your chest movements or your stomach, uncontrollably. For what feels like ages and ages.

7. CHICKEN CITY

I saw nothing. My script is prepared. My facial expression's ready. I know fuck all.

OK, I know exactly who whacked the new lad. I can name the leader, his monkey sidemen and everyone who snapchatted it after.

If anyone asks me though, I saw fuck all. I walked out of school in a deep world of my own. Other things, of far more importance to me than any shit that school can offer, were on my mind.

Of course, I made a conscious choice to cross the road and walk straight ahead, oblivious. I know who punched that lad, I know who pinned him back and I know who sent his bag halfway down the road. Here's the twist... I hate the guts of all of them, the entire wannabee badmanz lot of them. I'd fucking welcome the sight of each one of them sweating in isolation outside the heads office, waiting for the coppers to call in or the governors to all come in for a meeting that kicks each of their spotty smelly arses out of school forever. I'm pretty sure I'm not alone with my level of animosity for them.

I'm not budging though. Whoever asks me anything is asking the wrong person. I've never been that bothered about fights anyway. You know that stampede when violence kicks off in school cos everyone wants to see two kids, who they probably don't know, hammering the shit out of each other? I've never cared and, unless it involves one of the very very tiny circle of people that actually mean something to me, I don't see the point of watching it, let alone stepping in. Right now, half of Yorkshire's teenage population is stalking profiles to find out what happened at the school gates in such a way that the preceding juicy scandal, Jamie and Chloe at the Pizza place, less than 24 hours ago, is old news, cat litter news, no-one cares news, proper September the 10th shit. I could probably do the "£20 cash and I'll tell you a little bit and make up some more" act that Shelly did when she spotted her mate Fyza's stepdad exiting the multiplex holding hands with some random woman. Considering that Shelly came home from Meadowhell that weekend with several dainty looking shopping bags, paid for by someone who either wanted her to say nothing or say everything, doing the same is very tempting. But stuff that. CBA.

I could pull that trick off no bother. I have a more than reasonable level of influence amongst my peers, a position most kids envy, and even if they deny it, I know deep down they're talking shit. They'd love to be where I am. They know this, everyone else knows this, and most importantly, I know this. I can happily live with just knowing I have that power without ever being bothered to do anything with it, which in turn gives me even more power and influence. I know that the most powerful people never have to do anything to show anyone they're powerful. From the hairiest sweatiest sixth-former to the tiniest most timid year 7, from the head master to that old lady who picks up all the litter cos she failed the dinner-lady exam, everyone agrees that Sam Blake is capable of killing any other pupil gruesomely using just his bare hands if he could ever be angry enough. Not only is Sam Blake my mate, for another year or so, but he totally eats out of my hand. He's not needed to put a finger on anyone since he came back to school, not now that his shoulders and arms and chest went into beast mode from all that time in the gym, but he could be king of the jungle if he wished. He could walk onto the headmaster's stage in assembly, put himself in the middle of it and it'd be like Mufasa on Pride Rock. The Sam Blake I knew in year 7 would never have dreamed things could ever be like this.

Bronson Pierce is hard as nails too, and proper connected. He has an uncle doing decades in jail for punching some bloke so hard outside a nightclub that he got proper brain-damaged and has to have all his dinners liquidized so he can suck it through a straw. Some people say it were a punch, some people say he had this bloke pinned down and just kept slamming his head onto the concrete til his mates pulled him away to avoid the case for the prosecution being murder. I reckon most of the people doing all the talking weren't anywhere near, there's always some nobhead who adds his own little bit of story time to it before passing it on, so who knows. His Dads massive, proper bulked up, pecs, abs, all of it, and the giant fat-arsed jeep with the shady windows he drives around in has that 'don't fuck with me' vibe. You just know that one day, Bronson will be just as scary as his old man, his uncles, his brother, even his granny apparently. None of them need to go round in a fat Jeep, they could drive about in a yellow Inbetweeners car and still look proper badass. He's the school badass just cos he's connected. Some of the giant dudes that work on the door at Embrace are family. He's often with them, not using them to get let in through the door, or sorting enemies out or anything like that, he just sits around having a brew with them. There's a rumour that if he can't get any suitable backhanders, like money, weed, whatever he asks for, he points all the schoolgirls out that try to sneak in with a crafty make up job and flirty smile. He'll not admit this as he knows the law, and snitching on him is a proper death wish, but if he thinks he can get away with it, he'll take a blowie off some pretty lass here and there if that's what he's in the mood for. If they refuse he just tips his gorilla-sized cousins on the door which school they go to. He knows all the right people, and all the wrong people depending on how you look at it. He doesn't even need to go to school. He's probably making more cash already than most people 10 years older than him are. For some reason his whole family still live on the same estate, same street, when they could easily be living in some sick mansion out of town with a swimming pool and a shitload of woodland round the back of it. School even negotiates with his folks to get him to attend, like "If Bronson could attend school this week if at all possible, we've some activities lined up that might interest him, as well as a teaching assistant to keep him topped up with tea and biscuits and do any writing for him". Any other kid that doesn't attend gets some wagman banging the front door down with "Get your spotty arse to school now or we'll arrest your Mum and put you in foster care". No-one else gets offered owt like that, but no-one else is Bronson Pearce either. Me and him? Well, we're not mates, but were not enemies either. "Ay up" when we see each other, nowt more really.

Sometimes people wonder who'd win a fight between Sam and Bronson, but it'll never happen. Some idiots have tried to arrange it by trying to play them off against each other, but neither of them are stupid. When I've asked Sam if he's ever fancied the challenge and wound Bronson up, he thinks it's the most stupidly ridiculous idea anyone's ever suggested. Sam knows he's always being watched. One bad day, one daft mistake, and he's out of the gates with no exams to walk away with. He's year 11 too, so as he says, he's got nowt to gain from doing owt drastic which might get him get swat out when he's only 7 months away from walking out of the same gates that everyone else does. His mindset's like a prisoner that's on year 19 of a 20 year sentence. I've never asked Bronson, but I seriously don't think I need to. If you're on a deal so good that they only have to come to school 2 days a week, and even then spend your time in a mobile, on a mobile, telling the teaching assistants how many sugars, with no requirement to deal with idiots like Cory Hendricks, you'd not wreck that for anything.

Cory Hendricks will never have the presence of Sam Blake nor Bronson Pierce, but he'd stir-fry his own bollocks in Caribbean chilli sauce for it. His social media pages are full of him doing all the hand signals that Tupac and Biggie and NWA did back in my Dad's day, as if he actually lived in the Bronx or South Central himself, despite having no idea what they mean. Out of school he tries to pass himself off sometimes as one of United's or Wednesday's bad boys, but, as verified by Sam who knows exactly who's who in each of those thug groups, it's nowt more than a shit daydream. It doesn't matter how often he slaps the school geek about for no apparent reason, or how he blows his trumpet to everyone with bullshit bravado stories, there's fuck-all powerful or influential about any of that. Maybe some timid little year 7 might see it and think not to get too close, but i just see it and think 'wanker'. If Sam or Bronson could be Mufasa, Cory Hendricks and his sidemen would be those hyenas in the elephant graveyard that no-one wants to bother with. If I didn't have my status as the school Ronaldo, I'd have dealt with him ages ago, but I've got way too much more to lose than he will ever have, which is why him and his crew would enjoy it way more than I ever would.

The new lad's done nowt to piss me off. He poses no bother to anyone, but if he continues to walk into school in a Paddington coat, he's asking for grief. I know he's harmless, but I'm not putting my neck on the block for him either.

My phone keeps pinging. Shironda. She's looking for this Edward lad to check he's OK and that. I reckon she'd not normally give a shit either. There's nothing to benefit her, but I reckon she feels guilty cos she didn't exactly do anything when he stepped in for her this morning.

I get a PM. "*Off to Sam's gym. U coming?*"

I reply. "*K. 1 hr tho?*"

I think about it. "*y u goin there?*" I can't picture Shironda in a gym. As far as her PE teachers are aware, her periods last 3 weeks at a time, and when it's not chuftyplug time, its half term or inset day, which is as well, as I'd never ever pick her for owt if I was captaining. Whatever sport it was, she'd lean against the fence bored, checking her nails, not seeing the point. She'd go into hiding if the rest of the world realised she was capable of sweating. I make a mental plan to go to Sam's gym, but I'll get this maths out of the way first. Calculator can do it all. Teacher won't like it as I'll get this back with "*show all your workings out*", but hello? my phone's got a calculator on it? It's not the 1950s anymore, why would I need to do owt like that?

Breezed it in 5 minutes. Time to get changed. Black Jeans (Primarni). White t-shirt (Primarni), tracky top (always Adidas, never Primarni), spray some smelly then check my hair. Wet it, a very slight fingertip of gel on the front and I'm good to go. I'm just exiting the house when Sam texts. No way on earth is he letting Shironda in his gym, insisting Rotherham will win the Champions League before that happens, but secondly that if he's soaked in sweat when lasses see him, it's not a good look. He's sacking the gym off for the evening and meeting me in town outside KFC then off to meet Shironda in her Mums work. Makes sense. Her Mum works in one of the fried chicken shops near The Arches, one of those that she says actually sells take away food and isn't a front for summat dodgy. Or so she says.

Archie was sat on a wall near the bus stop troughing a box of Oreos to himself. I notice that the Co-Op has Oreos on promotion right by the front door, too much of an invitation for someone like Archie when he's got his shoplifting jacket on. He really shouldn't be sat too close to the Co-Op for too long, so I offer him into town with me. Archie naturally didn't have the bus fare, so, realising that if he goes to prison I end up having to commute to school on my todd, I pay his bus to City Square. Sam's already there, much smarter than usual. Black jeans, ironed. Superstars, white, boxfresh. T-shirt, clean, ironed. Black hoodie, clean, no dog-hairs, and he's even gelled his hair a bit. I don't know why, not yet anyways, but you can bet your ass I'm gonna find out.

I catch a whiff of poncy aftershave. I'd be making the effort like that if I was going to bump into someone on my to-do list, but tonight we're meeting with Shironda's crew. That's the bit I don't get. They've been friendzoned by me since year 7 and until forever. I've never ever imagined any of them in a romantic situation. Even if I was out with them at a party and they were dolled up in cocktail dresses and looking magnificent, I couldn't imagine not sitting and chatting to them like I always do, like I do with all my male mates. If I ever daydream about girls, which everyone does sometimes, it's never ever them. The idea's too weird, so, in a way, Sam's freaking me out a bit. I'm wearing whatever was first out of the wardrobe, and Archie's simply grabbed whatever's lying on his bedroom floor plus the usual beanie to hide his gingerness away with. Neither of us much look like decent wingmen right now.

Shironda was with Beth and a couple of other lasses from some other school. One's Tonisha, who I've heard Shironda mention before, and another lass with long dark curly ringlet hair and some mixed ethnicity going on but no idea what. I deffo wanted to know her name, but she was quieter, and it took a while to work out it were Jodie, but even then it might have been Josie and I'd heard it wrong. She seemed happy to let everyone else do the talking. Looked a bit Italian or Portuguesio. Actually, I were talking shite earlier. I definitely would like to see her in a dainty black cocktail dress.

Chicken City stands between Flamin' Burger and Indigo Tandoori. On the same street there's the Spitroast, Chicken Palace, Lucky Luciano's, Bengal Grill, Ali Baba's, Big D'z, and Chicken Express. Even if the street's rammed with drunken punters in party mode, only maybe a couple ever get anyone through the doors. Step inside any of them and you'll not be greeted with "Can I help you?" but "what the hell are you coming here for?" Ali Baba's attracts a few students cos the guy on the counter is the spitting image of Tupac, so they ask him for a wrap, like they're the only people ever to crack that joke. Shironda denies this, but I've never seen any customers inside Chicken City, not even the drunks who salivate for deep-fried crap at 2am. Right now, there's a couple of overly crispy drumsticks sat looking lonely in the warm roasty thing at the counter, and even though they sell kebabs, that elephant foot that slowly swivels round in every other kebab shop is nowhere to be seen, nor is the chicken one, which is enough to tell me to stick to Nandos as usual. Most of the menu is deep-fried, so we should enter and be overcome by the stench of deep-fried fat or whatever, but nowt stinks at all, apart from Sam. Shironda goes into the back room, and appears again with a multipack box of Coke cans. I've got training tomorrow, so I ask Shironda if there's owt else instead and she replies with "council pop or go home", so I hold onto the unopened can then pass it to Sam. He's gone proper quiet. Shy even.

Shironda's mum appears with a ruffle on my head, a "Here you go sweetheart" and a bottle of designer water. Shironda rolls her eyes, and whispers "twat" my way.

In fact, the only creatures that ever eat out round here are foxes. They say that if you show up here at about 4am, you'll see them tipping all the bins over, feasting on any discarded food lying around near the bins. I bet the Arches is like a massive free banquet for them, plus they don't have to look for rabbit holes anymore. Everything they hunt for, chicken, sheep, whatever, is freely available on this one street, with added spicy coatings. The other reason these places are empty is there were two murders round here a year or so ago. According to Shironda, cos she knew all about it, one was some guy who owed money to the wrong people, proper stinky debts that never get paid off. Whoever he owed to caught up with him in the car park round the side of this street, and he got found with his throat slit, blood everywhere. It was definitely a halal-style slaughter. No-one knows, or I should be more honest here, anyone who does know has made a point of losing their memory, blaming alcohol, drugs and the fact they've slept since then as reasons to remember only the most basic or useless details for the police to go anywhere with. The one big bit of news that did break that night was that all the cameras that point towards the car park are dummies. As a result, no-one in the know parks a car there anymore, and anyone who fancies twoccing a car easily now knows they no longer need to venture to the darker bits of the lower level car parks at Meadowhall. There was another murder soon after, a shooting, but Shironda gets all defensive about this one. She used to shout she knew nothing about it at all so stop asking her anything, and why would her Mum know anything about it when all she does is fry chicken. It's obvious that she knows nothing of the one she talks about, and knows plenty of the one she claims to know nothing about, but in reality she's only doing the same trick that I'll do in school tomorrow if anyone asks about Edward Geek.

The guy that owns Chicken City walks in, confused to see he has customers. Once he clocks it's Shironda's mates he greets us with a slightly concerned looking glance at the fizzy pop we're sipping on, then smiles a little and laughs out loud "Even you lot won't touch my food!". He's smartly turned out, not suited or owt, but his trousers and shirt look carefully chosen and made to fit. He walks to embrace Shironda's Mum with a kiss. I'm not an expert on reading kisses, but I'd score detective points if I said that this fella and Shironda's Mum might be a bit more than boss and employee.

I know a bit about this fella, more than he knows I know, or would want me to know for real. Ali somebody. Shironda describes him as a family friend, and like a Dad to her, even though I never hear her mention her real Dad much. She says he works away, but there's a rumour her Dad's doing 10 years in Nottingham prison, and because he's taken the rap for someone who'd get twice as long, and suffers memory loss whenever the police ask him questions in return for an earlier release date, Shironda and her Mum are well-looked after by random people. Might be fairy stories, though. Every now and then Ali will throw money at her, not a tenner or £20 like I get when I do something well, but a big solid wad of it. Her nails, hair, bag and whatever bling's adorning her wrists are all you need to see to know she's been endowed financially. Sometimes gifts appear from nowhere, Pandora bracelets, snazzy smartphones when it's nowhere near her birthday. There's deffo a reason for those gifts and if she ever says it's for getting good grades then she thinks I'm daft. School even fetched social workers once as they thought she had that CSE grooming going on, but everyone knows the kind of kid that gets pulled into that stuff, and it's nowt like her. Besides, for as long as her Dad's good at keeping secrets, then she's got family friends like Ali here to ensure that if anyone tried to groom her they'd disappear mysteriously, re-appearing in small pieces years later at a variety of locations. She's talked about Ali before. He's got a used car showroom on the outskirts of town somewhere, and Shironda says all the cars have been "recycled", whatever she means by that, and he sells about as many cars as he does chicken burgers. About once every 4 or 5 years, the whole "showroom", which is actually a portakabin with a few manky cars parked around it, goes up in flames. Police never quite worked out if it were an insurance job or an arson by someone who doesn't like him, but with him being a bit of a wrong'un with definitely a shitload of enemies just as dodgy as him, and despite it not needing the FBI to work out that he probably burns it all down himself before setting up another portakabin in a slightly different postcode, a few more dodgy cars with rushed paint jobs and a fat bundle of insurance money in the bank, they never seem to be too bothered about dealing with it.

With us, he's always friendly. Sometimes if there's a party he'll drop Shironda and her mates off, in his flashy car, one of those BMWs that can be convertible too, electric blue. Having said that, you just sense that through the gifts, the friendliness, the welcoming father-figure type he plays with us, there's no doubt another side to his personality that we don't get to see, that's not so amiable. Dad, Mum and Shelly all know of him. Their advice is identical, "Be polite if he speaks to you, but don't get too close, and if you know anyone who pisses him off, then don't be too close to them either." They give the same advice to dealing with Shironda too.

The conversation moves at ADHD-level from whether Archie's carrying weed or not (he isn't, I believe him cos I'd have smelt it by now, and I'd have also caught a whiff of 50p body spray too. Though he could do with spending the saved 50p on some chuddy to get the stench of Golden Virginia off his breath) to why Sam's looking so dapper. Tonisha's complimentary, Shironda's impressed, Beth doesn't appear to give a shit, nor does Jodie, and Shironda's Mum has already told him how lovely he looks when he makes the effort, and how he should do it more often, especially now he's toned up a bit and the ladies are going to love him. It sent Sam speechless, scarlet with embarrassment, which were hilarious, until she finished with "Ooh if I were 20 years younger", which sounded a bit wrong. Imagine a 40 year old bloke saying that to a teenage lass. Beth then moved the conversation to a repeat of her earlier lyrics at me and Sam for crossing the road from Edward earlier. I try arguing my case - I'd still be 1 against 4, I didn't see owt, I'm not risking my football career on a twat like Cory Hendricks - but Beth's having none of it, Shironda neither, while Archie's sat in deckchair-popcorn mode on the basis that for him, watching me and Sam taking a bollocking is top entertainment.

Archie chips in, "So, I'm not in no lessons wi' Cory Hendricks, and apart from one of his goons trying to nick me hat off me in year 8, he's never bothered me, but I've seen him in action and, if it'd bin me he'd griefed, I'd've dealt wi' him already. So why not you lot?"

"Much as I love you, Archie, especially your genius ways to successfully conceal stolen goods and your choice of headwear, I see you more as a stoner than a fighter, love." Beth chips in.

Tonisha scrolls through her phone and pulls up Corey's Facebook page. "Is this him?" Badman scowl on his profile, picture of 50 Cent with "Trust Nobody" inscribed. That's the homepage alright. Can't even stick a decent rapper on his page. Fuck it, if Tupac and Biggie hadn't got shot, 50 Cent wouldn't have been heard of, but I'm drifting here.

"Yep." I chip in.

"So you're saying none of you can tek care of him?" Tonisha looks our way, specifically to Sam.

"I'm out of school in 6 months. I've already stuck one lad in hospital and nearly got swat out. I need to see me time out peacefully. Joey gets it. I'm on a yellow card, 5 minutes from full time and the ref's watching my every tackle."

"It'd tek you 10 seconds, Sam"

"It'd tek the governors 10 seconds too."

Sam nods at Ali. Father figure. Could easily be a Godfather figure. Shironda looks a bit Italian or Mediterranean regardless of what colour she does her hair. Her Mum doesn't at all. I'm not asking.

"What about your Mum's buddy over there, is he aware you've been getting disrespected? I'm sure a dude like him has connections?" Sam asks Shironda.

Shironda looks at Sam like he's a moron. "Do you know anyone in your gym who's up for going to't infant school and tekkin on't badlad in reception class?"

Beth backs her up, "It's only Cory Hendricks. And we're sitting watching him savage everyone."

I'm in. "He were reyt disgusting to you earlier. If that were my sister getting griefed like that, my Dad would be scribbling the kids 16th birthday in his diary and booking time off to visit him the day after without any doubt."

"Like it'd happen wi' your Shelly. Does she know anyone?"

"She left school last year, why would she care?"

Beth's in, "Well the reason you get such an easy ride has fuck all to do with being a fancy-dan footballer and everything to do with her being hard as nails."

Shironda laughs at me "How come she's such a badass and you're such a fucking pansy?"

The answer to that's easy. Shelly inherited Mum's streetfighter shit. I inherited a fantastically high ABC and a markedly less aggressive demeanor from my Dad, who was also quite a handy footballer in his time. For a centre-back, he didn't get that many yellows or reds, and has no recent history of brawling. There were a time when I were 6 and Shelly were 9 that we both did karate. She went through her belts dead quick as she was shit-hot at doing the fighting, and went competitive for a bit. I got to blue belt cos I could do all the katas and stay on my feet. I weren't bad, but football started taking me on nice holidays and karate wasn't so I gave it up. Anyways...

"She did all that karate way back, but I had to rag it all in cos of football."

"Bag of toss!" Archie laughs.

Sam chips in "Your Dad played centre-back. Non-league 'n all, so he's no lightweight. Unlike you"

"Eh? Since when?"

Beth's back, like a stuck CD, "Since you saw Cory Hendricks twatting Edward and walked by."

"There were hundreds walking past, plenty of year 11s too, why are you singling me out?"

Sam's in. "Mate, them hundreds of kids don't have your influence. I heard about you giving Jamie them lyrics earlier. There's about 3 kids in't whole school that can pull that off. One's Bronson. He's not around. One's Bronson's sister in year 9, and one's you."

"Is this about dealing wi' Corey for't shit he gave to Shironda, or to Edward?" Archie asks.

"Is Edward sat wi' us getting us free drinks and margaritas right now?", Beth throws back.

Tonisha's mate, Jodie, joins in. "Is this Edward Pendlebury you're talking about?"

"Do you know him?" I ask. I need to know, before anyone twigs that my Mum knows his Mum.

"He were in my school in year 7. Big bushy hair. Got savaged daily, bless him. Summat happened in't PE changing rooms and we never saw him after that."

Shironda's scrolling, as is Beth.

"Nowt on Insta."

"Nowt on Snapchat, neither."

"Facebook! No profile pic. Thirty-two friends. Bless!"

"So he dun't do social networking. So what?"

"Dickhead. How many year 10s do you know like that?" Beth snaps.

"Loads." I reply.

"Name one?"

"Tyrell Jones from my footy team. Uses Insta for his footy pictures and CBA wi' owt else."

"So he uses it, just not much?"

"What about that lass who catfished hersen on Tinder wi' pictures of some model, then when her folks found out they put all her technology on factory settings, flogged it all and put her on a pay-as-u-go ten-quid brick?"

"And how many kids do you know who do shit like that?"

Jodie backs me up, "I know a lad who's on nowt cos he's got baby brain and can't use IT."

"Isolated cases then."

Jodie's eyes would be beautiful if she hadn't drawn black eye liner shit round them, but I'm not telling her that today. "Do you know Edward well?"

"Yeah, he had one of them businessmen bags. Kids would throw it all over. Someone photo'd the caretaker on a ladder getting it off the top of a basketball net one day and it went viral."

"His bag were in't middle o't road earlier. Some car had to slam't brakes so it din't get crushed."

"Oh, bless him!" Jodie says.

That's twice she's said that. I actually fancy her a little bit, but I'm not letting on, not when Sam's clearly in the mood for love with someone and I've not sussed out who.

"So this grief he's been getting's nowt new to him?"

Sam thinks I'm trying to excuse it all. "Yeah, but it's still not reyt. I heard he stuck up for you today for no reason at all, Shironda."

"I know, that's why I want to collar him to say thanks. I've seen his page, I'll get him on that."

"He last posted in 2013. He probly stopped bothering wi' it, like bullied kids do."

"So, if he sticks his neck out for you when he dun't need to, then why are you delving into me for not sticking me neck out when you've done't same?"

"Joey, you don't risk owt for anyone. Shola and them dollies she knocks around wi' were all saying you proper savaged Jamie for being a sleazebag. You'd not have done that for nowt, it were either to get in Shola's knickers or just to be Billy Big-Ones."

Beth interjects, deadpan, "I can't see you fancying her, Joe. She's all Mac and Pandora and not much else. She's made a note of you though, just in case you get to play for England then she'll be all over you so she can date a footballer, or forgetting you if you don't. Whereas your real mates, like me," she fake smiles "have no issue wi' snapping both your ankles if you start acting like a wanker."

Sam laughs. "Shola's Dad's at every City game, home fixtures at least. Knows the score of every game since World War 1, first team, reserves, all of it. Knows every player, especially you, and which lessons you do with his little princess."

"Why'd anyone be that bothered about their kid being in lessons wi' me?"

Shironda rolls her black-lined eyes, looks to Sam, Archie, then to me. "You don't even know do you?"

Sam turns to face me full-on. Alongside, Archie leans forward to face me full on too, just for the piss-take. "Right, fella. Are you listening?"

I pull a face.

"How many lasses in year 8 do you know?"

"None really. A lass who lives further down my street but I know her brother better. Why?"

"Have you ever been around when some dippy lass boasts that she's your friend on Snapchat?"

"Or, get this." Archie's in "You know that lad you walked to year 7 the other day, that chubby little ginger who fell down't stairs. Have you seen him lately?"

"Year 7s all look the same to me?"

"This one swags down't corridors in boss mode wi't shoulders swinging cos the rest of his year think he's full-on buddies with you. Think about it. Fat. Ginger. Clumsy as fuck. And everyone leaves him alone. As a fellow ginger I more than appreciate the scale of this." Archie laughs.

Sam adds more. "Somehow I'm popular. You think it's cos I do boxing n that. Nah, that still meks me a possible psycho. I'm one o't popular kids. Me, Sam Blake! Any idea how that happened?"

Archie's back. "Every lass in year 9 added me. I added none. When does that happen to a ginger? When I'm up at me Dads, I can't even get't kid next door to say hello to us. I'm not even Archie Connell. I'm Archie Joesmate. I don't particularly like the idea right now, but once I've used it to win ther best-looking of these fools over wi' me irresistible charm and had a few sexy sleepovers, I'll happily go along wi' it."

"But half an hour ago you said that if it weren't for Shelly I'd have got ragged about too?"

"Yeah, we'll do that. We've known you years. None of us idolise you. We all know the real you, which, tekkin all that Lionel Messi nonsense away, is basically a bit of a twat."

Beth's backing up. "There's others knocking about who don't like the fucking fandom you get and would love to see you fail. I feel the same when you get cocky cos you've won a footy match or," she pauses "whatever. I don't want to say well done or boast that I'm acquainted with you. I'd rather smash your ankles. If you did smash your legs tomorrow, there's kids about who'd fucking love it. Cory Hendricks's one. And his mates are 3 more."

"As if I even asked for any of that?" I try to counter

"Well it's not like you're ever bothered about anyone. It's why I call bullshit on you even caring how Chloe Evison were feeling. You savaged Jamie cos it were entertaining, you could get away with it, and you knew that most kids would back you over Jamie any day. It were just a laugh to you."

Actually, she's bang on the money with this. But am I fuck agreeing with her.

Shironda's back. "If you can savage Jamie, who's a nice lad but just fucking daft, and back Chloe up, who, thanks to you and your gob, in't a slut any more but just a bit dippy, why don't you use your fandom properly, like breaking 4-on-1 fights up?"

"But I weren't the only kid in't class who did nowt"

"No-ones got your profile. Or your sister. I've heard no-one messes wi' your Mum either."

"So you want me to be Superman?"

"How's about you back Edward up? You don't have to pal up with him, just step in."

"What's he ever going to do for me?"

"If he can step in for me, a stranger, why wouldn't he back you up too?"

"He's go no chance. He's not even big."

Sam's in. "Hello. School psycho in the house. Your mate. Guess what weight I bench-pressed last week?"

I accept my fate. If Edward Pendlebury gets whacked by Corey Hendricks again, I agree to step in. It won't happen, cos I'll put myself nowhere near him. Everyone's happy, especially Sam. I spot Tonisha checking Sam up and down, eye to eye, then up and down again. I study him studying her, just to see what he looks like when he fancies someone. A bit of a twat, to be honest.

I get the bus back with my cheeky sidemen, paying Archie's way again. Sam splits at the nature walk, and Archie at the original crime-scene, the Co-Op. I add Jodie on Facebook, Snapchat and Instagram. By the time I'm through the door, she's accepted all 3, and my red box is full from her liking all my photos. Well, the photos with me in it. Just me. When she finds the sick action shot of me from a couple of years ago, she sticks a love heart on it. Get in! I repay the compliment. Quick nosy through her photos. She looks awesome without all that slap on. I go through and like all the photos where she's not slapped up with Mac or whatever. Oh yeah, she doesn't do that duckfacing thing. I don't get why lasses do that? One day their kids will see those photos and the future won't be kind. Elsewhere, on my news page, 20 questions about Cory Hendricks and Edward Pendlebury.

Fuck it. I still know nowt.

----

8. The Mother Of All Fridays

School must have expected Mum's call, bang on 8.45am, as they put her on hold, and when, at 9.00, the hope that she'd hang up and go away hadn't materialized, they let her leave a message for the Head of Year. Mum's given Mrs Frogson until 11.00 to call back. At 11.01 Mum intends to drive to school and sit in reception until she's seen either the Head, the Head of Child Protection, or Mrs Frogson.

As always after I've been cutting, I have that curled up in cotton wool feeling, but it won't last. From the impenetrable bubble of this living room, and the cosiness of this old raggy sofa, the undeserved evilness I encounter daily feels far away. I don't really want to leave it or think about anything outside it, but eventually I'll have no choice but to go and face it once more.

So how did I get here? I mean, the whole world hates me and I've no idea why. I came home having never felt so alone and defeated. If there was a motorway or a railway line along my walk home, I'm sure I'd have stepped forwards and made myself something that could only be scraped up. If I was on a tall building or bridge then I'd have taken the Humpty Dumpty option without hesitation. If a big bag full of heroin or crack was available to me, I'd have taken it all. I don't even know how to take it anyway, I know smack's injected but have massive areas of innocence in this area, so I'd have just sprinkled it all on a pizza or in a bowl with ice cream and chocolate sprinkles, but I'd have taken it anyway.

Hard drugs will never solve my shit, but they'd take me to a nicer place than I'm presently in, if only for a short while. Yes, I know the risks, but last night I'd have happily blown myself away from the present, whether by mind-bending drugs or a dangerous weapon. I know that unhappy zone too well now, the one where you can't see anything clearly, can't see the future, think everything's hopeless and see ending everything as a positive move. I've tried escaping it before. Last year, aside from cutting across my wrist, I took other, paracetamol flavoured steps, to put my escape plan to action, thinking I'd be doing everyone a favour. I thought nobody would care too much and the tiny minority of people I can count on one hand who did actually care about me would be saved no end of bother.

I didn't quite reach that stage last night. This is because we no longer have a bathroom cabinet. Wherever the pills are kept, Mums ensured that I'm not party to that information. Similarly the kitchen knives, tool box, and even the washing line are all kept somewhere only she knows. Even my shoes are slip ons, as I can't be trusted with shoelaces apparently.

Last night, the more I shredded my arms, the more detached I became from everything around me. I wasn't cutting where I could crack an artery open, but I was so focused, so concentrated on drawing blood, giving myself that bit of pain, that I'd shut everything else out. There's 10 parallel lines across each of them, I'll cut downwards next time and make them into a waffle pattern that maybe I could play hugs & kisses on if I had a friend to join in. I've scratched a few across the base of my wrists before, just to let everyone know I'm really not happy with life. The first time I did this, everyone thought I was trying to kill myself. I don't think they realise how deep I'd need to cut to reach that big vein. A mathematical compass isn't capable for that kind of job, and even if it was it'd take an hour or more to wipe me out. There's just a few scars now, but I know that when people see those scars, they take notice, and I quickly learn who cares, and who doesn't.

Like other people see wanking, self-harm's a private thing for me, well, the arm-cutting is, so, when I lost that privacy, I also lost control and yelled at Mum for not leaving me alone. I'd rather she'd walked in on me dancing naked in glittery body paint whilst watching tentacle hentai. I threw some stuff across my room – nothing major, just the things that were closest to my hands at the time. Thankfully I don't keep African spears or hand grenades in my bedroom. That could have been messy. Once I stopped throwing, I collapsed into tears, but they weren't normal tears. I wasn't really upset any more, it was like each tear was me becoming one step closer to being calm again. Mum tried to grab both my shoulders to stop me throwing things, and kept saying "What's got you like this?" and "Ed you need to talk to me!". Nothing could be said that was welcome to my ears at the time, so whereas I didn't mind her sticking an arm round me, I really wanted her to shut the fuck up.

By this time Lara was wanting to know what was going on. Nothing good ever comes from her and Mum didn't want her anywhere near, so while they argued, I calmed down all by myself. I ripped a page from my exercise book and doodled a figure similar to that Scream painting that Edward Munch did. Apparently he drew it as he got fed up of being teased about having such a crap surname. It was no masterpiece. In fact after a few wavy outlines it looked more like the Starbucks mermaid than the scream figure, and I just kept outlining and outlining until the figure was nothing more than just the very small centre of something that looked like a big fingerprint. I don't do a lot of this, as I'm not the most creative of kids, but doodling kinda worked for me at that moment. Mum asked later on if she could have my doodle, probably to psychoanalyse it to see if I was batshit, but in asking for it, I thought she was batshit. I was emotionally exhausted by then so I thought yeah, whatever, take it, it's just a doodle. This is a woman who, in the same way that I stash old comics, has stashed mine and Lara's pre-school splodge splodge messy time artwork. She thinks they've got some kind of artistic merit. I think her knowledge of artistic merit might have a few gaps here and there.

I don't think either Mum or school know as much as they should about yesterday. They know about those chavvy boys lacing into me outside school, but probably won't know about the two complete strangers calling me a weirdo for no reason at all, or the year 7s fancying a go at me, or any other abuse I suffered. What annoys me most is that someone is going to say that I make myself a target, and it's my issue. I don't see myself as the problem at all. It's a bigger problem. Teenagers are generally fucking horrible. Our society conditions this. I prefer the adult world. I watched a YouTube programme once about the world's worst prisons, the American ones where you spend your whole life alone cased in a concrete space the size of a toilet cubicle, the South American ones where rival gangs share a space the size of a cupboard with gangster cockroaches and gangster rats, and the Russian ones where they just put you in a cell with no heating in the middle of Siberia, throw the key away and put you in stress position if you even think about sitting on your concrete bed. I reached the conclusion that I'd gladly swap secondary school for any of these and feel better treated and in more pleasant company.

At 10.58, Mum's phone rang. I logged off everything instantly and cocked my ear to one side.

"Hello, Mrs Pendlebury, its Mrs Frogson. I've heard Edward isn't here. Is everything OK?"

Mum has the speaker on, for my benefit, and is immediately fast-bowling. "Absolutely not. It's his second day in school, and he's already been assaulted by a group of pupils. He's in a terrible state, and having seen the state of his arms this morning, I'm not risking him coming back into school to be made worse until something positive gets done about it."

Teachers still polite for now, "Well, I've no record of anything happening in school, so I'm not sure what we can do about it. There may be aspects of the school environment that he may need to adjust to, but he needs to come and talk to us himself."

Mums back in, "It's his second day. Of course he has adjusting to do."

Teacher's still polite, but I can tell she's having to work hard at it. "If, as you've suggested, he's been assaulted on school premises, then that's something we need to know about so we can do something about it. He hasn't, and no-one else has mentioned it to me."

Mum bowls again. "Why don't you come around and have a look at his jaw. Then his arms. And see who has a responsibility then."

I think there's a call for LBW there maybe, but Mrs Frogson bats again. Play on. "I can't, but we do need to talk about this a little more. Does Edward know the names of who was involved?"

My turn to bowl. "The lad that hit me was in my form. There were other lads with him from my form, who sit with him."

Mum passes this on, just in case she didn't hear. Mrs Frogson, batting a bit better, just safety shots. "OK, and would Edward know the names of anyone who may have witnessed it?"

I'm back in. "When I walked home I saw a girl from my form with multi coloured fingernails, a boy in my form that's grumpy and late to all his lessons, then this massive lad with a beanie hat and stubble. I don't know their names. They were at the bus stop when I walked home. The girl had been picked on by the lad that hit me in registration that morning. He was having a go at me, too."

Mrs Frogson comes back in, "Well the problem we have is that we don't have enough people who saw anything so I'm not sure there's much we can do about it."

Mum bowls another fast one, "With all due respect, you fully explained to me, only 3 days ago, your schools policies on behaviour, bullying, and the rest. Your schools bullying policy clearly states that school has a responsibility to act in loco-parentis and guarantee the safe passage home of every pupil on its roll. Whether this assault was in school grounds, or in the street after the home time bell has gone, is irrelevant. It remains your responsibility."

Which translates as 'I've just smashed your middle wicket, but stick it back in and carry on?'

Mrs Frogson remains polite, but only just, "I understand your frustrations, but if it's not on school premises, without witnesses, I'm not sure how we can take this forward."

Mum takes a deep breath, as if it was a massive run up before hurling the final ball of the over, "I need to remind you that in addition to a copy of your bullying policy, I have contact details for the head, and, should I not get a suitable response, the contacts for the chair of governors, the LEA office and the referral officer for those lovely Ofsted people. I'm also on chatting terms with the parent partnership. I don't wish to go this far, not with Edward being a new pupil. I'd rather give you the chance to ensure the satisfactory and safe education that, according to the United Nations Convention on The Rights Of The Child 1989, Edward has a natural entitlement to. With the fact that Edward has seen fit to slash his arms again after a reasonably calm settled period, how do you suggest we improve this situation to mutually benefit everyone, particularly Edward, the innocent victim suffering amidst all this?"

Howzat! Bowled by Mum, Penelope Georgina Pendlebury, demeanour of a damp lettuce, heart of a lion. Stuff the supermarket, I'll go wherever Mum wishes this afternoon and not complain at all. Mrs Frogson is still trying to play for a draw at best. "Ok, I think we need to meet face-to-face. Are you free to come in today so we can sort this out?"

"After the few days he's just had, Edward needs a period of calm. I'll see you on Monday, but Edward will only return when you can guarantee a safe learning environment."

Pastoral meetings have been a fixture of my adolescence so far. I know from experience that only two possible outcomes exist. The long odds are on everything resolving properly with a wonderful solution being agreed that make my problems disappear quickly. Based on multiple past experiences this has been at best a very temporary, slightly partial success. The short odds are on me sitting in a year heads office with multiple adults who all consider themselves to be experts on me even though they've barely met me. I'll then get frustrated, walk out of school, avoid going home to face even more questions, then spending interminable hours shuffling around the park or fountains in town wondering what the fuck to do with myself for the rest of the afternoon/day/term/life. Option two's more likely. There was this time when I spent an afternoon sat next to the fountains next to the station, the one's that look like urinals, chatting to an old man who, whilst sat feeding the birds, told me how he had no money, no family, was banned from even walking down the street they live on, half his teeth were missing and he was probably 20 years younger than he looked, but still insisted on giving me reasons to enjoy life to the full. I bump into many adults who profess wisdom, but it was some rough old fella, one of life's losers, that made more sense to me in the simplest possible way than any professional or "successful" adult could.

Mum looks like she actually enjoyed that conversation, "Get ready, we'll get groceries, then we'll go for cheeky cappuccinos somewhere afterwards. Chocolate cake too."

The poncy coffee is very much a treat. A treat for her. But, after her telephone advocacy, if she wants to reward herself by sitting in a poncy cafe being overcharged for hot drinks in ridiculously impractical cups with John Legend or Arianna Grande providing an inoffensive but unremarkable background soundtrack to it all, then she's earned it. Stuff it, if she wants to browse lingerie shops then lunch somewhere where a stuffed olive with a walnut next to it costs £50, it would usually be the end of my life as I know it, but today I'll happily go along.

If there's 100 different types of bread on the shelves, Mum will check the labels of each one, check the ingredients, check the country of origin, whether it's GM free, and whether it's made by a corporation with a poor track record in any kind of ethical or environmental issue. I'm one-sixth of the way through my life already and it's all time I'll never get back. If there's only 20 different types of loaf of bread on offer, Mum will check for the same tick points, but will waste 80% less time doing so. When Mum turns left at the bottom of the street, I breathe a big sigh of relief knowing that it's the opposite direction to the giant Tesco. When she goes straight on over the roundabout, then that's Morrisons discounted, and I only have to worry which way she turns in about 5 minutes time. It's either Asda or Aldi. A giant monolith of a store that doesn't just sell 500 types of bread but sells fucking everything, versus an import bargain store with 20 types of bread. As she takes the left turn into Aldi car park, my heartbeat slows a little.

Though Aldi has infinitely less merchandise to inspect, there still remains the aisle of wonder to navigate a way around. If I don't exercise a level assertiveness in this area, I'll be watching Mum peruse and inspect every gazebo, golf club and screwdriver set that she never knew she ever needed. Sometimes it's a telly, sometimes a bike, sometimes it's just something completely useless like camping gear or inflatable dinghies or flip-flops that no-one needs in September. Today Mum wastes 10 minutes of what is left of my one and only life inspecting each single one of the multiple varieties of packet plant seeds, on offer at 50% off, reduced to 45p each, choosing one packet only.

I'm supposed to be 'helping' Mum, 'helping' as in standing idly by, feeling as equally useless as the disabled pensioner dressed as security guard, stood behind the till, massive gut, wonky hip, bifocal glasses. I ponder the idea of grabbing a bottle of vodka and tapping his shoulder as I run out of the shop with it, just to see if he suddenly morphs into anything like Captain Yoo Si-Jin, but each time I set off towards the vodka, Mum shouts me back with a ridiculous question, like "What colour peppers shall I get, red or green?" as if it matters in the slightest to me. Then, just as I'm about to walk off again, it's "Ed, be a love and get some bananas." Can't really get that one wrong, so I grab the greenest looking ones with a Fairtrade sticker on, and that's me one small step closer to the exit door. She trusts me far too much with the crisps and biscuits. It's a cruel chore, beautiful in its simplicity, as I don't even choose the stuff I like the best, but the stuff I can cope with and Lara won't touch. Jellybeans, Chilli Ridges, and some poncy French biscuits make it into the trolley. Lara's beloved Pringles, Galaxies and Smartie cookies don't quite get there. Damn, she's gonna hate me. Actually, she does hate me already, so it doesn't matter. This might make me a bad person, so I compromise, very very slightly. A big bad bag of big bad badboy chocolate buttons goes in. I've seen her eating them before, when she was 2. I even placed a handful in her bed once so that she slept on them, they melted and in the morning she woke up horrified thinking she'd shat the bed and couldn't remember it. The charade continues. She checks the bags of rice for one that says "produce of India" on it. Until he decides to change his name, poor old Uncle Ben has no chance, bless him. She doesn't spend too much time in the meat section. Everything in there still looks too much like bits of dead animal. She'll get meat in the frozen food bit, where it's all nicely packaged so you can continue thinking that lamb chops came from a lamb chop tree, and sausages come from the sausage plants that grow out of the ground and no-one could possibly imagine that they're the left over bits of scrotum and arsehole scraped from the slaughterhouse floor once the donating animal had been sliced to manageable pieces. In fact, the animals that contributed to the frozen section weren't even slaughtered, they kinda froze to death naturally in a green grassy field and the frost was so severe that they didn't just die, but they disintegrated into manageable pieces. Only when they were found in such a state did they get wrapped in polythene. A bag of chicken legs go into the trolley, once she's checked the water content and, the way she's twatting about, whether the bag has a big green suitable for vegetarians V on it. Once she's made her selection, she'll successfully equate none of it to be anything like the carcass of an innocent animal that had inadvertently lived a premature unfulfilled existence purely to donate its limbs and organs to a large supermarket chain to make a small profit on.

I'm happy to say that Mum did rummage through the camping gear and rubber dinghies, and, after the required amount of sarcasm from me, "Yes, Mum, a mini-trampoline is the exact thing our household's missing, it'll be so useful this winter", she came away with nothing more than a pack of marker pens. I knew that I'd have to be on point quickly or I'd be the mug bearing the weight of a tent or a rubber dinghy across my zitty shoulders, all the way home.

I get within sight of the till. Only one checkout's open, so I persuade Mum that it'd be a good idea I join the queue and she joins me in a minute. She agreed, though she was so engrossed with the back of a water bottle I could have said the same thing in Vietnamese and she'd still have nodded just the same. Clock checked. 35 minutes. Standard for me, pretty good for Mum though. This would have been 2 hours in Morrisons and 4 hours in Asda.

I'm one from the front of the till, everything loaded. The couple unloading their groceries behind me are complete strangers to me, but Mum knows them both, and is chatting away. This means I'll not just be loading onto the conveyor on my own, but also bagging up while she chats away. In fact she's so engrossed chatting that I do the whole charade, even paying for it all with Mum's card. I even try to guess her number, but it doesn't accept, so I interrupt her to get her to key it all in, then the conversation turns to me.

"Well he started a new school last week. It's not gone well. Been there 2 days, been assaulted on day 2. We're meeting the head of year on Monday morning."

"Which school has he started?"

"St Kevin's", Mum pulls a face.

"Our Joe's there. Never had any problems. Shelly before him neither. What year's he in?"

The lady looks nosy. The man looks like one of those tough guy alpha dudes who doesn't do chit-chat in supermarkets. "Just started Year 10."

"Our lad's in that year. Joe. Do you know him?"

Idiot question that one. "Erm, I'm not sure. Only been there a week, like"

The lady's in, like she's boasting. "You've probably seen him. Friends with Omar and Archie. Captains the school team."

I bet there's 30 different school teams, but only one that gets mentioned. "Football?"

The Mum looks back at me as if there's no other kind of school team that it's possible to be captain of, "You'll know him. Plays for City. Costs me a fortune in school shoes and hours wasted sewing up kneeholes. Keeps him out of bother though."

So your son can control a moving spherical object with his feet and then kick it in a straight line or maybe even a bendy one. That obviously makes him a superior being to the rest of us. It also makes him a boring bastard. However, these strangers seem to know my Mum well and I don't know how, so in the light of some valuable information being missing, I stay civil. "No, I don't think I know him."

"We're going for lattes over the road once we're done. You free?" the lady asks.

No, Mum. I'm not free at all. Not to chat to some tosspots smugly self-satisfied parents.

"That'd be lovely, why not?" Cheers, Mum. The Dad's in. He hasn't yet blown his trumpet yet about how he shot the future captain of Real Madrid out of his nutsack a decade and a half ago, so I'll give him a chance. The mystery kid, his beloved son, is probably a total arse. I've not met anyone at this school yet who isn't, and I've never met a footbally kid worth having any form of conviviality with. His parents, however, are happy to lavish £3 each on ridiculously overpriced frothy drinks that I neither want nor need, and I've no say in the matter. The car gets loaded up and over we go to Café Aroma. Mum asks what I want, which in an ideal world, is nothing. I live in a far from ideal world, so I choose the fussiest, most stupidly expensive drink in there, hot chocolate with squirty cream, marshmallow lumps and hazelnut syrup. The choc chip muffins are enormous and look like a full bag of self-raising flour went in the mix, so one of those too.

I trust only myself to get the best seat in these places. Window seat? Check. Comfy sofa chair, like in Central Perk on Friends? Check. Plug socket? Check. Do I have a laptop or tablet with me? No. Will I be happy right now to see someone unable to check their emails because I'm in the seat they want? Check. As far from the toilet as possible? Check. Well away from the noisiest gobshite in the café? Check. In full view of any attractive females? Not applicable right now but I guess there's a chance later, so, check. Is there anyone sat voluntarily poisoning their brain with a newspaper, and am I a safe enough distance away to avoid a conversation with them? Check. Mum would miss each single one of these finer points. Hence why she has the duty to pay for the goods while I set the ambience.

The couple that know Mum enter. The Dad slaps a note on Mums tray. Mum does that "Oh, put your silly money away, I'll get this!" charade that adults always do, like they'd actually argue about who pays for a drink. They never do fight of course, but I've always found that particular adult argument ridiculous to listen to. For God's sake, Mum, just let the ugly sod pay for it all, then you can invest the £20 you don't spend in here on me and maybe Lara, but mainly me. The argument ends with Mum handing the dudes paper money to the barista instead of the plastic card she's still holding in one hand. I can't really work out if he's rich, pretend rich, or skint and bluffing. Neither of them are dressed that fancy, but at the same time there's no labels to give away how they like to pigeonhole themselves. Her ... jeans, green sandals, horizontal stripy top, like a Frenchman might wear, with a necklace that's slightly Indian or Chinese looking, not too sure which, but it looks way better than wearing one made out of onions I guess. Him...boots that look like work boots, but having clearly never visited a building site, boring looking jeans, plain white t-shirt, open shirt. I'm anxious to get Mum to get over to me before her friends do, so I can ask her who the fuck they are.

Mum and her mate carry drinks over and talk incessantly throughout. The fella, being male, will be incapable of doing two things at once, so has the responsibility of fetching stirry stick things and sugar packets and swatting them onto the table. He parks himself opposite me with a thud and the chair creaks. Unfortunately it doesn't give way on him.

"I see you like the window seat too?"

I've just helped spunk away £20 of his money that he may or may not have in abundance, so I'll be polite, and keep the conversation away from school, or his superstar son. "I just like to people watch." Right now, no-one's walking by, and if they were, I wouldn't care, even if Lady Gaga was pushing Donald Trump along in a bright yellow wheelbarrow, but hey, small talk, keep it polite, etc.

"Like you'll check people out and they'll look back and think to 'emsen's how come that dude's not in school?" He cracks a crap quality joke.

I'm not into small talk, and he's obviously crap at it, so I ask the question that's bugged me for the last 20 minutes. "So, where do you know my Mum from?"

"Cait knows her mainly. She did me a big favour once when I had some stuff going on. I say hello in't street and that's it really, but they go back to school, college, work, some night classes they did together when you'd have been a midge. I remember them night classes too painfully. It left me home alone wi' two wee rug rats who preferred their Mum to me, so they booed their eyes out solid every Tuesday night. Proper useless I were."

I know nothing about any of this stuff that Mum did, college, night school, all that. I don't think I've ever asked her anything about her life, she's always just been "Mum". The ensuing silence should be uncomfortable, but it isn't. He certainly doesn't look too uneasy by sitting waiting for me to speak, and he seems to have all the time in the world. If I just gazed out of the window for the rest of the morning, I doubt he'd be bothered.

I can't describe in detail what's on these trays. I'd be a shite barista. Anyone asking for a skinny hazelnut babycino or a slowly infused chai latte would get a proper wakeup call if I worked here. I'd bin that giant machine and be much more efficient via the use of a kettle and a jar of instant granules. I'd have a laugh and a half with it. Mums chatting incessantly with this other lady, who keeps beaming smiles my way. I'm uncomfortable as to why. Even when I was an infant I wasn't the kinda kid that anyone, apart from Grandma occasionally, would beam a big toothy grin at. She's inoffensive enough, but she could do with being a bit less Essex and a bit more S6 instead. "Surely I must know her Joe?" she keeps saying. There'll be 15 Joes in my year. I don't care. For all this kid's achievements at balancing a ball on the end of his nose, he sounds a proper boring bastard. She has a million questions. I look at my Mum, hoping, silently imploring, that she'll answer everything without giving away all my inner secrets. Unfortunately, she's so animated that everyone in the place can hear, word-for-word, every source of my current angst, with not many stones being left unturned. "He was in top sets at Moor Vale, but a target for bullies from day 1. I spent nearly as much time in the place as he did. Eventually, I went to the headmaster and said that if he didn't deal with the bullying I'd move his school. He was really affected, it was sad to see him barely wanting to leave the house, not even in the middle of summertime. We knew people whose kids went to St Kevin's and they spoke highly. He had a bad day yesterday, but it might just be because he's the new boy."

The other 15, maybe 20 people in this building, all strangers, can hear everything. I'm a walking audio story, for fucks sake.

I'll provide the ending.

I roll up my sleeves. The 3 adults around me fall silent in an instant.

"Edward????" Mum explodes, embarrassed.

"Saves you narrating a whole novel about it, I guess."

Caitlin, and everyone else, looks on in silence. No more questions. Not from her anyways. Her quiet husband says, "Don't worry chap. You did alreyt there."

"Eh?" I reply "What's well done about that?"

The guy replies, "I'd proper struggle to do that. I'm not as strong as you, so well done."

The conversation and the dynamics immediately change. Mum and Caitlin move onto Lara, someone called Shelly, people they used to know, Mum's childhood dead dog. I keep an ear open to see if my Dad is mentioned. Not a word. No-one mentions him. I thought that when I just did my angst display just now that one of them would be shocked (no), or turn into some psychobabbling counsellor (no). The conversations not up to much, but I've worked out that after days of hostility from strangers, I've become receptive to anyone who'll talk respectfully to me. Damn it, if they offered me sweeties and told me they had some puppies sleeping in their white transit van that they'd show me if I got my tail out, I'd probably go and have a look.

"You like footy at all, fella?"

Like I'll ever be some billionaire's bitch. "No way. Everyone turns stupid with it."

"Aye, I get that. I have to slap a bet on before I can get interested. Any other sports?"

I shake my head. I then get "You play X-Box much?" I answer, with not enough information to enable him to develop a conversation any further. I then get "What music do you like?" I should say Stormzy or G-Dragon just to kill the conversation, but what's the point? I give him a chance. I think of the old stuff on my iTunes, so he might know that. I say I like electronic music, and his face comes alive, like he just common ground with me. Next step, "Which artists?"

"Kaskade, Phish, Objekt." The bloke's got no idea. I've just sent this conversation down a dead end street. I need to go back in time or change the subject.

"Skrillex?" That stuff's about 5 years old. Blank expression.

"Maybe Chicane or goosebump trance sometimes." That stuff's older than me. Glazed eyes. What's that ancient band called?

"Kraftwerk, then I listen to a Japanese dude whose name I can't even pronounce."

His eyebrows raise and he leans forward, slightly startled. "I remember them from when I was your age. How did you get into them?"

I know nothing about Kraftwerk. I just like a couple of their songs, but he's excitedly telling me about concerts they've done, a collaboration they did with some rappers back in 1765, offering to lend me CDs, boring me about how modern music's rubbish compared to the old days, and, just as my cynical side is about to take over, I remember, he's not spitting on me or cracking me a right hander. "I found them online. I like stuff with no voices."

"Like you'd want it as a background, but would rather stick your own words in?" he asks. He's actually not far off the epicentre of my feelings on this, to be fair. I let him carry on speaking, pretending that I'm interested, and I'm sure he thinks he's done his good deed for the day in getting me to smile. That smile conceals a more complex bundle of thoughts and emotions that anyone like him could ever understand, but I let him have that.

With that, the rest of the afternoon passes peacefully. Mum, in particular, is happiest. That evening, when Lara was in front of her laptop, picking at a tube of Pringles that she fetched from the local shop as Mum had bought crap nibbles from the supermarket (witnessing the drama over this was quite pleasing), and I was playing a very old skool car racing game, the door was locked, the curtains were drawn, the light replaced by a dimmed lamp, and I felt happier too. Mum cracks that same joke she makes every Friday evening "Ooh look it's wine o'clock!" getting no response from either of her two dependents. Once she'd nearly emptied her first glass, a glass the size of a fruit bowl, she did the unusual thing, for her, of logging onto Facebook. She has 48 friends and 22 photos, 20 of them being her flowering baskets, and her last activity was over a month ago, but within seconds was typing frantically and intermittently giggling to herself but not sharing the comedy with either of us. She doesn't really do social media, or any kind of social, or any kind of media really. When she nipped to the loo, which, with the mediocre quality supermarket wine she was emptying from ridiculously oversized drinking vessels, was increasing in regularity through the evening, me and Lara had a bet on what she was giggling about. My 50p said she's found an old friend and was reminiscing, with an outside chance it may be that Caitlin woman from earlier. Lara's £5 said she's joined Tinder and some random fellas trying to flirt with her, and she's enjoying the fuss.

For a mother who was last night dealing with the trouble and turmoil of me losing my shit, it was nice that she was in what looked to be a good place. Lara was civil. I guess she'd been specially briefed by Mum to be so, with either a reward or maybe even the risk of losing out on something important to her if she didn't. I'd no objections. Our living room was a cosy fluffy bubble, cosier, fluffier and bubblier than anywhere else I'd found myself recently, and, having had a day away from hostility, and 2 more days to enjoy of a similar ilk, I was much more content. Quite soon, I have to leave that fluffy bubble, face the multitude of enemies that I'd built up unwittingly in the space of several days, so I welcomed the break from all that.

With each hair ruffle and each girly giggle emitted, it's clear that Mum's up to something. I've no idea what it is. Lara's convinced she's chatting to a dude. I'm not sure that she'd get that light-headed just by chatting to a dude. She'd freak if we ever acted dizzy and stupid like that, as much as she did when I redesigned my arms last night. It'll all come out soon enough, I guess.

9. Missing The Train

I'd rather pedal to bloody Leeds on a Teletubby scooter right now than sit in the slow lane on this shed of a bus. Anything else I could be getting triggered over, I'm not. Whilst everyone else my age is smoking weed, sharing bottles of cola laced to fuck with vodka or sniffing that plant food crap and snapchatting pictures of their privates to randoms each Friday night, I'm going to bed earlier than I would on a school night, not envying their party lifestyle one bit. Switching off FIFA when everyone else is loading up? Yeah, I can cope with that. Getting up before daybreak, going online and seeing where everyone else was at 1am, who was off their face, who copped off with who, while I was tucked up dreaming sweet ones? I'm happy to forego it all, but 2 hours depriving my senses in the slow lane on a fucking bus? Grim.

I'm bored shitless. I forgot to charge my phone and it's on 20%, so I've put it away til the trip home. There's us and the under-11s on the bus. The under-11s are all at the front watching a movie. The coaches, on the coach, have annexed the back seats. Everything we do they can see from behind us, goalkeeper style. If anyone's gonna get a bit over-excited it'll be Brodie or Tyler, sat together sharing a tablet, and every 15 minutes or so they shove each other and getting reprimanded. I'd try and sleep for a bit if I could, but the fucking air-cons making that impossible, so I've got my English homework, "To Kill A Mockingbird", that I'm pretending to read. Beside me, my usual buddies. Brad, as bored as me, with homework out but in reality drawing half-arsed and badly, and Ben, next to Sam, sticking his headphones on every now and then, but whatever he's got playing he's not really into it. Mo and Hassan sit in front of us looking out of the window at nothing in particular, bored shitless. Jamal and Tyrell sat behind us, probably doing the same. The trialist is sat near the front. They've given him Kyle, Oscar and Dan for company. I'm working out who, if the new kid shines, will be sweating over the dreaded white envelope. One in, one out. Every time.

The trialists are an unpredictable never-ending cascade. Many of them get too overawed and freeze, but this Naz lad didn't at all. Things are going to be a bit edgy for a few days. A lot of the new kids tend to notice Brodie yelling relentlessly at them and decide there's no fun in listening to his shit 3 times a week, so they go away and wait until another club offers them a trial, if they ever do. Loads of kids and parents think greatness beckons once they sign. Fancy mansions with swimming pools and all that shit. The reality is that as soon as you sign, the whole clubs scouting network immediately goes to every corner of the world, be it Mexborough or Mexico, to try and find someone good enough to replace you.

Football's a cruel sport, end of. Any parent wanting to educate their kid about hard-knock life shouldn't bother making them do chores or any of that stuff, they should just show their kid how to play football well, ideally at an early age. That way they can lose precious childhood weekends trapped on a manky bus like this all the way to Newcastle or Norwich and once there, sit on the sidelines for 85 minutes, or even get spotted then spat out for the unforgiveable sin of being "not strong enough" or "not tall enough", at an age like 9 years old when you're not emotionally able to cope with rejection. That size thing proper pisses me off. We've been playing on adult pitches since age 12. Keepers try, and mostly fail, to keep clean sheets in adult goals high and wide enough for their Dads to need a stepladder to tie the nets on. I'm not joking. Then we play some teams where the kids are the same size as men. No-one seems to care that they're one-footed and have no comprehension of the idea of spatial awareness, as long as they're 2 metres high at age 13 then that's good enough. Barcelona, meanwhile, have Iniesta, Suarez, and Messi, all about 5 feet 7. Before them, the great legends, Pele, Maradona, Cruyff, none of whom were more than about 5 feet 10. If they were English, League 2 teams would turn them away for not being big enough. For football reasons, I watch Barcelona on the telly every time they're on, and cheer for them too. They're all skilful guys like me, none of this "not big enough" or "not strong enough" with them, plus I love how they play. The coaches tell us to watch their games when they're on telly, then feed back to them what we notice from them. I love the Bundesliga teams too, Bayern, Dortmund, Schalke, which I get told I can't do as it's like cheering on Man United, Man City, and Chelsea together. There's this unwritten rule that people have that say you can only cheer for one, which, to me, is just daft. You either like football or you don't.

I trialed at both Wednesday and City. I wanted Wednesday as they were the bigger club. I did OK, but not well enough to get past the Shadow Squad. City asked me to sign after the second session. At first, Dad thought I was too young to commit to that level of intense training, too young to handle the rejection if it came my way, and thought I should enjoy playing with no pressure for a bit longer. However, I'd totally fallen in love with that high-level intensity stuff, having to test myself both physically and mentally at every training session. I were well up for all of it. Plus, hello, this is City. Granted, not Wednesday, not United, but also not a grassroots team skipping round dogshit doing piggy in the middle birthday party training drills in a public park. It didn't matter how many friends I played grassroots with. Scoring 10 worldies against a bunch of beginners was nothing like the buzz you'd get scoring just 1 tap-in at a proper club.

When clubs miles away picked me out, all the other kids and parents on my grassroots team were all "Good luck!" and "Ooh well done Joe!". When Wednesday and City, clubs who these people supported, came in for me, that totally changed. It didn't matter that Forest, Bradford and Rotherham had also tapped my Dad up and he'd politely declined them without saying a word to anyone, people got aeriated that it was me that kept getting picked out and not their kids, and quickly went from being Mum and Dad's friends to obnoxious adversaries. Many of my friendships started turning ugly too, and Dad wondered why he was donating his time to help run a football team for the benefit of people who secretly hated him, and so he left the gobshite obnoxious parents to sort out their daft ambitions and their jumpers for goalposts team and we signed shortly before my 9th birthday. One of Cory Hendricks' hangers on at school, Louis, was in that team. Even though it were years ago now, the intense dislike still remains. When we catch glances, I know straight away he'd love nowt better than to see me crippled, or preferably dead.

I must have seen hundreds of kids turn up here on trial, then walk off with the dreaded white envelope, never having a clue exactly what information is in there. I soon sussed whatever was in there wasn't good, as every kid who got given one, I never saw again. I've seen kids leaving in floods of tears as sometimes you see them open the letter immediately, and even though I'm sure City word it well, like "regrettably your son isn't ready for academy football immediately", or "your son's ability is without question, but unfortunately we cannot make provision for him into our programme at this time", it's still enough to crush the dreams of hundreds, probably thousands, of schoolboys, and schoolgirls too.

Now we're under-15s, kids get brought in on trial from all over the UK, sometimes the world. When they fetch a grassroots team in to play us, we know there's maybe 1 kid in there that they want to watch. When we're on the sidelines we try to guess which one it is. If we're not pasting the grassroots team, you're unlikely to impact much against Arsenal or Man City so it's time to start worrying about being got rid of. If the older teams are anything to go by, then when we hit 16 most of us will get the same envelope all the other kids have had, released to dismal pub football in soggy lumpy fields, replaced by kids from miles away, even overseas, once they're old enough to relocate to the rainy, dismal little island that is England.

Supporting a team died for me once I actually became part of a real club. Football fans have this obsession with being a 'proper fan', loyal and true to one team from childhood to your dying day. Any player who breaks that loyalty and signs for another team is a traitor. These same loyal supporters would dump their miserable jobs immediately if another employer offered to double their wages or relocate them somewhere with brighter lights or brighter sunshine. 'Proper fans' would hate my team. That blind loyalty's not there. Hardly any of us had watched a City match before we signed. If you asked us how the first team got on last weekend, we'd have to look it up. I sell all my free tickets, Dan doesn't even bother doing that. He leaves them in his Dads car and forgets about them, which I find annoying as I could get £20 minimum for them and split the proceeds if only he'd ask me to. We're all just using City as a stepping stone to making our dreams come true.

Hassan should be the one shiting it over this trialist. He was watching his shoulder when Oscar trialed, but Brodie's probably the most paranoid. He's got aggression and little else. With more skilful players around him, he can just do the dog-work and still look good. He's comfortably familiar with us, so any new face is especially a threat to him. I'm guessing that today, if we're bossing it and cruising, he'll play proper wonky balls through for the new lad Naz to try and get onto, which, if Brodie's balls are as wonky as he plans them to be, he won't. It'll always be onto his weaker foot, or just that little bit too long or too short to latch onto. If we're not ahead, he'll opt to pass to anyone on the team except him. Even if Naz's unmarked, in space, in a shooting position, he'll go sideways to me, Tyler or even go backwards, giving Naz no opportunity. Once Hassan's on, he'll check who's marking him then find a way to whack him a couple of times so that Hassan gets a psychological edge. I really shouldn't be second guessing any of this though. Two seasons ago, they brought Dan in, played him on the left wing, and he was uncatchable when he got in full flow. I were convinced I'd be on my way, but they signed him, switched me across 3 different positions, moved Brad to left back and gave a special white envelope to the kid who'd been playing there, which none of us guessed.

There's nowt to see from this cramped-up stinking bus. If this were a train, we'd at least go through real places that are nowt more than a signpost here, the bits where there's money and the bits where there's none, the bits that look interesting, the bits that look just like any other shitty little anytown, twee little towns where the houses have big leafy gardens and outdoor jacuzzis, rough areas where kids play in old containers and abandoned cars, rows of boarded up terraces, then rivers, lakes, wildlife, mountains sometimes. I'm usually a good traveller. I adore flying. It's like a proper roller-coaster type buzz for me. The stewardesses are always so drop-dead gorgeous that I've pretended to be air-sick before just to get their attention. Unfortunately Mum's wise to me, and I'm youngest child and only boy, so there's no way she's ever approve of any girl I'd bring home, so she always steps in and totally destroys my chances of getting an air-stewardesses phone number. I'm not telling anyone this ever, but if a lass said "I want to be an air stewardess when I'm older" it'd be the biggest tick-point on the tick-list for me, right up there with "doesn't spam Insta with duckface selfies or talk endless boring shit about eyebrows" I've been on a boat before, on the top deck on a windy day and thought it were awesome, even though it proper messed my hair up. The train's fine, even Dad's car's fine, but I can't cope with the bus. No chance of sleeping, nothing to see, nothing to do.

300 years later, we're off the motorway and entering some mundane town that looks the same as every other no-mark small town anywhere else you go in England. The same order whichever way you enter the place...golf course, giant supermarket, after that a hospital or industrial units, a load of boring identical-looking houses, a pub that looks exactly like any other pub followed by maybe a drive-thru, then a shitload more identical houses but not as big or leafy as the ones you passed a minute ago, then finally into a long driveway where you can only see for trees, then suddenly a big bulbous dome appears. At last. You rarely see the first team, the famous ones, at these places when the kids are playing, but we always get a good view of what they drive about in as the car parks full of big beefy Range Rovers, shiny 7 Series Bimmers, the odd Porsche or blingy Lexus. The bus gently pulls in and with a hiss, the electric door slowly opens. I check to see if Dad's here. He usually drops me at the bus, and though he drives like he's 85 years old, he gets here before us every time. I spot him chatting to Hassan's Mum, lattes on the go, looking proper relaxed, probably because they've not had to sweat for 2 hours in this shed of a bus.

We're ushered straight into the changing rooms without even speaking to our folks. Brodie bagsies the centre of the bench, Tyler next to him. I check where the toilet is and sit at the other end from it. Half of us want to check our hair in the mirror, but the coaches are old skool. They'd slaughter us.

If you're doing sport, what you look like shouldn't matter, but it does. Image is everything. For me, it's not the hair, it's the shirt number. Most kids want 7, Beckham's number, but I've been on YouTube, so as well as Beckham I've watched Pele, Messi, Maradona, Zidane, Cruyff, Platini, and decided that the number 10 suits me quite nicely. Only a certain type of player can live up to that number. Strength, size and speed combined are never enough. If you're wearing 10, you're the artist. The number 10 can win a game with one touch that inspires by-standers to write beautiful poetry. Pele's dummy, Maradona's dribble, Cruyff's turn. The number 10 puts the beauty into the beautiful game. The fella you pay to watch. The fella you talk about for months afterwards. The fella who never tucks his shirt in nor pulls his socks up. The spicy rice in a banquet full of mashed potato. The perfect 10. Some people think it's the 7, but that's just English people being weird. Whoever wears 7 in my team is welcome to it. The perfect 10 never thinks about his opponents. They think for days in advance about him instead. Overseas, 10 is the cherished number. Don't believe me? Play an Italian side and see who their headcase defenders try to kick up into the air. In their eyes, you need something special in your locker to wear that number. You're the one who might make them look daft, so kicking the shit out of you well away from the penalty area is their way of acknowledging your status.

Stevie squats in the centre of the floor, looks round us all, and starts his speech. I've heard it before, countless times, know it word-for-word, but the message is bob-on.

"The South Yorkshire Junior Football League has 6 divisions for each age group, each with 12 teams, and 15 kids signed on each team. That's roughly 1000 kids who'd kill to be sat where you are now. Add the kids playing in every other league within an hour's drive and it rises to 10000. Then add the kids who kick about in the park, don't play for a team but would gladly sit where you are, and you can double it to 20000. Our scouting network has watched every single one of these players and what we have is you, with another 20 in the shadow squad waiting for you to slip up and swap places with you. The development centres have another 50 paying to train, then overseas there's another hundred or so kids we might hopefully fly in one day. Even though you're all here due to various talents we think you have, for each one of you there's a thousand kids who would kill to be here. When you cross that line today, remember that."

No-one fancies mathematics on a Saturday. The other one he does, same type of maths, which also makes sense, goes...

"There's 100 football clubs in England that employ full-time pro footballers...On average each one has a playing staff of 40...40 x 100 = 4000... Most players are between 18 and 34, so divide 4000 by 16 and you get 250... This means that just 250 kids your age will ever play professional football ...There's 50 separate branches of the FA... 250 divided by 50 = 5...That means 5 kids from our local FA will get to be footballers ...And I've not yet included the Irish and French and Scottish lads who'll all move over as soon as they're old enough, so, counting them in, let's say not 5, but 4...50 percent of 18 year old professional footballers will not be playing professional football by the time they turn 21. They'll have been either let go or got injured and be doing summat else. That leaves 2...Those 2 could be anyone from the England captain down to the reserve at Tranmere on a 1 year contract and the same pay as a shelf-stacker."

The reality maths lesson ends there. One day, be it next week or be it 20 years from now, like life itself, all this will all come to a crushing, devastating end, back to the same mundane reality that everyone else away from my football life currently wakes up to. It could be a white envelope, a bone-shattering knee-high late tackle that condemns my leg and also my dreams forever to pieces, or just that I'm 43 years old and can't be arsed anymore.

Stevie continues, "The hard work never ends. I don't care how big a character you are," he looks towards Brodie, "what magical twinkletoes fairy dust you can pull off" he nods at me and Brad, "how many goals you can score with your eyes closed" his head moves towards Naz and Hassan, not sure which one, "before any of you get excited if we go one up, I'm telling you now, I don't care what the score is."

He's blatantly fucking lying there. He's got a footlong Sheff Wednesday owl tattooed on his upper arm ffs. He desperately cares what the score will be. Next time he's at Hillsborough, singing his lungs out on the kop to whatever their brass band decides to play, he'll be itching to blow his own trumpet about how many goals we stuff Leeds United by in the hope that someone collars him and offers him a job there instead. His veins burst through his temple if we concede a corner for fucks sake. "It's't work rate I wanna see. If I see anyone stood on't sidelines wi't hands on't hips, I'll have you back to Sunday league proper quick."

Benny again. "We've played these before. Expect aggression, nowt dirty, just competitive. You'll need to give the same back or you'll get punished. Press 'em, give 'em no time, starting from the strikers. I want to see plenty of movement. Use every bit of space. As soon as we win the ball, I want to see the wide players spread themselves far and wide. I want to see movement that pulls their players all over't place. Don't think just about where you need to be that second, think where you need to be in 10 seconds time and get there. Be smart."

Stevie's back. "Reyt! Oscar in net. Tek control. Don't anyone backchat him if he tells you where to go. Brodie, whatever he says, back him up. Centre backs. Kyle, Sam. Kyle to mark, Sam to drop off. Keep the ball, simply and sensibly. No lumping it."

The little white board comes out. Stevie continues. "Full backs, Ben on't right, Brad on't left. Tyler, Joe, cover when you see 'em go forrads. I want plenty o' movement on each side. Mo, defensive mid. If no-one's moving for you, then scream at them. Give nowt away, but keep it clean. Nowt daft. Simple balls can work better than fancy diagonals. Brodie, same as I just told Mo, Tyrell just in front. These guys are strong in't middle so expect a good test. Put everything in. I don't care if we don't get a result, as long as you've worked hard, and done't best you can. Brodie, captain, go easy on't ref. Think of Cloughie's teams, he never let his players question't ref and they'd end up getting all't 50:50s in their favour. Be tough, but respect the ref. It works"

Brodie was born in 2001, Brian Clough managed in the 1970s. I'm sure he knows all about him, mate.

"Joe left. Tyler right. Be sensible. Their defenders won't read everything you do, but they'll read most of it. Know when to pass, when to skin your man, when to shoot. Joe, if nowt's coming to you, get infield and help out. No prima donna stuff, not early on anyway. We're not Stoke but we're not Barcelona either. Tyler, watch your challenges. I've seen them crafty ankle taps.

Hassan….."

The one we're all intrigued about.

"Up front. Tyrell's just behind, 'n men wide who can cut in and shoot. The big blonde lad at't back reads everything well. If he's marking you, tek him for a wander, let one o't others in. Stay alert. Work hard."

Hassan nods, but his eyes are proper glazed. Stevie could've talked to him in Mongolian, and he'd have nodded his head the exact same. We walk to the pitch. Dad's leaning against a post just down from everyone else as usual. We spend the warm up alternating long then short balls in groups of 6, moving without the ball to a new spot, quite lazily until Stevie comes over and we up the tempo.

Brodie and their centre mid wind each other up straight from kick-off, crafty taps on the back of the legs, full on shoving each other, every now and then a sneaky punch to the side of the rib cage. The ball's not coming wide much, so I'm spending the game drifting in to get extra bodies scrapping in midfield and trying to avoid getting a whack on the ribcage myself. Brad's reading things well so the does come our way, he's tearing forward while I drop deep. The first couple of times he can't get past the right back, so he loops overly hopeful crosses towards the back post that go out. Brodie suddenly remembers he dislikes Leeds, which, in his mindset, is a wholly legitimate reason to whack his man's ankles, not too far from the penalty box. He'll get a proper bollocking later for that. The ref spots it and the Leeds dude loops his free-kick over the wall, looking like it's going to drop under the crossbar, but Oscar times his jump well and gets enough of a hand on it to keep it out. The loose ball falls, gift wrapped, to their striker, who thinks he's got all day to bury it, and Ben slides in and puts it out for a corner. Oscar yells at me to get the front post. Brodie stares at me like he'll punch me if I don't. I get the front post. I spot their full back running for the short ball. I know my way forward when this breaks. This doesn't happen. The corners a good one, high, and dropping to the edge of the 6 yard box, enough to trick Oscar into coming out that bit too far, and Kyle to challenging for it. Both of them go for the same ball, no shout. Both me and Ben shout "Oscar's!!" a split second after Kyle heads it, not too well, past his own keeper. Me and Tyler both slide in, but in vain, their striker sees his chance quickly and drills the ball in. 1-0. Stevie and Benny stand on the touchlines, silent. They don't need to say anything. It doesn't take UEFA level 4 coaching qualifications to work out that we're hopeless at crosses at either end.

The first game ends. Bit frustrating. I've counted down to this all week, and spent all game doing dog work so far. Stevie's ready to do the talking, but I've learned that trick where I can look at him so he thinks I'm paying attention but my eyes are totally glazed over and I'm daydreaming. I do this shit at school every day. I'll get an A level in it. It's only when Stevie says "Joe, sit this one out, mate." that I pay attention. I don't get aeriated, near enough all of us will sit a bit out and play most of it. It means I can get a good look at their defence, see where they look vulnerable, and when I get back on it'll be like they've sprung me at them to proper freak them out.

Everyone returns to the pitch except me and Ben. Benny comes over. "No criticism, Joe, I whined at you in midweek not to hog the touchline when things get tough. It's been hard work so far, but you've gone where I wanted you, so well done for that. We're going to 3 defenders in a bit, so there'll be an extra body in the middle. Have a look at their lads at the back, and tell me in 5 minutes what you spot."

He then turns to Ben, but aside from he's going defensive mid, I'm not listening. We're not getting past their defence, just shooting from distance. Their keeper's got that habit of going a little bit dramatic, giving every catch a bit of a bounce, or finger tipping each shot onto the floor before falling on it. I recognise their centre backs. The tall blonde lad is easily their best player. I can't do it with my own team, but I can watch opposition teams and work out who'll make their first-team one day. He doesn't slide in, in fact he doesn't make many challenges, he just gets in a position when the attackers about to turn, steps in and within seconds he's stroked the ball away to his midfield or wingers. The other lad, they call him "T", spends his time giving nudges out, perfectly timed enough to put Hassan off, but not enough to knock him down. Not so great with his feet though, some of his passes land anywhere and look a bit toe-ended. If the chance comes I'm gonna pressure the fuck out of him. The right-back's decent. Brad's not taking him on at all, but instead trying one twos. Once Naz plays the right weight on the return ball, Brad will be in on goal. The left back doesn't play like a left back at all. The only thing he has in common with Jordi Alba is that they're left footed. I thought it was just grassroots teams that stuck all their left footers at left back. Going forward, he picks his runs perfectly, but goes a bit too far forward and needs his centre back to cover him. Though this centre back's nailed on becoming their pro and the rest of their kids are clearly playing to fit round him – I spot a way through.

I shout over to Stevie. Twice. He's not listening. He probably thinks I'm gonna nag him to get back on the pitch. I yell a third time, but instead of going "Stevie!" I shout "I've sussed it!" he still pays no attention. Ben quietly mouths the word "twat" my way. The match drags on. Brad plays a corner – MY corner – short to Sam, who shoots from the edge of the box before anyone works out where the ball has fallen. The keeper gets a hand to it but that shot had power. The rebound goes too far for the keeper to land on it, Hassan stretches for it, but so does the tall blonde lad. It breaks away, but Mo's first there and lashes out at the ball. The back of the net bulges, which is just as well, as if anyone got in the way of a shot like that there'd be injuries. Stevie clenches both fists, yells "Yes! Get in son!!"..."I don't care what the score is" my arse.

Benny beckons over to both of us and says "Get ready".

I stroll over and tell him that the left backs the weak link, he'll crumble if we press him enough and if we go 4-4-2 or even 4-4-1-1 we'll thrash them. Benny replies with a "yep". I want attacking mid or right wing so badly right now, but I get sent back on the left.

I'm curious as Hassan's off, and Naz is up front on his own. If Brodie looks out for his mates as usual, it'd suit me as I'll see passes that Naz should be having instead. Two minutes in, Ben sends a free kick long from just inside their half, on our right, and Brodie is in the box, stepping on the toes of their defensive mid, I can see them pushing each other about. I get myself out of the box. There's no need for me in there. I can do more damage if the ball comes out. Ben's ball goes high towards the far post. The big lads all run in, one of them gets their head on it. It's not pretty, but it's in the net. Brodie rushes to congratulate Kyle, as does Tyler. I think debut boy might have had that. I shout his name and just give him a well done. Brodie gives me his second death-stare of the game. If Naz doesn't get signed, that goal could be the highlight of his football life, so fuck it, let him have it.

At 2-1 to us, at their ground, the tackles get that little bit more fierce and the elbows and studs are coming out across the pitch. The right back's looked composed so far, but each time he gets close to me I feel a shove, enough of a shove to help me decide whether to fall over or not. I choose not to the first couple of times. Let the ref think I play fair. There'll be better places on this pitch to fall over. A couple of minutes later, I drift inside as Tyler plays a simple pass to Mo, who plays a diagonal my way. I shout "get ready" to Naz, not actually meaning "get ready", but shouting "one-two!" is a bit too obvious really. My backs to goal, I knock it towards him, one-touch style, with the outside of my left foot and feel a shove in my back. I drop to the floor, not as if the dude's pushed me, but more like he's emptied the barrel of a shotgun at me. The ref buys it. Free kick just outside the box, left hand side. My kingdom. Brad runs over for it, and I gesture him away. "Don't think so". I'll sing this song, you do the backup vocals. He's left-footed anyway. He'd spunk this miles away. He pleads, "I'll have it you get wide!" As if I'm that soft. He'd shoot. With his left. Nowt will happen. I reply "Tha can get stuffed". This gets followed by "Brad, go away!" Brodie to the rescue. Brodie lines himself square to the right of me, hoping I'll tee him up. He's too close to two good centre backs for me to even remotely consider sending a pass anywhere near him. Both of these centre backs are cleverer than him, in their own ways.

I used to watch David Beckham line these up. Place the ball down then 4 measured steps back, to the left of the ball. Other kids watch Cristiano do that action figure pose of his and try to copy it, but none of them really have a clue what they're doing. I've studied Beckham on YouTube, then practiced on the back yard. He'd stick the base of his toe at the base of the ball, just to the right of it, running in from the left. That'd lift it, and curl it, at the perfect angle with just enough strength and speed into the top left corner. However, Beckham's a bit old skool nowadays, and my free-kicks are that little bit sicker than his. I've spent years practicing at home, curling them over from next doors front drive, over the fence and in to my playgoal, on target. Mine look like they're curling nicely into the keepers arms, but swerve away from them at the last second, late enough to give them no time to fly for it. That's what'll happen here.

Dad has his phone out on the sly. He's not supposed to film anything in here, but no-one's watching him. All eyes are on me. I'm about to set this dome on fire. Watch this. Mum used to give me £5 if anything like these went in. I'll score this one for her for free.

The run up's standard. I hit the ball exactly as I described. Once I follow through, I watch the ball rise over the wall. The curl's fucking excellent if I say so myself. The keeper bought it. He thinks it's coming to his arms, so stands still for a split-second too long. Once the curl kicks in I spot his footwork, those couple of steps to the side before he springs himself to his top left. Too late. Even in full flight, the ball's too far to his right, beyond him. It doesn't matter how fast he chases after it, the train's already out of the station. For a split second I wonder if I've put too much spin on, as it looks like it's curling away too far, but it drops just inside the left post, and, ladies and gentlemen, I proudly announce that football should not always be described as a sport. When I have the ball, its art. Picasso has fuck-all on me.

The euphoria kicks in immediately. It always kicks in when you hit a worldy in like that, I run over to my Dad, then Brad's Dad, Hassan's Mum, Naz's Dad, Ben's little sister, Kyle's little brother and hi-five the whole lot of them. I'll probably get bollocked for this, but hey, that was a creation of such devastating aesthetic beauty. I'll get away with it.

The rest of the game went by in a blur. We scored 2 more. They got one back, but who cares. I'm not sure I got past the right back any more. I didn't need to. Brodie got subbed late on, and when Hassan dropped to centre mid and looked just as strong as Brodie does, I could read the anxiety on Brodie's face, and his mind ticking over."Naz in, Hassan in't middle and bye-bye me"...but I've learned never to second guess this shit.

One day, some reporter will collar me and ask "What's it feel like to score a worldy in a big game, Joe?" I'd love to give a realistic comparison but, being a 14 year old virgin who's not done drugs or dangerous sports before, I'm not sure I have a description. What I imagine base-jumping, having orgasmic sex or mind-bending LSD is like, or surfing a 60 foot wave, being on the space shuttle when it blasts off, or flying a plane through lighting, I'd still possibly be nowhere near if I combined the lot. I could spend ages trying to find the words and get nowhere near describing the buzz, so, for now, having no chance of finding the words, I'm not going to try. I do, on the bus home, ask everyone around me what my goal looked like, to see if they, as witnesses to the great event, had the words. Apparently it looked like "shut the fuck up", "get stuffed" and "don't be cocky". The best I got were from Benny, "not bad at all, fam", and Stevie, "It dun't matter how it guz in as long as it reaches the back o' t net, lad".

Much as I hate buses, an away win made the trip back euphoric and quicker than the trip out. Dad texted to say don't make plans for tomorrow as he'd lined something awesome up. I asked if I could go somewhere in town with my mates to get some food, and he texted back that Shelly was in the Peace Gardens with her mates so I should collar her to sort me £10 out and he'd top her bank account up.

Me, Ben, and Brad headed straight into town when we got off the bus. The City first team match was 3-2 at half-time when I checked my phone. If Sam Blake was actually watching the game and not stood staring out cockneys, then he'd picked a good game. If I'd known, I'd have asked 30 for the tickets.

Between us, we agreed that beating Leeds should be celebrated with Nando's window seats. Then I remembered I needed money. The walk through town wasn't a walk, but a proper swaggy strut. I wanted to stop and tell passers-by how sick my goal was, describing the full journey of the ball from foot to net in glorious poetic detail, but the reality is that I'm back in the big world where anyone I told about it wouldn't give a shit. There's usually some quirky sideshow going off here each Saturday afternoon, dance crews, singers, buskers, beatboxers, artists, all that. People stop and watch if it's really young kids doing stuff, not so much if it's the Uni students, as most of the stuff they do's a bit twattish most of the time. Some of the performers are awesome, some a bit crap, some a proper car crash, but still entertaining. If it's young kids, everyone claps them anyway even if it's shite. I always look to see if there's anyone I know performing, not to take the piss, but to see if anyone has a talent anything like as good as mine, or at least trying. I spot a girl from year 8 breakdancing with a group of other kids. I don't know her to talk to, but she's good. Some kids walk past and take the mick. Not me. I think it takes guts to do this in front of so many strangers, so I stop and watch for a bit, til Ben reminds me that he's ridiculously hungry. So we keep walking, past crowds of shoppers, past some wedding party that's decided for some reason that the City Hall is a much more idyllic location than Venice or Mauritius to commit yourselves to have sex with exactly the same person and no-one else, even if they're proper fit, for the rest of your life. I reach the top of the steps to the Peace Garden fountains and run straight through, not giving a shit about getting wet, and over to Shelly. Ben and Brad, in the euphoria of winning away against illustrious opposition, follow me straight through the fountains without thinking twice.

"Dad says you need to gi' us £10 and he'll sort it out later."

"Here. Now piss off. I'm busy"

"Beat Leeds 5-2 and scored a worldy just in case you wondered." Ignorant cow.

"Glad you won. Hope you played well. Now piss off."

I clock the dude she's blatantly throwing herself at. Skinny jeans, check shirt, converse. He looks like one of them swaggy K-pop boyband fellas. The penny then drops why she's so anxious for me to be out of here. I move towards him. "Hi, I'm Shelly's brother. Be nice to her or I'll have to kill you. Everyone will make me do it."

The dude smiles. Shelly scowls. The last time she deathglared me so angrily, I'd encouraged the cat to sit and shed black hairs all over her prom dress on leavers night at school while she were upstairs sorting her hair out.

Shelly's expression very suddenly changes, happy about something. Not sure what, but if she's smiling at me like that, it's never good. "Who's Edward Pendlebury?" she asks.

Why's she asking me that? "Oh just some geek kid. Proper loser. Why?"

Yeah, WHY? You've left school, for starters.

"Have you been giving him grief?"

"Like you've ever seen me bullying?" I reply, also meaning 'Like you've ever seen me talk to anyone like him?'

"You'd get a proper fucking slap if you were!"

"Not my style. I mind me business. Other kids are giving him bother, but no-one I'm mates with. He is a bit of a twat though."

Another beaming smile from Shelly, "OK that's nice. He's coming round ours for tea later."

Yeah right, love. Whatever.

Shelly laughs, then looks at me, obviously checking my reaction, "I've invited him."

She must be on a piss-take, though her expression says otherwise. I know that big cheesy grin usually means everything's legit, so that's unsettling. I doubt I'll be chilling with a billy like him anytime soon. I've not eaten since breakfast though, so only Nando's matters.

"Yeah whatever." I take the £5 off her. I'm sure Dad said £10. I walk off, paying no further attention to any of her crap.

----

10. Every Day Is Like Sunday

David Attenborough probably won't be filming any ground-breaking documentaries about Mum's campanulas anytime soon. Mum sees enjoying the garden at daybreak as one of life's treats, a theory she's enthusiastic about, but very much alone with, as me and Lara, who agree on little else, unilaterally buy into none of that tree-hugger shit, surfacing only when we're totally ready, which, on a Sunday, is around lunchtime. Sharing a rare mutual interest, such as not being woken to look at flowering plants, means that sometimes even me and Lara will do things together. There is a limit to this. It'll be a cold day in hell before I watch Love Island whilst telling Mum I'm watching Frozen. Mum disapproves wholeheartedly of our lethargy. She wakes at daybreak, makes herself a fancy breakfast, not a continental croissanty job or a fry-up, but more like something she's seen on Pinterest, then turns poetic over how awesome it was before making us something simple like toast or Coco Pops. When we do surface she'll tell us off for being in bed on such a glorious summer, or spring, or autumn, or winters, day. The only resident here who can enjoy a perfect lazy day is the cat, and, as far as she's concerned, to quote an old song by some miserable depressing band that Mum sometimes plays, every day is like Sunday.

Mum's been baking. It smells OK, as in "not a total disaster" kind of OK. She's made a lump of something, then chopped small pieces off. I prod it a couple of times, to check it really is dead, then, realising it's never really been alive, take a piece.

"Mum, what's this?"

"Ooh, try a bit, I've just made it. Coffee banana cake. I found it online and gave it a try."

I notice the absence of the bananas that were sat in the fruit bowl untouched for several days. They had hit the zone of brown-black confusion that all ageing bananas eventually hit if you leave them lying around uneaten for too long, and seem to have been denied a natural end decomposing on that DIY compost heap thing that Mum's got behind the shed. I say compost heap, but I actually mean an old toy box with a few holes poked in it, with some rancid dead vegetables going fizzy inside. She moves away from her plant pots and runs inside to tell me all about it. I don't need to know the recipe. It has that nice, warm feel that makes anything that gets oven-baked attractive. I do make the mistake of asking her what she's up to today, which she interprets as "Mum, tell me the exact jobs you're doing in the garden right now, in obsessive detail, taking every opportunity to use Latin names for plants that could more easily be described as tulips or pansies." Though she's convinced it makes her sound good, she actually sounds a bit ridiculous. The Latin language is extinct for a very good reason, simply that when compared to the languages that aren't extinct, it was crap. I mean, who's ever going to say 'gluteous maximus' when you could just say 'arse' instead? Now, if Mum could name all her plants in Spanish or Italian, I'd be impressed. There's a beauty to those languages that I appreciate.

"I've planted some tricolor violas ready for spring, then I've cut some of the dead flowers so the new ones can start poking through. If there's time I've got some heliantus annus seeds to get started on later. Anyway, don't be long getting changed, we've got visitors later."

"Oh yeah, who?" Like I ever get any visitors. Or her, come to that. Not counting Grandma.

"You'll see. I'm just waiting for a text."

It's probably Grandma. No-one else visits. Mum's scared everyone off with her unnecessary Latin plant porn. I glance at the cake. It's free from the addition of Nutella, chocolate drops, smarties, Haribos, jelly tots, cannabis, strong liquor or anything you'd hope to find either on or in a cake. But I can see Mum's put a heart and soul kind of effort into this. It's not every day that people say anything nice to her, so, knowing that feeling, I take another chunk of it.

I bite in. There's a big soft doughy bit in the middle that suggests it may be underbaked. There's also the distinct possibility that it might be a big soft lump of geriatric banana that should ideally be fusing together with last month's potato peelings behind the shed. I've told Mum that it can't be healthy to leave food waste there. It stinks to high hell and always has a squadron of flies getting busy round it, probably rats too, but Mum describes her compost as if it's a treat for her plants, like she's giving them pepperoni pizza. She's lucky her plants can't talk to her. I visualise all the pansies and whatever else she's bedded in lately growing faces and mumbling to each other "If that soft twat thinks I'm going to digest that gunge so that she can eventually rip my head off and stick it in a jam jar she can piss off!"

I'm still uncomfortable about biting into stuff that I can't identify, and, for a cake with coffee in it, I'm drinking more liquids than I really wish to just to wash it down, to avoid it forming a big dry doughball at the back of my throat and blocking my airways. I spot Mum looking my way, pleased with herself, in that I'm eating a second piece. Its just an act from me, but for all her shortcomings she's one of the very few people willing to make an effort to consider my self-esteem on a regular basis, so it's only fair that I reciprocate.

Lara appears.

"Hey, try this cake Mum made, it's," I pause til there's eye contact, "amazing!"

Lara looks at me in a way that suggests she knows I'm blatantly lying, possibly the very heavy emphasis I put on the word amazing. Subtle enough for her to get the message, discreet enough for Mum to remain oblivious. Nevertheless she looks briefly at the brown uneven lump, declines to indulge, and changes the subject immediately.

"Where do you know Joey Barker from?"

"Who?"

"Is he mates with you?" she knows it's unlikely, but I know she's hoping I say "Yes, bezzies."

Stuff that.

"Who?"

She shows me his Facebook page. The first thing I notice is the "add friend" button. My sister's a creepy stalker, and yes, I do recognise him. The one whose chair I got sat in, obnoxious, aloof, thinks he's better than everyone else for some reason, not someone I want to think about on a non-school day.

"Yeah, I've seen him."

"Mum says he's a mate of yours. I called bullshit. I insisted that if you had somehow managed to make friends with anyone it'd be a Star Wars fan with a droopy shoulders and bad breath, but she insisted you and him knew each other. Who's right?"

"Have you seen the state of your friends lately?"

"Hello? I have friends. Make some yourself before you criticise mine."

I try the stare of death. It doesn't even shut her up, let alone shit her up.

"Or even, if you could get him to be friends with my friends, especially Libby, who plans to marry him when she turns 16, using kidnap or blackmail if the situation demands it, then spend the next few years having all of his babies, then we'd be grateful. He doesn't need to be friends with you, just enough of a familiarity with you to get him into my social circle, so I can then get him and Libby introduced as soon as possible. It shouldn't be too hard."

"Lara. You don't even know him. If you did you'd know he's nowt but a grumpy obnoxious streak of misery."

"In your eyes, maybe. Now take a look at his eyes. They're not eyes you look at, they're eyes that you melt into before blissfully drifting off to the next world. Whoever designed them combined just the right amount of hazel brown with just enough dreaminess. If you look at them for too long, you'll just feel helplessly overpowered before falling into them and drowning yourself. Or at least Libby does. She's already c+p'd all his photos into her secret files."

"Which, I'll suggest, is very creepy and quite scary. He's a stranger, and you're a stalker."

"She has it all planned. She's gonna find a way of drugging him then when he drops to the floor, bundle him in a taxi all the way to her house, then rope him up and keep him hostage in her bedroom until he gets that Stockport syndrome thing and falls helplessly in love with her or some crazy shit like that."

"Stockholm syndrome. Like I said, have you seen the state of your friends lately?"

"He plays football for someone. Like, a proper team. Like Wednesday or United?"

"You're still assuming that I care. I've met him. He's a total arsebiscuit."

"How is he?"

"Like I said. Looks down at everyone, and spends each lesson looking out of the window."

"Well that's cute?"

"Whatever. The people in school he does talk to, he couldn't give a toss about. They're doofers to him. He uses them so it looks like he's got mates. As soon as school ends, he'll never think about them again. He's got one proper mate, an enormous hairy gibbon of a year 11 that looks like one of those sweaty roided-up gorillamen you see coming out of the gym, but with hair and no bulldog tattoos. Between them they're grimness on legs. He'll talk to the girls he sits next to, or should I say the girls he's probably been made to sit next too, and even then I could see him blanking them if he ever saw them out and about at weekends. Basically, if he was made out of chocolate he'd eat himself. Did you say his name was Joe?"

"You have been listening then?"

"I don't suppose you know who his Mum is?"

"She told me to mind my business. I'm sure they work together. Or they have done. They've definitely got history. That's who Mum was messaging the other night."

F.M.L. Even Mum has a social network with friends on it. I dread to think what crap she posts. Here's me too scared to even reactivate mine, all 24 friends on it, for fear of being slaughtered and it going viral. Seriously, me going on there would be like a sausage going for a swim in a piranha tank.

"Was it someone she met in the supermarket or in some poncy coffee place?"

"Can't remember. Not sure it's something I'd care about, maybe. Erm. Why?"

"When I went to the shops with Mum we ended up in that café near Aldi with some couple she used to know. They said they had a lad in my year. Joe..... shite!"

"Girlfriend?"

"If there's any romantic fabulousness going on between him and anyone, I've not bothered spotting it."

"Single then."

"Not something I've taken much priority in finding out, what with him being a miserable unfriendly twat that I have no interest in knowing about."

"Perfect!"

"Whatever."

"Do me a favour?"

"Nope."

"I'll do the shopping trip with Mum next week if you do."

"Try a full month and I'll listen."

"That's harsh?"

"Take it or leave it."

"Two weeks."

"Three."

"Two."

"I'm bored of this. Four."

"OK, three."

"The ears just opened."

"Spy on him. Find out where he hangs out, who with, what he's into, anything."

"Got to be four weeks, that."

"OK. I really hate you. Four weeks."

"OK."

"At least ten bits of info."

"Can give you ten now."

Mum walks in. "Shouldn't be hard, that. We're off out in a bit. Barbecue at Caitlin's."

"Oh lovely, enjoy yourself," I say sarcastically

"You seemed OK with Jim the other day?"

"I'm OK with anyone who doesn't punch me or push me into moving traffic, but that's not evidence to suggest I like him."

"I've known Cait since school. His hearts in the right place and he means well. If Cait wasn't alrite I'd not be chatting to her."

"She thinks her kid's Ronaldo. She's not seen you for decades and the first thing she talked about was her lad and his football team. She looks like she failed an audition for TOWIE."

"A what?"

"Don't worry. I'll come along, but I'll spend my time looking at my tablet instead of any human interaction. She may be your mate but her lad's anything but a mate to me and I can't see that changing. "

"OK, 1.30 at their house. You coming, Lara?"

Course she is. She looks brassed off. Mum will think it's because she has to get out of her onesie and go out. I know it's because she could have waited thirty seconds and saved herself a month's worth of grocery shopping. I look her way and smile, in return receiving a half-hidden hand gesture where the medial finger is crudely extended.

I've showered, inspected Gerald, and dressed within 5 minutes. Some people have baths on

Sundays, like proper long soaks with multiple poncy oils going in the tub. I always choose the shower. I've always thought getting in the bath is like having a big bowl of hot water then you put yourself in it, like you would a teabag into a cup, and marinade yourself in there until you're lying in what is essentially a big pot of dirt tea. I've never thought it's hygienic either. Like, when you're in there, all the bacteria that live in and around your bumhole swim out and relocate themselves everywhere else that you don't want them to go. In the shower, everything travels south towards the plughole so not so much of a worry, really. Lara takes a month longer getting ready. Hair, eyebrows, make up, whatever other shit she has to do just to feel able to leave the house.

"You know the plan for today?" Mum asks.

"You've been organising something, in that sneaky way that little girls do. I won't slate it as yet, I'll keep an open mind for now." That sounds like a complete pile of tosh. I regress. "Actually, I haven't got the slightest clue what you're on about."

Mum sits down. 90 degrees to me, on the other sofa.

"Me and Cait chatted loads yesterday. When I say chat, I mean Messenger, but you know what I mean."

"Ok" I want her to continue, as I'm unsure what's she's on about, to be totally honest.

"They think they need to repay a favour I did them once. They don't. But I'm going to let them try anyway."

"So you've not thought they might be clueless busybodies more likely to make things worse? And if their kids who I've worked out who he is, then they really don't need to."

"Then at least someone tried to be nice to you. People generally don't care a toss about anyone else. While you're young and people are willing to show you kindness, go with it."

I look at Mum like she has two heads. She continues.

"When we became friends, people were surprised because we were so opposite in a lot of ways. We were never full-on virtual sister types, just friends, but our paths keep crossing, and we've never fallen out."

I don't know why I say this, but the words just fall out of my mouth before my brain can call quality control, "Did they know my Dad?"

Mum's tone changes. I can tell she didn't really want that question. "Yes, but back in the day. Really back in the day."

"So how come they haven't asked you where he is, then?"

"The conversation hasn't gone in that direction yet. It may not."

Twenty seconds of uncomfortable silence.

"My big favour to them was nothing out of the ordinary to me, but massive to him. He was once a train driver. Loved his job, or should I say he loved the free travel pass he got from it. When him and Cait were dating a night out at the weekend for them would be in London, if not there then Amsterdam or Dublin or Paris. They'd be gone every time he got a couple of days off."

"So you helped him how?" I said, not really getting the point of what she was talking about

"That was a big passion in his life, just like you and I get passionate about things. One day he pulled out of some station, started picking up speed, heard a bump and his windscreen got splattered in blood and eyeballs."

OK, maybe I'll reduce the sarcasm.

"He didn't stand a chance, he was doing about 70 miles an hour, a figure just stepped out. He said he heard the thud. That was the guy's skull shattering, like an egg would if you threw it at a wall. By the time he'd hit his brakes and the train stopped, he was two miles down the line. To call stepping in front of a train a messy way to end it all is a bit of an understatement. It makes so many more victims. What was left of the head was found half a mile away from the rest of the body, and even that was scattered along the lineside bit by bit. Jim saw it all. It messed his head up too, in an altogether different way."

"Nice story, but I still don't get what any of it has to do with me. I've no plans to become a train driver." Actually, a free Eurostar travel pass would seriously help me get through my bucket list if they still do them.

"You're missing the point. I had my counselling qualifications. I did bereavement but I knew the basics of trauma counselling. Jim told me that even though he'd never seen the guys face before, he visualised it in his sleep, woke in the middle of the night to find it sat at the end of the bed staring at him, and for ages afterwards, it looked at him in the mirror, delivered his mail, served him in the chippy, and whenever he turned the telly on it was there reading the weather forecast, the news and the football results. I supported him at the time, but eventually it got to the stage where he'd see me and subconsciously think about that incident straight away. So, though Cait was my longest-standing and most reliable friend, I purposely lost touch with them so he could move on. You weren't aware of it, but that time we were with them on Friday was a massive bonus for all of us. It told both me and Cait he'd moved on."

I still can't see the relevance. I mean, Mum still thinks I want to kill myself. I've no intentions of the sort. I've a massive bucket list to work through before I consider walking onto train tracks and shuffling off to the afterlife. I can see the end of the tunnel. It's called leaving compulsory secondary education. I'm not so depressed that I can't see brighter days in the future. They'll reach me, just not yet. The cutting is just my way of coping with it. I don't have to cut. I could squeeze ice-cubes like the basket-weavers suggest, or punch something really hard and get that numb sensation you get when you shatter your knuckles, or I could burn myself, stick pins in myself, whatever. Last Thursday I cut, but it was just the right thing to do at the time. Explaining this to Mum would be impossible.

Lara's back with us, looking more like Saturday night than Sunday lunchtime. If it makes her look more ridiculous than me, then fine. Hair down, with a bit of bendiness in it from the curling tongs. To be fair she's not made a total mess of her make up, it looks alright, but she's way too young for it to suit her. At least she's not done that stupid shave-the-eyebrows-off-then-get-the-bingo-pen-out nonsense. I know what all the efforts about. I've already tipped her off Joes' an obnoxious bellend and she hasn't listened, so in terms of brotherly advice, I've tried my best. I'll sleep well tonight.

Everyone sub-consciously judges others. We do it before that person speaks or lets us anywhere near the content of their character. I'm judged constantly for my height, weight, haircut, how I walk, how I sit, whatever poxy label's on my coat or bag, all of it. I hate it, but I'm no different. Lasses get it even worse. I judge people, but I use a criteria unique to me, even though I don't see myself as unique. I think everyone has their own set of rules with which they form opinions of others. We pulled up at Mums friend's house, somewhere I'd never been, and these snap judgements that the brain makes for us, were in total overdrive.

Mum takes three attempts to park in a straight line, but, as I'm at least 2-3 years from getting a driving licence, I'd not do any better. I expected to pull up outside one of those spotless houses where the kitchen looks like no-one ever cooks in it, and the living room has nowt in it apart from a big fuckoff ugly sofa and a big fuckoff ugly telly on the wall. Instead, there's a bit of clutter dotted about, not unhygienic, just unorganised (box ticked, they've not frantically cleared the house up like Mum would if these people were coming round to ours). Jim beckons us to the garden. I can't see a home-made compost heap (a relief) anywhere. Instead I see half an oil drum pretending to be a barbecue, with more distinctly-fragranced smoke belching out of it than you'd expect backstage at a Snoop Dogg concert. Cait and Mum are sat together girly-chatting already. I can see ridiculous wine glasses in the kitchen that must be the size of my head, but I also see the kettle steaming. Mum did, briefly, do a sneaky glance our way when Cait was pouring herself a glass of something alcoholic, as if to check we weren't looking before sneaking a crafty glass of something, but we sneaky glanced back at her and she knew her limits there and then.

"What do you lot like on barbecues?" Jim asks.

Lara's already glued herself to her phone, as she does everywhere. She looks over to me.

I speak for both of us, "Anything except fish. I love spicy stuff, but Lara's a lightweight"

Lara's straight in. "You need to watch him. He can eat that curry that's hotter than a vindaloo, and if you've got any of those tiny Thai chillis that can kill you, Edward can eat them raw if you don't stop him."

"Really?" Jim asks

"He thinks it makes him look awesome. It never does. Specially next morning."

Looks awesome my arse. It's actually something I've done instead of cutting myself, when Mum's hidden all the knives and scissors.

"Well when you're ready, nip inside, everything's out, spice them up how you want, get creative. Coat a chicken drumstick up the same for me, and I'll see if I can cope wi' it."

I smile. "Bet you don't. No-one has yet."

I walk inside, get a bowl and throw in peri-peri powder (box crossed, it's the lemon one. That stuff's really tame. Proper peri-peri will strip the enamel off your teeth). I add Jamaican jerk, then lob a big dollop of chilli flakes in the mix too. I then throw a bit of oregano in just to make it look a little less deadly. I spot rosemary. It doesn't suit this mix, but I like the smell of it, so just a pinch, mind, then a bit of olive oil. Once mixed up, I take 4 chicken pieces one by one, then dunk each one into the magic deathmix then coat any bits I missed with the back of a tablespoon, then sprinkle a bit more chilli on them, just to add a little more flavour.

"What are you up to?" a young female voice suddenly enquires, as in "whatever you're doing looks interesting, and also batshit. Tell me the finer detail" (box ticked, she's being civil, at least). That'll be Shelly. I remember her name getting mentioned.

I decide good manners are the best route here. "Your Dad asked me to spice some chicken up as hot as I could. These are the deadly ones."

Shelly just smiles, in the same way someone would smile if I was stood there with my flies undone. "You'll probly kill my Dad, but as long as there's a couple of less dangerous ones left, then I'll let you off."

I start lying, to cover my back. "He told me to coat 3 or 4 up then leave a couple bareback for someone else when they arrive."

"That'll be our Joe. Forget him. He's on his man-period. Come on then. Give us a hand." (box ticked, she doesn't idolise that fool)

It's like she's been paid to be nice to me. She comes across as very self-assured, but most of all, she's got a green hoody on that, which I thought had a cheesy logo on the chest, but, on second glances I realise its Rin Okamura from Blue Exorcist. She acknowledges Mum, like they already remembered each other from somewhere. Not much between her and Lara though. Maybe if Lara put her phone away that might change. If I was five last time I saw her, Lara would've been 3 if she was there. Too far back maybe.

personal qualities of which none have been inherited by his arse of a son.

Joe looks down at his feet, "Dun't matter," then turns towards the back gate. "I'll see you later." The gate slams with quite a clank as he vanishes.

Shelly's now having a go at her Mum "You're too soft on him, Mum. You give him his own way all o't time, just to keep him sweet. It just meks him obnoxious"

Cait tries to turn the conversation to a goal he scored in football match. Unlike gardeners Latin, football is a foreign language to Mum that she neither understands nor cares about. Unless it involves Cristiano Ronaldo with his top off, Lara doesn't care either.

Shelly steps in, "My brother can chase a ball, then run wi' it and keep it so close to his feet that no-one can get it off him. Apparently this meks him summat special, summat more wonderful than the rest of us could ever dream to be, and everyone thinks it'll mek him into a millionaire one day. Unfortunately, my mate Fyza's dog can do exactly the same stuff wi' a ball, but faster. Every time her dog does this, no-one cares. Buster the King Charles Spaniel is never going to be exiting a nightclub with anyone out of Hollyoaks any time soon. The best the poor dog will ever get out of it is a pat on't head and an occasional biscuit."

"He could be sat on GTA all day or smoking weed in't bus stop instead." Cait retorts.

"I don't care, if I ever have to watch him do exactly the same thing a dog does, I'll chuck a biscuit at him and pat him on't head. And, no-one ever smokes weed in't bus shelter."

"Didn't you do kick-boxing or something once?" Mum tries peacemaking between the hosts.

"Got bored of it."

"I heard you were good, got black belt in primary school didn't you?"

"Got into other stuff instead. It's on me CV though. Black belt karate. I'm happy wi' that. A million quid couldn't get me doing katas again. Anyway...what you were on about, the real world? The real world," she stretches her right hand out. "Our Joe." The left hand moves out to the left, "When they finally crash into each other, what do you think'll happen?"

The conversation moved on, but the stage was set. I was hoping to see loveable Joe and big sister take each other on. This Shelly lass is so going to use me to annoy her rival sibling. Mum wondered otherwise, and thought that my chilli concoction was aimed at old Joey tidy-feet. I watched her struggling, taking delicate nibbles interspersed with big gulps of water. I think it was water. If it wasn't, her driving would be all over the place. I'd been diplomatic about her cake so if she complained I was ready and waiting. On the way, we drove past Joe perched on a wall two streets away, pretending to be mates with a couple of chavvy looking lads that I'm sure he'd cross the road from on a normal day.

I was dreading school tomorrow, but I'm OK with it now. I've decided that as soon as I get grief then I depart the premises. I've thought it through. I remember seeing school's bullying policy on the reception wall last week, they call it "the respect charter" or something. It basically says that I'm entitled to be treated with respect, and, if I'm not and they don't sort it, then they break their charter, so I'm entitled to walk out. Mum doesn't like it, but that's how I'm going to advocate for myself. I went to bed feeling a little more confident.

----

11. The Itch That Won't Go Away

Was it all a dream? Did I used to read 4-4-2 magazine? I barely slept, opting to try to picture how my worldy looked from the sidelines, and as morning came, lay staring upwards, pretending the ceiling to be a big-screen showing my goal on repeat, for ages.

The work of a true artist. How did I do it? Well, I can answer that easily enough, Gary. Art ably assisted by science and maths. 4 well-measured steps towards the ball from a point at around 250 degrees, west-south-west, 40 minutes past the hour. Then a very particular part of my right instep, just where the big toe connects to the rest of me, connected a specific part of the ball, just below the centre of the sphere, slightly to the left, with a strong but not overdone level of velocity, forcing the ball upwards and forwards, with side spin that, in time, brought the ball downwards at an angle that only a distinguished professor of applied mathematics and physics could predict. This perpetual motion created an optical illusion for the goalkeeper, who himself thought he'd left a reasonable gap for me to aim for, one he thought he'd reach easily. Naturally, after this pointless mind game, he realised a split second too late that I'd not aimed where he expected, and that maths, physics and art, when combined, always beats psychology. Realising his elementary but forgivable miscalculation, it didn't matter how quickly or how far he sprung himself over towards the ball, it wasn't enough. He were catching chuff all. The ball would be forever behind him. A penguin could have a more successful flight than him. My grandkids will hear about that one, at least twice a week, every week.

Had I skied it, my team-mates would've taken the piss all the way home. When I produce the goods, there's silence. Each of them would donate their right kidney to charity if it got them free-kicks within shooting distance. They know me and Brad share them. Me from the left, and the right when Brad's off, Brad vice-versa. His aren't bad. Mine are better, in the same way that the Co-Op sell nice chocolate cakes, but if Delia Smith makes one, you'd choose hers. Call me Delia, Gordon, or maybe the little Chinese fella off daytime telly that can smile and karate-chop onions at the same time, whatever he's called.

I have downstairs to myself. Shelly must still be in bed. Or out. Like I care. Breakfast's a disaster when I do it. This week, I've cocked up cheese on toast, and even after simplifying it to toast, I've messed that up too. There's milk in the fridge, and Jaffa Cakes on top of the bread bin. Job done. I put Match of the Day on record last night. I don't go to many matches. I'm too busy doing the business on the pitch to be ripped off by any football club. A cheap seat at a Championship match costs £30. Spending £70 gives you the pleasure of going up a division and watching never-ending disappointment at Anfield or St James Park, or maybe watching Crystal Palace or Watford scrap desperately not to drop to a level where they'd have to charge you less money to watch them. £100 guarantees you a seat watching Arsenal finish 4th or 5th. Plenty of people can't whip out the plastic quickly enough to spunk their money on this like total mugs. My Dad isn't. He knows it's cheaper to get on a Ryanair to Munich or Milan, watch the very best, then fly straight home after than it is to get a decent seat at any Premiership game. So, with that in mind, suckers can pay to watch me instead, and I can't be arsed with finding out the scores until I'm home and chilled out.

This goes totally wrong as soon as I go online. There's always someone trumpet-blowing or whining about 'their' team. According to Facebook right now, United's squad aren't worthy of wearing the shirt, although some fat lardarse sat ranting online who probably can't kick a ball, is, apparently. It's not that great a shirt anyway. I mean, you're not exactly going to see some slinky lady wiggling her arse down a catwalk in Milan or Paris draped in stripy polyester, are you? A 1-0 defeat away to MK Dons is apparently a calamity on the same scale as a Boeing 737 crashing into a playschool, if you read the shite that's on my feed. The Massives scraped a 1-0 at home against Forest, which, according to Facebook, means they'll now breeze the Championship, then the Prem next year, then obviously Barcelona and Juventus will get blown away in the Champions League the year after that. Nobs. Rotherham stuck four past Grimsby. Despite it being 0-0 until Grimsby went down to 9 men, which no-one seems to have noticed, that's awesome. City drew 3-3. Apparently the defence is hopeless. Evidently it's about the same level of hopeless as their opponents.

Match of the Day. Gary from the crisps adverts, who I think played for England in a World Cup once, is sat with Alan, who played for Newcastle for a bit when they were good, before they became a cheesy sub-brand of Sports Direct, and Wrighty, sounds proper Sarf Lahndan, retro Arsenal legend. I've seen him play, on a retro compilation, tangling the legs of some centre-back, rounding the keeper then slotting the ball away a few times. I've studied not just his footwork, but what he does with the rest of his body, where he looks, how he times everything. Then I've gone on the backyard, mastered it, practicing first with strategically placed wheelie bins and water bottles, then, once round them, whoever was available until they got sick of falling over and looking up to see my smile as wide as a watermelon with a slice missing. Anyway, let's see if anyone scored anything better than Joey the wonderboy.

First up. Chelsea v Leicester, described by the commentator as "Cheese focaccia vs Cheesy wotsits". Whatever. Costa twats the keeper and Hazard taps in from 5 yards, then Costa twats 2 defenders and taps in himself from 5 yards. 2-0 Chelsea. When I scored, no-one got twatted. My goal wins. Next up, Man City v Spurs. End to end. 2-2. The 3 v-neck legends bang on about how the result affects the top of the table, but nowt about the football. There was some, too. Silva went on a bit of a magician dribble and squared for Aguero, who couldn't miss. 5 minutes later, Aguero had his back to goal, two men on him, turned, curled a shot from nowhere and whacked the post. Had that gone in, he'd have deffo matched my goal, but it didn't. It hit the post. That loser Sergio's got nowt on me. Spurs came back. Kane got a couple but, being honest, the aged centre-back who was supposed to be marking him made him look good. If I was against him I'd have hit 6 in. West Ham v Stoke next. 1-0 Happy Hammers. Even when Stoke's defensive mid gets sent off in the first half, and they decide not to even bother with a midfield and just lump it long, it can still go either way, especially against a team like West Ham. The goal was a free kick, but proper central, 5 man wall and it deflected in off one of them. Central + deflection means mine's way better. Next up. Newcastle v Man United. 50000 people emptied their current accounts for that. Fellaini in centre midfield. 0-0. Grim. Really grim. Mum and Dad walk in with groceries. Mum's making a fuss, ruffling my hair, "How are you this morning, sunshine?" Dads quieter, sticks his head round the door, says "alreyt?", then cracks on with unloading shopping bags or whatever he's doing. I stay put. I'm not that awake yet, just mellow, like I can be on a Sunday. I miss Liverpool v Sunderland, catch some player being interviewed. Players never say anything interesting when they're interviewed. It's like they're told what to say (never much in the script), and what not to say (such as anything interesting or anything that involves thinking for yourself). What's left? Everton v Southampton's on today. That leaves goal-only highlights. Norwich win 1-0 when their winger latches onto a truly shit back pass and lifts it up over the keeper as he spread eagled himsen far too early and watched it trickle over the line. My Grandma could have scored that. West Brom v Swansea last up. 1-0. Dodgy penalty. Enough. Forget the football league show, it's clear. Goal of the day came from Joey B, for real.

I scan the channels for any decent foreign matches. Bundesliga. Get in! German footy canes the fuck out of English football in every way possible. The style of play would suit me down to the ground, way better than all this headless chicken nonsense you get in English games. Dad sits down while the presenter's talking. "Gettin't barbie out in a bit. Got visitors. You might know one of 'em. You alreyt with that?"

Teams walking out. Green shirts, yellow shirts. Wolfsburg v Dortmund. I hope Mum and Dad aren't going to try and talk through this.

"There's a lad just started in your year. Edward Pendlebury. Have you met him yet?"

That hopeless case again. Shelly and Mum have both asked about him since I got off the bus yesterday. Dad completes the hat-trick. "Aye, I've seen him."

"Be nice to him when he comes round."

"Eh?" WTF?

Seriously. What. The. Fuck?

"You had a blinder yesterday, so if you don't fancy a barbie I'll get pizzas in instead, no worries."

"Lovely." Both of them read the sarcasm.

Mums in. "Don't be like that, pet"

"I don't like him that much"

"It seems no-one does. I met him wi' his Mum on Friday and he seems a reyt nice lad, if only you and your schoolmates give him't chance."

Like I care. Back to the footy. Wolfsburg playing keep-ball in their own half.

Dad asks, "So why's he getting grief Is it cos he's new or cos he's got't wrong labels?"

What business it is of my parents is news to me. "No idea at all. You know whatever drama goes on wi' other kids in't my business. It's Cory Hendricks, Louis, that lot. They're at him."

"So have you stepped in, or even tried to mek life easier for the kid?"

I seriously don't believe this. "Why would I?"

Mum looks at Dad. Dad looks at me. I look at a group of German footballers in yellow celebrating a goal that I've just missed seeing. Thanks a fucking lot.

"I don't know," Dad says after an uneasy silence. "I just thought you might have tried to be a good considerate human being maybe?"

Where is this going? "I thought I might like to stay out of bother?"

Mums back. "If you're seeing bullying, then it is your business. It's everyone's business."

"I really din't mean to be such a disappointment to you, but I've not made it my business. Just out of interest, what exactly do you reckon I can do about it?"

Mum and Dad look at each other. There's silence. They look at me. Still silence. Back to each other. Fuck this. Dortmund corner.

"So you and every other kid in school are going to sit by and let this kid get slaughtered?"

I maintain my policy here of in-your-face honesty. "Near enough. Yes."

"You sure about that?"

"Sorry, but yes. It's not my business."

Big mistake. I turn back to look at the TV, but forgot that when I went into the kitchen a bit back, I left the TV controls on the other sofa. The screen goes off. Dad looks at me. No point yelling at him to stick the TV back on. He'll throw it through the window then climb on the roof and smash the aerial, before hitting the big switch on the electric, before he even contemplates meeting me half way with the telly.

"Right. You both know that City are on't phone to school loads to check that I'm behaving and doing my work and that?"

"Yes, although I'm really hoping you're not using this as an excuse"

"And you're expecting me to step into a load of bother between a kid I barely know and a load of other idiot kids I mek a point of having nowt to do wi'?"

I hear Dad whisper "for fucks sake" under his breath. "Well, it's a bit different, this".

"How is it? You and everyone else always told me to choose me mates carefully, don't get too involved wi' people, keep me nose clean, play my cards close, and now you're telling me to do the opposite?"

"No, no we're not saying that. What we're trying to say is..."

This conversation isn't getting the TV back anytime soon. I'm outa here. I make my way upstairs, slam the door behind me. Get the phone out, stick the Dre's on that Shelly handed down about a year ago. They might be fakes. I don't care. Hit 'shuffle'. Ed Sheeran isn't really suiting my mood. Skepta next. It'll do. Start scrolling. And scrolling. And scrolling. No-one I really want to talk to. Suddenly, the red box flashes.

Sam Blake. "*w u u 2?*"

"*Mum n Dad got visitors. Mite fck off out. U doin owt?*"

"*Gym til 2*"

"*Mums visitors r twats. Mite call in?*"

"*K*"

Job done. As soon as that freak and his freaky famalam show up, my shoes go on and I'm off to the Power House. If I was going to use a gym, I'd not use that sweat pit ever. There's more than a touch of the roids about it. Loads of gorilla shaped baldy blokes, massive shoulders, puny legs, tiny penises, so everyone says. Needs must though.

Back to Fifa. Start loading up, then I hear voices downstairs. Shoes ready, jacket not too far away. Sam Blake is my escape plan. Archie's my plan B if he's knocking about anywhere. The ice rink is my last resort, not cos I wanna skate, but I know all the ice-dancers practice there on Sundays and they're all fit. About half of them have added me online, (take note people, they added me!) and my future long-term girlfriend, the special one who'll get to have all my babies one day, is amongst that group somewhere. I've just not decided which one it'll be yet.

I log everything off and eavesdrop. Mum's got the giggles with his Mum. I want to know what they're talking about before I go. My goal yesterday hasn't been mentioned in any way shape or form. Shelly's there too. I catch her asking "What's our Joe like in school?"

A truly loaded question. Rupert needs to be very diplomatic how he answers this. I can easily make things my business, and not in a way that Mum and Dad are wishing for, either. I think he's playing safe, mumbling something about paths not crossing, whatever that means. I don't catch it clearly, but I temporarily adjourn my plans to push the squirrel-faced little twat in front of a bus this week, on the basis that I've no solid evidence yet. I grab my shoes, phone and jacket. I listen a bit more while I do my laces up, but I don't hear Tarquin say anything careless. Shelly's now having a disagreement with Mum. I never interrupt those. I could stay longer and watch this gathering implode disastrously from a cosy distance, but, fuck it, none of my business. Sam's in the gym, Archie might be around, and it's eye candy time at the ice rink.

I go outside, keeping my gaze away from the geek. I can easily avoid the kid sister who's with him. She's probably as embarrassed as I'd be, and I doubt she'll look up from her phone much if she's got owt street-wise about her. Mum keeps asking me to join them, her selling point being that there's loads of food. I reckon the foods all proper spicy, as in full-on. There's English person spicy, like you get at Nandos or the Chinese buffet, then there's proper spicy. This lots definitely option 2. I'll wait til later. Shelly's too friendly with them for my liking, more friendly than she'd ever be to anyone else who came round. You'd never catch her saying hello to any of my mates, but when it comes to people who she knows I'm not keen on, she can't do enough to ingratiate her fucking self. Shelly's all "*your mates really cool!*" and "*why don't you join us*?". The adults don't suss her out, but in with all that chilli and stuff cooking, I can also smell a rat pretty easily. That game she's playing can fuck right off right now. I suspect she's been paid off by Dad again. She's usually only this nice when someone pays her to be.

One smarmy look back and I lose it totally. "He's not my mate. I barely even know him. Just cos he's at school wi' me dun't make him a mate does it?".

I turn and I'm straight out, not even noticing the bins in the passageway that I walk straight into and swear at. I keep walking, through the estate, past the shops, over the main road, and cut through the nature walk. If you believe what gets printed in the paper, this is supposed to be the greenest city in the world. If you live in a snobby mansion in Totley or Owler Bar, maybe so, but round here no-one's looking through their windows in awe of the glorious splendour of the Peak District or Ladybower. We have the "nature walk" to savour instead. It's simply a path that cuts through some warehouses and units, its practical use being a short cut from the houses on our estate to a dodgy pub, a playground, a bookies and a few crabby take-aways. It's also the place where everyone goes and pisses when they won't get home in time. More than that, there's deffo people who shite in there, people have trodden in the evidence before, and there's all sorts of stories about people who've had drunk sex in there, taken drugs, whatever, despite the place being toxic with half the estate's bodily waste fluids, all varieties. I can see why, in the sense that it's one of the only places for miles free from the glare of coppers or cameras, but

OMG the stench of it. I'm walking like I'm playing hopscotch with myself just to dodge all the dogshit lying around, and holding my breath at the same time. You have to stay on what there is of a path through it, as stepping off it into the weeds is a proper gamble with your trainers. Even now, amongst the clump of weeds to my right lie an orgies worth of used johnnies, broken glass, dogshit and every brand of beer can and voddie bottle that's been on offer on the last 3 years at the Co-Op, either empty or occasionally left with dark yellow piss inside. The amazing thing is, thanks to some town planner being off his tits on mind-bending shit, when you make it to the end of the nature walk, the next part of this short cut is through a kiddies park where absolutely nothing works - the swings have no seats, the slide has something smeared down it and the rope ladder thing has been proper doctored. Someone's got their hands on some yellow spray cans, and not bothered with the side of any of the warehouses, probably due to the fucking stench of it, but instead covered everything here, even the paved ground, not with any decent artwork, but just badly drawn spunking cocks, really crappy tags, not even tags, unless someone's name really is 'SUFC' or 'cunt'.

A couple more minutes hopscotching and holding my breath and I reach The Power House, a grim ugly sweathouse next to some industrial units. For £40 a month you can choose from using a boxing ring, some free weights lying around, a couple of exercise bikes and a water-cooler. There's no pool, no sauna, and, looking at the state of the ape men in here who could probably raise an articulated lorry over their heads but wouldn't last 10 seconds if they had to run or swim anywhere, I doubt there's much demand here for aerobics. It'd kill them anyways. The room ventilates itself in vain with one of them fans that Argos flogs for £10, the ones that topple over if you walk too close to them. I reckon half the people in here are roid-ragers. You can spot them a mile off, always look temperamental, grunt a lot, wear similar kit to each other. Sam denies it. If I ever saw any of these baboons out and about, the first thing I'd do would be to take a quick glance at their girlfriends, check for black eyes, teeth missing, all that stuff. I spot Sam shoulder pressing, must be pumping 9 or 10 of those metal bars up and down, deffo more than I could do with my legs. He's got a City shirt on as usual, an out of date one, identical to this year's kit except it's got a collar and not a round neck. An estuary of sweat's flowing down his back, dark patches under his arms, I bet he mings to fuck. I'll go see the ice-dancers on my todd, thanks.

"What's brought you here? Haven't you got some free-kick to shout out about?"

I half-tell him the truth. "You know that geeky lad that got whacked by Cory Hendricks?"

Sam kinda half-listens. He looks my way briefly then looks at his shoulders and feels them. "Yeah?"

"His Mum and my Mum are mates. I only found out today. They meet up for crappucinos and message each other non-stop."

"I know already. They stroll in here looking fabulous while you're out at footy, clear the ladies showers out then drag me in for a steamy soapy threesome. Then, once I've fully satisfied them both, they walk out and go for coffee, humming happy show tunes together. That's what they chat to each other about. Everyone knows. Except you."

Here's one muppet who won't be on stage at the Apollo anytime soon. "Mate. You can't even get Shironda to meet you at a weekend. Not even wi' a pocket full of "Free Nando's" vouchers. It's blatant you want to. She would, too. You just need a bath, then some plastic surgery, especially on them squirrel eyes. And a washing machine. And a haircut." Sam looks at me like he's ready to floor me, but my status as the next galactico from his beloved football team's youth system prevents that. I switch the conversation to footy. "Match alreyt yesterday?"

"Weren't great. Probly brought 300 wi' 'em tops. Not worth waiting about for."

"So it were a waste of time 'cos you din't go head-to-head wi' anyone. Din't it finish 3-3?"

"Bumped into a couple of them on't tram. Not up for owt"

"You think every London teams gonna be same as Millwall"

"There were two of them on't bus, surrounded by us. Someone started chatting wi' 'em and they said they used to go to Uni here and they'd support City cos they did student discounts, all that wibble. We're their northern team or whatever. They were like, proper friendly, up for a chat. Whacking them woulda bin wrong. I heard you scored a lucky one yesterday."

"How did you know? I've not posted owt, or told anyone?"

"Your Mum put summat on Facebook. Med it sound like you'd hit a worldy in or summat. I bet it were a tap-in, weren't it?" I deathglare him. He continues "I guess Leeds are shocking if we beat them by that much?"

"We" indeed. He really thinks he's part of all this, just cos he had a season ticket once. "Nah, it were closer than that. They were ahead at one bit."

"Dirty?"

"Nah, not really. Physical. But every games physical at this level now."

"How do you cope with that then? You're not exactly the scariest bastard I've ever seen"

"Mate, no point me pushing and shoving me way about. I'd lose. But my technique's a gift. Imagine marking me. Your girlfriend, Mum, Dad, all on't sidelines watching, and your biggest nightmare is reyt there leaving you on't floor without touching you, like that Mahrez bloke does for Leicester when he can be arsed. Eventually, tha's gonna launch into me hard enough to mek sure I don't get up after, so, me tactic's to know how and where to fall over. My goal were art, mate. Me Mum's not bullshitting."

I watch him trying to work it out. Falling over's just falling over to him, but it's actually an art. Brazilians know it. Spaniards know it. English dudes, not so much. I go into detail about it a bit more, but in reality, I'm not that much into the conversation, plus Sam's been sat chatting too long. He really needs to get a shower. When he sweats he smells like cabbage or summat proper rank like that. The nature walk smells sweeter than he does right now. If he's gonna hang with me for a bit, which, in essence is a preferable option to that freak family currently sat in my back garden, he needs to get a fucking wash. I hint at it, pointing out some random lass who keeps looking our way. She isn't, but he's got his back to her and I'm facing her full on. He's got to rely on me for the truth here. And he does, blindly, stupidly. As he turns to go, I spot him smiling at her, and I spot her turning her head round and giving him that "What are you looking at you ape-faced grunter?" look in return. It makes me smile anyways.

I don't know what the fuss is with most lads my age to get laid at age 14. The ones who are having some kind of douchey competition to see how many lasses they can get into bed are the worst, or, I'll rephrase that, how many totally imaginary girls a lad can invent and then lay claim to getting laid with. It's always girls they met on holiday, or that live miles away, or on some social networking page, but never the same page that you're mates with them on. Sam claimed a bit back that he'd been with 6 lasses this year. Suspiciously, as I attend the same school as him and see plenty of the lad away from school, I'd never seen any of them before in my whole life. One were from Barnsley, another from down south, another one he'd just so happened to meet randomly on a day out in Skegvegas with his folks. Pure random chance stuff, or, more likely, some porno he'd looked at and dreamed about acting out. Archie's not so stupid. He claims to have had the one girlfriend in Scotland, which he can account for that as he's up there at his Dad's every school holiday, and his pages have quite a few Scottish people on it and there's a few photos he's got where he's hugged up with a couple of quite pretty lasses so, as he also uses my very own "my love life's my business" line, no-one will accuse him of anything. That line is one of my smarter moves, even though the honest truth is I'm doing no business whatsoever. I don't really think any of the girls I'm in any kind of contact with are that bothered about me, anyway. The year 8s and year 9s maybe, but the year 10s are probably sick of the sight of me, or, look at me in the same way as I see them. I knew them in year 7, so it's physically impossible to fancy any of them purely because of that. In any event, any lass I get together with in future, I'd have to be friends with them first. It comes before any being fit, looking good in a black dress, any of that eye candy stuff. With this, my mind drifts to the skating rink. There's people there that I need to make friends with.

Sam's out of the shower. Grey trackies, blue hoody, grey NY beanie. Though he now smells of Lynx and not B.O, no lass is looking at him at all today, or, by association, me. Not even one from Barnsley or Skegvegas. A relief, as if I sit here on this old leather sofas any longer then my arse crack will end up sweatier than the chap in the corner who's been exercise biking for the last half hour and there's a fat sweaty line vertically down the back of his trackies, right where his bum crack is. We leave the gym. Hopscotch on the nature walk again. We stop at the Co-Op. I'd never ever sit on the wall outside there, but Sam's fashion sense has made the ice rink a bad idea. It's downtown central scallyland here but it's better than going home. Becky from the slow class is there with a lad from year 11, don't know his name. I don't know what her learning issue is, but she's one of those kids that'll innocently talk to strangers, never sussing if they're dodgy or not. I've known her since primary so I feel a little responsible for her, so, with the joint hardest kid in school alongside me, I look the lad up and down. Then, disaster strikes.

"Joey, I've just seen that new kid coming out of your house."

What the fuck? And why are kids I never talk to stalking my house all of a sudden?

"What's he doing round yours then?"

Think quickly for fucks sake.

"It were about when Cory Hendricks whacked him last week. He got given my name, so his Mum went looking for me and got wrong identity." I'm a crap liar. Anyone with half a brain will see through this feeble bullshit.

"Really?" Becky replies. Thank fuck I got collared by one of the slowcoach class.

"Yep. Mek sure Cory Hendricks knows I've covered his back and said nowt. He owes me."

"Why didn't you drop him in it? I don't like him"

"Well" I breathe in, and lean forward a bit. "I don't grass. Just mek sure them twats know I've said nowt." Year 11 dude smiles at Sam when I say that. They both know. If Sam weren't stood next to me, I'd be half the tough guy I'm pathetically trying to be now. "Have they gone now?"

"Brandon saw them. Kiera too. And that Josh Illingworth who lives down from you. I saw them, they left and went that way." Becky turns her right arm out. Right and left. I learnt it when I first kicked a football. I check her trainers are on the correct feet, and her laces are done up.

Lovely as it's been to chat with the special class, I'm starving, and the urge to shower before I start scratching my arse in public and hoping no-one's looking, has intensified. "Laters."

"You off then?" Sam steps in. "What were all that about going to't ice-rink for a bit?"

As if I'll meet my future wife with Sam as he is. He's no wingman. "I wish. Was hoping to tap my Mum up for a fiver. No chance. Another time tho?"

"Should've told her you were wi' me. She'd have given you £20 to tek off for an hour or two while I..."

Fuck off Sam. You're not funny. 1) School geek socialising in my back yard. 2) No money 3) My entire family, 4) Scored a worldy against dirty Leeds this weekend and no-one gives a shit, and 5) Currently sat outside the Co-Op like a scally. If I was up for banter right now, it wouldn't be this feeble shit I'm listening to. I'm gone.

I should be feeling ecstatic today, for fucks sake. I scored a worldy against Leeds yesterday, but, thanks to everyone else being dicks, that buzz isn't there. All I've had is questions about some geek kid with no significance to me at all. I just wanna walk in, eat food, then shut me bedroom door and stick Fifa on for a bit. Next door's cat is sat on our front fence. Even she's looking at me to suggest I'll get savaged when I go through the door. I give her a pat, then take a deep breath, getting plenty of oxygen in before I walk in. I'm starving. I check the obvious places, microwave, grill, oven. It's only when I open the fridge that Mum actually enquires what I'm up to.

"See yer Dad. He's saved you a bit. I wun'ta bothered."

Full-on outstanding parenting there. I step outside. Dads leaning over his oil drum that he tries to call a barbecue, spraying and scrubbing like he was shining the bodywork on some beloved custom classic car. In the absence of badass car ownership, his current whip being a Peugeot with the badge missing and a few scratches along one side, this is his pride and joy. His head never rises from the task in hand and points at a plate buried under a couple of tea towels, without word or glance. I look at him cleaning his ridiculous oil drum contraption and decide to offer help, though I've no idea why.

"Want a hand with that?"

He points at a plate with a tea-towel over it and carries on scrubbing. At least I tried. I take the plate into the kitchen. There's chicken legs, big ones, but black as fuck and stone cold. Some sweetcorn on a stick thing, black as fuck when you'd rather it was yellow, also ice-cold. A burger that looks homemade, green and red chilli lumps in it, probably someone's special recipe or summat, also dead, half-cremated and ice cold.

"Is there owt else?"

Mum appears. "Just swat in in't microwave and mek best of it."

"How long for?"

"Don't think it matters. It's black as the ace of clubs. 3 minutes max"

Mum returns to her riveting online conversation, probably with mother geek. I stick the plate in the microwave, hit 3 minutes on it, and wait quietly for it to ping. I open the door. "Microwave's bust Mum. It's still cold."

"It were on defrost. Put it on cook."

Forget it. Too complicated. "Is there owt else instead of this? It's all burnt and it looks rank."

"Tough shit. You chose to tek off just as we were dishing up." Dad's clearly had an ear cocked to everything, and now volunteering his side of the discussion, not that there'll be much of one. I leave it all. I spy a cornflakes box on top of the fridge. I reach over to that.

"Good luck finding any milk." Dad chips in. "Your tea's on that plate, lad. If you don't like it, tough shit. Like I got told when I were a nipper."

It's 1 v 2. I'll lose. I decide to forget eating, but get my sweaty arse and empty stomach upstairs. Shower and Fifa, or Fifa then shower. I choose the order in no time at all. I go straight for the bathroom. The hot water's off. They're on a wind up. I'm not triggering. It's what they want me to do. Cold shower, cold shoulder it is.

----

12. FLYING ON FOUR ENGINES

You can tell by the severely slopy ceiling of the Head of Year's Office that it's good for a mop, a bucket and maybe a vacuum cleaner at best, but somehow it accommodates me, Mum, Mrs Frogson, and her assistant, a busybody with the build of a long-retired weightlifter and a smile so fake you can see the wild grimace behind it. I don't know her name so I'll just give her a cheesy name like Mrs Wotsit for now. Mum and Mrs Frogson both force out painful-looking pleasantries, but the hostility in the body language is unmistakable. The meeting starts with the inevitable useless question, the ancient chestnut I've been asked and infuriated by a million times before.

"Well, Edward, what do you think the problem is?"

Mum's straight in. "Edward's not the problem. Your school is."

"Let Edward tell us in his own words."

One day I'll have to fight battles like this alone. This can be a practice session for the day when Mum's not sat next to me anymore. "As my Mum just said, I'm not the problem. Your school is."

Mrs Frogson and Mrs Wotsit adjust themselves as well as they can within these restricted confines and pull that "heard it all before" face at each other.

"The problem lies with the people that assaulted me, not me."

"Ok. So what happened for things to get to that situation?"

Is this woman for real? ... "I'm not sure what you mean?"

"Yes, what do you mean?" Mum's gaze towards Mrs Wotsit is intense and not shifting anytime soon. She's well up for this.

"In my experience, for incidents like this to take place in school so quickly, there must have been a trigger factor, a tipping point even. We need to establish what that could have been?"

"Edward's the new kid in school. How's that for a trigger factor?"

"Edward is by no means the first new pupil we've had join us. It's just been a long time since we've had a new student encounter such issues so quickly."

I see what she's doing. She's projecting the blame for all of this onto me.

"I see what you're doing. You're trying to project the blame for all this onto me."

I think that Mrs Frogson was expecting this to come from Mum, not me. She pauses. "Not in the slightest. We have a rigid anti-bullying policy and a responsibility to maintain and uphold this. Pupil safety and well-being is of paramount importance."

Mum's in 4th gear now. "Can I see a copy of this policy please?" She's already obtained a copy, but no-one said she can't have another one.

"Pardon?"

"Your bullying policy. Can I see a copy please?"

"Oh." Mrs Frogson fake grimace smiles. "Right". She looks at her little squat-bodied sidekick, sat with shoulders back, arms folded, "Yes, that shouldn't be a problem." She nods at Mrs Wotsit, who struggles to adjust her swively chair to face her computer.

Mrs Wotsit sighs, turns the computer on, then sighs again, loudly "What's my password again?"

I can see now why she's a school pastoral assistant and not a cyber intelligence operative for MI5. If I'd made porridge for breakfast, I could have mixed a full bag of corn flour in and the end result still wouldn't be as thick as she is. She rifles through her diary, flips through a couple of pages then starts typing. If I have to take things that far, I now know to hack the school system via the flowery diary of the weakest link here. Awkward silence all round as we all focus on Mrs Wotsit staring at her screen, she knows we're intently focused on her. She knows she'd have to offer millions to my Mum to get her to change the direction of that intense stare right now. She wants to tell us loudly to fuck off, I can tell. Instead she picks up the phone, waits for an answer, and then goes "Hi Debbie, it's Wendy here, can you print us a copy of the school anti-bullying policy off please? I'll come fetch it in a couple of minutes."

There's some kind of muffled reply, to which Mrs Wendy Wotsit replies "Yes, I know it's lengthy, but it's important we have another copy."

Mum senses the perfect opportunity to create mischief and consolidate control, "While you're at it, if I need to see copies of your policies on drugs, safeguarding and diversity at some stage, is this the way I go about it, by arranging a meeting, or are they more easily accessible?"

If looks could kill. "They should be on the website" Mrs Wendy Wotsit snaps back.

"Excellent. If there's no satisfactory outcome to Edward's issues, I'll ask for them. I may also need copies of your policies on behaviour, attendance, head lice and threadworms if necessary."

If I was neutral, I'd watch this whilst alternating between a bucket of popcorn and a big fat Cuban cigar. But I'm not neutral, and while Mum's doing the absolute business here, I gain confidence.

"What my Mum's trying to say, is, that under the United Nations Convention on the Rights of the Child, I'm not sure of the exact part of this lengthy but informative document, what with me being 14 and that, I'm entitled to an education free from persecution."

Mrs Frogson doesn't know whether to scowl at me or nominate me for school council. She stays polite to me though, a little more naturally than she's managing with Mum. "Edward, it's what we're here to do. We're still learning about you, but we know you have potential to go far."

"Thank you. I hadn't finished. I'm entitled to education free from discrimination, harassment or risk to personal safety. Your school policies will confirm this, but more global legislation exists that comprehensively reinforces my insistence of a natural entitlement to this."

Mrs Frogson smiles. Mrs Wendy Wotsit follows with a smile too, once she's taken that extra couple of seconds to understand everything I said. I did use some words that were several syllables long. I also believe that off-duty she could be one of those gammony people who thinks that freedom from harrassment and persecution is some kind of liberal snowflake touchy-feely bullshit.

Mum's backing me up again, which is nice, but right now, I think I've got the upper hand by myself. "And its schools responsibility to ensure that you get an education safely."

"So what happened on Thursday?" Mrs Wendy Wotsit asks. "What's your side of it?"

"That's simple enough. I walked out of the gates as everyone else did, and within seconds I was ambushed by at least 4 boys. Some of them are in my tutor group, but I don't know their names. One of them pinned me by my arms and went face to face with me, then someone else pinned my shoulders back from behind while the first one threw punches. Another one kicked my bag down the street."

"So it happened outside the gates?" Mrs Frogson asks, folded arms, head cocked to one side.

"Yes. I got out of the gates, and was about to turn left to go down to the bus stop."

"How do you expect school to solve this? It happened off-site with no witnesses."

I'm back. "There were witnesses. Loads. I just don't know any of them."

"Any you recognise?"

"One's in some of my lessons. His name's Joe. There was a bigger lad with him, and a girl from my tutor group, dark hair, dark-skinned, bright-coloured nails."

"That'll be Shironda. Were they witnesses or assailants?"

"They just saw it and crossed the road. The girl had been abused by one of the boys when they were waiting for tutorial the other day, so they might have got assaulted themselves had they stepped in."

"And Joe, about this tall?" she raises her hand a little off the ground, not too high.

Mum's back. "Caitlin's Joe, who we were with yesterday?"

"Yeah, him."

Mrs Wotsit turns suddenly, as if something unbelievable happened. "Joey Barker's your friend?"

"No! I don't really know him but I don't like him much. My Mum and his Mum are mates though, and I'm mates with his sister, sort of."

"Shelley Barker would have this over with in minutes if she was here. In her own legendary manner."

Mrs Frogson scratches her chin, like pretentious artistic types do sometimes when they stare at sculptures, head cocked to one side. She takes a few seconds, and then speaks. "I was planning to reassess Edward's lessons anyway. I said I would when he first joined us. I also considered allocating him a buddy in lessons. I didn't have Joey Barker in mind, however."

Mum gets nosey. "Is Joe a bad one then?"

"I think you'll understand the confidentiality rules here, but no, he doesn't create any problems. He can be influential amongst his peers, as was his sister. He's not necessarily a character to avoid, but I wouldn't say that he exactly goes out of his way to be anyone's closest advocate either."

I just know that description of Joe will be getting typed online later, word for word, in the little chatty box at the bottom right hand corner of my Mums Facebook page, which, I've noticed, has become more active than usual recently.

Mrs Thingy's back in. "So, Joe and Shironda both witnessed it. The big lad, short dark hair?"

"Not sure. Two of the kids that assaulted me sit at the back of my tutor group. They were giving that Shironda girl some grief on my first day. No idea what about, but it wasn't good."

"So you witnessed that?"

"Well, it sounded like sexual harassment so I stepped in."

"Stepped in? So you tried to be a hero". Mrs Frogson sighs, as if she's disappointed with me and

I've done something wrong. What is she on? I can see what she's doing here. She's now angling to try and find a new way to project the responsibility for this shit onto me.

"Well it wasn't right. If I heard people talking about my sister like that I'd flatten them." If that doesn't get me extra brownie points with Mum, nothing will.

"Do you imagine this girl would ever back you up in return? As you say, she crossed the road when..."

"So you're saying I should do nothing?"

"Well, it might be wise to wait until your feet are under the table."

"So if this was a year 7 being harassed, or a special needs kid, I walk past, right?"

"No, that would be different"

"How would it?"

"Edward, we're trying to help you."

"No you're not" Mum steps back in "You're trying to find a new way to project blame onto him so that you don't have to take any action."

Mrs Frogson returns to the snarling grimaces. "I really don't think..."

I interrupt, shocking manners I know, but I'm getting emotional. "Mum's right. You're looking for a way to sweep my beating under the carpet. My last school did exactly the same. Would you like to see what it took me to get anyone to take notice?" I start unbuttoning my shirt cuff, but I read Mums expression. I realise that they already know what I'm about to show them. "That's probably in my school records. I really hope I don't need to explain anymore?" I feel my voice go a little bit there. But I want to hold all that emotional stuff in. I take a breath, send some fresh oxygen in, and wipe my eyes, to check for tears. Got there in time.

"Oh Edward, of course not."

"Right it's established. I'm entitled to an education free from victimisation, harassment, and bullying. As long as I treat everyone else with respect, as I've tried to do so far, then I'm naturally entitled to expect the same of others. And your job as head of year is to make sure this right is upheld for every student isn't it?"

"Yes. It's something I take great pri..."

I've interrupted again. I can't help it. Bloods pumping. "I'll go to lessons when this meetings done. I'll stay whilst I'm treated with respect, regardless of what the little label is on my coat, shoes, bag or whatever, all of which is immaterial to my requirement to learn. Agreed?"

Mrs Frogson opens her mouth to say something. I feel like one of those political interviewers on the TV do when they're haranguing a government minister. I'm bossing this.

"I also missed school on Friday due to recovering from my injuries. Hence I've missed a day's education. I'll do my catching up this week, instead of P.E. I'll work somewhere quiet like the library or an empty IT room instead. I expect to be kept away from the thugs who assaulted me, too. I have an entitlement to that."

Mrs Frogson takes a big sigh, and gently lays her hand flat, fingers outstretched, on her desk "Edward, how do you expect us to be able to implement this? We dont even know who attacked you, you can't give names yourself, and currently, no-one witnessed it who can back your story up."

"As I've said already, they're all in my form."

Mrs Frogson and Mrs Wotsit glance at each other. I still don't know her name, nor do I care to learn it. She can stay Mrs Wotsit. Mum's sat next to me, arms folded too, her popcorn moment I guess.

"There were plenty of witnesses. It was right outside the school gates as soon as the bell had gone. I'm trusting you to catch up with this and deal with my assailants accordingly. If this was a police matter, which, being that level of assault, it could easily be, they wouldn't dismiss this, and I could press charges. I don't really want the police to come into school and arrest anyone. I just want to come to school, get educated and not be slaughtered for it. That's where I expect you to help me."

Mrs Frogson wants to speak, but I'm in full flight here. All four engines, me.

"I'm now going to leave this meeting, and naturally going to fulfil the behaviour levels that you expect of all your pupils. At the same time, I have expectations that if somebody interferes with my opportunity to learn, I'm going to naturally expect you and all your colleagues to challenge this immediately. If you don't challenge any of this firmly, promptly or consistently, I'm going to get my coat on and walk straight out of school. If you can't fulfil your obligations to me, I won't fulfil mine to you. If you can't guarantee my personal safety, I have ways of guaranteeing my safety that I will employ."

Mrs Frogson is back in "But Edward, if you do that the only person that loses out will be you."

"In which case I'll hold you responsible. I'm still a child. As well as the potential you say I have, I have aspirations too. I expect you to help me on this, my next step towards these. That's why you teach isnt it?"

"What exactly are your aspirations?" Mrs Frogson asks. Her tone just warmed a bit there.

"I'm still working on them, but they're grand, awesome, and if I get there, there might be a photo of me in the middle of the wall in school reception, and you'll be boasting to everyone you bump into that you taught and inspired me to my level of greatness."

"Politician" Cheesy-corn-snack suggests. I'd discounted that one ages ago. I'm not dishonest, and I'd actually prefer my life's vocation to be one that makes life better for more people than just myself. I'm not sure there's a political party where I'd fit in.

"Criminal lawyer?" Mrs Frogson suggests. She says it like it's a good thing. Taking this setting into account, I'd only be willing to work for the prosecution.

"I've got a bit of time, haven't I? I don't even know what I want for my tea tonight, let alone what to do with the rest of my life. I'll work it out. And you, as teachers, can help me along the way, as you're paid to do." It's hot, cramped, and both my knees and arse ache from sitting at such a ridiculous angle. "As I said, I'm off into my lesson. You get paid to sort out bullying, so I'm leaving you to it. If I get anymore, I'm straight through the gates for the rest of the day. See you later Mum."

Mrs Frogson wants to speak, but I'm halfway out of the door before I realise the meeting wasn't over. I thought it was all over. It is now.

I was half-asleep before that meeting. I walk into the English class having never been so awake, with none of the nerves or trepidation that I really should have, bearing in mind the last time any of these people saw me I was getting punched in the face. I just grabbed the nearest chair, as I said I would, this time next to that chunky lad with no social skills who school tried and failed to buddy me up with last week. I feel him move his chair a few inches to the left, and when the teacher beckons this Joel lad to share his book with me, he moves his body to the edge of his plastic chair, and his book a clear 10 centimetres closer to me, and whispers "Are you fucking serious?", just quietly enough for the teacher not to hear.

So, I rise from my chair, ready to walk towards the door, next stop home, when the teacher asks what I'm doing. I should keep to my word, but unfortunately I'm still on four engines.

I raise my voice. Towards Joel. "Excuse me. I don't understand what you mean?"

The goofy lad looks at me, startled.

Time to go a step further. "When the teacher asked you to share your book with me, your response was to ask me if I was, in your words, fucking serious. Why did you say that?"

The quickest minds in this room don't function on full power on a Monday morning. He's got no chance.

"I'll ask you again. It's an English literature lesson on a Monday morning. Please define how you need to know if I'm serious or not. I suspect you meant this with unprovoked hostility."

The Shironda lass drops in. "I think he's got grumps on cos you've sat next to him, love."

The teacher's trying to say something, but I'm still on top form from taking Mrs Frogson on. If I can destroy her with reasonableness, I can hold my own with anybody, verbally at least.

And if I can't, I go home.

School won't like it, but they'll learn.

"Do you really think I sat next to you by choice? Like I walked in and thought "Wow, there's a seat free next to whatever your name is. How marvellous!" Take a look around. There's three free seats in here. One next to you, one next to the window that, if the sun comes out, will blaze my eyes out, and one underneath the teachers nostrils. No offence sir, but those seats are like the ones at the very front at the cinema. Instant neck ache."

The whole class focusses on me. Good for them.

"So, yes, I'm serious. Seriously serious. I need somewhere to sit. And sometimes the seat I need is bang next to someone I'd never even go near in any other part of my life. Like just now."

The teachers back in. "And on those succinct words, page 35 please. Rhiannon, you can narrate."

Some blonde haired girl I'd never seen or heard speak before reads to the class. I can spot looks darting across the room, aimed at the numpty next to me, not me. I quickly scan the class. Joe has his head down in the book, though I doubt he's reading it. Shironda and her mate smile my way. That might be a good sign. Another lad who looks like he's not slept, with a wristband on with a cannabis leaf pattern, stares at the lad sat next to me, like you'd look at someone who'd just proper full on embarrassed themselves.

When the lesson ends, I catch this wristband lad and a couple of others whacking the Joel lad on the back and saying "He made a proper bitch out of you there". I see Joe taking ages to fill his bag up, extra slow, deliberately. I don't really want to speak to him either. I see this as my chance to exit the classroom easily and painlessly. If anyone gets hassled, it's the lad who I've just faced down. I'm still on four engines, though. I really should think about making a safe landing soon. I'm in with the boffins for the next class. I thought I'd prefer being in the boff class, I don't. Even though there's barely an aggressive brain cell in the room, no-one says anything, and the lesson drags for an eternity.

This teacher should be buzzing. When all the science teachers got the year 10s distributed out, he got boffs class. He should be loving this. Even if his teaching's useless, they'll still all pass his subject with A's. He could have had the engagement group or nurture class instead. He looks like his life would have been happier if he had. I soon learn why. When he asks the class questions, he might as well ask "Do you mind if I sit here and pull all my teeth out?" It's that painful. I think about answering, but then I decline at the last minute. I realise that none of the kids dare answer anything as there's probably some kid in here that knows the subject way better than they do. Fifty minutes with all the sponges did help me though, as I've landed safely back to earth. I play safe at break time and stay in the science lab, reading the "To Kill A

Mockingbird" book that I've got behind with. I get to page 42. My hearts not totally in it, but I should finish it without getting too bored I think.

When I get to Graphics, Shironda decides to say to me. "Are you fucking serious?" There's a laugh there, and from her mate.

"Absolutely" I reply, deadpan.

"You're mad as badgers, you!" Again, I interpret friendly fire, not hostility.

"Well, he was very rude to me and I'd done nothing to him."

"Oh you did." The girl next to her adds. "You sat next to the grumpy twat."

"The seat was free. Did he expect me to stand up all lesson?"

"Erm. What do you think?"

"I think he needs to learn some manners."

"Ha ha yeah that as well. Do you do that with everyone that throws shade at you?" Shironda asks.

"Do what?"

"Rip them a new butthole? You did it wi' me last week."

"No I didn't."

"Erm, when Corey gave me grief and you jumped in? Listen, I know you're gonna get some grief and that, cos..."she pauses, changing her mind on what she was going to say "cos you're the new kid and that, and I don't want to be rude as you seem alrite, but you do need a new hairdresser and stuff, so you don't keep setting yersen up."

"Why?"

"Are you alright?" Shironda's mate asks. She's not enquiring as to my health and wellbeing here.

"No, why would I need to be careful? If people give me abuse, I'll stand up to it. People should respect each other."

Shironda's back in. She's clearly the mouth of the class. "Yeah yeah, be careful anyway, don't get yersen in any bother you can't get out of."

I nod back. Half the class are in awe of me for wrecking some kid with words. The other half look at me like I'm a prize idiot. The two groups are interspersed. It'll take a few minutes to break it all down. I turn the screen on. As I'm logging the password in, I hear Joe walking in with some other kid, "Did you see that round the world I did back there?" his mate asks.

"Bitch, I were freestyling them off when I were..........oh bloody hell!"

I sense trouble. The whole class does. I'm in his seat again. But I'm confident. Its not his seat. Its where he chooses to sit, and I was here first. If this was a tram or a train or a cafe, he'd have no argument. I look at him, making no effort to move. I was sat right at the end, away from anyone. Safe choice. Clearly his choice too. Joe looks at me for 5 seconds, then looks around the room and puts himself at another desk, I can hear "for fucks sake" under his breath. Everyone focusses on him instead.

The lessons a double, but passes quicker than the single lesson with the boffs. Talkative kids. I actually don't mind listening in on them, even little more than just gossip about other kids. I've no interest, unless it affects me. Apparently, Joel's always been a cunt, so say his closest mates, clearly distancing themselves from him now that the new geeky kid's produced a level of public ownership that the Labour Party can only dream of. I say nothing. I've already made my impact. I leave the lesson having learned less about graphics than I did about who's got ebola, who smells, who's been smoking crack, who's a pervert, etc etc etc. I got asked twice if I was at Joe's house yesterday. I noticed Joe deathglaring me. I made up some bullshit that my Mum was mates with someone who lived on his street, so someone must have seen me coming out of there instead. As if I'd choose to call round for someone like him anyway?

My school day lasts till lunchtime. I keep to my word. As soon as I'm disrespected, I'm gone. I do school the service of informing them of my departure. The Head of Year's room is locked and empty, so I rip a page from my exercise book, write down why I'm not staying for the afternoon, slide it under the door, face down for confidentiality, and get on my travels.

It wasn't that massive an incident. Joel stepped out in front of me from the queue outside the lunch hall and shoved me in the chest straight away. I didn't move. I just stayed face to face with him, studying every red veiny noodle in the whites of his eyes, ingesting the stench of his acrid breath and stale sweat, until...

"Don't ever fucking sit near me, or even look at me again, weird cunt!!"

I don't do threats. "I'll sit where there's a space, thanks."

"I'm warning you. Do it again and you can get ready!"

"Warn me as much as you want. I'll disregard it."

The reaction from onlookers tells me this lad is barely above me in the pecking order... "Pick your toys up, man", "Get back in't queue you fat twat". I wouldn't call him fat, but he's not overly dainty either. I stand my ground. When last week's idiots harassed me, everyone went silent, like they feared being harassed themselves. I see enough to know this isn't the same. The look on his face is intense, but incapable of stopping me sleeping well tonight.

I whisper "Listen to your friends. They're trying to help you. Go and join them."

With that, comes a shove in the chest, nothing painful, but I topple backwards, into a group of younger girls who immediately start yelling at me, "Cunt, nobhead, fuckin weirdo, freak", all that kinda stuff. I didn't deserve any of it. A dinner lady and a teacher were stood chatting to each other, seeing everything, doing nothing, neglecting their duty of care. My form tutor, whatever his name is, was also within sight and inactive. I'm out of here with no particular place to go. The manga corner in Waterstones seems appealing, as does annexing Lara's bit of the sofa, slobbing my way through Rick n Morty or Bobs Burgers. Either way, I'm on strike.

13. A Community Champion

It's all over school. I expected plenty of "how did you get on against Leeds, Joe?" or at least "Can you get tickets for next week's game?". No-one cared. Everyone, including those I never even talk to, had more interest in why Edward was at my house on Sunday, or, using their actual wording, "Hey Joe, how's your new bezzie?". Don't worry, everyone got told, face-to-face, by me, to F.R.O, but whilst me and him are being mentioned in the same sentence, this crap is becoming a bit of a leveller on the social front. A worldy against Leeds United isn't enough. I need a hat trick against Real Madrid and Stormzy spitting rhymes about it just for me to maintain my rep.

Everyone finds it entertaining. Everyone finds him entertaining. He walked into English late on Monday and sat himself down next to some lad who were sat on his todd. This lad, Joel, wasn't best pleased to be perched next to him, so he chunters about it, like "What are you sitting next to me for, twat?" Within seconds, Woopert here's stood up and schooled him full-on. I must add, in fairness, that in formal situations like this, he's quite handy. He totally turned the whole setting upside down and made Joel his bitch, full set of lyrics, everyone else sat with popcorn out, loving every second. Even teacher gave it 20 seconds before calming it down. Anyway, as everyone leaves, Joel's got every lad in the class, and a fair few of the girls, totally ripping into him for getting owned, well not totally owned but definitely mortgaged on a long-term basis.

From everywhere, the classroom, the footy courts, the bus home, I'm getting "Tell your mate well done for us when he drops in for you later". So, you can imagine how I feel when Mum and Dad get home and ask more about how Edward got on than anything I'd done that day. I was expecting a bollocking anyway, as I'd tried to make myself beans on toast earlier this morning, forgot to turn the beans off on the cooker and welded them to the pan. Washing up liquid didn't work, even when I emptied half the bottle into the pan there were still beans welded on the bottom of the pan. I fetched shower gel and shampoo from upstairs, cos they both do the same thing as far as I care, but that didn't work. Only when I swat Cillit Bang into the pan, making a mental note to always beware of anything getting cooked in it, did I nearly get it clean again. Somehow, though I've wrecked one of her indestructible pans, Mum didn't mention it. I wish she did though. :-/

"You've not seen owt of Edward at school today have you?"

"Yeah, Mum, training went well thanks." If you're even bothered.

"No, seriously, has owt gone off?"

Erm, hello? Next set of fixtures are out? "Summat kicked off wi' him and some other lad on Monday. The teachers were around so I kept out of it, thought it best to let them deal wi' it." What with them being paid reasonably well with generous holidays to take responsibility for stuff like this, amazingly.

"Did you see it all?"

"The lad gev him grief in English, just verbal, nowt more, and Edward gev him some back. He's not too shabby at that is he?" I fake a smile, unconvincingly. "Edward was in't right, the other lad were being an arse. I'd've probly done't same as Edward if it were me."

"That's all, just an argument?"

"I might've missed stuff. I were in't other lads lesson straight after. He were tekking stick for picking an argument wi' Edward. Then he spotted Edward at lunchtime and started on him again, slap bang outside o't lunch hall, but there were a reyt audience and I couldn't see owt. Everyone scrambles round for't best view when trouble kicks off, and I'd have needed a piggyback at least, maybe even a stepladder, just to see over everyone, so I just carried on where I were going. No need for me to get dragged into owt." Oh shit, that'll start more grief. Quickly I add "If there's teachers about". World War 3 averted for now.

That was enough to change the direction of the conversation, so I could get upstairs and get showered. Dweebs Mum was having a good chunter about the teachers apparently doing nothing to help her son. I could have replied that he doesn't exactly do much to help himself, wearing that daft coat every day, but I need to minimise conversations about him, so I held it in. I could've said Barcelona away were my next match. It wouldn't have registered. I went up the stairs, having had no opportunity to make reference to the Cruyff turn I wrecked Ben with before squaring an unmissable to Mo that I did in training tonight.

The pressure was off me after a couple of days anyway. Josh Illingworth from year 8 will be landing in a very prickly hedge, or maybe in the long grass in the nature walk, on account of being 1) too nosy, 2) too talkative 3) a bit fucking disrespectful. But that can wait until the time's right. By Friday, new gossip appeared, then escalated. Proper massive serious stuff.

On the same day as I give Josh Illingworth a good towsing, I will also buy a massive thank you chocolate selection for Scarlett Ryan from year 9. She didn't actually do that much. She just wanted to get the broken screen fixed on her phone. She asked a lad called Jackson Holmes, who, before Wednesday, worked in an e-cig shop that also did phone repairs, laptop wiping, all that stuff, but combined it with a self-employment as the go-to man for anything that anybody needs that neither Amazon or Meadowhall offer, a community champion indeed. Cigs for £3 a packet? He had a mate. ID needed doctoring? £100, a week's notice, and job done. Laptop needs wiping? Ped needs an insurance document? Car needs alterations, either in a workshop or on paper? He knew someone you didn't. All I know is that when Scarlett asked if he could fix her screen, even though the going rate's about £40, he told her £80, knowing she'd never have that much even in her life-savings, so when she cried poverty, he offered her other ways of paying, which, as she's quite a pretty lass, I don't need to spell out. Of course, he were counting on the fact that teenagers are so attached to their phones that they'll do anything in the world to rectify them when they go wrong. In many cases, he's right. He'd fix the phone, then send the owners of those phones to run errands for him, which could be deliveries, or collections, or looking after a package or two in your bedroom for a few days, or, if you're female and he takes a liking to you, more intimate and physical, delivered behind the tinted-windows of his uninsured Subaru.

Scarlett told Jackson she'd think about it, but went straight to her older sister, who texted her Mum, who, within minutes was on the phone to stepdad, who stormed into the youth club with his big sweaty mates looking for Jackson Holmes. Jackson wasn't there, but they still shit the life out of the 10 year olds in there trying to play pool on a ripped table with tipless cues and 5 balls missing, and the two lasses from year 8 sat at the coffee bar chatting to the youth worker, who in turn was half-listening to them whilst clock-watching, brewing his 27th cuppa of the day and rolling his 17th fag up of the shift. Outside were 30 teenagers who'd declined to pay 30p to use miserably underfunded community provision, seeing better financial value in producing 10 times this figure each to pool together for cigs, energy drinks, and whatever variety of alcohol or soft drugs was a text message away. Jackson wasn't among them, either.

Having not found their target, the big sweaty mob asked the group of kids where Jackson was, all of whom said "no idea" whilst simultaneously nodding towards to the back of the building. At first they only found Kean Briggs and Kyle Danic, spice-zombies, freshly zombied in their usual zombie spot, but sussed that as acquaintances of Jackson's, he may be close by. They walked further along until, at the back of the car park, behind the bottle bins, things moved up several levels when they caught his souped up Impreza, and behind it, some lass 2-man skiing, with the lad to the right being Jackson Holmes himself. Jackson must regret not wearing tracky bottoms at that very moment, as he couldn't button his jeans up in time to avoid one of stepdad's mates filming the full scene on his phone for 10 seconds, as proof of the crime, before the big sweaty stepdad crew dealt with the entire situation in the way they knew best, before calling the police out 5 minutes later. What they themselves didn't realise was that the police, in wishing to use as much available evidence as possible to secure convictions for all crimes committed, would retain his beloved Iphone 7 in a sealed bag marked "evidence", to be returned to him once the court proceedings are concluded and his phone is a curious antique. To complicate things even more, while waiting the usual 3 hours or so for the police to show up, he sent copies of this evidence to some mate of his to store safely. Unfortunately for him, his trusty mate decided to save it all safely to Instagram and Facebook, from where the whole episode went viral. I'm not daft enough to go looking for the full story. I've seen enough in the past to make the rational decision to take the no-grief option, delete the video, delete the person, block them from everything. I'd no longer know them, they'd be dead to me.

Though many will miss the valuable services to the community provided by Jackson, they also realise that in his absence, there's always someone else willing to step up and become the new go-to man. No-one will miss the one type of person that can rally a violent mob together with a common purpose, a sex offender. Jackson Holmes's 20 years old. He's deffo getting put away, fraggle wing, watching over his shoulder for 18 months minimum, checking his meals for bleach and maybe getting a new special moisturiser made from boiling water and sugar. It's that major. The other lad's 17, in college, never been in bother before, but he's taken a proper sick whack on the jaw and has been seen coming out of the police station with a face like the elephant man's. The coppers are all over this. It's a long-time since a gift wrapped opportunity to smash their performance targets has been placed at their doorstep. They've graced a few other doorsteps, and about 5 other people, maybe more than that, are opting to keep their mouths shut and their social media de-activated, sweating over official cautions or a spot of Sunday morning litter-picking if they're lucky, on the basis of the act of sharing any footage where under-18s engaging in sexual acts also being a sex offence titled "distribution of child pornography". Scarlett has a half-brother that no-one knows, from somewhere round Manor Park, who has, even though he's got some job that he'll get swat out of if he gets done for violence, slipped a cash/weed incentive to a few of his old school mates with less to lose than him, to visit Jackson on his behalf. If that's happened no-one's quite sure, and if so, no-one's naive enough to confirm this anyway. Still, totally ignoring the fact that 2 lads are going to Wetherby borstal for indecent sexual behaviour with a child, and at least 5 more are also answering to sex-offence charges, all of whom have simply trainwrecked their life-opportunities for the next couple of decades, the good news is that once all that kicked off, no-one any longer gives a shit about the school geek eating spicy chicken in my back-garden, and my life became easier instantly, so in all that drama at least there's a happy ending somewhere.

Amidst all this, Edward found new glorious opportunities to embarrass himself. On Friday Shola and her Mac 'n Pandora crew decided to ask him if he'd been skiing before. Instead of telling them to piss off, he replied that he'd been to the dry slopes at Hillsborough before they burned down. He seriously didn't twig what were going on, thinking someone actually cared if he'd ever been to fucking Switzerland or not, innocent child that he is. So the rest of the class began asking him what his favourite technique was, whether he liked 2 man, 3 man, uphill or downhill, clearly oblivious to the fact they were talking about a sex act, not a trip to the Alps. He even tried saying that "uphill skiing" was physically impossible and everyone fell about laughing all over again before he realised his innocence way too late. The piss-taking became too obvious, so he got his stuff and took off home, which he now does every time someone gives him grief. I'm not even sure he does full days in school now. He shows up each morning then goes home when he feels like it, but still manages to make a cock of himself when he's in. Anyway, apart from his Mum and my Mum being girly-giggle bezzies, I'm still crossing the road from him when I can.

Anyway, once I got clean, I went back downstairs to get food. It's a bit late, past 9.00, so no point eating massive. I manage to get into the kitchen, but within seconds I'm shouted into the front room by Mum. She's already sorted it. No more wrecked pans. Beans on toast for main course. Juice to drink. 20 questions for pudding.

"What do you think of the teachers at school Joe?" Dweebies mum asks.

Stop. Take 5 seconds. Might need to be careful with this.

"Joe?" Mum looks at me, nods at me.

I take an extra 10 seconds to finish chewing. If only I had overcooked steak instead. "Some are alreyt. Some are nob...., I mean, not very good"

"Do you know how they deal with bullying and pastoral stuff"

"What's pastoral stuff?"

"Bullying. Problems with kids."

"Don't know." I wouldn't. This shit's never my business.

"Come on Joe, you've been there 4 years." Mum pleads.

"3 actually, I'm just starting't 4th."

Mum looks at me, puts her head to one side. I want to leave, but I need food.

I repeat. "I don't know. I've never had any grief/"

"What about any of your friends? How've they been treated?"

"Alreyt I think. I don't know. I never ask. I don't get involved in owt."

Mum chips in "Sam Blake."

"You've seen't size of him. Plus who's gonna try ripping the sh... I mean tekking't pi...I mean having a go at a competitive boxer?"

Mum recites the Sam Blake story to Geeks Mum, correct with about 50% of it, but I can't see the point in pulling her up on any of it. She tells how he were a chubby kid who got picked on, his stuff got vandalised, all to do wi' supporting the wrong football team, then one day proper lost his shit, stuck 2 older lads in ambulances (I only remember 1, but hey, ancient history, and I've not got that much time), enough to get him expelled, but the other kids, Shelly and me included, saved his arse.

"So if the kids themselves didn't step in, he would've been expelled?" Mrs Woopert asks

"Yeah, probly"

"Does that happen a lot?"

"I don't know. I try to mind me business while I'm there." I add, looking at both of them, cos I know where this conversation is ultimately going to go. "The best way to cope wi' school is to keep life simple."

"How's life simple for you, Joe?"

"Easy. Try not to mek yersen stand out. Don't be seen on yer todd too much. Don't stick owt daft online. Blend in like you're wallpaper, at least until you hit year 11 then no-one cares about owt what goes on in school as you're only bothered about leaving it all behind."

"Cait said you captain the school football team. Surely you stand out?"

"Yes. On't footy pitch. No-one minds that. Off the pitch though, low-profile." I actually make eye contact with my questioners for the first time "Too much to lose."

"But surely other kids look up to you?"

"Never thought about it." Actually, I have. Frequently. The year 9 boys all wanna be me, the year 9 girls all wanna be with me, and as for everyone else, if they don't all love me, then its cos they got that jealous rage thing going on.

"Come on Joe." Mum's laughing, "You love the adulation."

"Right. OK," I pause "In school I hang around wi't kids who like football. Guess where we are each lunchtime? Kicking a ball around. Out of trouble."

"Where does Edward go at lunch and breaks?"

"I never see him. He's in a couple of my lessons, and my tutor, but so are lots of other kids?"

"It's OK Joe. Me and Penny are just trying to find a way to help Edward out. He's on his third secondary school already. We don't really want to move him again."

Don't know why I asked this but I did, "Would he do that thing where they give him a laptop and send a teacher round to teach him one-on-one so he gets no grief?"

Mums at me. "Why should he be sat indoors because other kids keep being rotten to him?"

"I don't know. How am I supposed to know? I'm just a schoolkid mesen?"

"Do you do anything else besides football, Joe?"

"What like?"

"I don't know, do you do anything artistic? Or have a part-time job?"

"Football's my art. I want it to be my job. Owt else'd get in't way."

"What about when you're not playing. You can't play every day?"

"X-Box maybe?" especially once I get away from this. Mrs Dweeb's not horrible, but she's got too many questions, none of which I fancy answering. I'm off upstairs.

"Have you ever..." I don't hear the rest.

I should have stayed sat there. It's deffo in my interests to keep ears open when Mum and her mate are chatting. I think they're plotting. I can still catch bits of conversation, about someone they know from their old days, nowt particularly interesting. It might be in my interest to go back downstairs and rejoin their conversation, but I bet any money that as soon as I walked in and changed the dynamics, the conversation would change. My legs have started to get that heavy feeling, the one where if someone stood at my bedroom door and dangled a hundred pounds in front of me, I'd not be arsed to move anywhere to grab it. I'm cosy in that respect. But in every other way, I'm uncomfortable.

14. CIVILISATION

Since I made my decision, 3 weeks ago, I've kept to my promise every single day. Only twice have I lasted til the afternoon, and on 2 other days I was home by 10 am. Mum receives daily phone calls, as apparently my attendance record is now at 46%. School describes my poor attendance as "a concern", but what they mean here is that they have a target where 98% of their kids should be in school at any one time, so when that doesn't happen, my non-attendance becomes "a concern". Therefore they have to act concerned about my problems so that they can achieve their attendance target.

On some days, I've just gone home. People complain about daytime telly. Not me. I'm up to date on 'Big Bang Theory', 'Walking Dead', and I've started 2 K-dramas, one with soldiers and doctors in it, another about a female bodyguard who falls in love with the singer she's minding. Every single character looks flawless and the storyline twists constantly, though I need a break from non-stop subtitles. I'm timing it today so I can get in before Lara, thus bagging the telly remote and the best spot on the sofa. The worst I get back from her is verbal, which now includes the C-bomb. I only ever use that word on special occasions to people who fully fit the description, but it is a total ear-opener when you hear your little sister say "cunt" for the first time.

On other days, I've gone exploring, anywhere where I can spend time but not money. There's the convenient, like a library chock-full of mangas yelling out to me from the shelf, and if I can pull enough tokens from coffee cups, then I go to the Italian Coffee Place, trade them in and chill out in there for a bit. One day, I walked out of school by 9.30 and didn't fancy being round civilised people let alone uncivilised, I walked all the way up this big hill that overlooks the city centre, and just sat for an hour watching how tiny everything was beneath me. I love gazing at skylines and cityscapes and picking little details out, but unfortunately this isn't Chicago or Hong Kong I'm in, not yet anyway. Then there's the edgier places. I've spotted loads of knackered old buildings to explore, an old market hall, some old sports centre, a nightclub that the police shut down years back. I've spotted an abandoned ski slope that's now on my unauthorised absence bucket list, but I learned a new meaning to going skiing recently, like a sexual term, so if I go there, I'll not shout too loudly about it. It'll get misunderstood.

I've have loads of conversations with total strangers. I know all the rules about talking to people I don't know, and I know that if I did bump into Sylvester the Child Molester, or some grooming gang, they'd not be sat in a white van offering to show me puppies, but I've not come to harm from anyone. In fact I'm a hundred times safer out of school than I am inside it.

There's an old lady who chats to me in the Winter Gardens. I bullshitted her at first, saying I was on day-release to the university, but I knew she could read my facial expressions so I just told her the truth that I'd changed schools and was getting bullied. I learned via her that it's always better to tell the truth, as once I'd told her the full facts she bought me a cup of tea and an egg custard, which, even though I don't like them, was a nice thought anyway. She told me that she always drops in here as it was her husband's favourite place and he died last year. I could tell she was lonely so I asked her whether it was the art he liked, or the plants, or the giant Japanese goldfish. As I knew there was a free cup of tea in it if I listened, she told me her dead husband didn't know a single word of any foreign language, but he could name every exotic plant in here in Latin, and he'd often nick stems or buds from here to take home to try out in his greenhouse. I could have offered her round to my house for tea. Mum would've fucking adored her. Last week I talked to her, or, more accurately, let her talk at me, and offered to keep lookout for her if she fancied nicking cuttings from any of the greenery in here, and she smiled, even though her eyes welled up a bit with tears, grabbed my hand and put £2 in it.

Being given £2 and chocolate muffins is considerably nicer than being slammed into a wall in a school corridor, so the Winter Gardens is now the first stop on my travels. If there's no chance of free cakes, then next stop library. I did chat for a while to a couple of blokes who sit in there loads, but I try to avoid them now. There must be a million books in the city library, all free to read, all likely to broaden the mind, yet they choose the only literature available in the whole building that can narrow their minds, newspapers. I've observed them go from calm, slightly docile old fellas, to, 10 minutes of brain-poisoning later, confrontational gammons spitting bile about Syrian Refugees, the PC brigade, the EU, Madeleine McCann and Princess Diana. What they have motivated me to do is, when I'm there, collect any copies of the Daily Mail or similar lying around, and distribute them elsewhere, maybe behind the encyclopedias, maybe down the toilet. If anyone asks me what I'm doing, I'm providing a valuable service to the community. A little less hate.

No-one in my lessons bats an eyelid anymore when I go on strike. I walked out at 11.30 today.

Half the class singled me out for stupid questions, some of which were sexual, and, once I'd answered, kids who'd normally never even speak to me would laugh uncontrollably. When I twigged that "going ski-ing" was some childish buzzword they use for a dodgy sex act, I was ready to start breaking things, but I've learnt how to get out of these situations now. It's simple. I stick my tie in my pocket, put my coat on, button it up, pick up my bag and set off on a journey through the corridors towards the gates and into civilisation. Sometimes I get grief as I'm passing through, but today I got safe enough passage through the corridors. There were just a couple of 6th formers passing through. Sixth formers don't give a sticky shit about anything that goes on in the uniformed bit of school, so I kept walking and so did they.

As I passed through reception I saw some woman stood at the window with a walkie-talkie, and near the gates another woman, maybe a teaching assistant or similar, also on a walkie-talkie. This explained how she knew my name despite me having no clue who she was. She was all "Edward, do you really think walking out will solve anything?".

I stopped, looked her full-on in the eyebrows and simply but politely answered "Yes, Miss, I think it possibly will."

She was struggling. I bet every other kid would greet her with "leave me alone" or even "go fuck yerself". I'm much more classy than that. "Why's that then, Edward?"

"You weren't at my re-admission meeting so you couldn't possibly know that I did very implicitly say that if I was to be subjected to any more abuse, then this is exactly what I stated I would do. I've been subjected to abuse. Again. I'm keeping to my promise. I meant everything I said I'd do. As a school, you haven't listened and here you are now complaining that I'm doing exactly what I said I was going to do if you didn't do what was expected of you to help avoid these situations. Sort this incompetent approach out, and I'll return. I'll come back tomorrow and see if you can improve on your terrible record so far."

I turned and began walking away. Another daft question followed me. "Edward, where are you going?"

"I'm going through the gates. Just look over there. That's civilisation, that is!" and continued my quest to steadily shrink into the distance. I bet it'd look really cool on a foggy day. But it's not foggy. And I'm not supposed to be cool.

Dumb question number 3, "And what do you think it will achieve?"

"It's my only coping strategy right now. There are other strategies, like monging myself out on drugs, or stepping in front of a fast-moving lorry, but I'm trying not to employ those just yet. Be grateful I'm employing this one, and maybe find me some more safe yet effective ways of coping with my situation whilst also trying to give me the opportunity to learn?"

"Oh come on, Edward?"

"You have less than 24 hours to make my education safe or I'll do the same tomorrow!"

I continue to make myself distant. I hear a shout. "I THINK WE NEED TO CALL YOUR MUM"

I stop and reply equally loud. "YOU'VE CALLED HER 23 TIMES THIS MONTH AND NOTHING'S CHANGED!!"

Whatever she said after that I had no interest in hearing or replying to. I'd left it all behind and onto the next level of my adventure game of a day. Once into town, I felt liberated. Though I was surrounded by strangers, amongst whom there may very well be terrorists, paedophiles, serial killers, child kidnappers or even education welfare officers, I felt reassured to pass by crowds of people who couldn't give a toss that I was anywhere near them. More importantly, no-one could summon the slightest interest in how narrow my trousers weren't, what label my shoes or bag didn't have on them or how I wore my tie. I certainly wasn't the only person with impossible hair or a spot/forehead dilemma. This is definitely something I can't wait for when I leave school, no-one caring who I hang round with or what I wear or, if I think about it long enough, which I do on a very regular basis, being civilised.

So, into civilisation. I did that busy person walk, looking straight in front, walking at a decent tempo to look like I actually needed to be somewhere at some time. I passed the station and even stopped and looked at the big departure board, as if I was even going anywhere. To be fair, it's sunny, and I have no direction and no need to be anywhere anytime. The fountains are on, the one's that look like giant urinals, so I park my arse there for a bit. Someone's left a coffee cup on there, so I liberate the token from the side of the cup. That's a full five in the collection. I don't even like coffee that much, and the coffee from places like The Italian Coffee Company are at prices only a fool would pay, but when it's free, it'd be rude not to.

I don't know why, but I find the sound of the falling water quite soothing, so, with the sun out, and a grand total of 2 pounds and 41 pence in my pocket, this can be my entertainment for a while. It's good for 10 minutes or so, until one of those "city centre ambassadors" appears in the vicinity, a man in a badly fitting uniform who welcomes visitors and proudly represents his city by yelling at anyone who drops litter anywhere. I know enough about these guys to know they're not the smartest, so, coupled with the fact that I'm intellectually more able than they are and they can't whack me because I'm under 16, they're no risk to me even if they want to be. They might ask me why I'm not in school, but I can always ask them why they didn't go to school.

I keep him in the corner of my eye for now, and watch him hassle some homeless-looking guy who's committing the vile crime of sitting on the pavement on a sunny day, doing nothing apart from rest his legs. After maybe a minute, the guy picks himself up off the floor, and moves on, although not until he faces the ambassador fella full on and yells "CUNT!" at the very top of his voice. I'm a good 20 metres away and I could see the spit flying out of his mouth as he yelled. I've caught a fair bit of that from others before. Twice last week in fact. Then I studied this cunt-yeller, his back slowly being broken by a grubby backpack which probably had all of his life's possessions in, a bottle of water that he's probably concocted from the taps in some toilet, a couple of plastic covers pulled from some skip that is now the nearest thing he has to a quilt, sleep being his most realistic escape from a world where he questions his identity, wonders if life could ever be different, and wakes up involuntarily, depending which underpass he can stay safe in, teased cruelly by the smell of curry, burgers, and coffee every few metres. The more I studied him, and, I could have studied him all day, I began changing my mind about civilisation totally. It looks to me like the worst thing you can do in life is be poor, as the poorer you are, the more the world despises you. I don't get it at all, but that's how everyone in the adult world seems to operate. Each time I'm in the city centre, it astounds me how most people just step over these guys unconcerned whether they're just sleeping or have died of starvation whilst at the same time clutching onto some designer handbag they've spent £300 more than they really needed to, or some poncy coconut milk frappucino they've paid £4 too much for.

I've not seen anyone do it yet, but I'm sure it's probably happened some time, but if this guy decided to urinate in the fountains, I wouldn't blame him. After the way the agent of the fascist state just demeaned him publicly, he could drop his trousers, stoop down and lay a big solid poo there and I'd empathise with that, too. I watch him walk on without defecating anywhere at all, pause at the traffic lights, and pass the pub on the corner. Every few metres he tries to stop a passer-by as if to ask them something, but everyone brushes him off. I can't explain my curiosity, but I decide to follow. He plonks himself and his lifetime's contents on the wall that runs along the pathway outside the Uni building, looks around, and studies those to his right. Smokers. Students I'd expect, fresh out of some 5 hour lecture, desperate to spark up. I plonk myself down to his left, and notice him studying everyone but saying nothing. I thought students might be a bit less fascist than the ambassador guy, but all I see is them looking acting like he's not there, which I guess is what the whole of the planet does with this guy and maybe needs to change. I always aim to be a compassionate citizen of the world with a very upstanding and admirable social conscience, so I step in.

"Hiya Mister."

He turns his head, looking at me as if I'm picking a fight with him. Time to speak quickly.

"I saw those pretend policemen picking on you earlier and I was disgusted by them."

His expression loosens a little. He could do with a haircut, a dentist, and probably a doctor or two. He looked 70, but he could realistically be any age. His mouth falls open. I'm not sure a dentist could fix much in that mouth. I'd pull everything out, and start afresh with a full set of falsies at a guess. "Are you having a laugh?"

At least he didn't spit the C-bomb at me. He might even like me. "I'm sorry. I don't smoke, but..."

"How old are you?"

School uniform on. Not a time to lie.

"15" I lied anyway. My birthdays months away, but that's the least of his worries.

"I've got a....." then a pause "ne' mind"

Made no sense of that at all, but at least the chances of him spitting whilst yelling "CUNT!" at me are diminishing by the second. I walk over to the student group, "Excuse me, is there any chance I can buy a cigarette from you?"

The smallest by far yet the most striking of the bunch, a tiny lass with scarlet dreadlocks and a weird piercing under her scarlet-lipsticked thin lips. "Here, sure."

I've no idea how much cigarettes cost. I know they come in packets of 20, and they cost more than £5.00, so I pull 30p from my pocket, estimating she'll make a small profit maybe? And I still have money left in my pocket. I'll have £2.11.

"30p's no use to me, love, just take one". She holds a deathstick up in front of me. I thank the lady and walk away.

"Hey, mister, Are you after one of these?" I hold the cigarette up, brown bit in my fingers.

The fella stares at me for a good few seconds, probably bemused why someone like me is trying to have a conversation with him. I'm a bit perplexed as he's still looking at me like he hates me, like everyone else does mainly. "You still on a giggle, kid?" I think I'm imminently going to be the recipient of a swearing and saliva cocktail. Do I run off? He's maybe slightly bigger than me, but he's probably as unhealthy as could be possible in the light of sleeping in the street for who knows how long. I've caught that smoker's voice, rasping and gurgling in ways no human voice should. I could lose him in a running race if needed.

"You either want this or you don't? I've just bought it for you. Just a thank you will do."

A very yellow grin appears, with a few spaces dotted about within it where at some stage there were once probably teeth. He takes the cigarette with his spare hand, places it in his mouth then pats me on the top of my right arm. I notice the scars and dirt ingrained on every finger. "Thanks loads mate. You're a saint."

"Oh don't be dramatic. It's only a cigarette." As soon as I said this, I realised it was so much more than just a cigarette. It was probably one of the few pleasurable aspects of a harsh, miserable, pitiful existence. I gave it to him, in exchange for absolutely nothing. No-one ever does anything for nothing. Most people will see him and cross the road, worse if they're drunk. Fuck it, it's an evil world we live in. I bet there's people who'd play a game of swerve their BMW off the road to mow him down like it's a sport.

"Only a cigarette to you, mate. It's the best part of the day to me. Thanks again."

"No worries. Have a free cuppa afterwards too". I hand him some coffee tokens and turn to go. Still with 2 pounds and 41 pence in my pocket. What am I gonna do for the next hour and a half?

As soon as I decide to head home, I hear a voice. The red-haired student lass. "Did you really buy that cigarette just to give to that tramp?"

I smile. "Erm. Yes. Why?"

Her facial expression changes, from a beady-eyed lass looking like she's ready for a massive fight, to having eyes with an inbuilt smile in them, and a smile that would look magnificently sweet itself had she not stained her teeth with those cigarettes. "That's really sweet!"

I bet the scarlet dreadlocks and piercings and multi-coloured Dr Martens are her way of rebelling against something. The smoking too, is probably an extended middle finger to something or somebody in her life, or maybe just life itself. I don't think the cigarettes will do her slightly charming demeanor much good. But if she thinks I'm, sweet, I think she's sweet too, not sweet as in I fancy her or anything like that though. She's too full on for me. I've probably got nothing in common with her anyways. I'm no expert on girls but I doubt lasses like her spend much time on Minecraft, and I doubt she has a favourite YouTuber. Not one that I'd watch too. She shouts over the street sleeper fella. "Hey fella. Have you got enough cigarettes to see you through?"

The homeless dude, about to cross the road and disappear forever, turns, shouts something that I'm too far away to hear, but he moves his head in a way that suggests he's saying "What?" This is my entertainment. I've inspired something. Something cool. To me, anyway. Actually, I am cool, just not in a way that stupid people notice. He takes ages to cross the road back to us again.

"That guys homeless, right?" The girl checks with me. Can't place her accent but it's definitely somewhere posh, or at least pretend-posh. I'll bet her parents are probably devastated she's gone to Uni here while their hated neighbours spoddy kid got in at Oxford, so she's dyed her hair postbox red as a big raised middle finger to them too.

I nod.

"And he's definitely not spiced off his tits?"

I think she's on about drugs. I'm not much of an expert on drugs, but I'd say he was primarily under the influence of abject misery. "He was sat outside the station earlier, just chilling. I was too, and I saw the security blokes, pretend police ones, harassing him. It looked like bullying."

"Reaally? And he was just minding his own?" There's of emphasis on the "really". I know no-one who talks like her. She pulls a face when she talks too, either that or that piercing's painful.

"You really did that?" This tall very dark lad behind her asks.

"I get bullied all the time myself, so I saw him getting hassled and needed to do something."

"Dude. I'm doing computer science. Give me the names of all the bullies. I can infect their social networks with all manner of nasty gremlin shit."

The homeless fellas back. "Thanks again mate."

The sweet but grungy girls back in. "Listen mate, have you had anything to eat today?"

I spot a half-empty bottle of water. There's every chance it may be vodka in there, but he doesn't look pissed, and would stand out a mile at this time of day if he was. I guess that rucksack of his, on inspection, was once a creamy beige colour, nowadays not so much.

"Here." The girl offers him her packet of cigarettes, before he can answer. She then pulls one out and places it behind her ear. "Apart from this one, I've got a fucker of a lecture to get through this aft. I'm definitely gonna need this one. I can get some more later if I need them. Take these. There's not many, and go careful with them. I've heard they're really bad for your health."

The guy looks close to tears to be fair. "Yeah I should try to be healthy. I'll start my juice-plus diet tomorrow."

From nowhere, the girl's friends start producing stuff. I don't know if they're her friends or just co-students, but to a billy like me, those finer points don't matter. The tall dark hacker dude pulls out some coins. "I was going to visit the Colonel on the way home. You go instead." Another girl, a really thin girl whose only outstanding feature was her stripy jumper, on a day that was maybe a bit too warm for it, pulled out a bottle of some drink and said "smoothie?"

"You're all joking, right?"

This second girl smiles, "I was gonna take it into my lecture, but I'll not miss it to be honest. The vitamins and nutrients in it will counteract all that toxic grease from the fried chicken."

"You're all amazing, you really are."

As he talks, the security goons stroll towards us from the station, just at the base of the hill.

"Here's the guy that hassled him."

"What for?" the first girl asks. "Sitting on the floor wasn't it?"

As soon as I nod, she plonks herself on the concrete, crossing her legs like you do in primary school, at assembly. "Ooookayyy" she says, like middle class wannabee posh people do.

Her mates take a second to think about it, and follow her lead. I'm not sure what I've created, but I drop to the floor and cross my legs in front of me. The trampy dude is the last one into the circle, only taking his space when the main girl tells him to sit the fuck down or she'll take her fags back off him.

"So what's everyone's plans for this afternoon then?" the punky girl asks?

The other students answer first "Lecture", "Sensory deprivation", "Sleep".

The trampy guy replies with "If I smile at the receptionist nicely enough I'll book in at the Hilton, get a couple of hours in the spa, ring my stockbroker and then maybe nip for tea at....."

"Have you got anywhere to stay?" the mousier girl chips in.

"Some nights I get somewhere. Others I'm wandering round."

"Sorry, not a lot we can do. Students and that. Security's everywhere, and they make our rooms small to stop us having parties."

"Have your parties at Endcliffe. Three big holes in't fence there. I made two of them mesen back in't summer break." The trampy guy replies.

"We're Hallam. Endcliffe's full of Uni-Of wankers. I'd rather spend a night sat on this pavement than go to a Uni-Of party. If you break in there again, you really should...."

The security dudes take their time, partly because they think people will believe they're police, ie people who actually do have the power to hassle innocent people, and partly because they're bloated and well out of shape. This could get interesting. They pause for a couple of minutes, during which Nina the rebel student tries to start a conversation on how to pass the entrance exam for city centre ambassador. No-one joins in. She's funny initially, then her humour turns to animosity, and I can't be bothered with this anymore, and should really get up and politely say goodbye. Just as I begin to rise to my feet, the two ambassadors start walking away, well, it's more like waddling to be more accurate. Nina gives them a very cheery and sarcastic, "See you later, sweethearts", as they continue onto the next stage of their heroic mission to protect their wonderful historic city from the mortal enemy that is litter droppers and loiterers.

"Lovely to meet you all. I'm moved by your kindness. My names Donovan O'Donovan. When I'm back on my feet and CEO of Apple once again, I'll give you all jobs with amazing wages. God bless you all."

"You're welcome Sir, I'm Nina". Big scarlet-framed smile.

"Ollie Hubbard, but call me O".

"Actually I call you twat mainly."

"Whatevz!"

Eyes over to me.

"Oh, I'm Edward Pendlebury"

"Ollie meant it about the viruses. Just let us know." Nina smiles back. Today's adventure ended there. I walk home all the way, looking forward to that joyous experience of opening a locked door to an empty living room. After placing crisps, cereal bars, and a tap-refilled water bottle in my bag in case I bump into Donovan again, I secure the sofa, telly and remote control, firmly clasping it throughout. Lara walks in halfway through 'Bobs Burgers', assesses her lost kingdom, drops the C-bomb at me again, then Mum follows an hour later to confirm that she's had two more calls from school.

Later this evening, Mum's friend, Caitlin Barker, visits, escaping whatever football match her husband and bratty son are vegging on front of, and asks if I know anything about a teacher that the schoolkids say got spotted in Spearmint Rhino sticking twenties in some lap dancers micro-knickers. I realise that as the focus of negative attention in school might not be me tomorrow, I decide to return to school.

----

15. CITY AWAY

Man City Away.

This coming Saturday!!!

Get in!!

Yes Joe!

Clockwatching already. Neither the big hand, nor the little hand, are moving round fast enough. They never do.

Yeah, I know, played there before. But the buzz never goes.

Man City away. Get fucking in there. I mean, reyt in. Man City!!!!!!!!!

Benny announced it, just quietly understated enough for us to hear, not quite audible enough for anyone else to make out. As he relayed this illuminating news, we all spot, poking out of his jacket pocket, the only thing capable of draining any brightness from our complexions.

That little white envelope.

How cruel is that?

The adrenaline's kicked in, though. Everyone's going to buzz from now til Saturday.

Except one.

Which evil fucking sadist dreamt this up?

14 of us on hot dates. 1 of us staying home alone.

"Away to City". Announced so casually. I mean, there's no need to say the preceding word. We all knew. No-one ever thinks Stoke or Bradford. A slowcoach may think Norwich. A slow coach is the abiding memory of that fixture. Done it twice. Great game. Awesome team. Nightmare bus ride. 10 hours trundling behind a bastard tractor. Do that trip once, and "Norwich away" means, "If you're carrying a knock, get it rested". If you're newly-signed, or on trial, it's great. Otherwise, get some rest and let those strains and bruises die down a bit. Dad's face when "Norwich away" gets announced is one where every muscle drops as far south as possible til he resembles a Bassett hound. He knows that trip. He knows the pain. Bye-bye weekend. He'll fist bump the ceiling at this one though. So will Mum.

I've played City away twice before. Never won, never drawn, never scored. The first elbow in the face I ever got was against them, well, the first one that connected right. Anywhere else this good, you'd need to fly to. Even though Benny, with his envelope poking out, insists on telling us he's demanding 100% commitment tonight, and he wants us "throwing it all in", no-one's gonna risk more than 50% if can they get away with it. No-ones daft enough to risk an injury.

Except Dan.

He adores a wind-up. I know his mind works differently. He's already run a finger horizontally across the front of his neck and nodded at Brodie, the worst one of all of us to wind up, so of course, he's spending the whole session sending for him.

I doubt any of us listened to anything that Benny said. It doesn't stop him talking though. Dan's focused on provoking Brodie into Apollo13-ing everywhere. He loves this mind game more than he loves the idea of playing at Man City. He might have a point. Brodie's not moved out of centre mid for ages, and I don't really think he's fast enough to go back into defence. Kyle's winning everything, as is Jamal. If either of them got the captain's armband, it would seem sensible. Dan and Brad have more in their lockers than him and could both probably sweep or go defensive mid. Mo plays the same positions as Brodie. Mo looks like Yaya when he plays. Brodie doesn't. Mo can rest easy too.

It could be one of the strikers. Naz might get told he's not made it. He's scored in each game he's played though, not bad considering half the team are looking after each other by not laying any decent balls on for him. He's enormous, fast, with an amazing temper. He'll take sly punches and kicks through the game and never react. Dad reckons he's good enough. Ben's Dad, Brad's Dad, Kyle's Mum, all say the same, in fact everyone agrees except maybe the one's who think there's a chance they might not be visiting Manchester this weekend.

Hassan Fawaz's Mum posted a picture in his Facebook last week. All his family round a table at Pizza Hut. That bit doesn't matter, it's the comments underneath that matter more, especially the one where some lass asked him when he'd be back at school. He's not missed any matches, but Brodie and Ben have mates in his school, and they've heard that he hardly attends. He's not naughty or thick or owt, he just takes loads of days off. If the academy finds out, he's gone. He's put weight on, and when you try and send him on his way with balls that, maybe last year, he'd read before the ball even left your foot, he rarely does now. Something's not reyt.

Dan has a separate theory, in which Hassan doesn't feature. As we get up ready for drills, he runs past Brodie and slips in, under his breath "What you up to Saturday, COD or GTA?"

The training session starts how I hoped, non-contact all the way - shuttle runs, then possession drills. Brodie still managed to deliberately crash into Dan. Dan's probably the only kid here who wouldn't care if he got let go. We're all here trying to achieve the dream, and he's right next to us, with just as much chance of getting that dream, but not caring. Brodie will be destroyed if that letter's for him. Dan knows this. Most matches, Dan very quietly and very slyly disrespects whoever he's up against. I've seen opponents end up trying to swing for him, from which he always drops to the floor and waits for the card to come out. He's a master of it. Brodie's an easy target. The easiest target. Dan knocked a ball past Brodie and tried to outrun him, but, where Brodie would normally just give him a good solid shoulder barge, he lunged at his ankles instead. Dan smiled back and did this cough where he clearly said "cunt" at the same time. Training ends with a game, small-sided. I'd expect no-one to risk injuring themselves for this, it'll be tiki-taka all the way, pass and move, stand and block stuff, but, I know Brodie, and how he thinks. If it's him getting the envelope, I can see him injuring someone so he stays a little longer. Anyone will do.

My lucky day. I'm on Brodie's team, with Tyler, Tyrell and Naz. The others need to be careful, Dan especially. He's just asked Brodie how many cocks his Mum sucked before City signed him. Still priming that bomb.

The training game starts. No-one dare stay still. Everyone's on the move constantly, making runs here, there, everywhere. I started right wing-back but in reality, I'm everywhere except left wing. Brodies yelling at everyone. Simple shouts - "Pass", "leave!", "Go!", "Drive!". He's deep, too. Things don't go my way. I try to 360 Dan, he reads it straight away and comes away with the ball. Brodie hurtles towards him, but Dan's no fool. As Brodie flies in, Dan changes direction totally. Brodie flies into clear air, Dan plays Mo in to shoot. Brodie's close to exploding. He looks at me like he wants to violently murder me. I've had it off him before. I'm immune. I don't react.

The adults haven't sussed what's happening. "Last minute" comes from the bench. Some poor sod's last minute ever. No-ones really up for it apart from Brodie and Dan. Pass and move, keep possession, no risks, run those seconds down. Tyler reads my run and finds me in space, I control and play square along the floor to Brodie, who lets fly. Even in rugby that'd be high and wide. If that's his last ever shot for us, there's no hollywood ending. Dan puts himself near Brodie and whispers something I don't quite hear. As soon as Oscar rolls the ball out, sideways to Brad, Dan drops to the floor, "OW!!" We all think that Brodie's done something none of us saw, and all worry that Dan's gonna be out of it for Saturday and run over. He's not just putting it all on to make Brodie look shit, but burning time for the rest of us, saving anyone a real injury.

"Time lads please". I'm not hanging around. They can post that fucking envelope if it's me. I don't really want to be kept back for a chat. "6.30 Thursday. Training game. Grassroots team coming along", are the words I hear as I become gradually more distant.

Once I make it to the car, I study everyone else coming out, Brad, Dan, Mo, all looking perfectly emotionally composed. Naz and Tyrrell follow with no visible signs of anguish on their facial expressions that I can see.

Dad opens with "I've not eaten yet. Hungry?"

"Did you catch what Benny said at't beginning?"

"Yeah. City away."

He's clearly not as excited about this as I'd expected. Last time we went there, Mum spent as many pounds in the shops as Dad gained in an Indian buffet. He should be buzzing.

"Someone's getting let go too". I offered. No comment. No signs of anxiety either. Maybe I shouldn't be anxious. Have a bit more faith in myself. I dunno.

The car ride is pretty quiet, at least til we get to the Nandos turn off. Do it fatha! I listen for the click of indicators, watch for the speed dropping on the dial thing behind the steering wheel, and find only disappointment. KFC appears 2 minutes further down, so I settle for second prize. I was hoping for the drive-thru, but ultimately wasn't too fussy, got the window seat and told Dad anything but popcorn. I love chicken but the popcorn stuff doesn't convince me much. Dad drops a fillet burger, some chips and a bottle of water in front of me. I open up the burger and use the rim of the unopened wet-wipe thing to scrape the slimy mayo off. The whole splodge dollop comes off in one go. Just a slight smear of it left. I'll cope.

"Manchester then, you fancy mekking a day of it?"

"You usually do." I bloat my stomach and puff my cheeks out. If he gets to choose he'll sit and stuff himself in the Curry Mile or Chinatown while Mum and Shelly spend all day shopping for shit they don't need.

"OK. I've got plans, so leave 'em wi' me, but there'll be conditions."

That'll be homework. "I'm up to date wi' everything except French but it dun't need to be in til Friday"

"So get it done. You kick off at 10.30. Then't first team kick off at 3. Home to West Brom. Should be decent."

"It's only 4 days away, will there be tickets left?"

"Leave it wi' me. If I don't manage it, we can always go watch Stockport or Hyde United, maybe Curzon Ashton too. You'd like that one. Proper decent chippy round there too."

"Pushing't boat out there Dad. I might just get't bus back wi' everyone, thanks."

He knows I'm joking. Paying mega-bucks to watch City or United, or standing in a shed watching Curzon Ashton are both infinitely preferable to walking round shops.

"I've offered Shelly to bring a mate but she says she's busy. Mum's working, so there might be space for someone."

"Uncle Davie at a guess." He's the only family member on either side who hasn't brainwashed themselves that I'm somehow going to be playing for Barcelona in 5 years.

"Not Uncle Davie. Not Uncle JJ. And Uncle Ronnie can get stuffed, too!"

I was about to suggest one of my mates, but Dad read me before I could get the words out. "And forget about that daft lump of a mate of yours. He'll have us scrapping wi' both sets of fans."

Mum and Dads views of him are polar opposites. Mum sees a friendly chap who's always polite to her. Dad sees violence and criminality radiating from his chubby bumfluffy cheeks.

"Well there's not really anyone else I'd ask along. Archie, maybe?".

"Isn't he more into X-box and weed? I'll have a word with Mum and see what she thinks."

Mum. Why you asking her? I know who my mates are better than sh...

OH FOR FUCKS SAKE THERE'S NO WAY HE'S BRINGING THAT DILBERT OUT WITH US!!!!!

Kicking off will only inspire him. I know it. I need to argue this, but carefully. Not let my gob or my temper spin everything proper batshit.

"Have you tried getting kids my age out of bed on a Saturday?"

"Have you seen owt of Edward?"

Diplomacy is now the only way out of this. Especially if I don't want to be spending my weekend with the twat. "Nah not much"

"He's in some lessons wi' you in't he?"

"He is when he turns in."

"So he's going missing a bit?"

"I don't know, I really don't pay attention to any of that sh..."

"Don't pay attention to what"

"Y'kno. School nonsense."

"And if it's bullying?"

"Seriously? We had this the other day?"

"And again. This stuff matters."

"You and everyone else always said don't get involved in owt you don't need to. Keep life simple and save yersen no end of bother. Remember that? I were younger then, but even in year 7 I saw all manner of stuff going off wi' other kids, some of it proper messed up, so I mek the most o't fact it's not me."

Dads not angry. That's a start.

"I get that. But bullying's different."

"What's different abou..."

Interrupted. Rude! But I need to concede the battle to win the war.

"It's different, son, as you're in a rare position where you can do summat positive about it."

"So what d'ya expect to happen if I do step in?"

"To be honest. I don't know. There's millions of different ways to step in though."

"Ok. Do you want me to tell you how it really is wi' Edward?"

"Fire away."

"Reyt. He started in school last month, as you know. He looks a bit weird, like one o' them kids who hides in't library at lunchtime eating brown sauce sandwiches for lunch and hopin' no-one notices them."

"I went to school once, deep in't last century. It were similar then. He sounds like his mother used to be. How d'ya reckon they palled up?"

"No idea, what wi' me not being born then."

"Here's the interesting bit. Mum got grief in school too, but it were different. Most days she'd be sat outside the head teachers office cos she'd floored someone who'd been daft enough to try bitching at her. Edward's mum weren't getting grief, but her face din't fit that much either, bit nerdy, liked her books and crap bands. That weren't your Mum's style at all, so them two palling up looked unlikely, but they sat near each other in lessons, an' even though they had nowt in common, they respected each other. When they left school they found theirsens in't same bit of college, and they hit it off properly then. Since then they've worked together, done a night class here, an aerobics class there, that kinda thing. Then, when I had big difficulties a bit back, if you remember it, it were Edward's Mum who helped me sort me head out. I don't really want to go bringing all that back, but I always said to mesen, if there were owt I could do to repay her, I'd do it. Unfortunately for you, the one thing I can do is more summat you can do, or at least give us a hand with."

I were only about 4 or 5 then, but I know all that stuff back to when Dad were a train driver and someone suicidal stepped out in front of him. Dad's head were as messed up inside as the dead chaps were outside. I'm not going there though. This conversation needs to be about match tickets at the Etihad, unaccompanied by dickheads.

"So what is it you seriously think I can do? I don't think you know what schools like"

"Well, first off, not being a prat with him'd be a good solid start."

Piss easy. I can do that. And having him nowhere near when we go and watch Sergio and Yaya will make it even easier to not be a dick with him. In fact, not seeing him anywhere aside from a classroom will fantastically maximise my chances of keeping to this promise.

"Second, the school head-case is your personal pet. You know this already."

"Aye, but I din't ask for any of that. I just want to do my time wi' no fuss til year 11 ends, then sneak out the side-door quietly."

"Some kids want to see their time out quietly and never get't chance. You can mek stuff easier."

"OK, tell us your big idea, and I'll tell you if it'll work or not."

"It's simple enough. I want you to keep an eye out, nowt massive, no best buddy stuff. Just don't cross the road when someone whacks him. If you can't step in, then be a witness."

"I'd lose all me other mates. Have you seen what century his clothes come from?"

"So you're worried what all the other kids think."

"You've been in secondary school before, right?"

"Erm, I made Shelly look out for you when you started. Guess what she thought of that?"

"Cash, cinema, cheeky Nandos. She did well out of it. Are you offering me the same?"

"Sunshine, I could do way better than that. And way worse, too. What's it to be?"

----

16. Sssh L E B :-) X

I'm coping with life at the moment, not how others prefer me to, but my ways. I'm not cutting myself or punching walls, not yet anyway. Like with lots of things I do, I made myself a system. If I don't even get dressed in the right order, life becomes hopelessly chaotic. My new system is to promptly depart the school premises at the first sign of personal abuse.

I've been exploring quite a bit. I've passed time sitting around watching the real world pass by oblivious to my presence in it, wondering how the fuck I'll fit into that world when I'm older. I study things I've previously been oblivious to, like the gargoyles on the walls of the church, graffiti pieces on walls of streets I've rarely walked down before, the floors above all the shops and wondering who lives in them, and how they ever manage to get to sleep and stay asleep when they live bang in the middle of everything. I've gone in an art gallery whose existence I've barely cared for on the hundreds of previous occasions where I've walked past. I pay attention to everything. While the days are still clear and the rain and fog's not turning the whole city grey, everything's good. I may have to change my thinking once the depression of the grim and the grey kicks in though. Gerald's very much alive and thriving, having made a comfortable (for him) home on my forehead. He's not pro-created and fathered any new spots, a blessing I guess, but I wasn't expecting to grow any more, as I'm getting more fresh air than I usually do, and when I'm in the library I hammer the water cooler. If Gerald grows any bigger though, my Mum will have to disclose him to the housing association as a non-paying lodger.

I meet cool people, too. Not people who others see as cool, but people I see as cool, using my own observations of their character. Some people describe this as a vulnerable child talking to strangers, but I see it as there's enough people in my life that aren't strangers who are abusive to me when I come into contact with them, so I've got nothing at all to lose from talking to people I've never seen before. Very few strangers could be worse than the people I already know. Social networkings pointless to me, so I can't get groomed, and I doubt Sylvester the Child Molester would look at me complete with spotty forehead and find me worth the effort of abducting. Having befriended, sort of, a street-sleeper, an old widow and some uni students, I'm pleased to say that none of them have offered me money, sweets or a shiny new Iphone to get my tail out so far. I'm confident this will continue.

I've no idea what his real name is - Donovan's definitely made up - but I chat to him loads. He's been out and about giving out leaflets for some funky happy-clapping church that gives him food and clean socks. I always take 10 of his churchy leaflets off him as he said the sooner he gives them all out he gets fed. He doesn't take anything off me, though. Last week, I stuck a carton of banana milk and a cereal bar in my bag in case I bumped into him, and he declined them both, and asked me if I had a spare cig on me, but it's just a joke. I've got him coffee a couple of times. I'd found enough tokens on the pavement, so offered him into the Italian Coffee Company, annexed the comfy sofas by the window, and people-watched, not at by-passers but at the other customers sat indoors looking disgusted that we'd chosen to sit near them. I know bits about him, not loads, but there's definitely a story to tell, though I'm probably not the person to tell it to.

He's sussed out everywhere in town where there's free food, blankets and whatever else he needs to stay alive. Though the food at the soup kitchens awful, likewise at the funky church, he gets new socks, toothpaste, and his sleeping bags washed and dried. He says that as the people there are all deeply religious, they'll go straight to hell if they rip him off. When the weather's awful, which in England is 9 days per 10, he moves between the library and an adult learning centre to make use of the kettle, water-cooler and the roof, which they let him do as long as he attends whatever class they run. As a result, he can speak basic Spanish, and, should his life ever depended on it, make a basic flower arrangement or an ethically-sourced bead necklace. I told him my GCSE English list, so he sat in the library and read "To Kill A Mockingbird" and "Romeo And Juliet" all the way through. He said it took him about a day. He has a Facebook page that he checks when he's in the Library, to see if anyone from his old life is asking after him, primarily Naomi, his 12 year old daughter that he barely sees but he messages online. He says he's no use to her as he is at the moment, but he keeps in touch and when he gets back to normal life again he'll be booking her straight into Euro Disney.

He's not clear about why he's homeless. I know he had a flat and lost it somehow. Sometimes he can get money from the benefits agency, sometimes he can't, but he hates going there, and hates using the Street Shelter too. He says that whilst sleeping in shop doorways at night, he's been threatened, happy-slapped, kicked the fuck out of, hospitalised, urinated on, vomitted on, spat on, had half a doner kebab scattered all over his head and even robbed of his ID and the sleeping bag that someone gave him at Christmas, it's still safer than sitting awake all night in the Street Shelter.

Donovan's used to people pretending he's invisible or frowning down at him as they step over him, but occasionally, someone will appear unexpectedly and do something kind. His friends are as random as mine, the odd churchy person, a couple of Slovakian dudes that sit drinking in the park on their days off then take him for the odd days work when they need a casual labourer. Depending on which underpass he beds down in, there's a posh old woman with a wonky hip who brings him a cuppa and chats to him for a couple of minutes while she rests a little, and then there's an Arabic looking lad who puts a carton of milk next to him, says hello then moves on. He's not keen on milk, as he thinks the Arabic lad leaves him milk as he thinks he's on spice, cos it's easier to drink liquids than eat solids on that trip, but he says he isn't. Even on the darkest days, he insists tiny rays of sunshine can appear. He says he woke up once ready to drop himself from the top of the same multi-storey he'd woken up in having taken shelter for the night in the same stairwell that random drunks had urinated in that same night. As he mentally prepared himself for his final act, he noticed a warm spot at the side of his leg, which wasn't piss, but a Maccy D's breakfast, all bagged up. He says that whoever left him that saved his life. For the abject misery he lives through, the fact that he still keeps faith in the world and finds good in people astounds me. His perspective on life is something I learn from. I've told him he can have Christmas dinner at our house, though I've not told Mum yet.

Sometimes he tells me, boasts even, about how long he's been clean, which I don't believe as his clothes are often filthy, but I nod politely and go along with it anyway, as I guess a hot shower or a bath is a luxury in his state. I'd be buzzing if I was on the streets and staying clean too. Isn't it weird how some of the richest most privileged people in the world, that people admire, are actually the most odious shitstains on the planet, but the nicest most saintly and considerate people are often close to starving. I used to think that wealth, fame, influence, big gold-plated mansions and all that material shit was something to aspire to. I've changed my mind. I'll cope without the full bank account as long as I get a full stomach every now and then.

I do my homework in the library sometimes. I can do Maths and French online, and I've finished my English books already, so I'm ahead. I'm behind in Science and Graphics. When I do spend a full lesson in either of those two, I leave the room with severe brain ache as I've missed loads and I'm struggling to keep up. I intend to apply myself wholeheartedly to these two subjects every time I climb the steps to the library, but then I spot the rows and rows of mangas as soon as I'm through the door. Temptation right there in front of me.

Yesterday, I walked out of school at break-time. Corey Hendricks, who hit me a few weeks ago, rugby kicked my bag through the corridor. A teacher saw it, but instead of punishing him, spent his time focused on trying to persuade me from walking out of school again. This resolved my mind to get on my travels and study Dragonball instead of Chemistry. It's not even my favourite manga. It's OK, but there's much better titles on the shelf. I read Prison School for a bit, then 2 Hana Kimi books all the way through. I was about to sign a third out, then I spotted a complete set of Death Note there, in order, so I signed the first 3 of those out instead. I thought someone would query my card as I hadn't used it since I was 12, but no-one cared, so I loaded my bag, left via the stairs, crossed the road, and who was coming the other way? None other than another cool and unlikely friend, Shelley Barker, with her mates.

I thought she might destroy her rep in front of her mates by greeting me, but she shouted my name out, ran over to me, spoke first, and introduced me to her mates, too. Her mates in hi-tops and snapbacks, me in a duffelcoat. Anyone passing by would have seen Blackpink chatting to Sheldon Cooper. The best bit? She snatched my phone and typed her number in. She said she wants to chat to me about something important. I've no idea what. I asked Mum later, to see if she knew, but she was clueless. I must have checked my index 50 times during the rest of the day. There was once just 5 entries, Mum, Lara, Grandma, Doctor and Chinese. Now there's a sixth, Shelley Barker, or as she typed it, "sssh L E B :-) X". How many lads would murder their grannies to get that number in their index? Lads infinitely stronger, smarter, better-looking, richer, cleverer, well maybe not cleverer, but you know, I'm not exactly Ryan Gosling or Cristiano

Ronaldo. How many got savaged whilst trying for that number? Unlucky.

Talking of phones, School are still phoning my Mum daily, sometimes twice-daily. She no longer answers and leaves it to the ansafone. Each message is near-enough identical, and Mum quite rightly refuses to discuss my welfare with either parrots or robots. It goes like this...

"Hello Mrs Pendlebury, its Mrs Cain from school attendance. I'm sorry but Edward's taken it upon himself to walk out of school again. We're marking this as unauthorised absence. His attendance record is currently 53% and a cause for concern. Thank you."

Mum says that when school calls and says *"Hello Mrs Pendlebury, we've got ideas to keep your son safe in school and resolve this situation"*, she'll return the call within seconds. So far, it hasn't happened. Sadly, I doubt it will.

In terms of both my academic progress, and school's ability to provide an environment free from harassment, no-one's learning. I'm taking the exact actions that I warned school I would do, demonstrating firm boundaries, and school aren't learning. They've had endless chances to react appropriately to this, but I've not done a full day in school since my first week, and I've only made it past lunchbreak three times.

On the day immediately after my meeting in school, Cory Hendricks's mate, Louis, walked to my desk in graphics and coughed up a giant ball of lung butter into my keyboard. The teacher was already in the room, did nothing, so I got my coat and went home. I returned the next morning, and some girl asked me if I'd ever been skiing. I thought she was being daft asking me that, but I didn't know that skiing, to her and everyone else, was a euphemism for a sex act. Being taken for an idiot just made me angry, so I walked out again. Some teacher stopped me to ask where I was going, and when I said "home", they tried that "No you're not, get back to your lesson." I said I was being entirely consistent with what I said I'd do if I wasn't treated humanely. They then shouted "GET BACK IN THE LESSON!!", but by this time, they could have yodeled into a ships foghorn and I still wouldn't have paid attention. Netflix beckoned.

This has continued. I've had stuff, food I think but possibly also phlegm, smeared over my coat, been told I look like anything from a circus freak to a paedo, pushed out of my chair in assembly, and had my bag emptied all over the floor. The kids that did all this have been told off maybe once or twice. The number of people who've stepped in? Zero. That Shironda lass with the big mouth and the mad nails, and her mate with the resting bitch-face, maybe once or twice, half-heartedly. Each time, I exit through the big gates. 20 different members of school staff, from teaching assistants to the head, have yelled at me to go back into lessons, and threaten me with exclusions, detentions, letters home, none of which change my stance at all. I reminded one teacher that when this wasn't dealt with by my last school I tried to kill myself. She couldn't answer that, so I kept walking. Mrs Frogson has called me into her office and twice told me that this can't carry on, and once offered to pull me out of P.E and instead spend an hour with the youth worker on a citizenship project, but I can't see how a trampy-looking 40 year old who prepares 20 black coffees and 40 roll-ups each working day is going to help when I can chat all day to a much more wordly-wise dude just like that outside the library. His youth club got shut down the other day, there's a big investigation on the go, so the bloke is now in school all the time and school are obviously trying to find him something to do. I got offered to see the school counsellor, too. I agreed an appointment for tomorrow. She's friendly enough, but I don't see how I have a problem. I just suffer from other people's problems, so I'll probably not turn up.

Tonight Mrs Barker was at ours, for hours, chatting with Mum. There's a lot of things that I've no idea what they're on about, probably stuff from their younger lives, but I did hear them talk about me and school. Mrs Barker said she'd "see what our Joe could do about it". I hope she doesn't. Her older child would be much more useful. I know there's a few dipshits out there in awe of him, but an entire generation is in awe of her. I can see why. She easily wears the best hoodies in the whole city. Her mates, male and female, all look naturally, effortlessly amazing. Wherever they walk by, you can see people stepping out of the way subconsciously to let them pass through. I don't even think they're even trying to be badasses, they just have that look that they might be, but I'm pretty sure that if anyone did give them grief, their comebacks would swift and savage. She wants me to meet up with her, for some reason. I know she's not out to destroy me. She might be out to destroy her brother, and I could be useful there maybe, but despite there being no love or respect lost between me and him, I can't see her needing my help to do that. Anyway, I need to plan this properly, so that it gets maximum coverage on the jungle-drums that go round school, that I'm a friend of hers, so I'll get left alone.

I went to bed without texting. My fingers were shaking too much, and whatever I'd type I hit delete immediately and not send because, well, a baby learning its first words could have been coherent than me. After maybe an hour thinking what to text, and getting nowhere, I pulled out Death Note 2 instead and read that, just to take my mind off it and maybe I'd come back to my phone and have something awesome to say. All I got was sleepy.

----

9 hours of sleeping like a baby did fuck all to refresh my social skills. The alarm went off at 6.30. I wasn't ready, so I reset for 6.40, then 6.50, then decided to stay comfy until 6.57. I looked at my phone. Still no idea what to say but it's a nice feeling having a new number in the index. If I could have my battered Samsung GTE with a cracked screen and her number sitting in the index, or a diamond-plated wonder phone with every single app and just Mum and Grandma's

wouldn't give up her seat on the bus. There was this one picture that I couldn't stop staring at, of a 6 year old girl, pigtails in her hair and those little girl ankle socks that roll up just above the ankle with bows on, walking out of primary school with 6 massive police alongside her to protect her from brain-poisoned white idiots. All that protection just to go to school. I should have taken history. I could do every essay on every topic in one sentence. "This event was caused in its entirety by white people being twats." Then this video came on of Martin Luther King doing a speech called "I have a dream", and a girl called Scarlett shouted out after about a minute "This is boring!" Saw this as my chance to get the necessary aggravation in order to vacate my desk.

"Don't be stupid! I've read about this bloke before. He'll be remembered forever, whereas you probably won't. Shut up and you might learn something."

The girls mate chips in..."Ooh, inspirational life advice from Edward. Please do some more."

I kept going. "When you're ready. I'm here all week."

Scarlett came back at me with "As if you'll even stay here past lunchtime", to which I thought "YES! This is my opportunity!", and was just about to comprehensively savage her when, from a seat next to the window where noise rarely emenates...

"Jeezuz! Edward's reyt. Either gi' it a chance or piss off."

None other than Joey Barker. Silent and docile all lesson, then he throws this in. Maybe this is why Shelly wants to meet me. Something's definitely going on there. The whole class looked his way, like he'd suddenly taken on a total character change, like you see on the news sometimes when some introverted accountant suddenly has something snap in their head and suddenly they're in the middle of Burger King with an AK47 going rat-a-tat-tat all over.

The teacher's in. "Scarlett, Danni. You're picking a fight with the wrong people here." He nods Joe's way, "Apart from the bad language, well done, Joe. Now, back to the video if that's OK with the rest of you."

How come he gets a 'well done'? I instigated all that? This is not working as I planned. Maths next, one of those silent boffin lessons that goes on for what feels like 3 times longer than it should. I'm still here and not overly pleased about it.

English next. Again, I think I've cracked it when a chunky lad I've barely noticed before, Travis Greenshields, turns to his mate and says "Look at't state of Dweebie's hair today". I see my opportunity. I'm escalating this.

"Erm, hello? Those bags under your eyes, if you got them at Aldi you'd be down 50p easily. What kept you up late? Was it Club Penguin or was it Pornhub?"

Travis is straight back "Before you say owt at me, look......at.......your......hair."

"Saw it earlier. It's not great, but I know it exists. Like how your stomach knows that KFC exists."

My credibility's up and I dont want it. "Oh. My. God! I'm practically dying!" squeals Shironda.

Beth points at Travis and adds "Bang. On't floor. Out cold."

Tom, sat next to him, looks him over and says, quietly "Goodnite mate."

Welshy backshoves Travis on his shoulder. "Edward's bitch.", then looks at me, smiles, and calls me a 'thug'. This is not the outcome I desire. Not today. The lesson goes painlessly. I make it to lunchtime, mission not completed. I look for Travis. Pressing his buttons will be like changing the gears on a Lamborghini. 0-60 in 3 seconds. I pass the footy courts, the y8 and y9 lunch hall, and through a corridor where some really loud girls sit, giggle and shout at everyone. Wherever I go, this lad is nowhere near. I plonk myself on the short wall outside the drama block, on my own, and stare at anyone who looks like they might come over and pick trouble with me. All I see are a group of girls in my year, none of whom I know, sat down from me, talking about another girl who they probably pretend to be friends with face-to-face, but in her absence, they're talking about her. Not in a nice way either.

I can't see an argument with them getting me far. Judging on their banter, they're unlikely to be abusive to anyone face-to-face, but needs must, I try anyway. "Do you always bitch about your friends when they're not around?"

They look at me silently, disgusted at me. One of them, asks "Excuse me?"

"I bet that yesterday, or whenever day she was last here, you were all lovely to her, planning sleepovers or movienandos or whatever. I really hope one of you is off school tomorrow. I'll drop over and listen in on your mates, if you can call them that, backstabbing you."

"Erm. Hello?" One of them, the one stood furthest from me, leans over and asks "What do you know about having friends?"

"If I had friends as disgusting and two-faced as you, believe me, I'm way better off being a billy. Way better off. You couldn't possibly know how much."

I have gained a small audience. Sophia and another girl. They walk amongst them, smile over at me and shout...

"Don't argue with this man. YOU. WILL. LOSE", Sophia smiles my way.

If she's backing me up, she can bloody well stop. Not today. She then recants how I demolished Travis Greenshields. I learn that when the bell went, he got roasted for being slapped down by the new geek, got laughed at for having an empty locker, got laughed at some more, then went and told the receptionist he had a headache, and as he's not known for bunking off, she let him sign out. None of this will get me out of here early. I seriously don't want it. Really I don't.

I resigned myself to a full day's lessons on the one day I wanted away early. Then, in graphics, my phone texted. Apparently the ringtone's so far out of date, hipsters use it to be ironic. It wasn't even that loud, but, like the after-effects of those farts you try to muffle publicly by sitting with your arse-cheeks squeezed together but still not preventing a one-cheek sneak at the moment you really don't want it, everyone noticed it. This is not what I want, but at the same time, for the purposes of my plans for today, it's actually the exact thing I want. I didn't answer it, didn't even look at it, but I know who it's from. Imagine the looks on these mugs faces if they saw me chatting to her. It'd also mean they'd see my phone. As far as I've seen, every single kid my age has a smartphone. My phone's a £10 Tesco replacement for a very similar phone that was tossed into the heavily-used urinal in the boys toilets at Moor Vale. That phone, also with a retail price of no more than £15, very lightly used due to a lack of internet, itunes, camera or any games apart from snake and battleships, was a replacement for another, similar phone which was emptied out of my bag in the PE changing rooms at Moor Vale, when all the contents of this bag were kicked across the changing room, just as some kid bigger and older than me decided to turn the showers on and soak everything. My exercise books were beyond repair, which hurt as I'd spent hours the night before getting my head around some very difficult maths, but I didn't care about the phone.

Phones don't matter to me, but to everyone else, they're like an extra body part. If Mum wants to punish Lara properly, confiscating her phone has a solid 100% success rate. It's like someone's amputated something. Watching her go into convulsions of raging desperation, followed by doing whatever's needed, and I mean, whatever, in the same way that a class A addict does whatever's necessary to get their gear, is always top-level entertainment. Even better is the fact that the same entertainment cannot be played on me or my no-frills Tesco value brick. Right now though, none of this matters. I ignore the phone, and hope everyone turns back round and stops getting curious. I feel my heartbeat returning to normal, sort of. I mean, Shelley Barker just rang me. There's nothing normal about that at all. I fix my gaze away from everyone elses, and focus on the teacher, who probably wants to say something. When he does, heads start to turn back to where they should be turning to.

For about a minute and a half.

Then it rang.

Not texted. It bloody rang. The ringtone belongs in a jumble sale, too.

I really don't want to answer this yet.

But it's Shelley Barker.

It kept ringing.

I wonder if the floor can develop a magic vortex just large and powerful enough to suck me into it for 30 minutes.

Then it stopped.

One issue over.

Then a new one begins.

Everyone knows my cheesy ring tone.

But it's quiet again. And the teacher's talking.

About all that very interesting graphics stuff.

For 2 and a half minutes.

It started ringing again.

"Edward, can you turn your phone off please?"

"I wasn't going to answer it anyway."

"Doesnt matter. School rules. Either turn it off or give it to me."

I'm gonna have to turn the bloody thing off.

How do I do this?

Oh for fucks sake!

Right, I think I can manoeuvre my hand into my bag and fiddle my way around. I lean to my right. I find it quickly.

FML, that's not the off button.

Different bloops going on.

"Have you borrowed your granny's phone?"

"I had one o' them when I were 6."

This is going wrong.

Erm.

Hello??

Wake the fuck up, Edward, chap!!!!!!!!!!

This isnt going wrong at all?? I'd forgotten. I actually want this grief.

I return to an upright position with my hand and phone free. As expected.

"What the fuck's that?"

"Edward, your Mum needs grassing to social services for making you carry that about!"

"What a spaz!"

What a spaz? What a fucking horrible thing to say. To anyone.

That'll do me. Cheers.

Check the phone quickly. 2 missed calls from Shelley Barker.

Shelley Barker.

I've had much more obnoxious abuse than this, but in my current situation, this'll do me nicely. Demeaning, lack of respect, humiliating, horribly insulting a large section of the population, anything else I can twist this with. Finally, I'm outa here.

The teachers out of his seat. "Edward, where are you going? The bell doesnt go till 3.15."

I'm making the most of this..."I'm leaving. Calling anyone, not just me, a "spaz" is disgusting."

"Omar, just apologise now and get it done with, for Gods sake!"

Before Omar can even open his mouth, I'm at the door. "You're supposed to be the teacher, and you've let this go. He'd be sacked from most jobs for using terms like that, but you've ignored it.

You have a responsibiity."

I've overcooked this. I could have stayed here and savaged everybody, but I dont really care about any of that. Shelley C's just phoned me. I'm away.

"WHERE DO YOU THINK YOU'RE GOING?" Mrs Wotsit shouts down the corridor at me.

Stuff this. Deep breath, then, raise my own voice back. "I'M MEETING SHELLEY BARKER!"

"What?"

Louder..."MEETING SOMEONE!"

"Shelley Barker? As in Joe's sister? You?"

"Yes, but none of your business. Bye!"

Half the school heard all that. Half the school would also gladly punch their Gran straight in the mouth in exchange for doing the exact same as I'm about to.

I stop, pull out my phone, and call. I don't even know if I have any credit, but Shelly answers immediately, like, on the first ring. Mrs Scrum-half appears squarely in front of me, left palm outstretched, expecting me to place my phone in it. I go to speaker mode.

"Hello Shelly. You wanted me?"

"Yes, mate. I need to chat to you about summat. Are you still in school?"

"Just on my way out". I look and smile at Mrs Trog. "Where are you?"

"In town. Going for bubble tea. Can you get to XOXO in 15 minutes?"

"IS THAT BUBBLE TEA IN 15 MINUTES, SHELLY?"

"HAND THE PHONE OVER NOW!" Mrs Trog tries to interrupt this awesome conversation, even lunging over to try and snatch the phone from my hand.

"OK. ON MY WAY!"

Some lass, in my year, no idea what her name is, not in any of my lessons, opens the door from her classroom, looks round, then runs back in. Yeah, I'm bringing the drama again, love.

"WHERE DO YOU THINK YOU'RE GOING?"

I can shout, too. "YOU'D BETTER ASK MR ROCCA THE GRAPHICS TEACHER ABOUT HIS DUTY OF CARE TO VULNERABLE PUPILS!"

Mrs Wotsit looks at me, takes a deep breath, about to say something. But I've not finished. "Do you really want this phone? Seriously? Look at it. I can't even talk properly on it, I have to shout down the line. There's no camera, and dream on if you want apps on it. Ask me nicely tomorrow and it's all yours. It's a bag of shite but it's also a bag of shite that I need right now. So, no, I will not be giving you my phone."

"EDWARD I'M GETTING FED UP OF THIS!"

"Poor you. I've had kids trying to humiliate me all day, and you've been nowhere when it's happened. And now you're trying to shout at me?"

"I'm going to ring your Mum!"

"Do it. She's expecting you. Whatever you tell her, make it interesting or she'll get bored."

"We'll have to bring her in again. Do you really want that?"

"Yes. I do. I really, really do. I don't think you understand how much I'd like that. Go and ring her. As soon as you can. I'm off!"

I turn towards the gates at double my normal speed, heart thumping like the opening beat to any speedcore anthem. The adrenaline propels me through town, all the way to XOXO. The first thing I see, staring my way from across the street, is Travis Greenshields. I didn't notice him following. He starts to walk over. I read his body language and facial expression. If looks could kill. He's going to come at me right here. I've got witnesses everywhere so let him hit first.

A voice calls out. Female. Young. Yorkshire with a little bit of faux-other stuff in the mix. "Edward!! Over here."

Shelley Barker. To the rescue. 2 other lasses and a lad with her. Strangers to me, but also strangers that don't look like they want to pound my face like pizzadough.

Travis Greenshields stops in his tracks. "She'll drop you to't floor in seconds. Dead man walking, you. Joe must've tipped her off how big a cunt you are." He's fully expecting me to be 5 seconds away from a beating, administered on his behalf. I hope he stays to watch.

Shelly puts her fist up, for a fist bump. "Hey!!"

Travis Greenshields's cocks his head slightly to one side. He can't quite work this out. This will fly round Snapchat in seconds. I turn my back to him, totally oblivious to the sneaky photo I know he'll not be able to resist snapping from a safe spot where he thinks no-one's spotting him. He'll Snapchat this, just among his "mains" initially, but it'll be shared and seen by every single year 10 in school. There'll be multiple questions, and Shelly's arse of a brother will also be questioned about this, pissing him off totally as he hates any attention that comes his way when his football boots are off. But I don't care about any of that. I've sensed the cordiality coming my way from a group of kids way older than the ones currently trying to make my life a misery. I've ordered nothing. I'm in XOXO and not even thought what I'm doing there. My stomach's in knots anyway, so whatever I drink I'll probably sick up soon afterwards or, noticing how much my hands are shaking, spill everywhere.

Mum has a framed photo on the mantelpiece, an old school old school photo of year 6 me and year 4 Lara. It's the first thing that comes to mind when I realise where i am right now, who I'm with, and how my life dynamics just changed in an instant, even though Shelly's friends must be wondering why they're chilling with a schoolkid with a giant zit protruding from his forehead. As Shelly starts to talk, I cast back to this photo as, in that shot, just as I am right now, I'm all ears.

----

17. TAKE ME OUT

Go to school, do the usual stuff, and if I spot someone ripping into Edward Pendlebury, I step in. This is the deal Dad put forward. I'm happy to agree, the unseen small-print from my side being that if he gets harassed and I'm nowhere near, it remains none of my business.

It's easy enough to not get the same bus as him, so I'll not need to pick him up off the roadside if some psycho flattens him. He's dodged PE every Monday so far this year, likewise he keeps away from the courts at breaks, so they're my kingdom too. So far this week, I've stepped in once. It weren't hard. Some lass whined at the teacher for putting a boring video on, so Edward had a go at her. Both were right. It was boring, but it was worth watching, this Martin Luther King speech thingy, and it were only 5 minutes long. Anyway, this dipshit lass upped the intensity more than she needed to, so I stepped in, killed the argument bang in the face, then turned round and got slightly sleepy in my seat again. I've done my bit. Man City on Saturday.

Before that, training game tonight. Some grassroots team have been invited for the game of their dreams. Our take on it is very similar to the attitude displayed by a pack of bored lions when a sleepy gazelle stops for a rest in front of them. It'll be merciless. Dreams will become nightmares quite inhumanely, but we can only play against whoever gets put in front of us. This is football. Dreams get shattered every single day.

Mum and Dad were both home when I got back from school, which translates to me as food and lift both sorted. Beans on toast with cheese on top. Mum still does the same trick that she did when I was small where the toast gets put at right angles to pretend it's a footie ground, with the beans being the pitch. I'm not 5 anymore, but at least its cheese over beans. I give it a minute to watch the cheese slowly melt and the entire plateful to slowly fuse together into very tasty goo. For all that nostalgic childhood shit, stuff that, I'm 14, always hungry, and, as we keep being told, food is fuel. I'm refuelling. I spill a bit, but it's only the school shirt. I'd be running laps if it was the training gear. I change afterwards, and get my homework done. Just English tonight...

"Write a letter to the school governors explaining why they should, or should not, re-instate corporal punishment."

...That's easy...

"Dear Sir,

As a year 10 pupil in your school, corporal punishment should only be brought in for terrorists and peedofile child killers, and even then only if the DNA evidance, is indisputably overwhelmable. *As long as there's no risk of an innocent person being executed, then fair enough. However, hanging people in school's very harsh. Some year 7s would be traumatized if they had to watch it. Bullying and taking drugs needs punishing, but not with corporal punishment. I read about that Malala girl from Afgganistan who got shot in the face for wanting to go to school, and we studied the little black girl in the Martin Luther King film who needed the riot squad just to get her into infant school safely. We're suppoased to be a civilised country, not Afgganistan or Texas or places that execute everyone."*

I got a C for my last assignment, but got a proper telling off as I'd spelt "analyse" wrong. It was only a spelling mistake but Mrs Frogson said that if I did anything like it again she'd ring my Mum and the Academy immediately. I was gutted as I thought I'd be on for a B at least for that.

Homework sorted in 10 mins, which gave me half an hour's X-Box time. All my mates would rip into me if I didn't have GTA, but I've not got time to play it, not as long as they do, whole days some of them. I CBA with COD either. I prefer FIFA, but I've been told that on footy days, if I play it loads I then end up playing footy like I play FIFA. It's been noticed before, so I'm not risking it, despite Archie texting me with "Fifa?" when I was eating. I put NBA on. The player I made is signed to Boston Celtics this year. I've made his footwork and movement 100%, put him in the playmaker role, and he uses a lot of the movements I use on a footy pitch. Just to complete the comparison, I've numbered him 10, my number. I just about get the first quarter finished, 32-16. My character doesn't score many, he can't jump for shit, but when he sets off on a dribble no-one can get near him. Proper wizard, like me in full flow. The wizardry comes to an abrupt end when Dad shouts me down.

Dad asks absolutely nothing about the City match, tonight's training, school today, my health or anything about me, just his little geek mate. I'm quite happy, proud even, to remind him that I backed his ass up in tutorial. He wanted to know more about the incident, like extra details, but there really weren't that many. I said some lass were being a dipshit, so was Edward, but slightly less annoying than she were, and that was about it.

We pull in as the grassroots team are taking selfies by the "Welcome to Sevenhill City F.C" sign. Bloody hell, two of them have had Maccy D's or KFC somewhere on the way. Whether it's pop or it's milkshake they're sipping at, they're gonna be sweating bucketloads, proper red in the face and stitched up to fuck within 5 minutes. One of them's proper chunky. When he sweats, he'll probably sweat gravy.

I walk straight in. Me, Tyrell and Jamal stretch off and watch the grassroots team kicking around, just to see if there's someone amongst them that the club want to look at. No-one we can spot. Their warm-ups comical. 10 of them in the penalty area, and one of them crossing balls in to them. Most of the balls get missed, none of them move for the ball, and when one of them does connect the ball can go in any random direction. The keepers like a statue on the middle of his line. The lad crossing in, wherever the ball is, manoeuvres onto the same foot each time. A couple of the kids are pretty chunky and look awkward when they run, not like they've got a mobility problem, but more like they're just not naturally athletic. It's going to be brutal, this.

"This could be boring", I say to the others.

"Can't see't point o' this, apart from a night out for them." Tyrell's in.

I'm back "Do you remember when you first went on trial? What did it feel like?"

"I went to Wednesday first." Jamal replies, "I remember going in their dome. Me whole family, Mum, Dad, Grandma, brothers and sister all came along. They buzzed about it more than I did, but no way were Wednesday letting them in to watch, so they all ended up in Morrisons getting groceries and a cuppa tea til it were time to fetch me home. All I remember was how fucking intense it were, just kept going non-stop with no time to think about owt. Time flew by and I proper loved it. When I came out, Mum, Dad, Grandma were desperate to know everything, and each of them had 50 different questions to ask me which I couldn't answer 'cos I were far too knackered."

While the other side do the Alamo drill, which is basically pass to the coach, who lays the ball back then you shoot, our coaches walk over to us, Benny's got another white envelope in his pocket. Everyone's here. Except Hassan. His Snapchat's been quieter than usual this week. I'm trying to think of the last time I saw him post anything anywhere.

"Right boys, City on Saturday. Their left winger's Dutch, their right-winger speaks Portuguese, their centre-back's Norwegian, their other centre-back cost a hundred grand, and they paid Millwall two hundred grand for their striker. That's two hundred grand for a 12 year old. We're playing their 14s. Don't be cocky about the age gap. If they couldn't play, they'd not be there. The space-age complex we'll be playing at is also where they all live and go to school. They spend more on schooling their kids than we do on our first team. You guys are in a good position, but these guys, providing they don't mess up big-time, have made it. These guys play Barca, Madrid, Bayern, Juventus, maybe a bit of futsal here and there. You've done well to get a game against them."

Benny pauses. Stevie steps in..."What do you reckon to these warming up now?"

Ben chips in. "Basic."

Others chip in..."One footed."

"None of them move anywhere."

"We'll finish this in 5 minutes."

Stevie raises his hand to silence us all, "When City play you on Saturday, that's how they'll think of you. They'll look at you from the same dizzy height as you look at these. They think they'll pass the ball around a bit, slot a few goals away early on then relax. Tonight you'll learn their mindset."

"We're changing it about a bit too. So......"Naz. Goalkeeper!"

"Eh?" Naz looks, like he's had a proper bombshell dropped on him.

"Hassan's played there before. When you find yourself in a one-on-one, it's worth having a clue what the keeper's thinking. You'll not have loads to do, but at least you can see the game from't keeper's perspective. Don't worry, tha's not in all night. Kyle or Jamal'll tek over a bit later. Centre backs can benefit from seeing what't keeper sees, too. It'll mek you think about your game a bit."

This could be an interesting night, after all. Any money I'm going defensive mid or full back.

"Full backs, Brad, start on't right, Tyler, start on't left."

Thank fuck for that. Defensive mid it is? Erm, no.

"Dan and Joe. You'll be moving here later on, Dan left, Joe right. This pitch will open up for you later on. I want to see what you do with all the space."

"Centre mid. Kyle. Jamal. Everything'll be at your feet with half o't time you usually get. Let's see how your decision-making goes."

"Attacking mid. Joe. You've had a lot of time stood out on't wing and I don't want you to start getting lazy. I want you to come infield and get a bit more involved. Tyler, listen in, tha'll be slotting in here later."

And so it goes on. "I ain't nobody's wingman." Brodie swears, under his breath.

Benny hears him, "No, you look more like a substitute. Stick a bib on and I'll talk to you in a bit."

Tyrell goes centre-back with Oscar. After Brodie, no-one's complaining. Oscar's beaming. He's only the keeper because City put him there. Centre defence is just as attractive to him as any position on the entire pitch.

Ben was going on the bench til Brodie threw his toys. Benny and Stevie look at each other, pause, one of them nods, the other nods straight back.

"Dan, defensive mid. We're going diamond in midfield. You OK with that?"

Course he is. He doesn't give a monkeys. He wants to be a pilot for British Airways. He smiles, sarcastically and slyly. Brodie knows that smile's aimed at him. He lives for that spot, sat deep, not much running, yelling at everyone and breaking people's legs. I struggle to see him coping anywhere else on a pitch. Centre back maybe, at a push, but only if everyone else gets injured. Dan's a psycho too, but infinitely smarter with it, much less obvious, and not quite in need of the same use of violence.

"No strikers. Two wingers. Ben. Don't laugh. You're on't left. Same reason Naz's in goal. Learn how the winger thinks when he teks you on. Sam, have the right wing. Be creative. Crossover as much as you want, but if I see either of you getting lazy, you'll be sat next to me."

Sam never says much anyway. He just nods his head and gets up. Ben follows suit.

"Right, on Saturday you'll not get much time on't ball. Tonight you'll get loads." Benny looks over at the opponents. "They're called Nethertown summat or other. Don't ask me what league they play in, cos I've no idea." Still doing layoffs and shooting. A Dad behind the goal, fetching the balls they've all shot wide, is clearly getting the best warm up. "When we have the ball, use it sensibly. If it's a simple ball that's on, then do it. I want everybody comfy with a ball, all 11. Four quarters of 20. So we'll change about quite a bit.

Eleven of us walk onto the pitch. Dan checks that the coaches aren't looking then nudges Brodie and says "Keep warm, fella". I'm too far away to hear Brodie's reply, but some stuff I can always lip-read perfectly every time. "Fuck off!" is one of these.

The opposition walk over and line-up to do that hand-shake thing. No-one does that at our level. Stevie shouts us over to do the same. Naz throws his hands up, he's just got his self into his 6 yard box. I shake the keeper's hand. His gloves are too big for him. Plenty of space at the end of those fingers. He's gonna struggle. Shoot on sight.

I forgot how noisy grassroots parents were. All their Mums shrieking "Come on Boys!!!", taking sneaky photos even though it's against the rules. We give them kick off. Touch back to centre mid, who plays it sideways to his winger, who'd already gone forward too soon. The full back's one of those grassroots ones who never passes halfway. Ben's there first, runs at the full back, does him for speed, and the centre back, one of the kids who was drinking coke when I turned up, touches it out for a corner. Ben can get stuffed. These are still mine. I tell him not to go far. I line it up as if I'm gonna send it long to the back post. Oscar's already making his run. Ha ha. He's loving this. I shout "Oscar" but play short back to Ben, just to wind Oscar up a little bit. Ben sends it in himself. Not bad with his left foot. Oscar's there, it's on the back post, and I'd expect the keeper to get something on it. He does but Oscar shoves him over and Jamal whacks the loose ball into the net. Disallowed.

I can see how things are going to go. That keepers got no chance with Mickey Mouse gloves on. His Dad's clearly the assistant manager and has kittens every time his lad has something to do. Over-ambitious Dad. In this man's crazy deluded mind, this is his boy's big chance. He wants him to be noticed, but can't even be arsed to get him gloves that fit. The kid's wearing Predators too. I bet he bought them especially for tonight. When did a keeper ever need Predators? Everyone in the Dome knows this is as good as it will ever get for this lad. The kid knows this. He's probably cool with it. But Dad knows best. If he does what Dad says, they'll sign him. In his batshit dreams.

With the pressure being put on him by his desperately deluded fat father, who seriously doesn't suit a retro-tracksuit now and probably didn't suit a retro-tracksuit in 1979 either, Joel (everyone now knows this kids name, it's all we can hear) lines up his goal kick, takes 5 steps back with his predators, 5 steps forward and curls his goal kick out for a throw-in. His Dad clearly wanted that goal kick to go to the same place that every Sunday league manager tells their keeper it should go, inside the centre circle, over the halfway line, same place that every grassroots keeper hits, and every opponent reads quicker than "Spot goes swimming".

"What was that?" Pushy fat Dad shouts. What does he expect sticking his keeper in Predators? It's like giving the postman a Ferrari to do his deliveries in.

Sam throws in quickly to me. I don't even need to pull a trick. I just drop my shoulder, change direction, and it's enough to wrongfoot the chunky centre back. I lose him. The keeper shuffles out, arms out, and his Dad's having more kittens. "Close him down!!" Idiot Dad doesn't realise that whatever this kid does, he's showing me half the goal anyway. I can slot this in blindfolded. I know Dan's not far behind me, so instead of shooting I square it with the outside of my left foot, so the defence can get roasted for it, not the keeper. Dan lets it run through his legs for Ben to hit it in. He scores one goal a season. He usually celebrates. This time I don't think he can see the point.

The Mum's on the sideline still shout encouragement at their kids. The assistant manager still delves into his son verbally, while the other manager's having a go at their centre mid, a big chunky lad who doesn't look like he runs much. I'm guessing that's his lad. This is why they're here, and this is why he's in centre mid. Best place to get spotted. I'll guess they phoned us for a game. All City will spot is two kids being forced to live their Dad's impossible dreams.

The game restarts. Kick off back to the centre mid again, out to the same wing again. Ben gets there first again. This time he plays it a yard in front of me, a dodgy hospital ball in any other game, but I let their centre mid get there first, the other manager's son. I don't challenge, I just stay close and deny him space, so he plays back to his centre back to do what grassroots centre backs can always be trusted on to do, lump the ball aimlessly down the field over everyone's heads. Oscar, sitting deep, has a quick look either side and lets it run through to Tyrell, who smiles as he gets his hands on the ball. He's having a laugh with it all. He holds the ball, not for tactical reasons, he just wants everyone to look at him. He throws over him to Kyle, who dribbles past his opponent effortlessly like he's not there. Kyle could have played me in, but instead plays out to Sam. Their left back hasn't touched the ball yet, and has no idea he's marking a defender that's never played right-wing before. Sam plays a square ball back to Kyle. I'm in front of the centre mid. Thanks to his gradually more anxious Dad, I know his name now, Harvey. Kyle plays along the floor to me, shouts for it back, but instead I flick with the outside of my right boot. There's a bit more spin on that than I wanted, but Dan read it. Through on goal, one on one. I'd actually put it somewhere where he could save, heroically, and shut his Dad up. Dan, however, doesn't care for that kind of bleeding-heart compassion, and adores pissing Brodie off if the opportunity arises. The keeper comes off his line. I'd hit it just wide if it fell to me, but Dan hits it hard and low into the bottom right hand corner, then turns to the nearest Nethertown player, says "amateurs", then runs over to Brodie and invites him to celebrate. 2-0. Both managers delve into their kids, yelling everything they're doing wrong. The keepers head's totally dropped. When teams pack in at 2-0, and player's heads drop this soon into a game, it soon becomes 12-0. I feel for this kid. I don't have Brodie or Dan's view on annihilating everyone. If we were playing someone that's a bit of a challenge, like Leeds the other day, or some proper edgy needle match, I'd be proper ruthless. Not here, though. There's no challenge, and no point.

I see it like this. This keeper has probably played nowhere like this in his life, ever. Unlike his Dad, but like everyone else on the planet, he knows he'll not play in the Premiership in this lifetime, and the idea's never crossed his mind. I'll go a bit further. This keeper probably just likes playing football. He's probably in goal cos every other kid refused, or because he hasn't got a hope of coping outfield, even in grassroots, or might even be in goal as he wants to play and this is where he's most comfortable. But, in his own way, he's part of a team, and probably enjoys that. He's never even thought of being a footballer, he probably thinks of little more than kicking about with his mates. He may only be in the team purely because Dad's the assistant manager. Other kids who could goalkeep better than him have appeared, and his Dad's seen them all off, as that's his lad's position and Dad has his impossible dream that he's not letting any other kid get in the way of. His Dad would probably turn Manuel Neuer away as his kid's the keeper, no questions. So, he probably trains once a week, then plays each Sunday, and when he plays, it's all for enjoyment, to feel part of something, to get off his X-Box for a bit and do something social with his mates, nowt more. In the big grand scheme of things, there's nowt wrong with that. It's all good. Everyone says we've got this generation of fat kids who live on chicken nuggets and Snapchat and sugary pop and COD and Netflix and Mars bars and pizzas with sugar on top. The adult world despairs of it whilst being the exact same people that buy their kids all this shit, so if there's room for every kid to do sport, even the one's with no talent who just like playing, and it doesn't cost a million quid to do, then that's good, right? So, yeah, this kid plays football, and is probably a bit less of a fat bloater for doing so, even though later on there'll be Mars Bars and Maccy D's after the game. When this kid got told him and his mates were playing a match at City's Dome, I'll bet not one of them even thought about getting noticed or signed, but just counted down to it all, took a few selfies at the front entrance, stuck them on Insta, then maybe looked out for first-teamers to get selfies with. The first teamers all train in the daytime. Unless the odd one drops in and does a session for some coaching badge they're on, we barely see them let alone any visitors. The kids in the Children's Hospital see more first-teamers than we do, which is how it should be. If I make it, then you can bet the wrinkles on your arse that I'll be there at least once a week, sat playing Fifa with some kid who's just lost a leg or something. No publicity, no getting sent down by the manager, I'll just do it. Anyway, I'm rambling. When most of these grassroots kids got offered to play here, they saw it in the same way as they would if someone offered them paintballing, so the obvious answer is "yeah, might be cool, why not?" So, what bugs me, is that tonight, just a training game for us, might be THE biggest milestone this kid's had in his life, will probably never play here again, or play anywhere other than the back of a primary school or some bumpy park pitch, so, this kid needs to enjoy having a game here. He might have gone to bed last night unable to sleep, unable to contain his excitement. And here's his Dad, trashing his self-esteem and totally destroying him in front of an audience. Wanker.

This car crash game is affecting how I think. I pick up a loose ball just inside my own half. Ben and Sam are in space, but the pitch opens out in front of me. I run through the centre and get my right foot ready. I can hear gobshite Dad again, so I loft my shot high, to the keepers left, close enough for him to get a hand to it, but far enough away to not get criticised by my experienced, level 5 qualified coaches. Oscar would take this cleanly, but this Joel dives Hollywood-style to push it away, then their full back lumps it away anywhere, like only a Sunday league fullback can. I say "Well done pal". He doesn't hear, his idiot Dad doesn't hear, but my own Dad does. He's seen this sort of shit so many times. I spot a sly thumbs up from him.

Their centre mid, Harvey, is pushing me about a bit. It's all he has. Each time he pushes me, I trick him straight afterwards. Each time I get the ball I can see Ben and Sam making runs quicker and more eager than a kid in a sweet shop. I can hear his Dad yelling at him "Closer Harv!", "Get a foot in", "Look wide!" In fact everything this lad does, is exactly what his manager Dad tells him to do. X-Box manager with an ultimate team full of schoolkids. With the last move of the first half, I get a square pass along the floor from Tyrell, and stop, wait for the challenge and side step it. I play a diagonal one through for Dan, who sends Sam on his way. Sam touches it forward and loses his marker for pace immediately, cuts into the penalty area, thinks about the shot, but plays back to me on the edge of the area. I decide to go for crossbar challenge. Of course I do it, and the ball hangs in the air for ages after it hits the edge of the crossbar. When it drops, it gets a touch off either Ben or whoever's marking him, and then bounces. The keeper shouts "Mine!" (we're banned from saying that), but the centre back still tries to clear it anyway. Kyle picks it up, has loads of space and lets fly with a thunderbastard from way outside the area. The keeper actually gets a bit of a hand to it, but not even Neuer could stop a shot like that dead. Sam's first to the loose ball and puts it low into the corner of the net. The goalie Dad's on his case again. I thought he did well to get a hand to it, myself. My Dad stands in the corner, minding his business as he does whenever I play. Damn, I'm grateful.

The whistle blows. Benny turns to Brodie. "Brodie. And any others of you. I pick the team. I coach you. I play you. Any of you that don't like it can go and sign for that crew over there. We ain't kids no more. It dun't take much to get let go. Ask Hassan Fawaz." Brad and Ben look at each other. "Anyone who fancies being a bigtime Charlie won't last another 5 minutes here." Benny looks at Dan as he says that. Dan looks back at him the same way he always does. There's a mind game going on. I'm not getting involved. I get my drink. Benny continues, "I'm giving it a bit longer as we are. Brodie, go attacking mid. Joe, go centre mid wiv Kyle. Keep that triangle. Dan, left-back. Brad, right-back. Tyler, well played, have a breather mate."

The game restarts quickly. Brodie plays the ball back to me. Manager shouts over at his son "GET INTO HIM!", and this Harvey lad runs towards me. I can see the boots flying my way, but I play under him, sidestep his lunge, wait for Sam to make his run, do a 2 touch turn, stepover past their player and I'm into the box. The keeper runs out, on the "GET OFF YOUR LINE!!" orders of his Dad, I play Sam in who lobs a beauty of a ball that hangs in the air. Ben, a shortarse like me, judges it perfectly and guides a perfect header in between the defender and the near post. 4-0. Their deluded manager is now yelling at his lad for coming off his line, "STAY ON YOUR LINE NEXT TIME!" I shake my head as I return to the centre circle.

Straight from kick off, the ball gets played back to the centre midfielder who lumps a long ball that Brad retrieves from near his own corner flag. "WHAT THE HELL WAS THAT?" his Dad shouts. Unlike the keeper, who clearly just wants to go home and never play football again, this lad gets ready to shout back at his Dad, but just as he opens his mouth, he stops. I can see him steadily losing his temper anyway. His nudges become pushes then become full on shoves. Won't be long before he lashes out. I'm in the same midfield as Brodie, who'll wind him up just that little bit more. I drop off him 10 yards. I've made my mind up not to take him on, just get in space, receive and pass. The tension doesn't take long to increase though. Brad plays a simple side pass to Kyle. I run to Kyle for a short ball, but he passes beyond me to Brodie. Brodie turns, tries the same trick on this Harvey lad that I did a minute ago, not as sweetly as mine, and Harvey gets a bit of foot on the ball. It runs loose, Brodie chases it, Harvey follows and when he gets close I spot Brodie stick a very sly elbow into the side of this lad. Harvey gives him a shove back which is more obvious, Brodie falls to the floor. Free kick to us. Manager tells his son. "THAT'S BETTER!

SHOW THEM WHAT YOU CAN DO".

These free kicks are usually mine, but tonight, anything goes. Brad wants it. I go wide. Dan's being marked by this Harvey lad. He says something to Harvey that I'm too far away to hear. The reply is "Piss off!" anyway. Dan's crossed over with Brodie and as Brad launches an impossible shot that actually goes quite close, I realise Dan's doing his "I fancy you" trick. I've seen him wind players up with it before, telling whoever he's marking that how awesome their bum looks in those shorts, and not to bend over in case he gets carried away and decides to feel them up. He'll keep quietly doing this until he triggers them to the level that they swing a punch for him then he laughs when they get subbed. If anyone questions him about it, he'll argue that he has no sympathy whatsoever for anyone with homophobic tendencies, as there's no place for such intolerance in modern society, and certainly not in football. He knows that once he's wound this lad up, he can get Brodie involved. Once that bomb's primed, he can then enjoy the inevitable explosion. When he tries this in grudge matches, it's fun. This is no grudge match. It's a training game against donut boys. Unless he's trying to trigger Brodie, I can't see the point.

My way of making Brodie look a twat is much easier. He's in attacking mid and hates running. I could feed balls through to him all night and knacker him out. I play balls 5-10 yards to the side of him or in front, even though there's players in better spaces than him. He gets to them all, but only because the opposition's slower than him. Harvey's chasing after him every time. Speed wise, they're a close match, and those sneaky elbows have now progressed to sneaky punches from both sides.

The third time I play these kind of balls, Brodie plays me a return ball in...

"TAKE HIM OUT!"...gets shouted from the sidelines.

Harvey only partially takes me out. He catches my leg, but not massively. I send the free kick to Dan on my left. He runs towards this Harvey at speed and nutmegs him before playing Sam in for a low cross that hits a defender then falls safely in front of the keeper who gathers it in the same way that my Mum picks pegs up from the laundry basket. Though it's not much of a goalkeeping technique, his Dad says nothing. Gets away with it somehow.

"I've heard you like it between your legs." Dan turns to this Harvey as he runs past him.

"FUCK OFF!" the reply comes. There's going to be a fight soon. I look over at the sidelines, just to see if anyone's going to blow a whistle. Now would be a good time to calm things down a bit.

The whistle, for me, didn't come on time.

When Benny said "Joe, I'm moving you infield tonight to get you more involved", I know it was a good idea at the time. When their manager yelled at his son "TAKE HIM OUT!" for the second time that evening, I knew why he shouted that too. When his son took one touch too many, just in our half, there was no blame on him when I nipped in, won it, passed to Jamal and then got into space for a return. When Jamal played a long diagonal ball on to Brodie, and this Harvey lad chased after him, with his Dad yelling "TAKE HIM OUT!" once more, I expected something to kick off again with him and Brodie. I made my run, shouted for the ball, and Brodie touched it to one side, a little too far in front of me, revenge for the balls I'd played to him. I got there, but Harvey's pent-up rage and frustration got to me first, specifically my right ankle. As I landed on the floor, I felt something go pop, I heard something go pop, and I knew that getting up again by myself would be a bad idea. Everyone crowded round. After a couple of squeezes of my ankle which were more painful than they promised me it would be, both Benny and Stevie tried to get me on my feet. I knew I couldn't. I spent the rest of the quarter, all 20 seconds of it, sat on the touchline dabbing away with a cold sponge.

Dad, along with Brad's Dad, carried me to an empty treatment room. There's never a club doctor when you need one. The first aid box contained a couple of bandages, a couple of dressings, and nowt else. I got strapped up then carried straight to Dads car. Neither Dad nor Brad's Dad have ever trained as paramedics, but the pain, now that I realise that no amount of warm baths or ice packs will revive my ankle for City on Saturday, is infinitely more emotional than physical. Once home, the manoeuvres to get me out of the car and the mood in the house were as awkward as each other. Tonight should have meant absolutely nothing. It now meant everything.

----

18. HAVE TWO BANANAS

"You havin' owt or what fam?"

I'd not thought about it. I'd been so focussed on getting here that I completely forgot that the bubble tea shop sells bubble tea. If I'd said anything to Mum she'd have deffo given me £5. I have 57p in my pocket. This place charges £4 for a drink that resembles very expensive, pretty milk more than tea. Oh, hang on.

"No, but I've got some Oreo biscuits in my bag. Would anybody like one?"

Shelly looks at me deadpan, eyebrows raised. The Asian lad and the girl with mermaid hair look up from their phones and study me, also deadpan, eyebrows raised.

"Is that what you say to all the lasses?" the girl sat next to her asks me.

Shelly slides a drink my way. "I sussed you wun't know jack about this place, so I got you banana wi' mango balls. Yeah, I know. It sounds rude. Pay me next time."

I check the price list on the back wall. Shit, I owe £3.90 already. I bet that's Shelly's big plan, get me running dodgy errands on their behalf to pay a debt off in vain, with interest accruing that never ends. I feel like Mowgli in the Jungle Book when King Louie sits him down and says "have two bananas!" I survey the group. If Shelly hadn't shouted my name so enthusiastically when Travis Twat was staring me down, or if the Asian lad with her hadn't stood up and gone for the fist-bump, or the other lad, a semi-lunatic looking chap wearing a padded coat that anyone else would wear in snowier, icier days, was a little more civilised and went for the handshake, or the two other girls with them, one heavily made up, the other not made up at all, given me a very calm but very polite "How ya doin, fella?", I could easily find these people scary. None of them give that vibe you get of potential violence. They're all calm, like, nobody's ever messed with them, or maybe, somebody did try to bait them a long time ago, and somehow nobody does any more, so that calmness comes from that kind of security, but there was something about them that inspired Travis Greenshields to step back from me. He's still visible, outside, looking like he's pretending to wait for someone, looking as lonely as I did 15 minutes ago, occasionally glancing in but rapidly looking away every time I look back. I don't need to worry about him ambushing me outside, not with my present company. I think if I got really angry enough I could probably flatten him. The problem I have here is that I take so long to reach any level of angry that it's all a bit useless.

I look so out of place. Let's be diplomatic here and call my dress sense functional. Everyone else has some kind of statement to the world going on, be it make up, some colour combination, a tattoo, some writing on the side of a garment. Shelly introduces her mates to me. Chelsea, Tariq, Jay, Maya. Everything looks platonic between them, but it's the bubble tea shop on a Thursday afternoon in a drizzly grey city centre. If there's any romance going on, there's better settings. Shelly and Maya have hoodies on that most kids my age would be desperate to know which shop to find them in. A dark green one on Shelly with some Manga character on the front that I don't recognise, some patch on the arm and something on the back. It looks two sizes too big for her, so I'm guessing it's a lads, boyfriend's maybe. Maya's is black with the words E X O on the front and 2 cobwebs across it, also 5 sizes too big for her, so I'm guessing she's dating a heavyweight boxer. If there's any dating going on here, it's between quirky and badass, and they're getting on famously. No labels, none of the total-waste-of-Mum's-money faux-material junk that other kids hissyfit at their parents for, apart from maybe the trainers, but only because I can't see them right now. Maya's hair is like I'd imagine a mermaids to be, like, really long, wavy all over the place. I could study it all day, every time she moves her head its mesmerising, but people would think I was weird if I did. Chelsea's hair, shorter with blue bits in it, like she's stepped out of a manga, most of it under a beanie that looks like it's been worn a fair bit, probably boyfriends again. I can see preppy, classy, swag, geeky, quirky, and 'don't fuck with me'. J's snapback, just with "84" on it, whatever that means. Tariq's possibly the plainest. Black and white all the way down, but there's finer details, an eyebrow piercing, some bandy stuff on his wrist, a Jamaican flag pattern on one of the wristbands, even though he's nowhere near being Jamaican. I could easily feel embarrassed about how I look. But again, I could wear exactly the same stuff as them and just look ridiculous. I really could do with finding a way of making the farty, geeky, dweeby look reasonable.

"You want owt to eat? I can stretch to a plain donut" Shelly asks.

I feel my heartbeat pounding away. Only thing is that right now, it feels like my heart's beating not in my chest area, but in my arse. Food's not a great idea. "No thanks, but i have some double chocolate Oreos. If you'd like one, you'd be very welcome."

"What about blueberry muffins, you got any o' them in yer magic bag?" Jay asks.

"Maybe tomorrow. I didn't bring anything for me, really. There's a homeless guy I speak to sometimes when I'm in town. I keep something in my bag just in case I bump into him."

"So you chat to strangers and they give you sweets. Seems legit!" Tariq laughs.

"Talking nicely to strangers is an easier way of getting sweets than robbing them at knifepoint."

"So, why aren't you in school?" Maya asks. She's got blue braces in her teeth that perfectly match her hair and trainers.

Shelly's back. "I told me Dad about you wi' them security blokes. He were reyt impressed. It's why I want to talk to you", she smiles, not the full teeth, but more like the smile my cat does when she's got a full stomach. I still have that sense I'm about to get blackmailed or threatened, like I've inadvertently stepped into a mafia meeting at the wrong time.

"Do you like footy by any chance?" Shelly enquires.

"Hate everything about it, why?"

"Have you ever been to a match?"

"I watched one at the park once when I was small. It got boring, so I went on the swings instead."

"No. Like a proper match. Big stadium, noisy crowd. All that."

"No. Why?"

"Dad's on about going to Man City this Saturday. He's offered me along, but I've got better things to do. He's getting a spare ticket in case I change me mind, which I won't."

"I'm sure your Dad's not gonna make you watch football all day if you don't like it?"

"No, fam, you don't get it."

Did she just call me fam there? That's what dickhead year 8s call each other.

"You've met my obnoxious billy big-bollocks brother. You've probly spotted that he acts like he's above anyone who can't balance a football on't end of their nose, even though, as you and I both know, there's millions of other people smarter, cleverer, and, most importantly of all, kinder than him."

"I've noticed that. I don't really go near him. Or his mates. I've nothing to say to them."

"I bet you go near nobody. New kid in school an' all that. I heard about Corey Hendricks."

"He doesn't scare me. He's the one with the problem, not me."

"Exactly. The problems someone else's but its gettin pushed your way. It always is. I've seen your friends, but think about it, old biddies, students, trampy beggars, they'll not stop you getting battered that much."

"Yeah, I know. I'm not that worried tho."

"Well I am."

"Why would you be that bothered about me?"

"My biz, that. You see me and my squad here?"

I don't reply, I just nod, and scan round at them.

"Well, we're gonna be your mates. You got my number. Each weekend when we're out, we'll fetch you wi' us. You won't need owt, you just come along n chill."

"Why'd you want me to..." I get interrupted.

"It won't be owt massive. If we've got money, it gets squandered on bubble tea like it does now. Tap your Mum up for a fiver. If you're wi' us she'll probly send you out wi a tenner instead. Turn up as you normally would, we're very accepting citizens of the world like that. We have rules, but you'd breeze them."

"Rules?"

"No Stone Island, no Jack Wills, no Hollister, no meet-me-at-McDonalds noodle dickhead haircuts, no talking bollocks about Fifa, Fortnight or GTA, no emo misery, no hipst......."

"Do I look like......"

"That Shironda lass helps her Mum out in one o' them gangster chicken shops near the Arches dun't she? Seeing as she's the school foghorn, we'll drop in. Don't expect us to eat owt from there cos it's rank. Even the mushrooms there have got mushrooms growing out of 'em. We'll tag you in everything. Word will fly round St Kevin's that you're wi' us."

I'm beaming at his, but shouldn't be, I should be a lot cooler with this. "OK, My rules now. I'm not running drugs, robbing cars or assaulting anyone. End of."

Shelly and her mates burst into squeals, "I'll assault you in cold blood if you do. You also know that my Mum and your Mum are buddies."

"Yeah I know right? I thought they looked a bit unlikely."

"The best friendships usually are. When I see you havin' banter wi a tramp or an old lady and whoever else I think of them."

I look towards the window. Travis clearly got fed up of waiting around. School will be interesting tomorrow. Suddenly, I feel a tug on my shoulder. I fall back. Something happens that people never do with me, something that I'd never even do with myself, something I've thought of in the past, but always changed my mind almost immediately after. Shelly presses the side of her face against mine, Chelsea leans forwards and rests the side of her head on my shoulder. Tariq, who was sitting next to me, is now leaning to his right, in my personal space, then, stretches his arms out directly in front of him. "Selfie!!" My first ever.

----

19. RICE AND PEAS

Dr Neale Konstantin, BSc Hons, DRCOG, DFFP (reg Cambridge 2006), whatever that all means, wasn't as scary as the mugshot on the wall suggested he might be. Well over 6 feet tall, one of those side-partings that only posh fellas ever have, a smile that actually looked like he was genuinely pleased to see me and not just paid to be, open-collared pinstriped shirt, no tie, no bowtie thank fuck, no white doctor coat, everything about him on first impression suggested that he would chat very politely to me using some very long complicated words then, once I was on my way, depart swiftly to some golf course. On his instructions, I lay on the recliner, socks and shoes off, trackies rolled up, noticing this medical professional had slightly colder hands than I hoped for. I could place his voice about as well as I could place Dani Marrero's Portuguese broken English, all I could describe it as was amiable-boffin. Despite having an accident report in front of him, he asked me to describe what happened. I didn't feel talkative but I had a go, and it sounded proper shite. "I tried to get on the end of a pass off Brodie, the other player got there before me and he did my ankle". He looked like it made sense to him however. He's probably too posh to have played football, he looks more a croquet kinda chap but probably has a PhD in year 10 bantz translation as well as medicine. A couple more prods with his cold fingers, the first of which proper hammered, then he was all smiles and "You can sit up now, Joe"

"OK, Joe, I'm pleased to say there's no fracture there. There's going to be some bruising, but once the bruising dies down, you'll make a quick recovery."

Get in! Sort of.

"You will need to rest this out for a few days, unfortunately."

Bugger.

"The ankle's a complex joint. Even on an average person it's responsible for coping with your whole bodyweight, so the first part of recovery is to keep your body weight away from it."

"How long am I out for?"

"From school or football?"

"Football?" I know he's a boffin, but come on. As if school ever matters that much?

"Ok. I recommend complete rest this weekend. I'm pleased to recommend spending the entire day on Netflix, or the X-Box, purely to keep you resting, of course. Or maybe a good book. Have you read the new Harry Potter yet?"

I was hanging onto every bar he was eloquently spitting out, but I'm not really into that wizard stuff. I've got the books. I've read "The Philosophers Stone" and skimmed through the others at some stage, but not because I like them, but because every other kid in school's read them. OK, well maybe not Cory Hendricks and his sidemen, and I doubt Brodie or Tyler would, but every other kid in my lessons has. Some of them proper adore it so I need to know what they're on about. If they've not read them, then they've watched the movie, or been to the theme park. I've watched the movies out of convenience, but taken one of the books with me on away trips and skimmed the pages half-heartedly, like I do with everything that's got nowt to do with football.

"No, not yet."

There's no way I'm pulling out £10 of my own money, and I'd need a good reason to be spotted in Waterstones, like if i were trying to impress some perfect 10 lass who just so co-incidentally liked bookshops maybe. I'll get it in the next few weeks however, only because Shelly's birthdays like, 2 months away. I could get Mum to fetch it, stick it in my bag for the next away trip, read through the main bits enough for me to not fuck up in classroom conversations, then wrap it up and give it Shelly for her birthday. 2 birds. 1 stone, on target as usual.

"Take a look at the bruising on Sunday night. The quicker we get the bruising out the better. Give it Rice." he looks at Mum. Mum nods. Both of them glance quickly my way to see I understand the situation. I'm happy enough with that. Chinese tonight, Indian tomorrow and Mexican or Jamaican on Sunday, and the big posh doctor finishes with "and the quicker everything turns purple the better", which I've no idea what purple rice is going to do to help me out here.

Sunday? That ain't good. "So when can I play again?"

"Right, this is how we do it. Are you listening?"

Am I listening? My ears are sticking out so much, I look like the Champions League Trophy.

"Do I need to write it all down?"

I wasn't being cheeky, but Mum just looked at me like I had been.

"Next week. Very light exercise. Walk the dog. If you've not got a dog, then if Mum runs out of milk, you go to the shop, that kind of thing."

He looks at me, checks for a reaction, then carries on.

"I'll do you a note for school next week."

At least some consolation. Bed and Fifa.

"Week 2. Back to school. No P.E. No break time kickabouts. I'm going to suggest swimming every second day. It's the best exercise you can get for this. You can do a good few lengths and not risk anything. I'll book you back in with me for 2 weeks today, get you a session with the physio, then once he says everything's OK, then back to light training for a couple of weeks, build the strength back up, then I'll look at it once more before you go on the pitch."

Shit. That's 4 weeks minimum. No City away. That Liverpool match that was getting talked about won't happen either. Is there not any magic bastard fairy dust in your cabinet that you can't just sprinkle over it?

"If we do everything properly now, the ankle will strengthen and you'll be back on the pitch with no issues. Come back too soon and you'll risk putting too much pressure on it and the injury can then create problems long-term. It's worth sitting things out now, especially when England are going to need you 5 years from now."

Yeah I get it. No City, no Liverpool. Watch me be fit for Rochdale and Barnsley instead.

The drive home was as silent and awkward as the drive out. Anxiety had gone, replaced by what I perceive depression to be. I've got Ibuprofen to take twice a day, but right now I'd rather it be spice or monkey dust. Even though she's been Superhero Cait Barker in the past, Mum has no chance at all of picking me up, either physically or emotionally. It didn't stop her trying for the rest of the morning, but I wasn't buying it. No-one turns Nandos down, ever, but I turned Mums offer down. That might never happen again. I'm not thinking straight.

There's 14 stairs to be climbed to reach my bedroom. I might as well try climbing Everest. After a few awkward minutes hopping from the car to the living-room by balancing my weight on walls, garden gates, the fridge, I fell on the sofa, not knowing when I'd be able to rise from it again. I don't know how Mum does it all. I'm like, coming to terms with being useless for a month, and within seconds the telly's on, tablet's charged, food's laid out for when I'm ready that I don't have to cook, or even get out of the fridge. Sorting all that out without an injury would take me 3 hours minimum. Mum leaves me on the sofa, my socks off, my ankles raised with 2 bath towels underneath and a bag of frozen peas on top of them, with another towel on top. I guess the peas is something to do with the rice thing they were on about earlier. There's a book next to me, "The Fault in Our Stars", but I've seen the film already. Tablet out. Snapchat. 3 streaks still running. Brad, Ben and that Jodie lass, the fit one. If she keeps the streaks going for another 2 weeks then I'll ask her out. Well, what I'll actually do is fuck Sam off with the free match tickets, give them to myself instead and offer her along. It's not exactly Venice, but if she doesn't like football, then she's totally incompatible with me in every way. If she does, I'll try and get the ££ that Mum was offering to spend on me in Nandos and take Jodie there afterwards instead. Again, not exactly a candlelit table but if she doesn't like spicy chicken either, there'd be no future for us. I've stalked her pages already. Some of her pictures have got bunny ears and cat whiskers shopped on, then there's some group selfies of her and her mates dolled up for a disco. They all look awesome, but the girls from the school down the road are always more awesome than the ones you go to school with aren't they? Little proper classy black dress. It might have come from Primark or H&M but its how you wear it that counts, not how much you pay for it. The shoes, black, heels but not big ones, might have come from Shoezone, but there's something about her wearing them that makes them look like they're Jimmy Choos.

Keep swiping. She's got a dog, a little one with stumpy legs that she proper adores. No detective work needed there. She's wrapped her arms round it for a selfie, and she's written "Monty" with six love hearts after it. I don't like dogs but I could probably cope with old scruffy ones that can't run fast and don't lick you, so I like the picture, kinda hoping she'll dump the dog one day and wrap her arms round me instead. 159 other people do too. Why is it that a fit lass can put any old shit on Instagram and get hundreds of likes on it, but I've got to do something amazing just to get 50? I got 127 once, when I took a selfie with Shelly. I only shared it so everyone knew who my sister was, but all these random older lads liked it purely because she was in it. Anyways, though this is so unfair, I made it 160 anyway. I move onto her Facebook. She's not got loads on that. She's probably got her folks on there so she puts just enough on there to keep them happy. She likes Ed Sheeran, Stormzy, and Lady Leshurr. Everyone likes them, though. It's like a golden rule, just like everyone also likes Fresh Prince, Friends, Rick and Morty and Stewie Griffin, plus the Harry Potter book thing. None of them count either. She likes Barcelona FC. That definitely counts. Massive box ticked right there! I'm only nosying for clues for when I ask her out though. I've got strict rules of what I'm looking for when I'm stalking, and she's passed them all so far. No duckfaces, no nudes, no nude selfies coming my way. If she sent me those, she'd send them to anyone so adios. No "rate me out of 10" or other vain insecure shit, no bitching about anyone, no trying to be a politician, or a relationship counsellor, no overdoing it with the make-up, no shaving eyebrows off and drawing shite new ones on with a bingo pen, no TyPiN sT8uSyZ lYk Dis as if you've never been to primary school, no photos of your dinner unless you're in some fancy or exotic restaurant. Jodie's got one where she's sat with what's probably her Mum and two massive ice-cream sundaes, but it's got "Happy Birthday Mum X" as the status so I'll let her off. Damn I'm harsh aren't I? I think about it, what does she see when she looks me up? I look on my pages...

I've put nothing on since last week when i put "City Away. Counting down. 9 Days", which is no longer happening. Jodie liked that. The last photo was from the first day back at school. New hair and all that. She liked that, too, on Facey, and Instagram too. Before that, some holiday photos. She liked them all, the action shot, the team photos, the poolside ones, even the pic with Mum outside a pizza place, all of them. There's not a lot to go through. I'm secretive like that. Some kids you can read everything about, no secrets at all. You could find one who's a stranger and work out where they live, what school they go to, who they hang round with, where to find them at weekends, those profiles are either a "this is how you break into my house" guide for burglars or a "how to find me and bum-rape me" guide for paedos. My page only says who I play football for, and I can't see any paedo squad getting past security at the training ground anyway. I'm safe and sensible. Ping! Sam.

"*Whr r u? Need tckts*"

"*At home. Anklz fckd. Got no tckts cos I wr @ treatmnt room. Soz*"

I'd forgotten all about them. It's a regular £20, that, double if it's Leeds cos I know he'll pay it. His thinking is this. "I fucking hate Leeds. Everyone fucking hates Leeds. Even Gillingham and Barnet fucking hate Leeds. So, if I twat some Leeds goon, everyone will love me". Unfortunately for him, this week it's Peterborough at home. No-one cares. Except for Sam. He'll find a reason to hate them somehow.

"*U around, Sam?*"

No answer back.

No-one's around. No-one's online. No-one's on Fifa. The TV's got 200 channels and 196 of them are shite. Fifa's shite on your todd. NBA's boxed up on the other side of the room. Not needing to sleep. Not hungry. Lying staring at 4 walls isn't an option. I'm depressed enough. Well, not depressed, not like adults who get depressed and sit and cry for no reason. I'm beyond crying right now. I should be able to without fail. No-one should miss City away. I lean forward and take a look at my ankle.

I may look a proper wazzock lying here with random shit where my socks should be, but at least the ankles turned yellow, with a little bit of blue and purple appearing. That's deffo gonna go multi-coloured. That frozen peas things kicking in, so I place them back on top. I'll look again in 10 minutes. If it colours up more, like green and orange and scarlet red, I'll do an ankle selfie and share it to see who's up for making a fuss. Jodie hopefully. Back to her photos. Two photos in. Ping! Dad.

"Mum told me. Never mind. Have a look on the mantelpiece :-)"

"??? On sofa... Mum said I can't get up"

"Ok. In a bit"

I look over at the mantelpiece. A couple of photos of dead family members, a picture each of me and Shelly from years ago, a few coins, a couple of boring looking envelopes. He's probably left me five pounds. He thinks he's the fucking tooth fairy of ankles. Don't need it.

Back to my ankle. I never thought being off school would be so boring. I don't know how Edward Pendlebury copes when he takes off. If it were a choice between taking an arseload of grief and sitting home monging my brain out with internet and daytime TV, I'd go to school and take a pasting, no questions. I lift the towel up, remove the defrosting vegetables and study the colour schemes appearing. It's spreading, around my achilles and even the bottom of my calf has a yellowy tinge to it. I study it in the same way an art boffin studies a Van Gogh painting, except I don't do that chin-stroking thing that Mr Johnson, my old art teacher at school before I dropped it, does.

I lean slightly to my right so I can fit the whole ankle area into the shot, and ker-click.

Snapchat. Insta. Facey. That way round..."*Man City can stop fretting now. Out for a month."*

Dad's through the door. I nod down to my ankle. He slowly lifts the towel, has a look, smiles.

Smiles?

"What's there to smile about?"

"Bruising's coming out already, pal. The uglier it looks, the quicker and better it heals up."

"Yeah, I'll be fit for Walsall away."

Dad reaches one of the boring looking envelopes from the mantelpiece and passes it my way. I pull the contents out carefully with three outstretched fingers.

Match tickets. 3. Manchester City vs West Bromwich Albion. Saturday 12th October. 3.00 kick off. East Stand Lower. Block 107, Seats 35, 36 and 37. That would have been straight after my match ended. I should be hi-fiving the ceiling.

"I can't play on Saturday. You might as well sell them on."

"Stuff that. We're going anyway. We'll call into't training ground if you want, see your mates play, but we'll not stay long, mek sure we get you through the doors at the Etihad before all't crowds roll in. Full strength team apparently, only Ya-Ya missing, but even then he might mek it onto't bench."

I still have no lyrics. But I should. City at home. Me on the East Stand. Unable to stand. Fuck it, I'll sit in the family section with the 6 year olds if I have to.

"You just need to decide where we eat. It's between Chinatown or Curry Mile."

Anything that involves curry is Dads idea.

"Whichever one's got a Nandos."

"Great. Overpriced chicken."

"They do rice there?"

"And they don't do rice in Chinatown?"

"Yeah, but the doctor said I've got to have rice for me ankle."

Dad starts to laugh, "Nah, keep the peas on fella!" and walks back into the kitchen, still laughing.

As soon as he's out. I pull the phone out, snap the tickets with my finger over the serial numbers, and upload, Snap, Insta, Facey, then check my ankle photo. No likes, no comments.

----

20. Safety Tax

I've firmly believed since infant class that anyone that follows football is a mindless moron with no hope of successfully engaging in meaningful conversation with anyone like me due to me being intellectually and socially above them. Everything about football, if I hear too much about it, has me ready to break things with a sledgehammer. I have no comprehension or patience for adverts that tell me to "Live Football, Breathe Football", the 50 plus men who pay 50 plus pounds for size 50 plus replica tops, and every one of those total cretins who defines their identity, life happiness, relationships and future emotional well-being by how intensely emotional they can be in dedicating themselves to some random bunch of millionaires. There's so many much more purposeful things in life to define yourself by.

Mr Barker called round yesterday evening, doing that jovial thing where he tries to be a bit laddy with me, despite being too old to pull that stuff off and I'm not exactly what you'd describe as a "lad". "Arreyt Edward lad, there's a free ticket wi' us for't Etihad on Saturday if tha fancies it?"

I was excited for about 20 seconds. I know the Etihad as an upmarket airline that flies out of Manchester to Dubai and Abu Dhabi. Yeah, I'd go there. Stuff it, I'd fly there with Cory Hendricks, let alone Joey Barker. Then I realised. Everyone else knows the Etihad as Man City's stadium. I wasn't exactly overawed, but to everyone else in the room, based on the reasoning that most kids my age dream of going there, I should accept.

I had no choice but to accept. Three reasons. One) I'd feel rude saying no. Mr Barker could have asked along any one of hundreds of people who'd buzz for it. He decided to ask me. Two) Mum and Lara were both staring intently at me awaiting a response. I could read the expressions of both of them that they wanted me away from them for the day, Three) It's not like I've got anything better planned.

I still can't abide football. It serves no purpose to me. It exists to prevent people realising how pointless, miserable and hopeless their lives are, and to stop the majority of the world from rebelling against those who rule over them, as well as keeping them pointlessly divided. While the masses are divided this way, focused entirely on battling each other, the ruling class can continue to screw everybody over with no interference. Red against blue, Town against City, nobody united. They don't just use football for this. I'm pretty sure that tomorrow night, more people will vent their uncontrolled fury at the X-Factor judges than some multinational company poisoning their water supply. The tools used by the powerful to seductively suppress disquiet are many and varied. 5000 crap TV channels, cheap alcohol, mind-bending drugs that the police never seem to quite manage to restrict the supply of, X-Box games that take months to complete, religions, soap operas, and a media that instructs us all to single out foreigners, single-parents or Muslims as the people we should blame for our problems. I'm one of the lucky ones though. I'm only 14 and can see straight through all of that bullshit. I've already made it my conscious life choice to brush aside football, religion, alcohol, drugs, crap TV, in order to one day rise up at 3am and crush the fucking bourgeoisie in between Bake Off and Coronation Street.

Of course, anyone trying to sidetrack me with football tickets is a lost soul standing in the way of this. However, I decided can make positives. I'll be out of town for a few hours, and out of my bit of town too. The change of scenery will be a drive over Snake Pass or a train ride through Edale. Views either way. Most importantly, Manchester beats Sheffield. The local tourist board's ideal advert should be "Visit Sheffield. It's not Manchester. Or Liverpool. But at least it's trying!" I'll cope with the football match. I'll people watch. All those idiots I was on about a bit ago, the 50 year old fat baldy men in the 50 quid replica shirts? I'll probably get some kind of amusement watching them misplace their life loyalties and render their lives meaningless by devoting their short time on this planet to worshipping a multinational corporation that, apart from regularly siphoning money out of their modest bank accounts, barely knows or cares that they exist. Joey Barker will be there. He's a prime example of such tragedy.

I lasted till break time today. Weirdly, I actually couldn't wait to get into school this morning. I wanted to see who'd pick a fight with me now that word had gone round that I was palled up with Shelly and Tariq and Chelsea. It didn't quite go like that.

As soon as I woke, I mentally did a stock-check of the events of yesterday, then thought of all the possibilities today might bring. I thought, and laughed, for a while, about nothing other than Travis Greenshields's facial expression yesterday. There he was, him and his other cockwomble of a mate, sniffing Pendlebury blood as I walked to XOXO on my todd, sensing easy pickings, then his initial glee at the idea of Shelly C doing the job for him, before watching his presumption turn to shit when he saw me park myself down in the company of Shelly and a bundle of older, bigger, infinitely more badass kids than he could summon together in his dreams. That open-eyed, open-mouthed stuck in mid-action pose of his as I looked round. If you can't picture how sweet that felt to me, imagine being given one of those bright yellow cakes they give out at Diwali, and dipping it in treacle before you bite in.

My shower lasted approximately 35 seconds. I even thought about going to school absolutely stinking to high heaven, plonking myself next to whoever gave me the biggest deathglare and seeing their pain. I'm curious to see if anyone treads a little more carefully around me. Breakfast didn't matter. I still have Oreos and some of those orange juice cartons that I liberated for my street-sleeping friend, as yet unopened, in my bag. If I get extremely ravenous I'll be OK. My brain's so scrambled that I didn't even notice the trip to school. Some weird adrenalin took me through the gates and into the tutor room. The main conversation this morning is about Joey Barker. Apparently he hurt his ankle playing football and he's off school for a while cos he's not allowed to walk, and school are cool about it. Apparently, being assaulted by a group of their very own disciplinary cases and left with facial injuries isn't something school can be cool about, so excuse my lack of sympathy for the pampered little snowflake.

"Prima donna", "Next time I fall off me bike check what school does when I turn in late", down to the more empathetic "If I were him I'd do me ankle EVERY time I played", "Nah, stuff that, I'd just fall to't floor 5 minutes in, limp into school, get sent home, then stop off for an ounce on't way."

That Joel lad who I roasted a few weeks ago still deathglares me. I reckon he's biding his time and waiting for his chance to try violence with me when the odds look to be in his favour. I can do without it, but if it comes to it, I'll fight him in full view of as many people as possible. I know the rules of the school pecking order. I used to wallow in my own self-pity as, being a little too unconventional for my peers, I'd be at the bottom of it. Now, half a childhood full of persecution later, I look at it slightly differently. I've nothing to lose whatsoever. I've already worked out he's not that far above me. He sits at the front, and the only kids he talks to are the ones who are all a bit like him, too.

Shironda turns round and asks me "Have you seen owt of Joe?"

"Erm, unlikely." I reply

"Well, you're mates wi' Shelley aren't you?"

She's just being nosy here.

"Not really. I know her though, she's OK. Better than him."

"Edward, love. Don't kid me. You got spotted wi' her squad yesterday. I'm not soft. Where do you know her from anyway?"

Now, my smart answer should've been "kick-boxing" or "ju-jitsu". But it's too early, and I'm not sure it's a lie I could get away with.

"Nowhere really, I just know them."

"Like mates?" Shabana asks, kinda hopeful. She's a bit of a loner too, in that her best mates are streamed into other classes above or below her. She's done me no harm, but she's done me no good either. This is the first time she's spoken to me. I'm curious. I sense I could change many dynamics now.

"Yeah, we're kinda mates."

All of a sudden, from a new direction....

"As if. Tha's chattin some reyt shite!"

Corey Hendricks crew. Not sure which one. They all grunt the same kind of sound.

"OK, I'm not then. Does it affect you particularly?"

"They're either shaking you, or they're leaning on you to keep quiet about summat."

Louis backs his mate up. "Man's getting his wallet shook, payin' safety tax. Everyone knows."

"Pardon?" No idea what he's on about.

"Shoulda thought that one up mesen 'n got in before 'em."

I'm not having this. "Dream on. You'd only try it when there were 4 of you." This could get nasty. Times on my side though. I can see the form tutor in the corridor.

"As if I'd not drop you one-on-one..." Corey does a Wealdstone Raider impression, badly "...if you want some, I'll give it yer". His mates laugh. No-one else does.

I stand up. "You don't do one-on-one. You'd not turn up anywhere on your own."

I feel the total silence in the room. I also feel the hairs sticking up on the back of my neck, arms, and places where I never knew I had hair. I feel a slight shaking in my leg. And arms. Adrenaline at a guess.

Corey rises forwards, his chair falls backwards, he does that arm-gesturing thing that has the same meaning as his words "Fancy a go now?" The adrenaline's mutual.

I stay calm for my reply "Ready when you are."

With both hands, Corey pushes me in the chest, but I'm expecting it. I push him back. He wasn't expecting it. He goes a good 4 or 5 steps backwards, the wall stopping him stumbling further backwards, and bounces back. This time I spot a haymaker coming. Now, I've never done any martial arts, boxing, self-defence, whatever, but I raise my right arm quickly and block his punch. I also realise that this lads never been a boxer or ninja himself. It connects with my head, but without any force behind it. I've nothing to lose. Anything I land on him's a bonus. I jab with my left fist twice into the side of his stomach. He's off balance and his guard is down. I push him again, this time he goes backwards, landing on one of the desks in the middle of the classroom awkwardly enough to knock him totally off balance and onto the floor. The door swings open. The teacher's in. Corey Hendricks on the floor, me standing over him. The teacher stays calm. He knows the true picture here. There's even a slight smile on his face.

"Edward. Corey. Sit down now, and I'll deal with both of you in a minute."

The rooms painfully quiet. I'm trying to work out if I'm going to be acclaimed as a hero, or going to get a full on pasting. My legs still shaking, and I can feel sweat all over my forehead, armpits, even that bit between your ballsack and your arse. I want to scratch. Ladies present though. I'll leave it a bit.

Me and Corey stay at our desks after the classroom empties. Another man, more expensively suited than the form tutor, puts his head round the door, and says "Edward, Corey, follow me please". I'm calm. I let Corey get up first. I want to see his every move. As we hit the corridor I sense a crowd, though I can't focus on it. Corey Hendricks is on his own here and vulnerable. He's got an appointment with the head, and probably thinks he has a full day of my company. Just me. He sits reasonably high up the year 10 hierarchy. I'm the awkward-looking geek. I fancy a mind game.

"If anyone else wants to end up on the floor with my foot on their face like this fool in front of me, then go ahead, wind me up!"

The crowd of kids, all shapes and sizes, none of whom I have any focus on, remain silent.

The head teacher isn't.

"Pendlebury. Enough!"

The crowd doesn't move. Corey walks in front of me, doing some exaggerated ridiculous strut where his feet poke out an extra 45 degrees and his legs are slower in speed and longer in stride. He thinks he looks a top lad, but nah, it looks ridiculous. I see another opportunity. I edge closer as I walk, in the same way I usually do, give his right shoulder a significant push forwards, and, in a much quieter tone than before, almost a whisper, "Stop blocking my stride. Move!!"

He stops dead in his tracks, faces me, starts to go into deathglare mode, but I see through it and smile back. I've got much less to lose than him. I could smile at him all day.

The Heads Office lies behind the main reception, identical to the adjacent deputy heads office, save for a slightly nicer carpet and a large fish tank in the corner of the room. I don't even give the option of choosing who to punish first, I push past Corey Hendricks and walk in.

"I was provoked, Sir, as I am every single day that I attend here. He's one of the..."

"I'm aware, but you cannot excuse your frustrations with violence."

"With every respect, sir, I have every right to defend myself. He's already assaulted me once, and tried to assault me on a separate occasion. When he walks towards me, I know not to expect a hi-five."

"It also means that I have to punish you as well as him."

"With all respect, sir, I believe that..."

"I've heard enough. I'm isolating you for the rest of the day."

"You just interrupted me sir. I'll isolate myself if you don't lis.."

"I'll isolate you for a week if you continue. You're creating far more difficulties for yourself than you need."

"So I'm isolated?"

"For today, yes. And I'll think about next week."

"And isolating means I sit outside your office all day?"

"There are worse places, Pendlebury."

"With him?"

"I'll decide that."

"And if he picks another fight with me?"

"Then you react in a more mature way."

"I don't see how more mature I can be than allow him to plant punches on my left jaw without retaliating. That didn't get sorted. Actually, I've no faith you'll sort this out, I'm going home."

Why did I need to say this? I caught a look at the Heads face and knew the reaction wasn't good. I'm not spending a day in isolation though. I deserve better. I head towards the door.

"GET BACK IN THIS ROOM NOW!!"

I keep walking. Cory Hendricks's waiting his turn. His head's down and avoiding eye contact. I ruffle his hair. He jolts to life, but he's never going to attack me here. I continue my exit.

"PENDLEBURY!!"

"Call my mother. She's expecting you!"

----

21. FANCY CUPCAKES

If Sergio Aguero gets injured, there's probably a legion of people, like personal chefs, masseuses, shoppers, butlers, translators, all of that, to serve his every need. That'll be me one day. Until then, I'll have to make do with my fat sweaty Dad in his Primarni jeans and antique sideburns helping me to a chair he's put in the bathroom where, in the absence of that stunning masseuse, I'll do as much as I can unaided thanks. I managed everything apart from my feet, so the pleasure of strapping my bad ankle and putting my socks and shoes on falls to Dad. Primarni socks, cos no-one cares where your socks come from, and Adidas Neo's, black with white trim. One day I'll be advertising them, but today I'm just happy they're on the correct feet.

Apparently my ankle's looking good, in so far as it looks fucking horrific, and the uglier it looks, the quicker it heals. There's purple and yellow, blue and black, a few different shades of brown. If you've ever seen the sky just before a massive badass thunderstorm, one of them crazy furious ones that blow the roof off everything, then you'd be quite close.

Today's big event. East Stand, Block 107, Row A, Seats 35, 36 and 37. Near the halfway line, 3 rows from the front. Three tickets. Dad got one for Mum, but she's having a girly day with Shelly, which means they're going shopping to buy Shelly stuff, then having lunch somewhere boring. Shelly will photo and upload her lunch onto Instagram and get minimum 100 likes from the same 100 lads who like everything she puts because she's 17, blondish and slim. Even if the food porn she uploads is a deep-fried rat, those 100 likes will still appear. We're going early so that I don't get my ankles whacked. Looks like it's just me and Dad. Dad's eat-out preferences are 1) Indian, 2) Chinese buffet, 3) Chippy. Mine are 1) Nandos, if someone else pays 2) Nandos, if I pay, 3) Spicy African chicken, somewhere with window seats that instantly make you boss of year 10 if you get them. There's some negotiating to do, and I guess Dad may have to concede a little.

I'm ready to go, waiting for Dad, so I get my phone. 33%. FML. Too much time online to Jodie Ramsden last night. I upload a pic of the match tickets. Only 1 comment on my status about missing the game. "*LOL*" (Brodie). 1 like (Dan). On what Brodie put, not me. From anyone else, nothing. Was just about to start scrolling, when suddenly......

"Ping!"

Jodie Ramsden likes my photo. The one of the match tickets.

"Ping!"

Jodie Ramsden "*kwl!*"

If she likes Barcelona, she might like Man City too. And she might even like me.

"*Might be a spare ticket. You free?*"

I stare at my phone. The minute that passes feels like an hour. 32% charged. But I care less than that than about whatever Jodie says next......

"*Rly?*"

I'd better check with my Dad...

"*Al jus chek wi my Dad*"

Offline. Dads downstairs. "Is one of these tickets spare Dad?"

"No. Spoken for now. Picking a mate up."

Silence. Heartbroken!

"Who we fetching?"

"I'll not be getting you into't Etihad in your state all by mesen, so I'm fetchin' a mate who can help me get you through't turnstile and into your seat. You're not as lightweight as you used to be fella."

"Never mind."

"You had someone in mind?"

"Aye but don't worry"

"Not that thug Sam?"

"No. A lass I've bin chatting to."

"You've been chattin' a lass up? You kept that one quiet."

"You know why. Mum. Shelly. Everyone else. You know what they'd be like."

"Oh well. Next time, maybe."

Back online. Jodie texts back

"Ur not jokin bout goin Man City?"

"Not sure. Not sure."

"Mum sez I gotta b bak 2 babysit by 6?"

Offline again

"Dad, what time we gettin back?"

"No idea, fella, I were hoping to get some food, summat hot and spicy."

"If we din't go for food, what time?"

"Dunno, not thought about it. 7 maybe?"

Back online.

"Not back til 7. Dat no good?"

Offline again. Dads on.

"Son, if you reyt like this lass, maybe stop floggin your tickets to Sam 'n tek her instead?"

"Is that how you dazzled me Mum and made her fall hopelessly in love wi' you?"

"Too right, Joe. I rolled up at her front door wi' a massive bouquet of roses, got down on knee and said "Coventry City at home this Saturday. Fancy it, love?""

I wiggle my finger at the side of my head.

"Ask her?"

She's in the living room. I could. She'd tell me a separate story, I know it.

Ping! Back online.

"Wt time u bck?"

"dunno yet. Txt u in a min. If u cn get bk 4 7 do u 1a go?"

Phone's now on 30%.

Dad interrupts my conversation with a "Reyt, we off then?"

I stick my phone and charger in my inside pocket. Dad passes me the crutches that I've avoided using yet. I give up straight away and give them back to him, electing to hop, placing my hands on whatever can support me through the door. I make good practical use of the blue bin, the fence and the wall. Dad holds the car door open, and I make use of his left shoulder as the best prop possible before grabbing the roof of the car, ducking my head down and projecting my arse onto the passenger seat, then rotating my arse 90% as I swing my dodgy leg in first, followed by the good one. The crutches go in the boot.

Ping! Online once more.

Jodie. *"I'll ask Mum. Do I need ££?"*

Offline.

"Dad, if we din't go for food, what time would we get back?"

Only once Dad's reversed the car out of the drive, and we're moving in a forward direction does he bother answering. "No idea. Depends on't traffic. All it needs is one tractor or a big fat sheep sitting in't middle o't road and you're crawling for miles."

"Would it be before 6?

"No chance mate, not even on a good day."

I'm off to City and I'm feeling stressed. I try to plug my phone into the cigarette lighter. Why do cars have these when it's illegal to smoke when driving? I go back to Jodie's page.

"Prob b more like 8 wen we get bk. Dat no good?"

The more I see of her, the more I think "wow, she's amazing". I've no idea what her ethnicity is, I'm proudly colour blind like that. I'll guess at a bit of Asian, a bit of Latina, a bit of Portuguesio, and a bit of Yorkshire in that family history. She's just updated her page. She doesn't just like Barcelona, like everyone does generically, she likes Man City too. That's on for me isn't it? With each swipe, her gallery reveals more awesomeness. In one photo she's got her hair up, but with a blue bow through it. I've seen other girls do it, but not like she does. She can bake cupcakes. I can't even make toast without the fire brigade being called. I can bring a forty yard diagonal ball down from the sky with one foot, and hit that same ball straight afterwards with the other foot, either way round, hard and fast enough to smash a crossbar in two, and make such destruction look like a work of art, but right now, none of that sublime craftsmanship can compare to Jodie's cupcakes, which I've never eaten but only seen on Insta. If I had to choose from Jodie offering me the last one, and crocking my good foot permanently, I'd carefully take my time deliberating over a very tough decision indeed. I must be in love. I notice other small but awesome details. She's got an umbrella with an ice cream pattern, and the handle looks exactly like an ice cream cone. Fucking hell, I've never even used an umbrella in my whole life. But if she was coming to City with us today, I'd hope it rained just so I could get under half of that proper sick brolly.

While I fall hopelessly in love at each picture on Jodie Ramsden's Instagram, I fail to notice the direction that Dad drives the car in. When he pulls up at the side of a street I vaguely recognise as being on the next estate, the horror hits me.

The worst possible outcome.

"Dad are you joking or what?!?"

He's straight out of the door without answering.

For fucks sake!

----

22. AN UPHILL JOURNEY

I do football about as enthusiastically as I do shitting in my hands and clapping, but here I am, on my way to Manchester, the Etihad Stadium to be precise. I appreciate that Manchester's like Mecca if you're into football, and I've read blogs from people who travel stupid distances, like Japan, Singapore, America, all that lot, just to watch a match there, and it really does feel like a sadbastard kind of weird pilgrimage they're making. As far as I'm concerned, Manchester's just a place where it rains all the time. However, Sheffield's grim even on a sunny day, so that's good enough for me. I could do with a change of scenery. I looked online last night. There's plenty of cool places, museums, galleries, whatever to explore there that have nothing to do with football whatsoever, but I'll not be seeing any of those today. That really doesn't matter, though.

I'm there with Unlovable Joe. Nothing in life has any more importance to his tiny little mind than spending a Saturday in somewhere like the Etihad, his life happiness dependent on the outcome of 20 complete strangers who may or may not be able to kick a spherical lump of leather into a designated space at the end of a precisely measured out grassy rectangle. It's guaranteed he's going to be an obnoxious arse when he sees me. However, I've learned over the last few weeks that he's encountered very few people like me. I'm the exact kind of person he'd cross the road from if he could. But then again, ninety nine percent of the population could fit that category.

Knowing that I can annoy him without trying, I'm curious about what I could achieve if I actually threw serious effort into this. The warm fuzzy feeling I gained from annoying the school bully yesterday can easily be recreated with the captain of the footy team. Like yesterday, the lad must be just as shaky without his squad around him, no-one to impress, no crowd to perform for. Paradoxically, I've never impressed anybody in my whole life, and people like him, I probably never will, so, it's not something I've grown to care about too much. With that in mind, I think I'll enjoy today.

The bell rings. Mr Barker. No winding him up, though. He's been OK with me.

"Alreyt Penny. Is the main dude ready?"

"Hiya Mr Barker. Do I need anything?"

"Just yersen pal. Reddeh?"

I say goodbye to Mum, and, with sarcasm, a massive smile and a very excitable *"See you later!"* to Lara, who's reaction is to not move her eyes from her tablet, I'm into the car. Joey Barker's in the front seat, slumped way down. I decide not to throw his crutches out of the window, but elect to employ the same strategy just used on the little sister, a very cheerful *"Morning, Joe!"* which he reciprocates with a grunt, no facial expression and a feeling that it took him his every last effort just to make that grunt.

Mr Barker makes the conversation. What starts out as "Have you been to Manchester before then, Edward?" moves swiftly onto discussions about my Mum liking Robbie Williams and Lara hating him so intensely that they argue about it. The conversation moves on to Oasis, quickly, as only Mr Barker listens to them, then museums, galleries, types of art, then onto World War 2, politics (Mr Barker's definitely left-wing. Passionately, too, if you set him off. I'm not sure if I'm left or centre or even a tad over to the right in some areas, but I don't think I'm alone there). I keep that conversation going a while as I know Joe's got no clue and no interest in any of these subjects. It'll piss him off at the same time, too. The banter is solid between two of the three of us as we leave Sheffield, and when the countryside starts to appear, and the Peak District views appear, then the car starts to go silent as we slow down to check out the scenery. Every now and then Mr Barker points things out like some stream with big rocks in that he used to walk inside when he was a kid and comes out with some story about how him and his mates upset a bees nest in there once. Joe looks bored shitless by it, so I make a point of being interested.

"What does a bee's nest look like?", "How do you sort bee stings out?", "How far does that stream go?"

Any old question, really.

A few miles further, Mr Barker slows down again to point to a couple of campervans parked by a field, the owners of which are searching the field for special mushrooms that if picked, dried out, then cooked later, will get you hallucinating. Joe actually looks through the window for that.

The conversation drops afterwards, as the road narrows, winds and the hills get higher, steeper, to the extent that you can see massive forests growing to the side of one and realise that just to walk up it would take a day, but maybe 5 minutes to get back down if you lie down and just start rolling. Mr Barker's like one of those nervous drivers that slows down for every bend, every traffic light, every built-up area. He's either had a bad accident or a shitload of speeding tickets before. Even when the scenery goes and we're running into the burbs, he's going 40 max.

Joe stays silent, brooding even, for over an hour until he finally spots the brown road signs with the little football symbol on. Then, like a very excited 6 year old outside a sweet shop that'd just found a tenner on the floor, he springs to life.

----

23. NON-UNIFORM DAY

How did I not spot this happening? I could have asked any one of my friends along and been paid immediately for the tickets at a very comfortable profit, if not into my Dad's pockets then deffo into mine. Fuck it, I'd happily empty my junior saver *and* my Nando's fund to bring Jodie Ramsden along and every single rugrat she's babysitting, but of all people, go ahead and bring that mugglewump Edward Pendlebury to the Etihad with us why don't you? He even wears his school trousers and shoes at weekends. I'm bored of this.

"I bet you'd dress like that on non-uniform day!" I manage to sneak in before Dad opened his door.

"I bet you'd still wear your shinpads to play chess!", straight back at me just before the driver's door swung open, and the car chassis heaved under the weight of 100 kilos of blubber in badly fitting jeans and hush puppies.

I thought Dad had missed the lyric battle, but he hadn't. "Any bother 'n we can always go look at the paintings in't Whitworth instead." Whatever that is.

Anyway, we're on our way, the sunshield's down and I'm slouched as low down in my seat as I can get. I keep my eyes open through town just in case I get spotted. No-one saw me, or that thing in the back seat. I need to be ready in case he pulls a phone out and starts uploading, and I need to watch out for Shelly, she's deffo in on this, just in case she sticks owt online. My phone's not charging quickly, still on 30%, so my Snapchat story can wait til we're in the stadium. Jodie's off chat, I were chatting to her until I got out of the house. I text her but she's not got back to me yet. So I'm scrolling. Ben posted *City away!!* a bit ago, which I'd have liked had I been playing, but seeing as I'm crocked, he can get stuffed. I know he's my mate, and as the academy lads go it's him or Brad for bezzies, but he's all brain and no speed on the pitch. He'll get skinned like a bunny today.

I seriously hope Man City stuff them today. Not just win, but spin everyone in circles, leave them tangled up on the floor and hit double figures if possible. I'm not a traitor, I always think like that when I'm off the pitch. Secretly, we all do. Whenever we score, you never see the subs cheering. They've got that creeping worry that the team are awesome without them, and that worry turns to becoming a team mutineer. The only person who doesn't is Brodie, but that's only for the very simple reason that he's got the armband, which deflects from the fact he's one-footed and his technique's shite, so he needs to milk that captain wannabee cult-hero status as much as he can. Brodie is to this team what Scott Brown is to Celtic. Play him against Barcelona and he'll get a total idiot made out of him, but when you've got a scrap against the hated local rivals, the team all of a sudden gets built around him and he plays the full game. Anyway, he's got City today. They're going to spin him round in extremely dizzy circles.

The drive over isn't as bad as the usual motorway brainblock, despite the geek in the back seat indulging in whatever shit conversation my Dad's making. It's tedious. We're on our way to the Etihad and they're chatting about hill-walking and some boring politics wibble. Edward's buzzing off it all. You should check his geek bantz out, "I've always wondered how they make dry stone walls," and "I quite like the Green Party's policies but I'm not sure they'll ever win an election round here" as in, who seriously cares? Every 10 minutes or so Dad slows the car down so we can see the view. I'm not joking. Views as in hills, sheep, not much else. Every now and then we go through some quaint little village that probably costs a million pounds to live in. Personally, I can't see any reason why you'd live here if you had a million quid. There's not even a chippy let alone a Nando's. Dad's talking about how lucky we are having all this on our doorstep, but I'm perfectly happy with a Co-Op, a kebab shop and a tram stop on the next street, thanks.

Check the phone again. Ben and Brad have selfies on already, together, outside the "Welcome to Manchester City FC Academy and Training Facility" sign. That one hurts a little bit. Understated. That one hurts a lot. Tyler's done the same, Oscar's got one that his Dad's taken of him stood proudly, shoulders back, arms folded, cheesy grin, outside the main entrance. Brodie's gone full smarmy *Proud and honoured to Captain Sevenhill City against Manchester City this afternoon*. He's only got 5 likes. I bet they were from his Mum, his Granny, his other granny and her two bingo mates. I bet he reminds his schoolmates every day who he plays for, and they all secretly hate his guts. Kyle McCullum. No photo. Just *Playeing at Man Sity todaiy. Wish me luc*, which he's gonna need. He's going to be busy as fuck in that centre back spot, but compared to Brodie's smarminess, I quite like his modesty so I comment *good luck pal,* which is the same as loads of other people have put on already. Here's the most interesting one of all. Hassan Fawaz is apparently going fishing at Rother Valley Park. His mates have tagged him in. I know that place as well. No-one our age goes fishing anywhere without alcohol or drugs. It's a front. I didn't see him get injured anytime anywhere, so he must have got the envelope. Which for me means I don't need to rush back to fitness.

"Dad, Hassan Fawaz got swat out."

"Didn't you know?"

"Erm. No. I don't do that guessing game no more. I always get it wrong."

"When were't last time he looked interested?"

"I dunno. He scored the other week din't he?"

"He couldn't really have missed that one. Do you remember how he played a year ago?"

"Well he always had that lazy side, but it were part of his game. Drift out of it, mek the centre back think he's got a comfy game ahead then all of a sudden turn and run from nowhere and find himsen one-on-one wi't the keeper."

"And when were't last time he did that?"

"Actually, yeah. Ages ago. Before we went to Spain."

"His heart weren't in it anymore, Joe. It were sad to see him some days."

"Why'd you not want to play, though?"

"How well did you know Hassan off the pitch?"

I'm interested, all of a sudden.

"So what's the crack with him then? His Mum were alright wasn't she?"

"Yes, I'd chat to her. Dad, not so much though."

"Why, what was wrong with him?"

"I played against him a few times back in't day. Big ugly centre forward, proper Billy Whitehurst type, same position as Hassan would've ended up. I always thought he were just a brawler, but he were good enough at that to sign for Rotherham and he made it to't reserves. One day, when he were supposed to be recovering from an injury, he went clubbing wi' his mates, got stupidly drunk, tripped down some steps, and his knee totally went. Guess what happened next?"

"The end."

"Yep. So when he has a son wi' owt like his ability, and having got so close himsen to mekking it, what do you think his attitude were like?"

"Pushy as fu..., I mean...owt"

"I were stood next to him once when Hassan put one wide. Weren't pretty."

"But we all worry about playing badly. You know how tense it gets when a trialist turns up?"

"Not all of you. Dan doesn't, Oscar just gets on wi' it too, but you know their reasons. Hassan were hoping to get let go as he were fed up of how his Dad'd be each time he made a mistake."

"So why didn't the club ban his Dad? They did that before wi' that other bloke years ago, him that wouldn't stop shouting."

"No idea. Hassan's Mum said he were wekkin up in't morning refusing to go to school. Mum needed his older brother to help her drag him out of bed by his arms and legs."

"What's that got to do with owt?"

"Well, the days he did this were always Tuesday and Thursday. Training nights."

"That's reyt sad."

"Exactly. There were no enjoyment in it at all for him. And like everything else in life, if you're doing summat you don't love any more, then you need to leave it behind. He couldn't walk away, as his Dad would've slaughtered him for it, but if he got released, then, seeing as near enough all of you will get released one day, there were no shame."

"I don't love school anymore. Do you think I should stop going?" Edward asks from the back.

"You already have, haven't you?" I reply.

"Well, if people respected me a bit, I'd stay."

"Respect's earned, fella," I reply. "I din't get to where I am without putting a bit of effort in."

"Edward. You're a bright lad. Do you hate school or do you hate getting educated?" Dad asks.

"I love education. I love learning. I hate school."

"So find the bits you love learning about, and focus on them."

"What if I don't find any?"

"Then keep looking."

"So what do you like, Edward?" I ask.

"I like lots of things. I'll not find them in school though. You might have worked out already I don't fit in."

"I hate school too. Still got to go though. Same rules apply to you."

"You fit in. No-one argues with you."

"Dun't matter, dun't mean I like it."

"I have principles. I'm just standing by them."

"Aye whatever."

Dad steps in, "Not long now, look." He points to the little footballs etched on the road signs.

Nobody from school will be bumping into me today, so I don't have to publicly deny that I spent my Saturday with him, so I talk to him. Normally, I wouldn't. But the opportunity of a Nando's attendance depends on it.

"Have you been to City before?"

"I've been to Manchester before but not the football."

"What's the best ground you've been to?"

"I've only been to Bramall Lane. Once. Back in primary school."

"Who were they playing?"

"I didn't see a match. We just went on a trip with primary school once."

"Any good?"

"We sat in this big room for an hour then someone handed out goodie bags."

This is going to be difficult. The good news is we're through all the countryside, and I can spot the stadium rising above the fog in the distance, so it's my turn to get excitable. I put my phone away and focus purely on what's unfurling in front of the windscreen. Two sets of traffic lights further on, I hear my phone ringing, but whoever it is isn't as important as whats beneath those floodlights I'm getting closer to. Whatever they want doesn't matter til 5.30 at the earliest. I let the answerphone deal wi' it.

----

24. GREAT WALLS

In any given school lesson, the feeble-minded idiot in front of me would be gazing through the window even when there's little more than a car park to look at. We're crossing the Pennines on a clear day, Ladybower, Mam Tor, Edale, craggy stone walls dividing the landscape into squares and penning in a million sheep randomly. Through the magnificence of this change from the usual greyness, this idiot has instead opted to admire the breathtaking view of some acquaintance's breakfast, pet cat and whatever other shit the algorithms on Instagram care to throw in front of him. Remind me never to fly over the Rocky Mountains or the Alps with him. He'd watch whatever shit was on the in-flight movie instead. You could take him to the Pyramids or the Great Wall of China and he'd say "OK, whatever, where's McDonalds?" This is what I'm dealing with today.

Anyway, after an hour pretending he's not sharing the same cramped space as me, he puts his phone away and tries to start an uncomfortably awkward conversation about football, safely in his comfort zone, something I've no wish to be in.

So, what is the best football ground I've been to? Erm, hello? Don't they all look the same? Big steel square sheddy things with a light tower at each corner? OK, maybe there's a couple that look interesting, like the one in Germany that glows red in the dark, or the one I saw on Buzzfeed in Slovakia or Slovenia where a steam train ran between the stand and the pitch. I'd even fancy visiting on the off-chance that something more interesting was taking place than just a football match. It really is like asking me which is the best branch of Morrisons I've ever helped Mum buy her groceries from, or the registration number of the cleanest bus I've ever shook my skeleton away on in sub-zero temperatures. I can't answer. I said Hillsborough but it could so easily be Bramall Lane. I'm really not sure, whichever's closer to the City Centre, with a bike shop at the side of it. I could actually say that that was the best bike shop I've ever been in. Anyway, I never saw the pitch, just this businessy room with long black tables that had orange squash, Mini Rolo bars and Penguin bars on every table. I was about 7 years old. I've done well to remember the Mini Rolo bars considering I don't like them.

He is, however, desperate to know where I want to go for food. I can be kingmaker here. His Dad wants curry, he wants Nando's. I see benefits and drawbacks to both. Indian food should win easily. Every mouthful's a total flavour adventure, you get to do the curry burp several hours later, which is much more enjoyable than even the smokey bacon crisp burp and I doubt Joe can handle much on the curry side. He looks like he's one of those people that hits their heat limit at tikka masala. Anything hotter would kill him. I can do a vindaloo without even touching a sip of water and make him look so fucking lightweight he'd not live it down. He'd need to stick a gas mask on just to watch me. Joe's ridiculously desperate for Nando's. I've never been, though I know a lot about it due to how many other kids bang on about it endlessly. The recipes sound good enough, however, and they're easy to cook at home. I've already done it. I went to Tesco's with Mum once and a couple of ladies in bright coloured t-shirts were smiling at total strangers and giving out free bottles of Nando's sauces, one that said "hot" which wasn't, and one that said "mild" which I liked better as it was more honest. Normally, as I'm not as good at cooking Indian food, I should choose that, but... another giant box of positives can be opened up by choosing Nando's, which is namely the whole status thing that goes with that place, and Joe, along with half of my peers, are willing victims to all that bullshit. Being seen in the window seats there matters way more to kids like him than what the food actually tastes like, how much you get or how much it costs. He'd be Instagramming his chicken desperately wanting all of his crew to know he's in Nando's, but no way will he want to let any of them see he's in there with me. That bit would be hilarious. I could agree to go in, annex the window seats, then laugh out loud at his new-found social anxiety. He'd soon be wishing he'd stopped for a crusty sandwich from a petrol station.

So, there's comedy on its way for me, at his expense, either way. I can't lose. I've noticed that when he turns to look at me, his eyes focus on Gerald every time. My siamese twin of a spot is now at Mount Krakatoa level. It could blow at any time now. If it does, it won't just take me with it, it'll take every occupant of this car with it, along with whichever place we're passing at the time. It'd be a national emergency. The awkward conversations end when Joe finally decides to look out of the window and suddenly goes into hyperactive mode. "It's there Dad!" Phone out, snapping away. "Get in!" "It looks proper mint, that." All I can see is a giant car park and some officey type buildings.

So we're at Man City. It's a smart enough place, like an Olympic village might look, but it's not quite NASA headquarters, though if it was, then I could be interested in something. Joe's eyes and mouth are wide open. He stops still, leans on his crutches, "Check this out, Dad, its proper sick!" To me, nothing glows in the dark, no steam trains chuff along the touchline anywhere, but Joe's too easily pleased, This is definitely his Great Wall of China moment.

---

25. LUNAR ETERNITY

I can feel a hammer crashing down on my foot with every step, but it doesn't matter. Netflix, X-Box tournament, whatever, I can rest it properly tomorrow can't I? It doesn't matter that geeky Edward also took 1000, 2000 steps alongside me, oblivious to being within the gates of the most amazing football stadium a kid our age could ever get to play in. In all honesty I'd have happily walked in here with Corey Hendricks, or whilst lovingly holding the hand of the most annoying lass in year 8 that fancies me. I don't really care that I'm on the sidelines watching less talented team-mates get destroyed by probably the best team in the country. Actually I'm lying, emotionally it hurts way more than the bloated elephant ankle ever could physically, but wasting the day on the sofa scrolling everyone else's inane shit would be even more painful. I'm happier here, making the most of a bad job, losing a tenner and finding 50p.

This should be my Cup Final. All those early mornings, All those hours sat on sheddy buses queuing on motorways to dull towns like Grantham and Sutton Coldfield that you'd never look through the window at let alone stop off. Every single one of the eggy, putrid farts I suffered that Brodie sneaks out on the bus for 'bantz', all in the knowledge there'd occasionally be days like these. I'm even tolerating Edward Pendlebury. To be fair to him, he's not pissed me off yet. Early days though.

There must be a hundred pitches here, each one a pristine, immaculate blank canvas laid out especially for a footballing artist such as me to produce the most wonderful works of creative genius on. Each one has a stand alongside that could house the same crowd as a decent sized non-league club. I spot my game, still doing the warm ups, though it'll probably tek me the entire first half just to hobble over there. Edward's saying very little. Dad, on the other hand, is in peak muppet mode........

"Tha's a lucky lad, I never got to play these. There weren't even an Etihad back then. City were crap back then. Their ground were bang in't middle o' Moss Side. Every house on't surrounding streets had metal shutters on and every pub had bullet holes in't doorways. Only a nutter would hang around for a pint after."

It's probably true, but also irrelevant to the moment, so I don't care. We reach the steps to the stands. There's even a space for the TV cameras on the training pitch, and shitloads of advertising adorning the sidelines in Chinese, Arabic, and other funny writing. I make it down a few steps with the help of Edward in front of me, holding my crutches while I put my weight onto the handrail. Getting mesen back up them will be fun, but I'll worry about that later. As I manoeuvre at snail pace to the seats, I notice MY team getting ready for a team photo. I could sit down somewhere, but I stay on my feet in case I get spotted and they carry me over and get me in on the photo.

No-one's looking over. At all. Unfortunately.

"I remember going to Maine Road in about 1990. Manchester were proper grim back then."

Shut up Dad.

My team's photo line up in full view of me, 7 at the back, 6 at the front, a coach at each end. They'll probably need to line up like that in the game so they can keep the score down.

"Got to Piccadilly then got proper drenched waiting for't taxi. Pissed it down as usual."

Dad. Who cares? Seriously.

Front row. Brad, Dan, Brodie in the middle crouching like Polish gopnik badboys when they're sat drinking in the park except he's pressing his hands on the match ball and not a bottle of something weird, then Tyler, Naz, Ben. Why the fuck's Tyler in the middle? That's my spot.

"Soon as we said Maine Road, the taxi drivers face turned white wi' dread, which were summat considering he were Pakistani."

Dad. Just. Stop. Now.

It's like I'm invisible or something.

"Drove like the clappers through Rusholme, he did."

Dad. Even Big-Bang-Theory Edward's not listening.

"It weren't long since Vinny Jones had signed for United from Leeds. If he were starting you knew it were gonna be a scrap."

Dad. Absolutely no-one cares. No-one.

I scan the line up. Normal squad, minus me and Hassan Fawaz. One unusual face at the end of the back row, stood next to Benny the tictac man. Clock him as Josh Smith from the under 14s. A good sign. It means there's no trialist trying to get me released. He's got my number 10 on his back. The master craftsman. The one with the magical footwork. The flair player. The inventor. Pele's number. Zidane's, Cruyff's. He can fucking dream on.

"He twatted City's centre mid straight from kick off. Booked in 10 seconds."

DAD JUST SHUT THE FUCK UP!!!

Photo gone. Not one acknowledgement from my team-mates. None of them. From the coaches walking towards us, Benny looks blankly at me, mumbles "Alreyt" then turns and faces the pitch.

Like you do with random dog-walkers that you pass by when you walk along the canal.Like the one kid in your highly-talented junior football squad who could make you famous, whose development could keep you in a very well-renumerated salary.

Dan looks at me then looks away before I say anything. He's got Brodie's cockiness, but uses it more smartly. Tyler arches his back and faces forward. Kyle and Jamal centre backs, quick fist bump between them. Brodie's doing his motivational gee-the-players-up gestures but no-ones paying attention. Brad and Sam on the left, Naz up front. The subs come over, Mo and Tyrell. No acknowledgement from them. I truly fucking hope Man City stick 10 in minimum. They can all trip up over their own fucking goosebump hair for me.

"10 seconds. It were a world record at't time"

Dad. Just go and jump in the sea.

I edge away from the front rail to find a space where I can fall back into a seat. I spot the players parents, chatting away, sipping coffees, watching the security guy so they can pull off a quick photo opportunity in order to make themselves Facebook-fabulous later on. The City parents are dispersed, scattered in ones and twos across the stand. Over the next 90 minutes Edward will home in on each one of them and, with inappropriate enthusiasm for this setting, tell me the languages they were speaking.

Oscar's Dad shouts over "Alright Joey lad, how's your ankle?"

"Getting' better thanks."

"Good lad."

Why did I just say that? It's fucking far from alright thanks. It's so swollen that it looks like it belongs to someone 5 times my size. Anyway. At least he could be arsed to ask. I was hoping for City to trash them not just because they're a bunch of ignorant smarmy cunts who can't even respect an injured team mate on the sidelines, but primarily because they'd learn how poor a side they are without me. It looked quite even for about 20 minutes. Then their centre mid, striker and attacking mid played 3 or 4 one-touch balls to each other, between Ben, Brodie and Jamal every time, that finished with a final diagonal ball going through to the penalty area that their left winger, an Asian looking lad who were too fast for Dan, let alone Ben, got to a good couple of seconds before Oscar could ever hope to, and slotted it under him into the net. No celebrations, just a trot back to the centre circle to restart. I guess they'd done that manoeuvre countless times against stronger teams. Just before half time, Josh Smith, my stunt-double, did my trick of knowing exactly where and how to fall over, and took the penalty even though he should've let Naz or Jamal make a proper job of it. The keeper pushed it away, but Josh was first in on the rebound. 1-1.

1-1 had "our" boys on a false sense of security. City put 3 subs on, clearly their match-winners, and no-one could cope with them. If I were honest about it, I'd probably struggle, they were that good, but as I'm sitting the game out injured, I don't need to be harsh on meself. The attacking midfielder had tricks that he made look so simple and effortless. Within 2 minutes he turned

Brodie inside out, casually skipped over Kyle's outstretched leg, put his foot on the ball with his right then slotted it wide of Oscar and just inside the left post with his left. As the game went on, he'd go from 0-60 in a second, not need to trick anyone, just use that bit of speed to make a bit of space and let fly. The other midfielder was like Stevie G, without the slipping over bit, just endlessly played from box-to-box, picked passes out that sent defence to attack every time, or went from 50-50 balls to safe possession every time. He hit the third, a screamer from outside the box that flew into the top corner. You could see Brodie losing his head with him, the pushes, kicks, sly nudges getting more intense but this lad just brushed Brodie off like he wasn't there. Brodie got subbed before he properly lost his rag, which were deffo the right move, so he can sit down, watch, learn. I bet he learnt nowt though. The striker, the most slender looking kid on the pitch, looked like one of those kids who'd just get knocked off the ball all the time, a simple well-timed shoulder or elbow nudge would be all it took, but Jamal, twice his size, couldn't put him down. He dropped into midfield later on, but even then, he dribbled round our entire defence and laid the fourth on a plate, then did the same a minute later but got greedy and scored it himsen for the fifth. They scored a sixth late on, I weren't paying attention. I were looking at and absolutely loving the faces of frustration on my team. They missed me, but they'll never admit it.

It were like an exhibition. The other parents fell silent, silent in that sinking realisation that their cherubs won't be in the Premiership or the Champions League, and had just been destroyed by the cherubs that will. Even the kids that City let go could just ring us for a trial and they'd be in after 5 minutes. No-one's buying that mansion in Spain in 10 years time on the back of their child's sublime talent. I'm glad they got stuffed. Oscar walked straight past, just his Dad said hello. Jamal, Tyrell, Mo, all left very quickly with one of their parents arguing about food or something. Brodie just looked at me and looked away, head down, Sam the same. Naz walked out with the coach. He's signed. Him and his folks were the happiest ones there. In all, I got "aye up" off Ben and a nod of the head from Brad. And they're supposed to be my closest mates, the ones I have 7 glorious years of all-conquering history with. The coaches pissed me off too. I mean, "How's your ankle?" wouldn't have hurt. I'm very much aware that Sevenhill City aren't the only football club on the planet. I could easily give Grimsby or Notts County a call.

Dad has a theory that each kid at the academy is merely a number to them. He compares the football academy system to a book he loves called Brave New World, which he keeps telling me I should read sometime, but I have better things to do. He often calls our training ground "The Hatchery", calls the kids the "Alphas", and thinks everything's a bit too sterile and too much is controlled, and sports training should be more enjoyable and laid back than it is. He restrains his opinions when he's on the sidelines of course, but he airs it all at home a fair bit. As Dad clocks the lukewarm greetings, he pats my shoulder and says "You look like you're ready for a bit of soma and a trip to Lunar Eternity, son"

I've no idea what he's on about. I wish he'd just call it the Etihad and stop chatting shit.

26. A Collaborative Vision To Harmonize The Wider Business Community

The Etihad Stadium, also known as the City of Manchester Stadium, was built in 2000 at a cost of £112million, for the Olympic Games, which then got given to Sydney instead because, erm, where would you rather go if you ran marathons? It has space for 55000 rabid football supporters each match day to cough up near enough their entire week's wages to sing show tunes in unison if a goal gets scored. Today that'll be 54999, because three rows from the front in block 107, sits an apathetic teenager who seriously couldn't give a shit which bunch of well-numerated total strangers scores the most goals. It makes no difference at all to my life happiness or contentment whatsoever. I'm here because I've never been before, and if I'm going to criticise anything, which I intend to do purely to annoy Joey Barker during his period of incapacity, then I need to know what I'm talking about. The stadium looks awesome once you're in it. There's so many possibilities for this place. Manchester should bid for the Olympics again, tell the footballers to chuff off, and then see what Danny Boyle could knock up for an opening ceremony. When Aerotropolis is finally built in 50, 100, 500 years time, the local sports centre will look something like this, but hopefully with a few things better to do than kicking a ball around. It probably won't be in fucking Sydney either.

Man City won the game. As I said, I didn't care. Joe was delighted. He seriously did care. His entire mental well-being depends on a team of hairy-arsed men in shiny shorts, all strangers to him, scoring more goals than another team of hairy-arsed men in different-coloured but equally shiny shorts, again, all of whom he'll probably never meet. He's being OK with me right now. I've helped him across the road, through the crowds and safely to his seat without further injury to his precious ankle, but I expect in time he'll default back to an insufferable obnoxious arsehole once more. He's cocky with everyone. His ability to perform circus tricks with a ball apparently makes him superior to anyone who can't do as many keepie-uppies as him. I can see why the other kids on his team don't talk to him. He was even more of an arse with them than he is with anyone in school. He needs to calm that Billy Big-Bollocks bullshit down. He's very dependent on his remaining functioning ankle being injury free right now.

Everywhere you look, there's advertising and corporate wibble. A shop the size of a large supermarket sells every kind of occasional shit you can imagine. Fridge magnets, baby bibs, hot water bottles, all with the club badge on, sell for considerably more money than Tesco could dream of charging. In any other setting, no-one would pay £7 for a teacup, but the football supporter's mindset isn't the smartest. Here, gigantic security beasts on the door allow a queue of maybe a hundred people enter the shop two or three at a time. Joe was desperate to join the long procession of the gullible, but his Dad, probably hoping to use his monthly salary on more useful things like food and electricity, persuaded him that he'd never get through the throngs of wide-eyed shoppers on his crutches. Joe does, however, get to choose where we eat later. I can predict kids like him every time. My money's on Nandos.

This is how much I know about Man City. 1) Oasis are their biggest fans. Old blokes love them. There's a bit more angriness in their dad-anthems than I prefer, but there's plenty of worse music out there. I can listen to them. If the Olympics ever do come to Manchester, and Danny Boyle gets the job, I'd recommend he gives them a slot on the opening ceremony, along with Bugzy Malone, The Smiths and The Fall. Take That can piss off though. 2) Their old shirts look better than their new ones. There's an old one, simple plain blue with a white circle around the collar, free from any advertising. If I was going to own a football shirt, I'd choose something like that. It's probably on sale in the megastore for the same price as a week in Tuscany, but you could feasibly get something similar from H&M and then stitch a cloth badge over it. 3) I can name some of the players. Zabaleta sounds cool, as does Kolarov and Caballero. Don't ask me what any of them look like, I won't know. I just heard their names getting announced, and I'm sure I'll have forgotten them again by 6pm.

All manner of dull shit went on while the stadium filled up, mainly with pale blue, and a few stripy Tesco value shirts in a corner to the right. Promotions took place for anything from bank loans to chocolate bars, some group of teenage girls danced with pompoms, some old man in a suit that I've never heard of walked to the middle of the pitch, waved to each side of the ground and got a massive round of applause. At least when the match starts, it can't get any more mind-numbing than this. The players' names were read out by an invisible man with a microphone, and Joe cheered each one. I don't get it. He might as well cheer each name that gets called in registration in school each morning. It's exactly the same thing.

Joe's programme, a brochure rammed with adverts and wanky business bollocks, cost £5. If anyone knows what a "collaborative vision going far beyond the club itself, but harnessing through key partnerships, an impressive platform to engage and harmonize the wider business community" actually means, please explain. I'm in top set English and it just sounds like toss to me. Joe's Dad sees what I'm looking at and advises that if I think that's bad, I should visit Newcastle where it's the same thing but with SportsDirect plastered everywhere. I expect every ground's like this. If your local stadium's called "the Emirates", or "the Britannia", or "The Sports Direct Arena", I guess you become a prisoner to all that bullshit if you let yourself.

If anything, this isn't what I was expecting from a match at all. Mr Barker was talking earlier about when he came here years ago and everywhere was dog-rough, people got stabbed if they parked their car on the wrong street, and everyone stayed standing and singing together for the full game, making the terraces stink of what was left of 10000 dodgy beers, burgers and spliffs. The manner in which he described it all, even the walk in the dark through a maze of backstreets in pissing rain where one wrong turning guaranteed a brick crashing into your face, was fondly nostalgic. I glance over at him and he looks bored stupid. 2 minutes from kick off, and whatever atmosphere Mr Barker said there used to be, isn't there today. I've worked that much out.

Joe's not thinking about any of this at all. He's focused on the pitch, and animated when the teams walk out. He stays this way through kick off, calms down 5 minutes in, then gets excitable when the first goal goes in. He yells again 5 minutes later when the second goal goes in. A really tall black guy called YaYaYaYaDory scored that one. I know that as everyone sang his name. He calms down 5 minutes after that, through half time, then tries to bounce around not long into the second half, when a blonde haired tall guy took a shot from quite a way away from the goal, the keeper dropped it and the little dark-haired guy scored from the rebound. Joe tries to join in with the singing, which there isn't much of, even for a team winning 3-0. The other team score one later on, where their small bundle of stripy fans jump around for approximately 30 seconds and then sit down again. The match finished 3-1. I know this simply because I can count, not that I paid much attention to the game. I people watched everyone around me.

For a football ground bedecked with so much corporate businessy stuff, the fans in the ground look like the people least likely to ever make use of it. Along from me, two teenage lads in pale blue tracksuit tops, short, gingery with permanent snarls and facial expressions similar to rats when they're just about to chew through something. The other side of me, a chunky balding 30, maybe 40 year old, with a couple of teeth missing and a MCFC hoodie that he must have earlier spilt his dinner on going by the gravy stains down the front of it. In front, a thin man smelling of beer, slightly red in the face and eyes, with his primary school age son, both of them occasionally getting up to clap or shout something, blocking my view at the same time, though I don't really mind about that too much. I can't see any of these guys sipping many cocktails whilst watching the corporate entertainment in the Platinum Lounge, where refreshments are complimentary for Gold Card Customers. In fact, I guess most of them would do well to afford a day in Blackpool, let alone fly off to Dubai on a swanky plane, but here they all are handing over a small fortune to advertise an upmarket Arabian airline for free across their chests.

The corporate shit never ends. An electric scoreboard reminds us that being here is a "lifestyle experience". I've seen enough. I think Joe's Dad has. He says little through the game, standing and clapping only when a goal is scored or a substitute comes on. I'm guessing that the actual "lifestyle experience" encountered by the old guys years ago, like he banged on about earlier - getting drunk, singing and swearing for 2 hours and getting your head smashed in by skinheads on your way home - was more attractive to him, even if the best bit of it was actually getting back through your front door with the same number of teeth you left with.

Sometime between Mr Barker's childhood and mine, giant mega-corporations bought these football clubs, trashed their identities and replaced them with new desensitised sterile ones that make them money with endless opportunities to scam whoever tries to share in this identity. Each opportunity, each premium rate text service that updates you with the reserve goalkeeper's loan move, is a slightly more ingenious scam than the last one, and the ways these businesses extract even more money from their 'loyal' supporters continues forever. Supporters my arse. It doesn't matter how fanatical these people around me are, or how few home games they've missed since they learned to walk, or whereabouts on their body they tattoo the club badge, their loyalty is as meaningless as their life-identity. They're just customers, consumers in the same way that Mum supports Aldi when she gets her groceries there. The only difference is that my Mum would instantly shift somewhere else if anyone tried to charge her £2 for a donut.

It were a proper slow trundle across the road, and then there were stuff like crowds and steps I needed help with, but if I really have damaged my ankle further and put myself on the sidelines for 3 years, I felt no pain and noticed nowt. Our seats, 3 rows from the front, next to the aisle, meant I could stretch my leg out a bit once the match kicked off. The only frustration is I can't leave my seat, not even to stand up, but I don't care. We got in the ground early. The club shop were rammed inside and queuing out, but I accepted it was a bad idea going in and will use the missed opportunity to press my case for cheeky Nandos later. I checked my phone. Might just get home with 23%. I managed to twist myself round so I could get a selfie in with the pitch behind me, without Edward's spotty mug in the frame, so I stuck it on my Snapchat story. Stuck "*Unlucky lads*" onto whatever the academy boys uploaded. Sarcasm and sympathy on one go. A smack in the mouth and an arm round the shoulder. No replies. Probably sleeping it off. They got educated this morning.

Message from Jodie. "*Where r u?*"

Sent 2 hours and 34 minutes ago.

Shite!! Got so occupied wi't footy I forgot all about her. Better text back. "*in MCR. U?*".

Scrolled for a bit. Some dippy lass from year 9 filmed herself and her mate getting thrown out of Maccy D's, giggling endlessly about it. Classy. Made Edward look not so bad. I expected Edward to be proper full on train spotter today, but he's not done much to piss me off, although, if he does start going into arsenugget mode, I'm not exactly able to do much about it in my incapacity.

It's a reasonable enough sacrifice if I think about it. I have the irritation of a full day with him, but it's also the irritation of a day sitting in the Etihad on match day. What does this compare to? Maybe like having double English Lit of a Monday morning, but the book you're doing is "The History of The World Cup", or you've got to clean up til the kitchen and living room are both spotless, 'cos Mum has visitors coming, but the visitors are the ice-dancing squad and they're all bringing cupcakes round. That kinda thing.

Anyways. This is the shit I dream about. If me pulling 360s on this turf less than 5 metres from where I'm sat never happens, I'll tell everyone it's OK, I know how difficult it is and how lucky I'd have to be and all that, but deep in my most private thoughts, it doesn't get any worse. All those other kids who say they want to pimp chromy badass cars up, or run YouTube channels with a million followers, or step into a boxing ring, none of that registers wi' me. I think more along the lines of employing one of them to pimp my car up, or manage my profiles. I consider this a bit more and realise how this unreformable geek sat with me would probably excel at all that boring shit, managing websites, doing accounts, organising my servants, and owt else I'd not be arsed with doing myself. If he gets through today without being an arse, I'll move him up the scale of possibility a bit. Needs to get himsen to a decent hairdresser, mind.

As the ground fills up, I imagine how mad this place must've been when they needed to win that 93:20 game on the last day to clinch the Prem. What it must've been like when the injury time equaliser went in and the commentator shouted *"Manchester United have done all they can... Wayne Rooney's goal good enough for the 3 points at Sunderland ... Manchester City are still alive here...... Balotelli......AGUERROOOOOO!!!!"* shirt off, diving into the orgasmic crowd, Joe Hart running round in madman circles in his penalty box. The commentator's lyrics were good enough for our living room. I remember Dad falling out of his chair, me dancing around the living room, jumping and manic play-fighting, then Shelly coming downstairs, looking at us rolling around on the floor like animals in a mud bath, whispering "for fucks sake" and returning upstairs again 10 seconds later. That's the buzz you can get from football, though only occasionally. When it does, it's never forgotten. I can pick out watching Liverpool win a Champions League final when I were really small and the buzz were electric. Then this match where Celtic did Barcelona with 2 lucky potshots and an hour of desperate backs to the wall defending and getting lucky deflections. When you're playing, there's more chance. I get that buzz every time I score. If you're watching, it's rare, but once in every blue moon, it happens. Blue moon indeed.

"Remember that QPR game, Dad?"

"Aye."

Aye? Is that it? I remember every fine detail, from the bounce off Zab's deflection to the total strangers hugging each other in the stands like long-separated twins who just got reunited. Fuck it, if I was a doctor I'd prescribe the last 5 minutes of that game as an antidote to depression, personally.

"Bet it were mint in here that day"

"Aye"

Enthusiasm. There's Dads policy of not supporting a team in action right there. Like, who in their right mind cheers for both United and Wednesday? Even when I score a worldy he resembles a shop dummy on the sidelines. No real passion unless he's been to the bookies or there's some ethical shit involved. I know most of that. Celtic over Rangers, Barca over Real, Wimbledon over MK, St Pauli over everyone, not that he ever bothers going to watch any of them. Even the 93:20 game needed a season long bet of £20 at 4-1 odds to get him bouncing about. I thought Balotelli were going to be daft enough to try shooting, but the nudge to his left with the outside of his boot was mathematically and scientifically perfect, Aguero took one on, then two, knocked it out of his feet, just good enough for his right to put a bit of power in it, keeper didn't read it, then the carnival that erupted straight after. I scan the stand to my left where the cameras focused, where it got proper messy, 57 varieties of uncontrollable human emotion unleashed. If there was ever a drug that kicked all that lot off, I'd rob my closest loved ones of their last pennies to try it just the once.

"Did you ever see that 93:20 match, Edward?"

"That what match?"

Bloody hell. "Dun't matter mate." Polite conversation. One more try. "What do you reckon will happen today then?"

"Oh City will probably win."

"What score?"

Edward looks at me a little disgusted, like I'm asking the resident professor of astrophysics at the University of Oxford his 3 times table. Dad steps in, "Personally, I'd expect West Brom to get battered, but there's always that chance that City could bombard them, the ball just won't go in, then Baggies could sneak a lucky break or a jammy deflection somewhere. Not a match I'd slap money on."

"I reckon West Brom will try and stick it out first half, not get ambitious. If they get to an hour at 0-0, then this place will get nervous, the big teams always do. We do at our level. City should go all out early. Get it all put to bed in't first half hour."

"10 defenders behind't ball, leave a little fast guy to run at the defenders til he's knackered by half time, then bring another little nippy lad on for't second half, hoping Di Michelis or someone, but probly Di Michelis, slips over like Stevie G."

Edward's out of this. It's only like taking me to the ballet and asking me stuff, so fair do's. It's not long before the grounds rammed, the teams are out, and I forget about my ankle for a bit. The goosebumps kick in. I hear, and feel, a roar to the left of me, then behind me, then across the whole ground. I want to get up like everyone else. The goosebumps prevent me more than the ankle does, and the shiver down my spine paralyses me further. I really should've gone for a piss earlier. There's every chance I could make my leg warm in an unplanned way during the next 2 hours.

As for the match, it took about 15 minutes to break the opposition down. Silva took on his man just outside the box, got to the goal line and curled a low ball in with the outside of his left foot that Sergio read before anyone else, and despite two brummie defenders who'd been double-marking him since kick-off, his foot got there first, their feet caught him, but the ball was over the line. The noise was deafening. My heart vacated its normal place behind my ribcage and moved northwards through my throat and into my mouth, beating at the same rate as that piss-poor clubland music that Cory Hendricks' mandemz play on their phones sometimes. Not long after, Yaya played a one-two with yer man Sergio, got himself 1 on 1 with the keeper who spread himself wide while Yaya just chipped over him. My heart beats now at a level where someone took the shitty music off Cory Hendricks' phone and did a speeded-up remix on it, like bassline DJs do with old R&B tunes. Apart from a sliver of stripy shirts kettled in the far corner, I'm the only person in the whole ground who's sat down, but to be fair I'm actually preventing myself having a heart attack. Early in the second half, their keeper spills a shot that DeBruyne sent in from distance, Sergio gets to the rebound, and seconds later he's diving into the fans with his shirt off just to my left. The ref dishes out a yellow to him for it, but he doesn't seem to care. He smiles as he takes his yellow, like Dan does when he's been caught winding his opponent up. West Brom pull one back late on. I don't pay much attention to it, it'd been game over for at least half an hour, and City were showboating.

Of all their showboaters, Silva's my man. If the coaches told me to sit and study someone today, it'd be him no bother. Not much point me studying Yaya or Sergio or Kompany, I don't play like them. Silva's only slender, but he's not even the artist, he's more like the magician when he decides to be. Of all the turns, through balls, passes he makes, any of the other fellas on the pitch could practice them all week and still not manage it. Whyever he's in England I don't know. Barca would suit him perfectly. Imagine him behind Messi. Of course the downside of this is he does the business for 1 game, then next week he'll go missing and get subbed off at half-time. But consistency's for less skillful players isn't it? At one stage he goes for a 50-50, flicks the ball with his right just as the opponent slides in, he jumps over him and before he lands he curls a diagonal out to the other wing, then keeps his run going before Nasri or whoever it was spunks an awful cross over to Sergio thinking he's 22 feet tall. I make a mental note of that one. I'll do that one on the back yard, the same way I perfected the rest of my repertoire. But for the last half hour, I study everything he does.

The ground wasn't that noisy, but when Blue Moon started, the whole ground sang it, except of course for the away fans. And Dad and Edward. Shop dummies. I'm surprised no-one checked them out and asked if they were Arsenal fans who'd got lost. I'll teach them the words on the way home.

----

28. Dribble and Pass

I saw the uncomfortable wriggling, legs double crossed, and recognised that body stance as the same one I used to perform in nursery. Mr Barker thought Joe would get trampled in the stampede out of the ground, so kept us back while everyone else left, unaware that his son, in the midst of his excitement at spectating at a football match, had a bladder even weaker than his knackered ankle. No way could he drop so low socially as to request to visit the boys room, not with me around to rip into him for it as remorselessly as I've been ripped into for not being identical to everyone else, a treatment that he hasn't taken an active part in, but has spectated with the same enthusiasm that he devoted to City's second goal going in. Watching him emerge from the gents toilets trying to hide that big wet penny in his trouser pocket made my day.

He knows. He's suddenly trying to be my bezzy. "What did you think o't match, Edward?", "What were't best bit?" even "You up for doing this again?" As if we'd always been mates. As if he'd ever thought about anyone out of his steadily shrinking bubble. As if he'd never talked to me like I was dogshit before. As if he didn't wee his pants 20 minutes ago. Frenemies at best, pisspants.

I can see all the way through him. I've accepted seeing him as the most popular kid in school, "popular" on account of the popular kids announcing loudly to everyone that they're popular whilst simultaneously giving the less "popular" of us a signal that they're actually obnoxious. I digress. Joe's popular in that all the younger kids look up to him, and teachers daren't discipline him too harshly just in case one day he becomes the kid that they tell everyone in the pub that they taught once. It's all a massive steaming pile of bullshit. Yeah, he's popular in school now, but on that glorious day in the future when everyone leaves school behind, he'll be left behind too. All the popular kids will, once the environment alters to no longer favour their vanity, where no-one anywhere cares who you used to hang round with or what label trainers you had. That slow, terminal decline in social importance has just begun, that first weekend party that they're unaware of until the following Monday, that drop, 1 or 2 at a time, in their online friend count, not knowing who deleted them or why anyone possibly would, all the way to that club night a couple of years from now that they'll be desperate to be seen at, but aren't on the guest list. He's still a couple of years from queuing outside the club in the rain jealously watching others strut in before him, but he started getting acquainted with that feeling today. He knows, but isn't letting on, and in his confusion of how to cope with it he adopts the tactic of gradually becoming nicer to me through the day. I'm reciprocating, but I know he knows I know he knows.

Firstly, let me repeat this once more. It sounds too funny to be true, but it happened. I witnessed Joey Barker do a big wet mess in his jeans. If I did this I'd be changing schools for a third time, to a boarding school miles away, which still may not be enough. It may need to be a boarding school on Mars, in a cave. All because watching the football was more important to him than emptying his bladder. He emerged from the loo with nowhere to hide. I have no empathy. He's a big lad now. He should know what to do.

Sensibly, he opted to delay food until we renavigated the Pennines. Give that big piss patch time to dry. I sat behind him and could see everything on his phone. Being the owner of a dumbphone with zero capability of embarrassing myself online, I should exploit this to my advantage. I watch his social standing, his revered place in the Champions League spots at St Kevin's Community Academy year 10 hierarchy, drop down several rungs over the course of the journey. He's been commenting on his team mate's pictures all day, with no likes or replies, and he's deffo not used to being ignored. I know none of those kids, but it was clear to see their indifference to their "mates" presence either during or after their match. He looks down on his schoolmates whilst classing these guys as his main buddies. They obviously see things very differently. One of them, I caught the name Dan, put in capitals *"AS IF I EVEN FUCKING KNOW YOU??"* The only reply he received. This could be uncomfortable.

Another text. Jodie. Quite pretty, though it's never clear how much editing goes on when lasses take selfies. *"Thanks for wasting my day. I cancelled babysitting for you. Tosser!"* If her photo's been edited, her correct usage of the English Language hasn't. Her name was faded out, so she's binned him out of her life. He was silent for ages after that, even looking out of the window to take some of the views in.

His fall from the popularity pinnacle continues. I witness him text Sam Blake and Archie Connell to ask what they're up to later or tomorrow or whenever. After 10 minutes of his phone being completely silent, he texts Tom Carroll and Omar Levy with the same *"WUU2?"* or *"Fifa L8r?"* with a continued lack of pingy noises or little red boxes in the top corner of his screen. Only after sending identical messages to Nathan Miller, Josh O'Connell and Ben Atkins does a solitary reply arrive, a very simple one saying *"busy fam"*. 2 minutes later, he pulls his silent and message-free phone out again and starts a text to Jodie, followed by Shironda, both of which he erases before switching to the football results, showing no major emotions as he glances down the screen. He's not in a good way at all, but this doesn't mean I'll necessarily empathise. I've learned to live without "friends", genuine or fake. There'll be a time when I'll consider having friends, but I don't think it needs to be now. I have a feeling Joe may try to develop a friendship with me that will last until someone appears who he deems more 'popular'. I will simply return any polite exchanges that he initiates respectfully with equal courteousy, but also have popcorn and a giant deckchair set up on the other side of the road ready for the moment his social issues suddenly escalate.

West Street at 7pm was host to students, office bunnies, Bugs bunnies, Easter Bunnies, Playboy bunnies, a few beardy hipster types trying too hard to look as innovative and original as every other beardy hipster type in every street in every city in the UK, groups of oldies with shoulder pads, baldness and polo shirts de rigeur, wobbling their soft bellies along to their 17th bar of the day, belting out some cheesy party song and losing a stiletto or two. It was that lull between the shoppers going home and the party people building their night up to its inevitably classy finale of brawling over taxis, vomiting on the pavement then using a doner kebab and garlic mayo as the most failsafe way to replace the vomit aftertaste. Briefly overpowering scents of some perfume that smelt like petrol passed by intertwined with occasional whiffs of Lynx desperation or hints of poor quality cannabis here and there. Joe had earlier pleaded incessantly for Nandos, though not so much on the way home. From what I've heard so far, ice-cream vans play better music than Joe does on his phone, so I doubt the African music in there holds much attraction, and there must be half a million different places in this city that offer some type of spicy chicken. The only attraction to him was the window seats. Just being seen in there raises your profile on the stupid school pecking order. Every kid who walks by glances at the window to see who's sat there. But today, he has a dilemma. He'd be seen with me. I never frequent the place, but I do know that the hottest chicken in the hottest sauce with the hottest chilli passes through my taste buds as if it's vanilla ice-cream. I'd savage him. I'd charge him £10 just to swap the little flaggy label over. Although I don't care about that school hierarchy nonsense and never will, it was all about avoiding embarrassment and maintaining his position. He forgets that I'm not the one who smells faintly of urine right now. When his Dad suggested the Chinese buffet next door, clearly a consolation prize, Joe very readily agreed.

I'd never visited Mr Woo's Oriental Buffet before, and I doubt many Chinese people choose to either. A giant community of wealthy Chinese students pays eye-watering amounts of money to live 5 minutes from the University just around the corner. West Street alone has five bubble tea shops, and the street-food stalls are disproportionately Chinese in influence. Everyone inside Mr Woo's tonight is white, and either too drunk or too hungry to care if the food's any good or not, so long as they can glutton on it and not pay top dollars.

Joe points his crutches, positioning his decapacitated body towards a table near the back. My physical health at present, not needing crutches to project myself anywhere, means I have more say where we sit, so I reach the one spare window table before he can even put his worst foot forward. I plonk my jacket on the chair with intent, and then smile at Joe as I offer him help to the table.

"Window seats? Are you havin' a laugh?" he asks,

"That table's next to the toilet. The worst seat in any restaurant." I pause, then add "Mate." Like I said, frenemies at best with this lad. "You always like the window seat in lessons. I thought you'd prefer it."

Joe's Dad's clearly aiming to stuff himself silly at minimal cost. He's already advised us to "skip the noodles n't rice on't first plate, lads. Tha'll bloat up 'n be too full for seconds". His advice to himself is somewhat different, "Fella, it dun't matter how much rice 'n noodles tha shovels in, tha'll be shitting a wardrobe out in't morning either way, so fill't plate up and enjoy thee sen."

This buffet is as quintessentially Chinese as bacon and eggs. A TV screen on the wall shows a Japanese game show where contestants win a plasma TV if they stand in quicksand with a family of scorpions in their underwear for 20 minutes. Very entertaining, but I'm hungry, of course. Joe's Dad can't reach the food fast enough. It's the quickest he's moved today. I wait to see what he brings back. If his plate just has a few items, then he knows his stuff and he's being selective. If the plates loaded then he's no connoisseur, just happy to gorge himself on whatever stodge comes out of the kitchen, no matter how congealed or lukewarm, so hungry he's forgotten he has an incapacitated child to feed. Option two wins.

I take Joe an empty glass over, leave it on his table, and walk away to sort myself out. Whilst I'm glad that this place isn't full-on authentic Chinese, as I wasn't really in the mood for boiled duck embryo in its shell, or live drunk octopuses that had been swimming in Saki all day, there was still a strange feeling that whoever the chef is, he quite possibly isn't altogether Chinese either, nor is he too enthusiastic in his work. I opt to leave the Szechuan style sausages and cast a more discerning eye over it all, then hear "EDWARD!"

Joe. Probably wants his glass filling. Fuck it. I'll do it in a bit, once I've eaten.

"Have they got salt and pepper chicken?"

"Yeh, owt else?"

"Aye, chicken balls, wi' nowt on though."

He can be my food taster tonight. I plate him up. Salt and pepper chicken, barbecue spare ribs, chicken balls, then just to freak him out, cold sweetcorn and the last spring roll on the tray that had probably sat there all day with someone's bogie on it. A few fire noodles by the side, not strictly Chinese but who cares. He'll need the fire brigade 20 seconds after he sends those down.

"There you go fella, fill up."

I turn and walk away before he can speak. My turn. Deffo off tonight's bucket list is Mr Woo's special chicken, and the ginger beef laid out in a sticky glop that I could tile Mum's bathroom with. It had, at some stage of the afternoon, been invaded by a stray noodle or two and a spring onion clearly rebelling against its intended role complementing a beef tataki. The longer I spent there, I realised every dish had unintended pieces of rice in there, except the rice.

Mr Barker was oblivious to everything and near the bottom of his first mountain. I watched Joe nibble a spare rib through to the bare bone, and once I'd noticed he'd not lost any teeth in the process I decided it there was no risk to me doing the same. As I did so, I caught a familiar face out of the window, sat just along from us, sat under a sleeping bag with a coffee cup on the floor, which I could already see held nothing but a few coppers.

Donovan O'Donovan.

Out I went, across the road.

"Alright Donovan?"

He didn't answer straight away.

I walk over a bit close and lean over him. "Donovan, it's me, Edward."

He looks up then beckons me to sit down.

I place myself, crouching, next to him. "You eaten today?"

"Cuppa tea at the church at lunchtime."

"I'm in that place across the road if you fancy a take-away, sort of?"

"Won ton soup's my favourite, followed by prawn curry, then black bean sauce on its todd."

"OK."

Hang on a minute.

He smiles. "Whatever you can get pal, I'm not fussy."

"On it. Give me 5 minutes!"

I walk back inside and grab the napkins that were laid out on the table. Joe's Dad, about halfway through his second mountain, stops eating momentarily and asks "You know him?"

"Yeah, I chat to him a fair bit when I'm out and about. I'll tell you in a minute."

I'm not sure about Donovan and those missing teeth of his, so I skip the spare ribs. I wrap up chicken balls, pancake rolls and samosas as they're the warmest, then one of those Japanese sandwiches that have rice instead of bread. I check to see where the waitress is. Coast clear. Back outside I go.

"That lot OK?"

"Nah I prefer Indian. Can't you fetch us a lamb biryani instead?"

"Are you having a laugh?"

"Buddy, you should live my lifestyle sometime. Detoxing's easy."

"Have you got somewhere to go tonight?"

"There's a hostel near't Uni. I try 'n avoid it. Always drama or someone trying to nick your stuff, but needs must." I scan to see what he has that anyone would consider robbing him for. I spot nothing. "You back at school yet?"

"I turn up each morning. It's complicated."

Mr Barker comes out.

Donovan spots him. "You best get back inside, Ed. He'll be wondering what you're chattin' to me about."

"OK Donovan. See you soon." So, back inside. Joe's Dad crouches next to him, chats and, after a few minutes, hands Donovan a note, can't see if it's a 5 or a 10 or a 20, but hopefully enough to send him somewhere warm, safe and free from drama.

"That your wingman then? I've seen it all!" Joe spits out at me when I sit back down.

"Given a choice of a street sleeper to chill with or anyone from St Kevin's, I'd always choose the tramp. He smells better than you do, by the way."

Joe returns a deathglare and a half.

I have my right foot under the table, ready to very accidentally catch that precious ankle of his if necessary. "Think yourself lucky your pissy trousers aren't on Instagram right now"

I check Joe's plate. He left the noodles. I'm glad he didn't touch them now. I could kick him while he's down, but I'm much much classier than that. I go for the peace offering instead. "Drink?"

"Aye, owt wi no rice lumps in it."

I take his glass, look outside, and see Mr Barker and Donovan still chatting, looking cosy while doing so. Like they already know each other.

----

29. Mr Woo's

My bucket list runs like this...the San Siro, the Nou Camp, the Bernebau, the Allianz, the Westfalstadion, the Azteca, the Maracana, that stadium in China that looks like a birds nest, that stadium in the Middle East that looks like a big massive fanny, Wembley, Parkhead on old firm day, Ibrox on old firm day, Anfield on a European night, Hillsborough, Bramall Lane, Elland Road (those last 3 to play and score at, not spectate). Then, aside from the footy, visit New York, then Sydney, Rio, Amsterdam, Tokyo too, own a black Porsche, marry a Venezuelan air-stewardess. Not far behind all of this, of course, is the Etihad. Just as worthy a destination in many ways, as long as you've not pissed all over your trousers.

Dad's stupid fault. I knew as soon as the third goal went in that I couldn't wait much longer for a piss, but there's no way I'd ever be daft enough to go to the loo when the match is actually on, ever. So I sat, hands between thighs, pelvic squeezy exercises all the way through to the final whistle, cursing the ref for every second of injury time he played, then, once the final whistle blew, Dad made a desperate situation even more intense by suggesting that we should hang on in our seats until the bulk of the crowd were up the steps and spilling out onto the street. The words "spilling out" didn't do me any favours.

So, helped upwards, onto the crutches, and Dad going "tek your time, lad" and "don't rush, son", it was either him or geeky Edward to help me through the door. Geeky Edward would probably watch everything. He's probably got a third leg downstairs. It's always the blokes like him with no chance of ever using it with a naked lady that swing like the pendulum on a grandfather clock, isn't it? The pain I was in as I hobbled up the steps turned briefly, once I was through the door and unzipped, to total nirvana. Then I caught sight of the damage in the mirror above the basins, and I'm now officially a tramp. I might as well go sit in a bus stop with a bin bag full of Buckfast and yell "CUNT!" at each passing vehicle.

Only now that I've wet meself in public can I begin appreciating the presence of geeky Edward. Anyone else would have uploaded and shared my dilemma in seconds. I've seen his dumbphone. No camera, no internet, no nothing. Nothing's getting uploaded. I pull my hoodie down at the base as if to stretch it a bit, but that's got no chance of that hiding my accident, and I can't cover fuck all with my hands clinging to these sodpot crutches.

Edwards looking out at something on the city skyline that he finds interesting, so I take this as he's noticed nothing. I make a point of walking behind him all the way out of the ground til Dad plonks me next to a ledge next to the main road, telling us to wait there while he swings the car round. I start whatever conversation that can keep his gaze away, asking what's in the distance that's so interesting, what's so interesting about the planes he keeps looking up at, based on the fact that there's no piss-soaked trousers to see in the clouds. He answers enthusiastically, and I have my hopes up that the biggest smile I've ever seen open out across his face is due to me triggering him on some excitable geek subject as opposed to him noticing I've pissed mesen. I've got doubts though.

I manoeuvre into the car and bed myself in for however long it'll take Dad to weave his way out of town. Phone out. 16%. Should get me home as long as I don't stream owt off. Check my pages. 1 comment, 1 like. "Are you playing there today? Looks like a nice ground Joseph. Enjoy the game. Auntie Bernie". No-one else. I know she means well, but, honestly, kill me now.

Onto messages. Jodie.

SHITE!!!!!

Forgot about her. Too wrapped up in the footy. "Thanks for wasting my whole day. I cancelled babysitting and everything else because of you. Tosser!"

Damn.

Can't message back.

SHIT!!!!! She deleted me.

Eh, WTF?

Seriously WTF??

No-one deletes me. Ever.

Check my friend count. 497. Yeah, two down from yesterday. Instagram. 260 followers. 1 less. That's her too.

Can't deal with this. No-one, I mean, no-one ever unfriends me. Like, why would they? OK, Shelly a couple of times, but she doesn't count. This one was even in with a chance of dating me one day. Well, she doesn't now, obviously, but that's her fault. I was at the football and my phone was on deathbed battery. She never thought of that. Selfish cow.

I gaze out of the window for a bit, wondering if I should tell Shironda that her mate's batshit. Not right now. Maybe later.

I really shouldn't care at all. But I do, it's like someone's took a stab at the core of my self-worth. Why would anyone dislike me, especially a lass?

Who does she think she is anyway? If she told the other lasses in school that she'd deleted me they'd think she'd been sniffing her nail polish for too long. Proper batshit.

I don't like the feeling, anyways. The feeling that someone doesn't like you and you've done nowt wrong to them. Another red box. Danny Alvez Flanagan replied to your comment. "AS IF I FUCKING EVEN KNOW YOU?" I'm not in the right frame for his twatpatter. I'm not playing his games. He'd win.

I need to get that dippy lass off my mind. Sam will no doubt be hanging round the train station, whichever platform the Peterborough train leaves from, deciding which unlucky soul is going home in an ambulance instead. Archie, dependent on whether he's noticed if his mum, brother and stepdad are at home or not, will be either on Fifa or Pornhub. I message them both.

10 mins down the road. No reply. Try Marcus and Omar next. Even if it's just Fifa or summat later on. Nowt back from them either. I send out to anyone else I'd consider talking to in real life, Nathan, Ben, that lot, then look out of the window for a bit, even though it's just sheep, stone walls, big hills, and fuck all else. After a while this gives way to a few buildings, then a lot of buildings, and I start fretting. 10 messages sent and 1 reply, like a "soz mate busy" and nowt else. Edward and Dad are talking about wildlife they've seen, snakes and weird spiders and whatever. I'm actually listening in. I predict by the end of today I'll be just the same type of total billy that he is. Eventually, the more we go through the burbs, gradually passing by rows of shops and bars and offices and whatever else, I make a big life changing decision.

No Nandos.

Seriously.

It's a bad idea. Nothing good will come of it.

1) I'm here with Geeky Ed. 2) My mates are being weird and its spooking me. 3) I stink of piss.

I probably look even worse. I check the vanity mirror, only briefly. Passable I guess, but not at my best. I'm best off going straight home and having beans on toast. It's definitely a day to be on the sidelines.

"Dad I'm not reyt bothered about food, me. We can go straight home if you want."

"Stuff that son. I'm starving."

Plan B. I'll sit in the car while he goes to the chippie or through the drive-thru.

"Oh OK, just KFC or summat'll do me."

"KFC? Aye right. Not on your diet list, that. No chance."

"Just thought it'd be easier wi' me leg an' that, that's all?"

Edward's smarming in the back seat. He sees through all this. We'll be sat for the whole evening at the outside tables of some poncy cafe that everyone walks past if it's up to him.

"Joey lad, same as I said, I'm starving. A KFC megabucket to mesen won't even touch the sides, pal. I'll park up in town and find summat better."

Another text thru "*Soz bud got plans*". Nowt more.

The same charade when we pull up in town. Let Edward walk in front. I have a sudden brainping moment when we get near the all night supermarket. Everyone else is kinda dressed up ready to party and I'm a scruff, so I manoeuvre into the shop, hobble towards the smellies, turn my back to everyone and spray extensively across my hoodie and especially my jeans.

Maybe I should have looked at the label on the can. Sure for ladies. FML.

On any other of the 364 days of the year, I'd be celebrating if Dad ever walked near a Nandos. I can spot a window seat free, and my dream setting is now my biggest nightmare. I don't want this at all, but Dad saves my life with the best bars he's spat out all day.

"Chinese buffet?"

"Get in!"

"Better than Nandos, even?"

"Aye, I only liked it cos everyone else did" I lie back, unconvincingly.

There's not many people in there, so I manoeuvre my crutches ready to move myself towards a table at the back where no-one can see me. I'm at snail pace though, so Edward overtakes me and, with movements defter than me weaving between two clumsy defenders, bags window seats. I seriously hate him.

"Window seats are crap in here, pal" I attempt to lie again.

"The seats where you were heading were next to the toilet. Worst seat in any restaurant."

He wins. Dickhead.

"Then again, sitting you next to the loo would reduce the risk of little accidents, maybe?"

He loves this. He doesn't just win. He savages me. I don't care how much this lad gets bullied, he's a dick. But so is everyone else I know. Mates? I'll let you know when I make some.

Check the phone again. 1 more text. Archie. "*Sorry pal, stuff lined up*"

Dad wasn't joking about being hungry. He's not even checking stuff out, just piling his plate sky high, loading enough on to feed every diner in here for a week, amazingly dropping nothing on the way to the table. I should really say "well done" for that, but as it becomes obvious that this is just his first plateful, I think more along the lines of "you greedy fat bastard".

Edward returns with an empty plate. He's actually offered to plate me up. I shouldn't trust him at all, but food's not my priority right now. It takes me ages to think of any food so I just say "Salt and pepper chicken" and let him guess the rest. Check my phone while he's gone. No point talking to Dad. Mouth full. If he speaks, I'd not get the news, I'd get the weather.

Aside from ignoring my messages, Shironda's had her nails done to look like one of those pink and yellow squared cakes that only weirdos like. Sam's shared a picture of 3 crates of tinnies. Omar's uploaded a picture of himself, Marcus, and some others sat on a bus. Edward's back. I change my mind. I actually am hungry. Not in the pig-at-the-trough way that Dad is, or the "all of a sudden a connoisseur on Asian cuisine" manner that Edward's giving off. He points at each dish....."Salt n pepper spare ribs", "Singapore noodles", like I'm learning the words in English for the first time. Dickhead. I grab a spare rib and pick at that while I keep scrolling. 8%. Might get home with that. The next time I look up from my phone, Edward's walking out of the building. I watch him cross the road as his weirdness moves to a new level. He crouches, gopnik style, and chats to some tramp who's sat a little further down, sleeping bag round him, cup out next to him for coins. For a split second, I wonder if there's any danger, but actually Edward and him look like they're having banter, like they know each other, like they're buddies, sort of.

"Dad. What's he on wi'?" I ask while the chances of a noodle explosion are reduced.

Dad looks from his second heap of unidentifiable fried things lumped on top of each other. I nod my head forward. Dad looks out, looks back to me, then looks out again, screwing his eyes and face up to get a closer view for a good 30 seconds or more.

"Shite!" he comments, projecting half-chewed beansprouts over to the next table.

"You know that bloke?" I enquire.

"I did, once."

"That in't his Dad or summat is it?"

"He's not seen his Dad for years. But he's sat chatting right there to a bloke who has."

Edward came back into the restaurant, then, believe it or not, smuggled him a load of food out. Dad went out to him too, and chatted to him for ages. They seemed to know each other too. I saw Dad slip him a tenner and then shake hands after. Dad didn't even wash his hands when he came back in, just casually asked Edward how he knew him.

That conversation carried on all the way to the car and into the car. The bits that I made sense of are...when Edward walks out of school, he takes off into the city centre and lounges wherever he doesn't have to spend money, the park, the library, wherever. I didn't make sense of everything, but he chats to random students, old ladies, and this trampy Donovan fella. He says he's not a crackhead, but one of those unlucky blokes that had a bad day once and lost everything. I always expected he walked out of school, went straight home and stuck the X-Box on like anyone else would. Most batshit of all, he chats to Shelly and her college crew too. They let him hang round with them whenever they see him. She'll be doing it to annoy me of course, but I'm not letting on that it's working.

Now, I could shout out, either in school or online "guess what geeky Edward does when he walks out of school?" and all this would be dynamite, but I'd really be better off not doing it. I'll use it all to blackmail him with later, though, listening to him, I don't really think he'd give a shit who knew. Dad's asking him every question going, like what does he know about the tramp guy. I'd read Edward if he was withholding. For all his oddities, the one thing I've deffo sussed about him is that's that he's honest and straight up all day long and in his sleep too. He keeps everything so real it causes him problems, like grief off Cory Hendricks and getting a pasting that he could've avoided if he were a bit more streetwise. In a way, though, I respect it. Though I look the other way when all that drama's kicking off. He just sees something that's not reyt and he can't help himsen but try and do the right thing. No idea why.

Dad decides to drop me home before Edward. I reckon he wants to know more about this tramp. I'd say it's obvious that if he was a kiddie-fiddler then Edward wouldn't be smuggling Peking duck on his behalf. The last time I saw Dad this triggered was when Shelly came home with a henna tattoo on her arm. It washed off in the shower, but he didn't know that.

I stopped caring about any of that as soon as Dad pulled up at a red light by Hillsborough Park. Just beyond the swings, I spotted a massive squad of kids my age. I recognise nearly all of them. Welshy, Charlie Woods, Chloe Evison all loved up, presumably with Jamie, Shironda shouting her mouth off, Jodie, Tonisha, Scarlett Ryan, George Robinson, Jassi Turner, Sammy Ahmed from the badass class, cans and bottles all over, spliffs on the go, probably other stuff too. Unfortunately, one of them spotted me, and before I could slink down into my seat, a few more did, then others appeared, some I knew, like Omar, Archie, Sam, wankers all of them, some I didn't. To rub salt in, they spotted geeky Edward sat behind me too. By the time Dad hit third gear, my phone vibrated the final 2 miles and its final 2% all the way to the living room, losing its capacity for staying alive at the same time I did once I found the sofa.

----

30) THE FOOD OF LOVE

"How was Joey yesterday?" Lara asked as she looked up from her phone for a whole 5 seconds.

"Boring as usual. He's not the most superdynamic personality on the universe."

"Nor are you. Anyway, Libby was asking me earlier what he was wearing?"

Lara needs to pack this in. It's not even year 8 nonsense. It's year 3 nonsense.

"Piss-stained trousers."

Lara rolls her eyes and returns to her phone. Mum perches on the edge of her chair, clasping her giant coffee mug with both hands, looking like she's seen a ghost, itching to ask me something, but unsure which exact words to use.

"What did you think to the football match, Ed?"

I'll keep this civil. The finer details aren't required here. Her interest in football is zero, same as mine. "Yeah, enjoyed it thanks." Honest verdict? I'd go again, providing the stadium was on the next street and the entry fee was £5 max. Otherwise, seen it, done it, moving on.

She chatted to Mr Barker for ages last night about Donovan. She wants to know what I know. I told her about the first time I ever saw him, when he got picked on by security goons. I told her that I chat to him if I see him in town. I told her I'd helped him give out some of his flyers that he hands out for some churchy place sometimes have a cuppa with him. She still didn't think I was telling her enough. I really couldn't tell her much more, but I could see how intent she was so I asked her a few questions of my own first.

1) Is Donovan a paedophile? Or is Donovan connected to my Dad by virtue of them belonging to the same filthy grooming ring? No, not that she knows of.

2) Is he part of a sinister death-cult using me as a way to get to my little sister in order to skewer her through her heart and offer her as a kebab-like sacrifice to their demon fire-god? No, and this really isn't a time to be silly, which is a shame, as I'd give Lara up for demonic sacrifice for a reasonable price indeed.

3) Has he, at any time over he last 4 decades, been known to indulge in drive-by shootings, acid bath murders or acts of terrorism? Not that she knows of.

4) What's the dodgiest aspect to his character that should advise me to cross the road when I encounter him? He's had various substance issues, associated mental health issues, may still have them, and, apparently the most concerning to Mum and Mr Barker, he knows my Dad.

My Dad. More of a sperm donor than a father, to give a more accurate description. A man who's absence, in my earlier years, affected my development to the extent that I actually developed Stockholm Syndrome on his behalf, explaining away his absence to anyone who asked after him in a way that didn't look detrimental to the content of his character, treating judgements of his character as something much more important than me having no primary male role model in my life whatsoever. A man whose name I defended in the playground countless times whilst at the same time being on the receiving end of every conceivable variety of physical and emotional bullying, with no-one standing by my side. A man I spent my primary years wondering where he was, my early secondary years wondering who he was, and what was too important for him to see his kids. A man who, despite not having been in prison, hospital, kidnapped to ransom, or marooned on a distant island surrounded by sharks, certainly hasn't been making a millionaire of himself despite contributing fuck all financially to my Mum to help towards either mine of Lara's upkeep. A man who, around the middle of January each year, still sends me Power Rangers or a Ben-10 t-shirt for Xmas, whilst Lara opens Lazytown DVDs or Tweenies figures. A man who sends birthday presents anything between a week and 3 months after that birthday has taken place, usually wrapped in a plastic bag and delivered via some Aunt I barely know to my Grandma's for her to bring round. Last year I got some Matey bubble bath, a bag of jelly babies and a make-it-yourself Bob the Builder Digger with a label still proudly stating "reduced to clear". A man who bought me an Airfix Spitfire kit when I was 3, a real coming-of-age milestone of a present that I can remember being told to sit quietly and not disturb him while he glued it together, put it on the mantelpiece and ordered me not to touch it in case I knocked it over and it shattered. A man who performs his responsibilities so badly that Mum often looks knackered from doing the job of both Mum and Dad, and apologises when she really shouldn't because she feels guilty that she's useless at doing 'boy activities'. A man who instantly changes whatever mood I'm in on so many Monday mornings when some kid talks about their "one day every second weekend" Dad taking them to Harry Potter World, Eurodisney, wherever. Actually let's go to the next level. The kid who meets their one weekend a month Dad and ends up going fishing, or to Maccy Ds, or for a nature walk because their Dad's skint, or even sitting bored shitless on a grubby sofa in a poky flat getting treated to a packet of Quavers and a fresh cup of shut the fuck up while Dad watches the Premiership, is having a parent-child bonding experience a hundred times more rewarding and developmental than I ever have. A man I used to ensure every last detail went on a father's day or a birthday card, nagging mum for the materials to create something just perfect enough for him to like it enough to decide to come and visit me and Lara, then come home from school each day for weeks afterwards, running up the front path in excited anticipation of checking the letterbox then finding the sweet sum of fuck all having dropped through it in return. A man who, even when he lived with us, changed my nappy once and once only, because I'd piddled while my nappy was off, as baby boys do. A man unable to cope with the same thing Mum managed to laugh about several times a day for 2 or so years, even if she'd been out all day and I'd been left with him and spent 6 hours sat in my own poo. A man who, despite being unable to give Mum money towards me and Lara, is tagged in blurry pictures across his pathetic Facebook page stood in some cheesy pub with either a beer, or a cigarette, or maybe even both, a Facebook page that Mum's blocked from despite being the person responsible for bringing up his kids. A man whose presence in my life is so beautifully inspiring I've tried several times to persuade my Mum to join Tinder and Match.com.

She still refused.

Anyway, Donovan, real name Darren, has history with him, once good, now irreparably bad. Mr Barker also knows Donovan, and when they chatted last night, got all the most recent info about my Dad, freely. It's not good. If he was in New Zealand or California or even living like the tramp life like Donovan, then I think I could find a way to eventually forgive him for not being in touch. I remember Donovan once said something that really touched a nerve with me when he said he had a daughter, miles away, that he didn't see, to protect her from embarrassment at the state he was in, but still manages to book onto a library computer where he can keep in touch with her online, and will starve himself for a couple of days to stick a tenner in a card for her when he needs to. My Dad's not in a massive life-crisis like Donovan so visibly is, and he's not marooned anywhere distant. He's in fucking Rotherham, in some bedsit where he shares his bathroom and toilet with complete strangers. He's also part of the reason Donovan also shares a bathroom and toilet with the entire planet. I typed Rotherham onto Routeplanner last night. 11.54 miles from my house. 18 kilometres. Wanker.

As I would if he was a missing person, or a sudden death, I still want closure. I could put my mind at ease, Lara's too if she actually cares. She heard the conversations last night, but she was more interested in Joey Barker, on behalf of her mate Libby of course, absolutely not her. I'll bet she can't even picture him. He's like a phantom to her.

Mum doesn't want to tell me much. She wants me to tell her what I know about Donovan first. I've already told her once, so I repeat the basics. He looks older than he probably is, has a very weatherbeaten appearance, but hello, sleeping rough, what do you expect? I've not seen him drunk, or, as far as I can spot, stoned, though he's clearly been both on many an occasion in the past. He's mentioned a daughter he doesn't see. He thinks it'd destroy her if she saw how he is, so he tells her online that he's in Manchester, but seeing as she's in South London I guess everything outside London is like a strange hazy blur to her anyway. He sits in the library a fair bit, in which time he's read Harry Potter, The Fault In Our Stars, The Hunger Games and clues himself up on other teenage stuff just in case he gets to see his daughter. He can identify Stormzy, Skepta and Bugzy Malone after 4 lines, likewise the Sidemen, Dan & Phil, and Logan Paul, and name the family members in both Bobs Burgers and Rick & Morty. When he meets her, he'll be prepared. I could tell it was all minor detail to her, so I added more. He smokes, could make good use of a dentist, a doctor, a makeover and a washing machine. He's attempted to kill himself before a couple of times but one way or another it didn't happen. He uses McDonalds toilets to clean up in if he has to, as they've got the cleanest toilets in town. I've been nicking food out of the cupboards when I leave home in the morning, just in case I bump into him, only the odd chocolate bar or carton of juice, nothing more than that. I've gone to the Italian Coffee Company with him, using the tokens from discarded coffee cups that I stop and pick up when I see one. One stroll through the train station and the bus station and I've usually picked up 20, so if she wants to join us, I've got enough.

"OK. OK. Enough!" Mum says.

Job done pretty well there, I think.

"Are you likely to see him again?" she adds.

"Well it's not like I go looking for him, but it'd be rude not to say hello if I see him. Is he likely to talk to my Dad?"

"Well, I'd like my mind putting at ease if possible."

"Mr Barker said they'd fallen out massively."

"Yes, but he could have been making it all up?"

"Why would he?"

"Bloody hell Edward you've some growing up to do yet!"

I'm not arguing. I've not eaten, but I've an idea where I can get some food. I still have the full £10 from yesterday. All I'll need's a bus fare. Shoes on. Coat on. "I'm going out for a bit Mum, I'll be back after lunch."

"Where on earth are you going?"

"Church."

"Do you think I'm that gullible?"

"OK you caught me, I was lying. I'm going to get a big bag of heroin and some needles."

"You've no money."

"I don't need any. They give it you for free when you first start."

"We've already sorted it with Mr Barker. Joe's off school all week, you can help him get caught up with his school work, and yours too."

"No Mum he's a dic.., I mean, a bit obnoxious."

"I can be obnoxious, too, son. You either do your Maths in school or in Joe's living room."

"OK maybe." That's maybe as in never. "See you later."

I walked into town, head spinning with the thought of me spending any more time with that little prat. Just because he's losing his mates doesn't mean I actually want to make some. If I did, there's a million people I'd pal up with before him. I found Donovan's church just as whatever service there'd been had ended, as the priest bloke was stood chatting and shaking hands with a group of old people, and briefly said hello to me as I walked through. "Hello" I said back, as I'm thoroughly polite in such surroundings. One man sat on his own at the front of the pews, a few more old people sat at tables with tea and biscuits, then a few more people in sight at the other entrance, just through the door, including Donovan. I planned on creeping up on him without saying a word, but he spotted me well in time.

"Edward! Robin Hood of Sharwood, I had a feeling you'd show on my radar today."

"Yeah, well, er, Darren, I never realised we were connected."

Slightly awkward silence.

"Listen buddy, if you're wanting me to get you to your Dad, then the news in't good."

"I've no interest in seeing him."

"So what is your interest?"

"Seeing as I've not seen him since I was 5, you'd expect that I've a head full of questions."

"How's your Mum doing nowadays?"

"Well she's usually OK. You know her too?"

"Since infants, Jim since college, and that gypsy lass he married since secondary. All before you were thought of. Hungry?"

"Not really". I'm actually fucking starving.

"I'm going for food. Can you cook?"

"Only if I have to"

"You can cook wi' me while we chat. Cooking's a life-skill. Thank me in a few years when you're knocking up your signature dish in't candlelight for the lady you love."

"Whatever."

Into the kitchen.

"This dish will win all the ladies, Edward my little apprentice, I promise you."

I scan the tins of corned beef, processed peas, gravy granules and instant mash. The food of love, without a doubt.

We barely mention my Dad at all whilst in the kitchen. Other volunteers, mainly the old people who were sat around sipping tea or chatting to the priest fella a few minutes before, come in and start doing their bit, "their bit" actually meaning taking over everything, pulling big trays out, preparing vegetables, filling big tea urns up, and gradually moving us onto more menial roles. I set the tables. I've no idea which way round the knives and forks go so I just place them next to each other to the left of where the plates would be. Gradually, the odd diner appears here and there, seats themselves and food appears instantly from the kitchen hatch, platefuls not far off the size of Mr Barkers noodle mountains last night. Donovan initially appointed himself head waiter, but happily gives way to some white haired old dear who's probably my grannies age. She brings 2 platefuls over and tells us there's more if we want any. The presentation and smell immediately makes me realise why this stuff's free.

"What's this?" I look over at Donovan whilst prodding around at the plate.

"It might be mashed potato, possibly. The brown stuffs definitely gravy. Treat it like a lucky dip, fella."

"What about this bit?" I prod around the plate. It looks like cat food.

"Corned beef hash."

"What's that?"

"It's what you can make wi't stuff that gets donated."

I take a mouthful of the potato. It's certainly not the type of potato that grows underground in a big field anywhere. It really, really isn't for me. I'll concentrate on drinking as much tea as I can for lunch instead. Darren, on the other hand, is fully focused on what's on his plate. I guess if you don't know when your next meal will be, you'll gladly eat warm cat food and chemical mash if it's going to keep you alive a bit longer. I offer him mine. He can't talk without there being an explosion of half-eaten poor quality food flying out of his mouth, but he takes it and beckons towards the table near the door. I suss out what he's pointing at. Tea and coffee's on free refill. I return to the table with a plateful of biscuits, casting back to the old Peter Kay sketch, annexing the Oaty Hobnobs whilst leaving the Rich Tea for everyone else.

The white-haired octagenarian waitress returns to the table with a bin bag and a couple of sticky labels and a pen, then another bag, with clean clothes and a toothbrush in it.

"Gi'z 2 secs" Darren nods to me.

5 minutes later, Darren dumps a knotted, half full bin liner on the floor near the entrance, then sits back opposite me in clean clothes apart from his coat, which I guess he never hands over, merely spraying cheap deodorant over it to freshen it up a bit.

"I'm gonna give mesen a headache with this. I did consider telling you to fuck off next time I saw you, abruptly ending our unconventional friendship but doing you the favour of being unaware of things you might be better off not knowing. However, I realised that if it were me, I'd want to know stuff too. So, once you've sorted some fresh cuppas out of course, I'll do my best. It's not easy listening, mind."

"I gave up on happy reunions with Superman when I was about 8."

"I also need to know you'll not go looking him up, or give your Mum grief over it."

"No worries". What does he think I'm going to say? I've given up a Sunday of laziness to sit here killing myself with shitty processed food if he'd not noticed.

"You're not expecting me to say nice things about your Dad are you?"

"I'm not that interested in him. My brain's like a jigsaw. I'm just after missing pieces, so I can finish the whole puzzle then put it away for a long time."

"Jim knows stuff, as does your Mum, obviously. I know stuff about them, too..." He catches whatever my facial expression is right now. I've no mirror. "...but I've no beef with them, so there's nowt bad to say."

"I know the bare essentials."

"What are they then?"

"That my Dads not a paedo, a terrorist, a serial killer, any of that stuff."

"Aye, fair play. He's not got many saving graces, but I guess if there are any, they're the ones."

"You really don't get on with him do you?"

"I did once, but like I said, I'm not about to spit out any Nelson Mandela stories."

"More tea?"

"I think it'd be a missed opportunity if I didn't, to be quite honest."

I fetch a fresh pot. Darren stirs it, studies it then plucks two soaking teabags from it, places one in each cup, and pours over them. "Gi'it 5 minutes. Too wazzy right now."

"I've made tea before."

"Right. When you're ready."

"Yeah I'm ready."

"Comfy?"

"Yep."

"Pen and pencil ready?"

"For Gods sake!"

"Right, in order to tell you about Nigel, I'll need to tell you my story too, they intertwine."

"Fine" I add, with a smile, "Darren."

He takes a glance at me, a little off balance now I've used his real name. "Use Donovan. I chose that. Darren's a bit of an unlucky a name for me."

"Ok."

"Right, you can have my rags to rags life story. Your Dad's bit will merge in along the way."

Last time I focused so intensely on anything, Harry Potter had found the last horcrux and was preparing for his final battle with The Dark Lord.

----

31. MR SHUFFLEBOTTOM

The ankle feels proper rough, deffo payback time for yesterday. There's all manner of irritating shit going on, but the best thing I can do is rest, get fit, get back on the pitch, and let my feet do the talking. I invented my own workout this morning. I rolled over to reach underwear from my drawer, got my boxers on by doing sit-ups, rolled over to reach the wardrobe, failed, so I grabbed the trackies and top that were lying on the floor. Then I moved most of the quilt onto the floor and rolled mesen over for a proper comfy landing. I could have happily done that a few more times. It were fun, like back to age 5 when life was simple. What everyone else calls squats, a 5 year old calls "sitting down". I crawled to the bathroom on hands and knees, ankle raised, used the side of the bath to lift myself up to position myself on the bog then did everything sat down lady-style. Whilst sat on the bog, I reached to the taps and scrubbed my hands, face and teeth. I left all my smellies in the bedroom, but Shelly leaves loads of hers in here, so I nicked some strawberry shortcake deodorant. I'm not going out today and she'll not wake for ages yet so I'll get away with it. I got downstairs by sitting and shuffling my arse 14 times with my bad leg resting on my good one, then crawled into the living room, pushed myself up on my good leg and landed on sofa cushions. That's me snug and sorted for the day.

Oh shite. Left my phone upstairs.

It'll stress me out checking out other people's bullshit, but I feel naked without it so I went back on my travels. Down off the sofa, onto the floor, then back up the stairs the exact opposite way I came down, shuffled my arse into the bedroom, grabbed my phone. 100% charged when I don't care that much. I could do with the X-Box coming down too, but there's no way I'll manage that.

And back down again, Mr Shufflebottom style.

Mum's already made bacon butties, but she's buttered the bread, and I'm not that fussed about bacon at the best of times. I'm definitely on the same team as Shabana and Mo and Kassam and every other muzzy kid or veggiepharian I know on this one. Pigs are proper filthy animals. Their lifestyle's every bit as scruffy as a rats, happy to roll about in their own shite all day. That can't be healthy, especially when the weather's proper blazing. There has to be summat dodgy like Ebola getting spread about by them.

I ask Mum if I can have something else instead, so she takes the filthy pig-laden plate and places it in the lap of the filthiest plate-laden pig in the house. Without even looking at it, Dad makes it invisible in seconds, not even touching the sides, as if he didn't do a good enough impression of a pig at the trough in Mr Woo's last night. Mum returns with Coco Pops.

Timed everything else bang-on. Match of the Day just started. City should be up first. Actually, no. Man United somehow seem to be more important, as if they're going to finish above fourth this year. A dodgy offside, a dodgy backpass, and a dodgy penalty gave them 3 easy goals in the second half. Chelsea next up. Home to Villa. I'll guess at 0-0. Close. 1-0 Chelsea. Hazard. Could have been 5. City up next? No. Liverpool. Erm, why? Away to Newcastle. 2-1. I could describe the goals but they're irrelevant. Arsenal next. As if they matter nowadays? 4-0 against Southampton. Sanchez turned his man inside out 3 times. He's got nearly as much wizardry up his sleeve as I have, but I'm struggling to care. If Tottenham show up next then the BBC can just fuck off. Yeah, here they are. Well oiled but trophyless machine of Spurs, bipolar West Ham. Two teams only a fool would ever stick in an acca. 1-0 Spurs, 1-1. 2-1 West Ham, red card West Ham, 2-2, 20 man scrap, red card each team, penalty, missed, 3-2 Spurs, penalty Spurs, missed, best game so far, by far, but I'm not in the crowd, so make it second best. Right, now for City. Finally. That Yaya-Sergio-Yaya one-two was a thing of beauty, aesthetically more skilful than the Sergio-Mario-Sergio move of 93:20, but less drama. Yaya runs from deep, Sergio uses the outside of his boot, near his heel, to put the defender a split second off the pace, his outstretched right leg just that little bit too far away from the ball to make any difference to. Yaya then draws the keeper out and places it just over his outstretched hand, covering defender running back to try and divert it away but the ball just nonchalantly trickling that little bit too far away from him. YaYa runs my way. I should be on telly here. Nah. Randoms bouncing about in front of me. Oh well. Another day.

I get a better look at the third, which went in at the other end of the ground to me. Apparently the Baggies defence was too slow reacting when the keeper spilled the shot. I see it differently, Sergio was running in as soon as the shot left DeBruyne's foot. Its nowt amazing, it's just being able to think a couple of moves ahead of what's actually happening. The Baggies goal. No-one cares. The game pans to the relegation battles, Crystal Palace, Burnley, all that lot. Shall I risk my phone? I've got a clear run at the TV for a while yet, so Bundesliga next, La Liga or Serie A later, depending who's playing. I decide to get all that online bullshit out of my system, then move on with my day in peace.

It's not good.

Two more messages. Both from last night.

Marcus "*Fifa lol, as if, just seen yer new wingman. Enjoy chess.*"

Sam "*Go fck yersen u cost me £30. Cunt.*"

Sam again, later on, drunk or drugged "*HJey Joe yua vcungt, c n e1 u kno?*"

Picture. Archie with Jodie behind him, gently draping her arms across his neck, cheek to cheek.

As if. Choreographed. What's the best way to piss Joe off? I know, fake-snog his mate and upload the selfie.

I'm wise.

I'm also learning who my real mates are. None of these.

There's photos and videos all over. Sam's tried to tag me in one where Jodie's all cuddled up with some random lad, don't know his name but he's in year 11 and deathglares me usually. He also wears the same £30 tracky top every time I see him out of school so I'm not dropping levels to savage him. Sam's too drunk to spell my name anyway so I'll save any lyric battles with him til he's learned basic English. I might need a doctor after but he'll need fire engines.

I've seen lasses do this before, to other lasses, like arrange a party and invite 29 of the kids in the class, purposely not invite the 30th, then after the event, spend hours chatting about the party that kid number 30 wasn't invited to. It's like bullying, but proper sly and pathetic too. I'd like to think I'm above all that and can just brush it off. If only my old man hadn't gone that way home with geeky Edward in the back seat, life would've been easier. Petrol onto the flames.

Comments everywhere. If I comment back it'll go viral. If I stay silent it'll die off as soon as new drama kicks off elsewhere.

"*PMSL Joe in his Dadz whip, wid da VIP in back?*"

"COULD NOT BREATHE!!"

"LEGENDARY!"

They can all go play on the motorway. I'm siding with Edward here, not that I'm ever gonna be his mate, but, like him, I could get on with life reyt better if I bin all this lot off as soon as.

Back to footy. Swansea versus who-gives-a shit. Some Asda Smartprice team. Blue tops. Could be Everton. Look again. Leicester. Mind's elsewhere.

"Mum, am I at school this week?"

"I'll ring 'em in't morning. Have tomorrow and Tuesday at home, then we'll see Dr Konstantine after. I reckon you'll be off all week"

YES MUM!

"Then I'll sort out getting some work sent home so you don't drop behind."

"Aye sound". I know for def that won't happen. I could be off a month before anything lands through the letterbox. It's happened with other kids before.

Oh yeah, more important stuff.

"What about football?"

"Doctor Konstantine decides that"

Dad's in. "See what't Doc sez. Probly some light walks, mebbee a swim or jogging for a day or two."

"How long do you reckon I'll be off school for?"

"Don't know Joe. You sound like you're gonna miss it?"

Just cornered myself there. Think with care here. "Not going to miss it" = they'll think I'm after a month off, so no football. "Going to miss it" = they'll know I'm lying. They know my enthusiasm levels. "Might fall behind" = I'll end up with one of them calling in and collecting essays, "I'll miss my friends" = I'm 100% lying there too. I'm a shit liar. They'll read all of it. Either that or they'll invite fucking Archie or one of those other fairweathered wankers over.

I choose option 3.

"Nah it's just me school work. I'll end up months behind and ne' get caught up"

"You're probably behind already. I'll sort it wi' school"

"Cheers" I reply in the understanding that I'm off for at least this week, maybe longer.

"You're welcome, son." Mum chips in with a glance over to Dad, which I don't trust at all.

Back to the telly. Bayern v Mainz. Everyone's quiet til half time, when Mum muses "Edward'll have some catching up to do 'n all, what wi' him tekkin' off each day". I finally realise what she's up to.

Not again.

----

32. NEW DRAGONBALL

Some things will never change. I had another one of those brilliant but crazy surreal dreams. I also woke up with a massive stiffy again, and don't remember anything sexy going on, which means now I'm subconsciously attracted to giraffes or skyscrapers or giant teapots, I'm not sure. Gerald now looks like a pus-filled headlight installed on my forehead, like I've got a miners helmet on. Won't be long til he starts glowing in the dark. I'm dodging the hairdressers so I can grow it over my forehead and he can stay warm in winter. I've certainly not gone to bed, slept, and woken up any more irresistably handsome, but I have woken up with a new identity, history, and heritage. From the moment Donovan took the first sip of his second cuppa, did that "aahhhh" sound that people do when they're making a warm drink sound something a lot more sexual than it could ever be even in one of my surreal dreams, sat back, put his hands behind his head with his elbows sticking out, and said "right, fella, you ready?", my existence, and the story behind it, changed immediately.

Barely any of its good, but I have closure, that missing 5% that confirms he's a complete waste of a man, and my respect for Mum is such that I've no need to ask her ANY questions she doesn't want to answer. I'll probably get on better with her. I no longer need to ask why we never go on holiday anywhere, or why the stuff Dad left behind, is in bin liners under my bed, out of sight. I understand it all. I know how other people fit in with my life, and how others don't. I know why I don't really know any family members on my Dad's side, and probably why I've barely met that many of them. Any bits that didn't fall into place straight away, are doing so now. Most of all, for me personally, I learned about myself, and I think I've learned how to be myself. It's not going to take that much, really. I've got that comfort of not looking at everything I do and wondering if my Dad would approve. From yesterday onwards I learned I don't need to please anyone. All I need to do is to just be me. I'm suddenly at ease with my identity. That fool's not part of it, so, if I was going to draw a big complicated diagram of myself to explain to people who I am, in the past there'd be a grey cloudy area that my Dad would occupy and I couldn't explain, but, since yesterday, I've managed to erase that bit so it's presently a blank space which, when I'm ready, I can re-design independently of anyone and anything. It's liberating.

I still look in the mirror and see Gerald on my forehead, the hair I can't even comb in a straight line, and anything else that I could beat myself up about. None of it matters that much does it? Everyone else has these problems, the only difference being that it's blatantly obvious with me, whilst , aside from a very tiny few people who get to model for Vogue or Men's Fitness magazine, and even they're airbrushed and photo-shopped to fuck, every single person on the planet has these insecurities. It's just they deal with them differently. I've decided that my spotty forehead is an essential part of my identity, as is my unbrushable hair, my love of things that aren't exactly the grooviest things on the planet, my lack of time for some of the things that are. They're all part of me. I can live with them. I've actually woken up with a much clearer head than I think I've ever had before.

Yesterday, for the first time, I walked to school, looked up at the sky, at the plane trail 50000 feet above me, and, knowing that my deadwood Dad, I mean sperm-donor, is neither creating it or sitting in it on his way to somewhere I'm not, meant I didn't go into the usual train of thought that I drift off into most mornings, wondering about him. There's no need to wonder anything. Instead I can learn about my Mum, and other adults, and work out what's going on with them. My Mum's actually my Dad too. Her own life's on hold, for my benefit, and in an ideal world, it shouldn't need to be. When she's trying to persuade me to go out for a walk somewhere, baking a cake that I don't fancy, picking the phone up and going into badass mode with some numpty at school, or trying but failing miserably to bring me back to normality when I'm in a dark place, the word to pay attention to is 'trying'. She's got no natural talent for any of this, and she's certainly getting fuck all out of it for herself. Anyway, her efforts are acknowledged, so I'm going to go easier on her from now on. Much easier. Maybe I'll bake her a cake. Lara can get stuffed though. She's still a pain.

I breezed through the gates, the corridor and into the classroom, shoulders up, head up. Last Friday I had more bother from the class psycho. I had the upper hand, at least psychologically, and he's probably spent the weekend angrily plotting how to destroy me properly. I'm cool with that. I could even say I'm getting confident. I've kept my word about going on strike if I get any abuse, and school are starting to realise I mean business. I can tell with the teacher's response to me that I'm not joking, and they don't have the responses. Mum got a letter last week about my attendance. I'm on 65% for the term so far. In GCSE terms, that's a solid Grade B. They should be happy.

Joey Barker has this bullshit mantra that his feet do the talking. My feet express themselves far better than his. They propel me into the civilised world at the first sign of any grief coming my way. Today I have options. There's new issues of Dragonball out. If they're not in the library, then Waterstones is quiet enough on a Monday, and the staff there are as unconcerned about my presence there as the baristas in the Italian Coffee Company when I bring a tramp in for free lattes. I fancy doing both today, but Shelly's been on at me to go round to hers to help Joe out with his homework. He's going to fall as far behind with his schoolwork as I am, but I have the world's tiniest violin ready to play a tune on for that. I much prefer the adult world beyond these gates, and I'm way more comfortable there than I could ever be in school, I think.

Anyway, through the door, into tutorial, 20 questions immediately.

"What were you and Joey B up to on Saturday?"

Ha ha. The school's running low on gossip. I'm too smart for this. "We went to Africa to wrestle a giant rhinocerous."

"Piss off Edward. You got spotted in his Dads car."

"Oh yeah, I remember. Coming back from Beyonce's hotel. Jay-Z was in town laying some new stuff down in the studio. She was lonely."

"You think I'm soft?"

Yes. Stupid enough to lose your shit and give me an excuse to go walkies again, hopefully. "You might not like the answer, though I'd hope you could find it in your heart to respect my honesty and openness, though."

"You were in Joe's Dad's car. We saw you when you pulled up at't lights."

"We did a drive by shooting. Contract job. That's why Joe had his head down."

"Joe said he were at Man City."

"Course he did. He's not stupid enough to boast to all his mates he'd just done a drive-by, is he? Why would I go to a football match anyway? I don't even like football."

"Just behave. Did you go to City with him?"

"No, we went to Chuttleborough Train Museum. It was Thomas the Tank Day. Joe loves Thomas, but keeps quiet about it. Gordon the Big Engine's his favourite. If anyone wants to buy him a birthday present I have suggestions."

Seriously. Is nobody going to throw my bag across the room and call me a cunt? I'm trying my best here.

"That'll be why he were tekkin selfies in't stadium at 2.30 on Saturday afternoon then."

"No, he left at half-time to go shopping with his Mum. He'd run out of underwear. Kept having accidents. He'll tell you he hurt his ankle playing football. It's a front. Big problems downstairs. I'm not supposed to tell anyone, he even paid me to keep schtum. Oopsidaisies. Oh well. I didn't even want to go, but couldn't resist having his ticket while he walked round Marks n Spencer. I felt sorry for him. Only slightly, though."

"Why? he dun't do feeling sorry for anyone, least of all you."

"That's OK. I don't like him."

"So why you spending your Saturday wi'im?"
"Favour for his sister."

"You're mates wi' Shelly?"

"Ask Travis. We go back years."

"Fuck off!"

"Travis. Remember last week when you waited in town to get even with me, found me at the Bubble Tea place with my good buddy Shelly and the rest of my squad then ran home to your Mum?" I smile. Squad for God's sake. Not good. I'm starting to sound like them.

Everyone looks at Travis.

He sighs, reluctant to talk to anyone, "I thought she were shekkin you down for protection"

"Why'd she do that? She can't do anything in here, this place is just me against the rest of you here. I'm ready when you all are by the way."

Me against the rest of you. 1 vs 20. Your chances are good. Hit me. Now.

"Why the fuck would Shelley Barker knock about wi' you?"

"Because basically I'm a lovely guy with irresistable charm and top-level bantz." A couple of the girls, Shironda being one of them, smile. Them getting charmed by me is unlikely to get me any closer to Dragonball, so I add, "Unlike any of you tossers."

"I'm a lovely guy. Love it!" Welshy laughs. Funny how the kid most likely to be off his face is probably the one who can make sense of everything.

"Irresistable charm?" Beth looks at me, shoulders half-shrugged and pushing into the sides of her head "Yeah, you maybe. But please, explain Joey Barker. He's a precious little buttercup at't best of times. And now you're palled up wi' 'im? Are you mad?"

By now every single person in the class is hanging onto my every word. I've also noticed that Cory Hendricks isn't in. I nod over towards his desk.

"Oh, he's isolated in't steamer all week." Shironda shouted above all the others and wanted to be the first to tell me, whatever that's about "Headmaster took your side the other day."

"Oh bless. I'll miss him." I do already. I'd have been on my travels 5 minutes ago if he was here. Why is it you can't find a good bully when you really need one?

I catch a look from one of his mandemz that isn't good. Come on, roadman, time to step up. He does nothing. What's up, not enough back-up?

"So why are you palled up wi' Joe? Can't see you two being likely mates."

"I'm not. I was doing Shelly a favour."

"By hanging round wi' her brother?"

"Yeah. I saved her life once."

"Yeah right."

I'm getting bored now.

Shirondas' in. "Finished 3-1 dint it?"

She knows. Much much more than she's letting on here, so I'll be reyt with her.

"Yep. Shelly gave me her ticket. They don't get on, and seeing as him and everyone in this class has basically been a wanker with me since I first walked through the door, I fancied levelling the score up a bit. So, each time he deathglared me, I tapped his ankle or trod on his heel with the point of my shoe, accidentally of course. It was fun. Excruciatingly painful for him, but way more entertaining for me than any football match could ever be."

"How many times did you whack his ankle?"

"Lost count. He respects me a little more now, apparently."

I see the remaining members of Corey's little shitty crew paying attention, looking confused, trying to mentally work out who they'd back up in an Edward v Joe fight.

I carry on..."20 years from now, he'll remember my name and his ankle muscles will tighten just that little bit more in horror."

"He'll love himsen whatever you do to 'im." Shironda comes back in. She knows. She's mates with the girl who blew him away then blew him out this weekend.

"Not right now he doesn't. You know why." I look at her, eyebrows raised. Yeah, she knows.

There's a few looks coming my way now, as if I'm making it all up. I'll hold back the bit about him pissing himself. That bit can wait until I've found something worth blackmailing him for. Anyway, the teachers in. Registration. Alphabetically from surnames. When it gets to Bradley, silence.

"Anyone heard from Joe?" teach asks.

I feel eyes burning holes in me from all angles. I feel like a walking talking Emmental.

"If there's any schoolwork that needs to go home to him, I can give it to his sister?"

The teacher's eyes move to me, and he pauses. Yeah, it really was me. I really don't have to do this. Believe me, I don't really want to either. I actually only said that to reinforce the fact that me, and Joey Barker's big sister, are pretty decent buddies, for the benefit of all the mugs in here that are still trying to come to terms with the fact that this geek here is actually way more up the social ladder than they could dream themselves to be.

"Edward, thanks for the offer. I just get the feeling that once I'd round-robinned all his teachers and got something ready that you'd disappear on strike again?"

"Sir, I'm uncomfortable with the idea too, but this offer applies for a limited period. I'd be quick if I were you."

"Ok, thanks for the kind offer, I'll bear it in mind."

I sit back. No-one comments or even looks my way. Things are changing, positively. I should be overjoyed. I'm not. DragonBalls out. I want out by lunchtime.

----

33. A HAPPY ENDING

Monday morning. The beginning of a full week on the sofa. I should be buzzing for this, but I'm hating it. My phone's silent. One red box. Some random's birthday. Nowt else. I don't like it. God knows what lyrics Edward will spit out today. I really should be there to limit the damage. The boy saw me piss mesen. No-one lives down stuff like that. I remember in year 7 when some teacher wouldn't let Rhys Kent go to the loo, thinking he'd bunk off but he actually had some health problem which made him shit himself, which he did in front of everyone. I felt awful for him. No-one knows where he is now. Then there was that lass in Shelly's year who everyone called "Mars Bar" when someone found her using one to do summat rude. The grief she got was proper savage. She missed school for months, til someone else called bullshit and said that some other lass made it all up because she had beef with her over some lad. Wetting mesen in public is deffo on that level.

Edward could easily announce to everyone that I can't piss reyt. Alternatively, he's a bit smarter than most, so he might say nowt then blackmail me instead, like make me do endless favours for the next decade to make sure he forgets everything. Right now, I'll take that, at least til school ends and I then disappear.

I made it down the stairs on my feet today, handrail all the way, and managed to dress mesen all the way except for the one sock on the bad ankle. I'm still hoping to light train at the weekend, then get back on the pitch the week after. Mum's all up for giving me the week off, she's also proper keen to see me getting schoolwork done, too. I never trust her when she's like this, and once she's fixed me something to eat - cuppa tea and toast wi nowt on it - she rings school with an eagerness I've never seen from her before when performing the same identical job in the past with either me or the big sister.

After 10 minutes of hearing her say, "Yes, Mrs Frogson you have my guarantee on that" at least 3 times, she re-enters the living room, snatches my tablet away, and sits facing me.

"So where shall I start, son?"

"If that's Mrs Frogson, she dun't teach me and I don't even talk to her."

I'm bang-on. Unless you're one of those timid kids that need an office to hide in at break time, why would you want to spend any time chatting to a grim old cow like her anyway? She knows nowt about me. Mum's looks at me, expressionless.

"Making the bare minimum effort."

"Eh?"

"Homework's usually basic."

"What?"

"Except for PE, which is on a predicted grade A."

"So there you go. Nowt to fret about."

"English is scraping a D and Maths even less than that."

"Have you seen the state of the..." Interrupted. Rude!

"Punctuality's OK. Doesn't misbehave. Seeks no responsibility. Passive learner in most lessons. Check these comments."

"Says who?"

"Thinks he's doing a GCSE in looking out of the window. Varies unpredictably between passive learner and passive non-learner."

"Eh? Who said th-"

"Shut up, Joe."

OMG. Shut up yourself!

Mum carries on. "Not creating any problems. Not creating anything of merit either."

"So that's..."

"Below target in every subject except PE."

"It's only Year 10. I've got a year yet."

"Shall I ring City up? Hiya, Joe's tossing school off, but it's only Year 10 so we're all reyt aren't we?"

"Mum have you seen the others? Kyle can barely spell his name. He teks Handa's Surprise onto't bus to away games. Everyone at Brodie's school say he's a proper ..."

"I'm not responsible for them. You've got catching up to do."

"Yeah, I'll do it. I don't see what you're..."

"Too right you will. You've a busy week lined up, son. The X-Box is mine all week."

"No way!"

Mum looks at me, smiles and whispers, "Fancy racing me up the stairs to see who gets it first?"

Fuck.

"X-Box off. Phone hanging by a thread depending on how much you argue wi' me."

She's carried the phone threat out before. I shut up.

"Mrs Frogson has offered to gather some work up from your teachers. I'll ring her back to accept her very kind offer."

"And by the time it meks it through the letterbox, I'll be back at school ag..."

She's already out of the room and on the phone.

"Yes, Mrs Frogson please, Year 10 office."

A few seconds silence

"Hi Mrs Frogson it's Cait Barker again, Joe's Mum. Yes, if you could send some work to Joe, that'd be great. He's got a friend in school who'll be coming round to see him later, so you can send it all with him."

Can't hear what Mrs Frogson is saying back.

"Oh no, it's not any of those boys. I'd call in myself rather than trust them. If you can give the work to Edward Pendlebury, then I'm pretty sure it'll get here."

More muffled year head's talk that I can't work out.

"Not yet they're not, but me and Penny Pendlebury are long-standing friends going back all the way to our own schooldays. You'll probably not be interested in this but once upon a time I was the new girl in school, getting similar grief that I've heard Edward's getting. The one person that stepped in was Penny, hence my eagerness to repay the favour. Give it to Edward. I'll look after him, and I can promise you that very soon, Joe will be all too keen to do the same."

Bollocks to that. I'd rather have no mates than one spoddy one. More mumbles. No idea.

"Yes. Anyway, lovely chatting to you, Mrs Frogson. Whatever you get, he'll get it all done and back to you by Friday, you have my word on that, and hopefully he'll be back on his feet a week from now. Speak soon."

Mum walks back in and sits exactly where she sat before. "History repeats itself son. You've got a friend coming over for tea. In't that exciting? You may not think he's a friend, but from where I'm sat, you know fanny adams about friends anyway."

Before I can answer, Mum walks off into the kitchen to get ready for work, saying to herself, "I've waited years for this. I do love a story wi' a happy ending!"

34 ON STRIKE

It's bad enough having to stay in school all day when no-one gives you an excuse to walk out, but Mum telling me to get ready for tea at Joe Barker's was enough for me to throw my toys. I had a belter of an argument with her about it. Words got me nowhere unfortunately, so I used footsteps instead. Shoes back on, coat back on, and on my travels. Can't remember where I went, I wandered for an hour then strolled home, slowly. Once through the door, Mum simply turned round and said "Ready to go then? We're running late". I said I was as ready as Lara was, sat snug on the sofa in her onesie with laptop, telly and phone to herself. Apparently it was just me she expected to go. I tried the "I spent all of Saturday with him, which was more than long enough thanks." argument. It failed. I then changed tactic, and asked Mum "How's about we play a game? It's called not seeing Joe Barker. If you can get me there, you win. If I don't go, I win". I then walked straight out the front door, into the foggy evening, winning the game emphatically.

A slow wander through some woods, returning along the canal path at 8.30pm, ensured I was conveniently late enough to go no further than my bedroom. A changed atmosphere greeted my return. Silent treatment. No tea made, but it's not like I ever ask Mum to cook, so I'll do my own in a bit. I can do silent too, so I put my shoes and coat away then went upstairs without words being traded.

Settled for watching some random YouTubers acting like attention-seeking dicks, til my eyes went heavy and I drifted off. I did dream of something, and it woke me up, but I went back to sleep, and forgot what it was when I woke up again. No shouting out loud. No stiffy either. Can't have been that good. Got up in silence, too.

Mum's on strike. No clean gear hanging up for me, so I fished my shirt out of the laundry basket and my trousers off the floor, had a quick look in the mirror, the shirts crumpled to buggery so I stuck a jumper over it so no-one notices. Then I realise I'm missing a trick, as a scruffy uniform will draw comments in the classroom that can enable me to go on strike myself, so I ditch the jumper back onto the floor.

Breakfasts easy. Coco-pops. Milk. No Haribos. The silence is making the whole house awkward so shoes on, coat on, and I'll make sure I come back here instead of town if I walk out today. Pick the bowl up and knock back the chocolate milk, scoop the cereal into the bin, and I'm away.

Nothing fazes me anymore. I choose the bus to school with most schoolkids on it, as this means more chance of some kid telling me to fuck off for no reason at all, which in turn means more chance of actually getting what I want, as well as obeying that particular command. Only a few kids get on at the same time as me. A really overweight girl and her friend, I think they're in my year, look at me, look at each other and giggle. I spot this as my chance. I get on the bus after them, follow to where they decide to sit, and put myself on the seat right behind them, in the middle of the seat so each time they look at each other, I'm in the corner of their eye, too.

Then my phone goes off.

Probably Mum. She's not communicating verbally, so it'd make sense to get a text from her.

Nah, not Mum. Shelley Barker.

"*1.00 outside that Coffee place. Don't fret about ££*"

It's a date.

I hope she knows I don't fancy her. For all that ruthlessly eye-catching awesomeness that she exudes effortlessly, she's also Joey Barker's sister.

"OK. Am at school. Need a way out"

"On it! :-)"

So, into school. Cory Hendricks is still simmering in isolation, slowly plotting revenge. I took it a bit far last week, shoving him about on the way to the heads office. He'll not forgive that quickly. Walked past the isolation room. He's sat there, front seat from the teacher's desk. Some year 9 with a black eye sat across from him, and another kid of the same age, no black eye, sat at the back. I stop by the window and face him down. He responds in kind. Stare warfare. For a full 5 seconds. Then whichever teacher's sat in there with him looks over, so I continue towards the classroom.

I try the same stunt at break time, but the reaction's not the one I want.

The reaction I do want appears in the corridor, less than a minute later.

Some lad from year 11, who's clearly been waiting for me, who I've never seen before, collars me and whispers "Shelley Barker told me I've got to say this."

"Eh?"

"Actually I've got to proper shout it out."

"Shout what out?"

"She gave me 2 cigs."

"Is she trying to kill you?"

"Don't tek it personal. I'm just earning a living."

"OK, fine, earn your slow death."

"I FUCKING HATE YOU, YOU WEIRD CUNT!!"

Oh yeah, I get it, my invitation to depart the premises. Cheers pal.

I reply, loudly, shocked and offended of Tunbridge Wells, "WHO ON EARTH DO YOU THINK YOU ARE? NO-ONE HAS THE RIGHT TO TALK TO ME LIKE THAT!!"

Silence.

"Cheers mate!" I whisper quietly, then head for the exit. I hurtle helplessly through the curious teenage onlookers, through the same school reception I walked through only 5 minutes ago, and past the sound of my name being called out by an adult I don't care to respond to. If they don't know the rules by now, they never will.

"Edward!!"

I keep walking, purposely, through the gates, down the hill, over the bridge, past McDonalds, past some shops, through some car park, across the road, through the bus station and into the crowds. Shelly's already there. Her, Tariq, Maya...

"You got your message then..."

"Yes thanks, really appreciate it."

"You're coming wi' us."

"Why, are you kidnapping me?"

"You bet your spotty arse we are" Smiles from all of them, "Back to mine!" Smiles just from Shelly. I smile back, thinking of how many lads have dreamed of hearing those words from her.

"What to do?"

"Bantz."

"What do you want to chat about?"

"A bit of this, a bit of that, and a little bit of family history."

----

35 Toast

Have you ever checked the sky out when things are about to get ugly, where the clouds go multiple shades of black, grey, purple, every grim colour, where you know there's a massive dramatic bastard of a thunderstorm on its way so you scrap any plans to go out, think yourself lucky you're not at sea and either stop in bed or waste your day on Fifa instead? Well that's how the entire area around my ankle now looks. The clouds start halfway down my foot then go most of the way up to my knee. It looks a reyt atrocious mess. This, of course, is an excellent reason, two excellent reasons in fact, to be more uplifted than I've been in days.

1) It's still ugly enough to keep me off school long enough for some new drama to kick off, so that once I'm back through the gates, my time hanging round with Edward will be cat litter news.

2) I can feel my mobility coming back, hence closer to resuming my journey to the Champions

League.

I managed to get dressed and get down the stairs by mesen, and I made my own food too. I've sussed how the toaster works. Plugged it in, swat some bread in, the sliced stuff fits best even though I hate it, and then watched it til it popped up. I've not managed to butter it properly yet. I had a go but it were rock hard and I ended up ripping the bread to shreds. I had another go, used margarine instead and I didn't just master it I nearly fucking Instagrammed it til I remembered that I can't stand people who upload their breakfast. I tried making a cuppa tea as well. I couldn't work out what order to do it all in, or how much milk you need to stick in it or which teabags to use. I used what Mum calls the posh tea. It smelt OK in the box but once the milk and water went in it looked proper minging, so I abandoned it til I've had another look what everyone else does again, and I'll try again another day.

Checked my phone to see if any new drama had kicked off. It's only Tuesday so there's plenty of time yet. I'm not up for talking to anyone anyway. I've always said my feet do the talking, so I've already decided I'm speaking to no-one from football until I'm back on the pitch. It took me a while to realise, but your team-mates aren't necessarily your mates. You're just kids chasing the same dream, so your mates are whoever gets put alongside you at the time. Personally, once I'm away from the pitch and changing-room, I've no desire to get too close to Dan, and Brodie's an unpleasant arsehole at the best of times. Of the others, Oscar seems bang on when I chat to him, but he lives at the other side of town. I've only really ever seen Brad and Ben as mates, and even then, if either of those two got released, I couldn't promise I'd stay in touch with them. I'll bet any money that Hassan's phone and pages have been free from any of us collaring him to see how he is. Though there's all these mantras about loyalty, team spirit, camaraderie, half of its bullshit. There's no loyalty between anyone, and, nowadays, I've more interest in watching Strictly Come Dancing than I have in getting to know any of these guys well.

Every single one of my schoolmates also has a sell-by date of the day after year 11 officially ends, a day to be remembered in history as "The Day of The Great Cull" - when 90% of my Facebook, Snapchat and Instagram disappear mysteriously. Shelly said she spent year 11 slowly deciding who she'd stay in touch with when school ended, who she wouldn't, who she trusted, who she never could, who was cool in year 7 but no longer, and who were dipshits in year 7 but were now cool. She had a group of six girly friends who were like a sleepover club in year 7, but by year 11, she was being polite to two of them who secretly she couldn't stand, and they were being polite back although they by now detested her. Of the remaining 4, there was one lass she adored but knew that all she'd be doing with her future would be hanging round with whoever grew the most superstrength mong-out weed and scraping the bits that fell on the floor, so she decided she was good for Facebook, a chat when they crossed paths, and nowt more. That left three, two that were loved up with older lads and racing each other to be the first to show off engagement rings, flats, babies, etc, etc, before the other, so she quietly edged herself out of their lives and let them get on with it. That left one, Fyza, who was going to the same college, different course. After a couple of days of meeting up with kids from 100 other schools, all undertaking the same exercise of dumping old mates and meeting new ones, they drifted away from each other in the loveliest way possible. Shelly's probably on meet-up terms with 3 kids from school. One's Fyza, who I guess, being a second year hairdresser, is a useful and economical friend to have. There's also Millie, who she was at primary with, drifted away from in secondary when they got put in different streams, then chatted again in college. The other friend she has from school is Tariq. They were never mates in school, but weren't enemies either, but found themselves in college, same course, same class. Though they barely spoke to each other in 5 years at school, you can tell they actually quite fancy each other now, like proper legit, not checking each other's legs and arses out, but more like their faces lighting up and animating when they chat to each other. Even though she's a twat, and he must be a twat for liking her, it's actually quite sweet to see but I can't see owt blossoming, because I reckon when college finishes, all those friendships will die off like foliage in autumn and new ones will appear like snowdrops in February when they get jobs or go to uni or wherever. Anyway, in one of her rare wiser moments, Shelly's words were "you think when you leave school you'll stay bezzies wi' everyone forever and ever, then once you're through the gates for the last time, the real world turns up in front of you and tells you it's time to bin 298 of those chuffers off and keep 2".

Since she told me all this, I've wondered which 2 I'd keep. I always thought Sam would be one and Archie the other, but as time passes, this is looking less likely. If I make pro, it won't be wise to be palled up with a hopeless replica shirt collecting wannabee top lad with a thug mentality like Sam. Archie? He's got a 50% chance of moving to his Dads in Scotland when school ends, so there'd be no point. I've no romantic interest in any of the girls here. There's something about spending 5 years in a classroom with someone that removes every hint of attractiveness from them. That, plus any of the girls in my year that are checking lads out, are checking the older lads out, the ones that have money, maybe cars, can get served alcohol, not the sadsacks in my year that are sat in their bedrooms losing on Fifa, or in the youth club sneaking smuggled vodka into their Panda Pops. Presently, I see a leave 300 kids behind and choose 0 situation. But then again, another thought creeps up on me, creeps up on me with bushy mad scientist hair, a duffel coat and Grandad banter.

Though Edward will probably get me beaten up and blown out in equal measure, Mum means business with this arranged friendship. City can ring school up whenever they wish, and if they get told that I'm doing nowt in school, then I'm on my way down the great pyramid of football to getting my legs broken on some Sunday league pitch, or trialing hopelessly and endlessly at Stockport or Halifax or somewhere miles away. Not worth risking.

So, I've got school work to catch up on, and their big idea is to send Edward over, as he's behind too. I've still no idea what the fuck to talk to him about. I don't even know what he's into. He's a geek, full-on. I can't see him on Fifa or GTA cos if he did he'd never log off. Minecraft's definitely his level of geeky, though he must a bit old for that by now, surely. Skyrim might be up his street, or any other niche no-mates strategy game that never gets completed but dictates the sad lives of many a billy dotted in bedrooms with the curtains shut tightly to the midday sun all around the world. He's probably one of those geeks with hundreds of mates spread across the world in New York and Hong Kong and Sydney and everywhere in between but hasn't met any of them in person and would be extremely disappointed if he did. I've heard him talking about comic books. That daft Japanese shit mainly. Doctor Who? Harry Potter? I asked Shelly last night if I could borrow one. She agreed, brought me down her copy of "Harry Potter and the Deathly Hallows" and told me straight away "He dies, by the way". She meant to annoy me with that, but she's also daft enough to think I'm actually going to read enough of it to be arsed to reach the end. I'll watch the film instead. It doesn't take as long.

I can't do geek. Dad and Edward can chat with no inhibitions about any level of sad shit - wildlife, politics, history, all of it - and all I can do was sit silently scrolling whilst avoiding getting into any conversation I've never been arsed to ever think twice about. Anyway, I've been told to expect the boring bastard anytime soon. Mum's been talking pizzas and donuts and whatever else is in the academy handbook's not-the-greatest-of-fucking-ideas list, but only once he's shown up and we've got pens and books out. He's behind too, mostly because he keeps getting out of his chair and walking off out of school every time someone calls him a name. He needs to grow a pair, or even better, go on trial at the academy and get megged in front of his entire family. That really hurts.

When the door crashes open, I've hit page 46 of "Deathly Hallows". As promised, Edward walks in with Shelly, Tariq and Maya. Shelly fancies the arse off Tariq. It's blatant. The fun bit for me is when Tariq comes round, he's more into talking about football with me than any of her daft shit, and Shelly both knows it and hates it. True to form, Tariq clocks my leg hoisted high onto the arm of the chair.

"Ankle?"

"Aye, shit tackle the other week. On't mend now, though."

"Not missing owt decent I hope?"

"Nah," Shelly chips in, "just Man City away, only one o't best teams in the entire universe, bless ya." condescendingly ruffling the top of my head. I raise my middle finger to the point that in my line of view, it rests squarely between her eyes. Observing silently, comically out of place, is Mr Pendlebury. Imagine your driveway has 4 cars on it, a Lambo, a Porsche, a Ducati and a grey Ford Fiesta, 02 plate.

"You'd better get a chair." I shout over to him.

"Anywhere?" he does that 'I'm-in-someone-elses-house-so-i'll-be-polite-and-painfully-sincere-manner. He places himself on the sofa I'm not sat on, taking up the left hand side of it.

"Got any school stuff with you?"

"Some of it. I'm having difficulties getting school to believe that I'm actually taking stuff to you. There's English, French and Food Tech. The IT teacher, not sure of his name, looks like Harry Hill, either Mr Jackson or Johnson, thinks I'm joking when I ask for your work. I've been to PE and he's told me not to worry as you're ahead."

"Mr Jackson. He's a prat anyways.

"Ok. Which ones are you behind in?"

"All't lot of them except PE, so Mum says. What about you?"

"All of them except philosophy. That's piss easy, though. We've got a new subject coming up. Do some research, then go to class and find someone to argue with. Its capital punishment I think."

"What's that?"

"Firing squads and hanging criminals and stuff. Decide if it's a good idea or a daft one, then write your view up and make some notes about the opposing view. If we agree the same way, we can write that one up in 20 minutes and breeze an A each."

"Ok, what's for't others?"

"That Mockingbird book for English. I've already finished it. There'll be an essay soon, so make sure you read it and don't just look at the pictures."

"Whatever. What's Food Tech? Are we mekkin owt yet?"

"No idea. It's all written on the sheets. You'll know some of this stuff cos you do all that nutrition stuff with football, so you can do the Food Tech work without me."

"Sounds like a good piece of business"

"Absolutely. I don't do social. Not with anyone from school anyway."

"Just jakeys. And my sister"

"Both of them being infinitely more well-rounded, interesting and pleasant personalities than anyone I share a classroom with. Including you. Don't ever forget that."

"Whatever. Business suits me. So when you're ready."

"Yes. So much to do. So little time."

Shelly quickly disappears into the kitchen, rummages through some cupboard and returns with a biscuit selection box, and some drinks of pop that no-one takes. I notice empty spaces where the Oreos should be. Me and Edward get busy. French is translating a load of childish stories, from some proper scrubby old books. They're second hand, maybe even third or fourth hand. One of them "Daniel et Valerie a la Mer", has each character illustrated on every page with either a giant spunking cock or a scribble as if to denote a hairy vadge, drawn by someone who I'm sure hasn't looked at genitals in much detail, not even their own. Luckily "Daniel et Valerie a la Campagne", "Daniel et Valerie en Angleterre", have no such embellishments, so we look at them first. Google should sort this shit very easily, but we stay busy, business-like, til suddenly, the concentration gets broken.

"What's crack wi' that Darren bloke, Edward?" Shelly asks, out of the blue.

"Donovan?" Ed corrects her.

"Mum calls him Darren", Shelly persists.

"Oh I don't know. He's just someone I chat to." Ed tries to dismiss the conversation, and fails.

"He's got history with your Mum, my Mum, my Dad. He even knows your Dad." Shelly looks over at Edward to see if there's a reaction going on.

"Yeah, I know. He's welcome to him."

"Go on then. It's famalam business. Nowt's going online" Shelly does this cheesy grin where she screws her nose up like a fucking rabbit or whatever

"Give me five minutes to think about it."

"How's about 2?"

Edward takes the full 2 minutes to decide whether to satisfy Shelly's nosiness, or to flee on his travels. I'm still not sure if I should care a shit about any of it. I was happy enough translating a story about little French people going to the seaside with giant spunking genitals bigger than the rest of their cartoon bodies. Shelly never did GCSE French, so clearly thinks otherwise.

----

36. UNACCUSTOMED AS I AM TO PUBLIC SPEAKING

Well, they did ask.

"Are you sure you really want to hear any of this?" I thought I'd best double-check. And see if I can actually avoid this.

"Why, is it boring?" Joe asks.

"It might be."

"Is it more boring than this fucking Mockingbird book looks?"

"We've got Shakespeare once that's finished. You've not even experienced boring yet."

"Ok, so let's wait 'til we're on that book then."

"Ok, sound."

"In your dreams. Get on wi' it." Shelley intervenes.

"Ok. I've only got Donovan's side of the story. What if he's made it all up?"

"Er, hello? He's an adult, so there's gonna be big stinking piles of bullshit to treasure hunt through, but the truth'll be in there somewhere."

"Aye, just spill it, we'll work it all out." Tariq backs Shelley up.

So, though I'd not planned it, I'm set to share parent history with their curious offspring. "Ok, but promise me something."

"Oh, I don't know about that. Making promises is never a smart move." Shelley replies.

"Not a single word to my sister. I've not even said anything to her myself."

"I dunno, I might go and find all her mates maybe?" Tariq jokes.

"I mean it. I've no idea what goes through her head, and she never mentions him. One day she will, and I'd rather tell her."

"Ok, Ok we all fucking promise." Shelley's getting impatient. I'm not far off a safe limit.

And so I take a deep breath, get as much oxygen in as I can without looking daft while doing so, noticing every face focused intently on me. I gaze back at each one in turn. Either eyebrows or the end of their nose. Unaccustomed as I am to public speaking, here goes...

"Right, you know my Mum and your Mum were school mates?"

"You've heard them, right? Put them together and they're like little giggly dipshit year 8s."

"Donovan was in the same class as them both at school. He'd been in primary school with my Mum, but never had much to do with her. No beef, just different mates, did different things at playtime, all that lot. Your Mum started there at the beginning of year 9. When she started, she didn't get much of a welcome."

"Like you right now then, Edward? New school, all't kids being dicks with you" Shelly asks, nodding over at Joe.

I look over to Joe, "Yeah, spookily similar. New school. Dickheads. Sitting comfortably?"

Shelly chips in, "Perched on't edge of us seats in wild anticipation of your curious story. I mean, just look at us all. Except for Joe here who reckons he can stretch himsen out on account of a poorly leg. Sit up ya little twat!"

With the turning speed of an ocean liner, and a couple of ouchy sounds that seem like he may be acting it out a bit, Joe slowly manoeuvres himself 90 degrees and deathglares his big sister.

I begin, "Right. Your Mum. I'll call her Cait, what with that being easier than going - your Mum my Mum your Mum - turned up in school in year 9. A few people knew her, but more people knew her brothers. They did boxing or bare-knuckling or something for money. A few kids in the class had beef with her straight away, on account of their big brothers having lost money and teeth to them."

"Yes. This is most informative. Continue at your leisure", Tariq's on a wind up.

"The girls were a different matter entirely. When they realised that this new girl had a short fuse and getting her from calm to furious was as easy as pressing that light switch over there, they worked out exactly what to say, and every time they hit the switch, she blew up so easily that any teachers knocking around only noticed the bomb that was Cait exploding, not the schemy cows that were priming that bomb beforehand. This went on for a bit, and school weren't arsed with bringing counsellors or behaviour support in. They didn't bother with any of that back then, they'd just sit her outside the classroom, or isolate her, or move her lessons. Because everyone thought she was a gypsy they didn't think she'd bother coming to school that much so they were going to put her in the slow class, then they realised that her writing and Maths and all that was just as good as anyone else's really, so they mixed it up a bit and stuck her in with the boffins for some lessons. She walked into her first lesson, and everyone in there had put their bags on any spare chairs so she had nowhere to sit. She sussed what was going on straight away, so when no-one moved their bags she picked the biggest lad in the class, kicked him off his own chair onto the floor and swat him and all his gear across the room, then suddenly just as teacher walked in this little voice squeaked out "You can sit next to me if you want?" Guess who that was?"

"Your Mum?"

"Yes. Let's call her Penny. It's what my granny does."

"Has your Granny got a proper hardcore name, too?"

"Whatever. Anyway. Donovan witnessed all that. He said Penny was one of those kids that no-one ever noticed. She never said much, hung round with the same one or two girls, didn't flirt with lads, just sat quietly and did her work. Even though he'd been in the same lessons as her for 10 years, Donovan never knew much about her. She was never out and about at a weekend, no drinking, no getting stoned, none of that."

"Sounds like a reyt nightmare."

"Yeah, I'd hoped she was a bit more thuglife too. Like me. But you can't have everything." Shelly, Tariq, Maya smile at that. Joe does, in a wholly different way. Like he's worried. Like he's worked out my banter's better than his, and his self-esteem falls another small rung from that mighty perch the world of junior football once placed him on. "Donovan said even when Cait sat herself next to her, he still expected nonsense to kick off, especially when he noticed Cait sat for ages with her fists clenched ready for action. The stories much longer. Don't know if I can be arsed though."

Shelly walks over to the back door to lock it, shouting over, "You'll not be mekkin it out of this house alive til you do!"

"Ok, but tell me if I get boring."

I look at Joe.

Joe returns the glance, "Er hello? As if I've anywhere better to go right now?"

I continue.

"So, they hung around together a bit from there, even they were into different things. Penny had that gothy indie band thing on the go, Echo & the Bunnymen, The Cure, all that lot." Blank faces. Yeah I guess it was a long time ago. "They weren't likely mates at all. Penny never got picked on. In fact she never got noticed, but when she started knocking about with Cait, she moved up a level or two. Donovan saw it all."

"How does he remember all that? Surely his heads proper amnesia'd to fuck from whatever he's been off his face on."

"He's got a story too. Anyone who sleeps in a shop doorway has a story, don't they? I've heard some of it. I'm sure there's bits he's missing out, deliberately probably, but I'm cool with it. He's been in the Army and got sent somewhere that's given him nightmares forever, drunk himself stupid and put whatever shit into his system that can help him get rid of whatever he can't cope with thinking about. That's his story though, and everything he's said about my Mum and your Mum, now I've thought about it, makes sense."

"How? Like palling you two up wi' each other like they palled up in school?"

"As in, Joe here's no fan of mine, and basically I think he's a bit of a prat, but here's our parents planning Nandos and football matches and probably Disneyland for all I know, the way they're going on at the moment. Why do you think they're doing that?" I look at Joe. His focus on my words is intense, more intense than he'd want anyone to spot. "Like I said, Donovan saw it all. Both him and Penny were in top set English, Penny because she actually enjoyed reading books, which Donovan never made sense of as he liked to read fuck-all in his spare-time. Reading was too geeky for him but he knew song lyrics, and could explain the deeper meanings of any song, and if he couldn't he'd just make it all up and still impress the teachers. He had to do an essay analysing the meaning and beauty behind a piece of poetry of his choice, so he analysed "The Message" by Grandmaster Flash. His teacher hated hiphop and gave him an "E", but the teacher from boffins class saw it and immediately shifted him into his lesson. Even when he left school with piss-poor grades, he left with passes in English, and English Lit too. I've seen the stuff he reads when he's keeping warm in the library. It's not Take A Break Magazine. Anyway, he ended up in the same College as Cait and Penny. Donovan thought Penny would go to Uni and end up a primary school teacher, cos he said she had one of those faces full of kindness and humanity like all the best primary teachers have, and she could play the piano a little bit. He can't remember what Cait was doing but they still both hung around together. Donovan didn't have a clue what to do so he put himself on an engineering course because his Grandad said it'd be a good idea. My Dad, lets called him dickhead, also did engineering, sort of."

"Sort of?"

"Yeah, he was a year older. He turned up late. He left his Mums house when school ended and moved to his Dads in Lincolnshire, in some tiny village in the middle of nowhere, went to college there, and jacked it after 2 weeks. His Dad got fed up of him sleeping in til lunchtime and doing nothing, and when he told him to either start work picking cauliflowers out of the ground or to go back to where he came from, so he went back to his Mum, who was shacked up with a new bloke that he didn't like that much. His Mum let him stay as long as he put himself into college, and if he missed a single day, he'd be sent back on the next rattly train to those cauliflowers. So he turned up, not caring less about what he was doing, and ended up sitting next to Donovan for two years. He kept telling Donovan he was going to be a pilot for British Airways, as his Dad had a mate who was one and would sort him a job out. Donovan thought bullshit straight away, but at the time he couldn't exactly preach sermons about honesty, as he himself was telling lasses he fancied that he was DJ Dippy D and was filling old warehouses up at acid raves, whatever they were. He said he even introduced him to Penny, but there wasn't much happening in the love chemistry department, not for a few years anyway."

"So Penny and Cait stayed mates then?"

"Right through. Penny would pick out concerts she'd want to go to, The Smiths, The Stone Roses, all that old stuff, so Cait repaid her earlier offer of friendship and would go along so she wasn't alone, even though she thought the music was rubbish. Cait got Penny bits of part-time work with her family so she could get enough money to pay for both of their concert tickets - frying bacon, cleaning windows, anything her brothers had spare. Eventually they ended up working in my Great-Aunts burger caravans at the football grounds and pop concerts, United one Saturday, Wednesday the next, then the odd week night or two. After a while, Cait started dating some other lad from college who was doing sport, a lad called Jim."

"Ha ha. He's never been a lad, ever!" Shelly says.

"OK. Donovan didn't really know Jim, but said he guessed he played football as every footballer back then had this comedy mullet haircut thing going on. He'd been released by Wednesday just before he left school, and went on trial everywhere desperately trying to get someone to sign him up. He had a chance of going to America, got through all the football trials, just needed the education, so was doing college so he could get on the big plane going west. That was his big idea, then one day, not many weeks before he was due to fly out, both he and Cait witnessed something that changed them both."

"True love and all that shit? Cupid appearing out o't sky doing archery practice? This is my Mum and Dad. You're on shaky ground. Be careful." Shelly chips in.

"The Hillsborough Disaster."

Lead balloon. Mood killed. Like when you're playing Cards Against Humanity and someone lays the Madelaine McCann card out. I'm guessing there is stuff here that they don't know.

"Yeah, I know they were there." Shelly throws in, quite possibly lying. Joe looks at her alarmed. He knows nothing, obviously.

"No. They weren't. Cait was in her Aunt's caravan trying to sell greasy food, wondering why all the customers were going home early. Your Dad was playing a match out of town somewhere. Like Hillsborough it was a cup semi-final. He'd played the game of his life, defended a 1-0 lead through to full-time. He was due for some big celebrations, £200 in his pocket for making the final, and clubs offering him more trials over the summer. The final whistle went and he couldn't understand why nobody was bouncing up and down celebrating."

"Yeah. Mum mentioned it."

"You know owt Joe?"

"Bits."

"Right. Her Aunt's caravan was across the road from the New Barrack pub, where all the other team's fans were, not Liverpool, but whoever they were playing. She expected to be rushed off her feet until the game started, then would clean up for a bit ready for another spell of running round like a blue-arsed fly at full time, then clearing up again. When it wasn't exactly happening like that, and people were walking out, but the game had barely started, she ran to the ground to see if she could work out what was going on. She was able to peek through the turnstiles and saw everything, ambulances all over, people frantically running round the pitch or laid out on advert boards which were now death beds. The memories never left her. The hopeless feeling of watching death and being helpless to do anything. That feeling probably stayed with everyone that was there. Donovan mentioned another kid he knew whose Dad worked there who ended up drinking himself to an early grave because he didn't cope with what he saw and didn't think he did enough. Your Mum's response to all this was to become an ambulance driver, so that if she witnessed any of this again, she'd be a bit less fucking useless than she felt that day. Guess what she's doing now?"

"You're seriously not gonna call that a happy ending are you?"

"Donovan didn't. No-one did. Jim's response was to pack up football immediately. The whole lot, playing, his college course, going to America. For 19 years he'd been living for it, and couldn't understand people dying for it. He wanted nothing more to do with it. You know that saying people have sometimes "Football's not a matter of life and death, it's more important than that?"

"I hear it every day I go to training and twice on match days."

"Not from your Dad you won't. Ever. Someone said it to him at college not long after. Donovan said he swung a punch at the bloke and sent him flying. He got interviewed by the police for it, not charged, but it went on his record. It would've stopped him going to America, visa rules and all that, but by then he didn't care. Donovan remembers asking him about that one punch that sent the guy flying. What Donovan got back was that Jim realised how seriously he was taking what was just a game, and decided that people dying just to cheer a team on no longer made sense. Not to him anyway."

"That'll be why he barely talks to anyone at matches then."

"It's also why, if you get released, he'll not care. He sees the real world. You will one day." Shelly looks over at Joe.

"I like that world because you're not in it." Joe throws back, starting a new sibling scrap with no chance of winning.

Shelly snaps. "Shut your stupid little mouth. It all meks sense to me. It's why you and Eddie the legend here are getting palled up, and there's nowt either of you can do about it."

"Since when has he been a legend?" Joe protests.

"Since I decided he were. I know one when I spot one."

"Anything more, legend?" Joe turns to me. If Shelly loses her shot with him, I'm so not getting involved.

"Shitloads. You not bored yet?"

"Something about the way you tell a story, Edward. Just think how mint News At Ten would be if they sat you at the big desk?" Tariq digs the feuding siblings out of a hole.

Deep breath. "Oh he started on about what happened next and I stopped listening for a bit. Sorry."

"So that's it?"

"I'm sure he went on about himself from there. Are you sure you're not bored yet?"

"Nope. Crack on. I love stories me", Tariq sits on the floor, legs still crossed like he's back in reception class.

"Right, so your Dad and football finished with each other there and then. Someone tapped him up for rugby league. He trained a few times, thinking he'd might travel somewhere that way, but his heart wasn't in it. Donovan lost touch with everyone soon after that. He had to move out of his Mums house, and had nowhere to go. He didn't fancy going to the council, as they stuck all the young single lads in the shittiest bedsits in the roughest bits of town, so he joined the army instead. He'd never planned to be a soldier, but he had some certificates from college and he thought that if he signed up he'd have a roof over his head. He did, what he didn't realise is it'd be in Kosovo and then Iraq waking up in a piss-filled trench with rats and dead comrades with half their heads blown away next to him most days. He cut a lot of that stuff out, about what he'd done and seen, but I got why. I realised whatever happened to him there sorted out the next bit of his life, and why he is where he is now. He did mention that when he went into town and signed up for the army, my Dad, was talking to the RAF at the same time. He was still telling him he'd passed college with distinctions and the RAF were fast-tracking him to be a fighter pilot or some bollocks. This bit does me emotionally, not in a good way, but gets me proper angry, so bear with me."

"He's not a sex case or a wife beater or owt is he?"

"No, none of that. I clung onto this idea that he'd be in touch with me one day. I thought that in spite of all the overwhelming evidence that said otherwise, there probably was some excellent reason I never saw him."

Nods.

"Right. Donovan was in the army for a few years. He'd been sent somewhere grim, and whatever he saw or did there, he didn't cope and it mashed his brain up. He had a baby with some lass he met in a disco one time near his army base and when he came out, he didn't cope living with her as he'd never had to, and she didn't have a clue who he really was without the fancy uniform, and even less idea what having PTSD was like. Not many people do, do they? She just liked the idea of copping off with a soldier. Men in uniform. All that bullshit. It didn't last. He had some money that the army gave him, which he spunked on whatever drugs could block his nightmares out, as well as a car he was always too out of his box to drive. He ended up homeless, hundreds of miles from home, with addiction issues and no chance of getting a job that he could turn up on time for, what with his brain being on another planet."

"But he's been a soldier and that, so he'd get looked after, right?"

"As if. The one's who got out of his regiment in one piece all had their heads fucked up and no-one giving a shit. Donovan says he knows some old mates doing long prison stretches for losing their heads one day, some others who stepped in front of trains or loaded a pistol up and also lost their heads in a whole new way. He thinks he's one of the lucky..."

"Stepped in front of trains?"

"Small world, like I said. You know when Jim was slipping Donovan a fiver on Saturday night, you saw that?" I look towards Joe.

"Yeah, I saw that."

"That was your Dad making sure Donovan wasn't going to lose it and step in front of anything but the front door of wherever gave out food or shelter."

"He freaked when he saw him."

"I freaked too. I'd no idea they knew each other, but then again, they're both quite old, so i guessed they'd both know loads of people anyway."

"So that's why he's here now? Cos he knew people? Seems to me like he's got no-one?"

"Well he had a few people once. He got a bedsit off London Road, and though he was struggling to get a job, he was getting counselling off someone who Penny also knew. He'd not got clean from drugs, but he was managing to go longer periods without. He thought he was getting past the worst and he'd be OK, eventually. Then my Dad bumped into him, with nowhere to go and needing somewhere to stay. If Donovan knew that he'd not long since ratted on Penny, or had even been in a relationship with my Mum, he'd have said "see ya later" and crossed the road. Unfortunately at the time, the Jobcentre and Child Support were having difficulty understanding how he'd managed to get rid of £18000 from his bank so quickly, so the offer of £30 cash to have some old acquaintance kipping on his floor was very useful indeed."

"So he's mates wi' your Dad?"

"My Dad's a mystery to me in many ways, but I've learned I can depend on him for two things. One's lying about everything, and the other's fucking other people's lives up with minimal effort. Donovan let him on the floor of his bedsit. Donovan was trying to pull himself together so he could face going back down south, finding his toddler and say "Hi I'm your Dad" He heard all the stories about how cruel everyone had been to him, how he couldn't finish his computer game without some kid yelling at him for food or a clean nappy. More than that, my Dad had borrowed money here, there and everywhere. He'd spun my Mum this fairy story that he was training to be a pilot for Easyjet and was in training every week, when he was actually working in Skegvegas in some amusement arcade, or not even bothering to do that if there was some daft scam going on, blowing the little money he had on shit that he didn't need, when he could've been chipping in for baby clothing. Penny didn't take kindly to it. She'd had to drop university when my grandad died and get a job, quick. She worked with your Mum somewhere til your mum went off to have you. My Mum tried to get herself education and keep a job going, then, on a drunken night after some concert she'd been to, she bumped into my Dad, chatted for ages about old college times and ended up having drunk sex, which led to me. Anyway, popping me out meant that my Mums ideas and dreams of her own were on hold for years, but she still talks about them. Hopefully she'll do them one day. Anyway, she relied on my Dad being sensible and responsible, if only for a few years. He bluffed her endlessly that he was, even when she started finding letters that he'd never opened from people she'd never heard of that he'd borrowed from that she'd never seen turn into anything useful. The people who wrote those letters became visitors, so he responded by taking off without letting anyone know where he was. When she gave up trying to find him, she got the child support agency to have a go. When they found him, he responded by jacking his job in so no-one could get any money off him. Donovan knew nothing, didn't even make the link that this "Penny" lass that was giving his lodger a hard time was the geeky bookish lass he went to school with, just like he's been chatting to me for weeks and not knowing who I am. It was your Dad that pointed that one out for him. Anyway, one day 2 ugly roided-up gorilla men turned up to his door threatening violence if he didn't pay his debts. My Dad had been borrowing money using Donovans address. Of course, as soon as Donovan messaged him to ask what the fuck was going on, my Dad legged it into thin air once more, and Donovan ended up locked out of his bedsit with what was left of his life's possessions in the back of some strangers van."

"At least you're more like your Mum eh?" Shelly replies.

"Yeah thanks for that."

"You're not planning to visit him are you? You could do without the head fuck surely?"

"Nah, I know where he is. Donovan's told me. But I'm happy to leave him where he is for now, in his sweaty bedsit eating Rice Krispies for Sunday dinner, but one day, when I've got the swanky job, the shiny car, the material shit, plus my Mums got her bills all paid, or the nearest I can get to it, I'll knock on his door. When he answers, clocks me looking 100 times better than him, I'll hi-five him for supporting me with fuck-all and then turn round, go, never think of him again, and leave him to an old age of loneliness."

"Yeah, karma."

"So now you know why I'm happy to be mates with a tramp? Why I'm perfectly happy to be the school billy? If my Dad can let me down, anyone can, simply."

"So you're gonna do all that "trust nobody" mantra?"

"Nah, I might be able to trust some people. I'd need to see something from them first. People think I can't handle school cos I keep getting picked on. Wrong. I'm used to that. I just think life's too short to spend it in the company of cunts."

Tariq reaches to fist-bump me. Shelly and Maya turn to each other as infant school kids do when one of their classmates ever drops the C-bomb. Joe turns, clearly triggered. "Everyone in school? Everyone? You can't name anyone that isn't?"

"Joe. Can you name anybody in our school, yourself included, who isn't?

----

37. Fifty Shades

Fifty shades of grey. Not just a shit wannabee freak-porn book read by short people unable to reach the real porno books on the top shelf, but also a good description for the colours on my ankle today. There's a fair few yellows and browns there too, but barely any black and blue. I'm walking, not yet running, but three days ago I needed to shuffle up and down the stairs on my arse so I'm happy. The amazingly awesome Doctor Konstantin said he was quite happy with how it's recovering. He thinks that running might be alright by the end of the week, but for now I should swim, as the water would support my ankle as I exercised the rest of me. So, Dad threw a day off in, Ponds Forge were off the agenda, as were Donny Dome - he said it had to be a proper pool with no waterslides and stuff - so he ran me to some grim looking pool somewhere the other side of town. Puddles on the changing room floor that you hope are just water but you're never quite sure, big clanky metal lockers, a fat ugly 50 year old lifeguard with bad tattoos, and a half-empty snack machine that may or may not dispense a selection of Space Raiders or Tangy Toms or nothing at all depending on how lucky you feel. Everyone else in there was minimum age 65, bobbing along doing lengths at turtle speed. I'd normally refuse to go in in case anyone saw me, but the last few days have taught me all about about judging people, so I entered the water via a seated position in the shallow end,. From then on, I did lengths til I got bored, and minded my business. I left breast stroke til last as that's the most boring, the most effort and the slowest speed, 2 lengths max of that. We spent maybe half an hour in the pool, and then at least an hour in the jacuzzi cos we kinda got chilled in there, I found a bubbly spot which was hitting my ankle bone just right and I could have fucking slept there, but I waited til I got home, onto the sofa and fell asleep on that instead. Not for long, however. Shelly rolled in with her squad, which now includes Edward Pendlebury. If Shelly wants to hang out with him, then go for it luv, but can't see any of her mates being ideal mates of mine. Tariq's good for a chat, but he blatantly fancies Shelly so he's just doing the groundwork, part of which includes keeping the little brother sweet.

Coach Stevie saw me when I were sat outside the doctors, and spat out the exact words I suspected but never thought anyone would admit - "Coulda done wi' you on Saturday, pal!" I could have told him at any time that if you're facing Man City you need something special in the lineup, and should have postponed the fixture til I were fit again, but hey-ho. He told me they've put the Liverpool game off til next month, clearly because their fire-starters ankles not quite back to full strength yet, so it's just some grassroots team coming over for a game this weekend so not to worry. If the Doctor and the physio give me the all clear, he'll sort me some game time for the under-14s this weekend. I won't get long and could be any position, wherever they need someone, but I'm cool with that. Normally, I'd find that insulting, but I'm just happy I'm being thought about.

Dr Kon's swimming advice couldn't have come at a better time. The living-room's turning to a prison cell and doing my mental health in. I've become receptive to the idea of the company of my sister, and even thought about having a look at the homework that Edward brought in. My main priority this week is to find any excuse to get myself straight down to the swimming pool at the first opportunity. I'd even offer Edward an opportunity to put his paedospaedos on.

I'm not anxious about going back to school either. Someone's got onto Alfie Heywood's phone, been through his gallery, search history, and realised that it's not a mobile phone that he owns, but more so an instant porno device that he can also make telephone calls with. It's proper filth too. "Lexxxy Lashes" is apparently his favourite pornstar. I image searched her. She could be beautiful but no-one's quite sure. If she's not got something rammed in her mouth then she's pulling some pained looking face because she's got something rammed in a long way south of her mouth. I guess smiling's difficult in that situation. Whatever's attractive about that, I don't quite make sense of. His searches invariably include the words "anal", "fisting" and, amazingly, "anal fisting", which, if it's what I imagine it to be, and is what Lexxxy Lashes is famous for, she'd be well advised to get a CV done, lie on it if she has to, and get a more rewarding job. Sweeping up at the abattoir or cleaning the pub toilets after curry night must be a more enjoyable day's work, surely? His folks spent £200 on that phone for his birthday, which was like, not that long ago. He's quite a gobby youth, has beef with a lot of people, and is known to most, like Lexxxy Lashes will also be known one day if she's not careful, for being a massive arsehole. "Caught with porn". It doesn't matter one bit that 99% of the boys and at least 50% of the girls look at porn at some stage, even though 100% of them will deny it, even though most adults say it's perfectly natural for a teenager to look at as everyone's curious at that age, it's good enough to make Alfie Heywood a pariah for the remaining 6 months ago of his compulsory school life, probably longer than that once Facebook, Snapchat and Twitter have wrecked him as only they can. Even if they don't, his little brother who, on the observation that they walk past each other in school and won't even catch the same bus home, has minimal concern for his bigger brother's reputation, will only too gladly tip his Dad off that he might want to exercise his parental responsibility in a robust manner. I remember Will Anthony from Shelly's year sent a dickpic to some random lass and ended up offline, no phone, laptop, tablet, nothing, and probably still is. Anyway, this beats the horrendous crime of messing a perfect 10 girl about to spend a day with Edward Pendlebury and getting blown out after, so I've decided next Monday's the day.

Edward's through the door without even knocking, and on the other sofa without me even offering him, by 12. He can think twice about getting too comfortable.

"Owt kicked off today then?" I ask. Probably nowt. Someone probably stuck their tongue out at him and off he went.

"Cory Hendricks's out of exclusion. He wants me outside the gates at 4.00. CBA."

"Just him or his whole squad?"

"Which do you think?"

"He dun't roll that deep. It's just him and a couple of sidemen."

"Deeper than me though. You seen the size of my squad?"

"I dunno, you seem to be good buddies wi' Shelly's crew."

"Nah. She's palled up with me for a reason."

"Like that thing with my Mum and your Mum?"

The adults have decided and I'm resigned to it. I am going to be fantastic buddies with the geek, regardless of my wishes and feelings on the subject. I'm not overly excited about it but at the same time my resistance to it isn't as high as it was. I've waited all week for Snapchat to explode about me pissing myself, and nowt's happened so far. Jury's out. If I go through my school day on Monday, and nowt's been said, then I know I can trust him. Archie or Marcus or Omar would have got it viral within 5 minutes, I think there's a message in there somewhere for me that I'm ignoring, but maybe I shouldn't.

"Nah. Can't you spot it?"

"Spot what?"

"Shelly's friendship with me. Do you seriously not know?"

"No. Not got a clue."

"It's easy. It's purely a gift of an opportunity for her to wind you up. It works a treat, and you can't get back at her."

"And what do you get out of it?"

"Not much, apart from an amazing blackmail opportunity if I wish. The chance to see you squirm very uncomfortably, alone, with no back up. Be grateful my phone's basic, or right now there'd be selfies. Your face would be epic."

I don't bite. "Edward, is your Mum at work?"

"Yeah, why?"

"I've got to go swimming. Ankle rehab. Do you wanna go?"

"I'm a shit swimmer."

"I'm shit at Science and French. You keep your mouth shut and I'll do't same."

"I'm not sure I can do that. I try not to make promises."

Until word gets out about Saturday at City, I don't see the need to react.

Edward's back in, "I'll ring her. You know what our Mum's are like. She'll not just drop some stuff off, but load us up with £20 to make a day of it, no bother."

"We'll need a lift too. It's got to be a boring pool"

"What kind of boring pool?"

"No waterslides, no inflatables, just a pool to do lengths in, mebbee jacuzzi or summat after."

"OK, hold on a sec." Edward gets his phone out and texts. Whoever he texts replies instantly.

"If she gets done at work early she'll think about it. She says get some work done."

"English. French. Food Tech. Pick one."

"French first. It's easiest."

He's already done his translation, won't lend me his book, and instead reads out what he's put and I write it down. We double check. I've spelt loads of words wrong and missed all them accent things off. He's happy wi' that. He makes me read it back out, then takes the piss, as I'm speaking French and pronouncing the words Yorkshire style. I could swallow a French dictionary, go to Paris and still no-one would know what I were on about.

"What's crack wi' English?"

"It's really easy. Just read the book. You read any of it?"

"A bit." I lie. "It's shite, though."

"So you've not read it then."

"Yeah I have." I lie again, "It's shite so far."

"Yeah, whatever. You need to read more of it."

"Why, does it suddenly morph into Green Street at page 26?"

"Erm, no. You've got to get into it, through the court trial bit at least, then it'll all sink in."

"You've read it all?"

"Yeah, of course I have. I want an A out of this subject."

"What's point of that? Just shit a C out, that'll keep everyone happy."

"Bloody hell I'll use something simpler that you might understand. Who'd you rather sign for, Manchester City or Lincoln City?"

"What's that daft question got to do wi' anything?"

"Well, I want to go to a Premiership Uni. Somewhere cool to spend 3 years, Manchester, London, maybe even Oxford if I wanna go all-out Champions League style. They'll want A's off me. B's mean somewhere not shit, but not great, just steady, like Huddersfield or York or somewhere like that. A "C", to me, equals Welcome to the University of Cleethorpes."

"And what are you going to do once you've got there? Like, is it gonna be worth it?"

"Course it will. Bloody hell, I've not even worked out what I want for tea tonight let alone what to do with the rest of my life, but it'll give me a bit more time to work it out."

I pause and think for a second what I'd decide to do if I got released. Then, realising the prickly uncomfortable place that my mind is travelling towards, quickly snap out of it. It's not a place I want to go to mentally right now. "So what's the best bit of this book then? Which page do I skip to?"

"You don't skip at all. It's not like 50 Shades, where everyone flips straight to chapter 7 or wherever the pervert bits start. Skip one single page of this and you lose any idea what it's about. Your B grade becomes a C minus immediately, maybe worse."

"What if you CBA? Is there a movie of it, like on Netflix?"

"Probably, but you watch that only after you've read the book."

"Why not just rip the reviews off the internet?"

"Your choice. Enjoy a mundane life spent ringing strangers up to try to sell them some shitty insurance they don't need, and getting told to go fuck yourself 100 times a day."

"OK, so what's the best bit of this book then?"

"Read it and see for yourself."

"No. Give me a clue"

"There's a message in it. I'd say everyone should read it, people like you especially. Once you see the message, it'll make you think a bit, hopefully. So write all those thoughts down, and who knows, Mr McGregor might just be ringing your Mum up to let her know you've pulled an A out."

"Can't see that. He'd think I'd copied it then hand out a C- like usual."

"Try not gazing out of the window wishing you were elsewhere?"

"Yeah, well, none of this lot sets my brain on fire. I'm not into reading anyway. It's boring."

"I know. That's why I'm gonna motivate you."

"As if."

"Ok, tomorrow, Shironda's got a big mouth, so I tell her about you being so excited at the Etihad stadium that you pis..."

"OK. You win. You're a proper cocksucker by the way."

"I'm actually a saint, but I live in world full of cocksuckers, so that's how I have to roll too."

"So what's the message in this book?"

"I'll leave a clue. Pay attention to Scout, the kid, and how she views everything. Pay attention to the lawyer guy. And it's not really a message I'd want to see you get from it personally, but more an outlook. See how the lawyer guy puts himself in another man's shoes and tries to imagine the world from that side."

"You're quite a deep meaningful kinda guy when you want to be."

"All part of my charm. The ladies love it. Looks only go so far, you know."

"As if."

"Trust me. Which of us will be dating Catwalk models and Bollywood actresses in 10 years?"

"Three guesses. Possibly the one of us without a volcano on their forehead."

"You sure about that?"

"Yeah, dreamer."

"It's simple. Initially, it'll be you they spot first. Maybe you'll get the real phone number off them, but a couple of dates in, after realising there's not much more than an ability to kick a ball and maybe a good physique to look at, there won't be much else to get interested in. In the midst of their boredom with you, they'll discover me. I'm not so aesthetically pleasing with my not so high cheekbones and not so toned physique, but they'll spot the untamed beauty that shines so brightly within my soul they'll want to stay close to that forever."

"£10 says you're dreaming."

"Make it £100. That'll be loose change to me by then, but will bankrupt you. Anyway, get that fucking book read by the weekend. It's not that bad, honest. We'll have Shakespeare soon. If you can't cope with Harper Lee, who wrote just one book which was so awesome she didn't bother writing another because she didn't think she'd match it, then you've no chance with Shakespeare, not even Romeo & Juliet."

"OK Boss. Fancy going swimming?"

"We're going tomorrow. Your Mum's taking us."

"How do you know?"

"I know lots of things."
"Yeah. That's what pisses me off."

"What did you think to that stuff I told you on Tuesday? You knew none of it. I could tell."

"Honestly?"

"I do prefer honesty, given the choice of that or being bullshitted to."

"Don't know. I'm still working it out. Ask me in a week?"

"You'll be at school by then, pretending you don't know me, and I'll be looking for any seat in the class that isn't next to you."

"I'm not going to sit next to anyone"

"Fuck off. Most year 8s would go to the ebola ward at the hospital and lick the floor just to sit next to you, even if you had diarrhoea too."

"No. I'm going to choose not to sit next to anyone. Well, as much as I can get away with."

"How long have you sat next to that Sophia lass in registration?"

"I got put next to her in year 8. She dun't smell, so I thought nowt of it."

"How well do you know her?"

"OK, she hates football, she's good at science......"

"That it?"

"Her folks have split. Her brother dun't go to work but plays Fifa and Skyrim all day instead, this being why she hates football and computer games, but all the girls do don't they?"

"Any more?"

"She's been off school a couple of times. Said she'd been on holiday but din't have a suntan, so I just thought she'd been to Bridlington or somewhere like that."

"So, after 3 years or so, you don't know anything about her?"

"If it's not my business, I don't ask owt."

"Which I guess is for the best, 'cos if she told you you'd be pretty fucking useless anyway."

"What do you mean?"

"Remember the first week of term? It was still summer. Everyone was melting in the classroom, the ADHD kids were all losing their shit, and she kept her blazer on while everyone else was shirtsleeved up and desperate to go home."

"What's that got to do wi' owt, and how's it my business?"

"You don't know do you?"

"Sounds like you do."

"I've got a bit of a clue." Edward starts to roll his sleeve up.

"So why would she do that?" I ask, in search of a proper answer.

"I don't know, but she's happy enough to sit next to you in registration."

"Why? Do I look like a nutdoctor?"

"No, she's happy because you're so oblivious to anyone else, so wrapped up in your daydreams of Cup Finals and flying elephants that you notice nothing about anyone else."

"So what else have you spotted?"

"You want to know?"

"I'm curious. See what else I'm not spotting."

"Cory Hendricks isn't the evil one in his little group. He's just the daft one that the others can put up to doing daft stuff. Then there's Shironda's nails. There's a reason for those. There's a lot."

"So I should feel sorry for Cory Hendricks?"

"Not really. But you should pay closer attention to those with him."

"I've got history wi' one of them anyway. Goes back years. It's not good."

"I'll have a guess. That'll be Louis, and footballs involved."

"How did you know that?"

"I just guessed. You're not the most multi-faceted personality I've met. It didn't take long."

"We played on't same team at under 7s. I got spotted and he din't. He fucking hates me. He's the only kid in the class I've not got online. Anywhere."

"He's the smart one. He manipulates Corey. Haven't you noticed?"

"I pay as little attention as I can to him."

"You know when Cory Hendricks is in kick-off mode? Louis puts him there. For little more than his own entertainment. You ever spotted those 20p cans of energy drink in his pockets?"

"Why would I care?"

"He never drinks them. He keeps them to give to Corey, then sits back and enjoys watching Corey start being a hyperactive cunt with everyone."

"So that's why you're not fighting Corey today then."

"I don't really want to fight him at all. I just want a day where no-one winds me up."

"But if you fought Corey or Louis, you might win, one-on-one you could anyways."

"I shouldn't have to. This shit doesn't happen in the adult world. Secondary school's supposed to prepare us for the adult world. If school can't do that then what's the point?"

"So you're going to get in at a Premier League university by chilling with tramps and reading Japanese comics in the library til they swat you out."

"Which is why my Mum and your Mum are palling us up."
"As if I'm going to sort your stuff out."

"You won't. But remember when your Mum got grief in school it didn't matter how good she was with her fists. It was my Mum who stepped in, who'd never got her fists out in her life."

"But that were in't last century. Everything's changed since then."

"Some stuff will have, but not everything."

"Do you reckon me and you could seriously be mates?"

"What do you think?"

"I don't know. There's shitloads I'm not sure of, that's why I'm asking."

"Not right now, no. You look at me and you've already made your mind up. I look at you, and just think "No". But things change don't they?"

I've thought about this a fair bit since the weekend. When school ends, I've got 3 separate lists in my head. People I'll be buddies with, people I'll just keep online, and people I'll delete and forget ever existed. The more I think about this list, the more surprises it throws up.

"Shelly and Tariq were in the same school, same year, and weren't mates were they?"

"They are in college though."

"They weren't mates, but they weren't enemies either. In school, she had her mates, he had his, they didn't mingle. Then school ended and those groups split. New groups formed."

"I remember her sat on that sofa announcing each person she deleted, laughing as she did so."

"You're talking to someone who doesn't do social networks."

"You must be one of two kids in the whole year."

"Like I even care? I'd have to add people I didn't want to add, then delete them all in a year's time, then add new people, and of the people in school I'd end up adding, I really don't care for anything they do or say. I might as well leave all that shit for now."

"OK. I thought about it. There's hundreds of people on there that I'll be binning as soon as y11 is done. I've spotted some already, but it might change."

"I've no idea who I'll be mates with that far ahead. Like I said, things change."

"What else we got?"

"What do you mean?"

"The reason we're chatting. Homework. Food tech weren't it?"

"Yeah. Get ready for a practical next week."

"What we mekking?"
"A dessert that can be made for less than £1.50, can be eaten by diabetics and lactose intolerant, and meets all cultural needs."

"Like what?"

"Well, break it down a bit more and it's easy. Cultural needs means keep pork or beef products out of it. We're making a pudding."

"So you get summat that can be eaten by diabetics and lactose intolerant people."

"Yep"

"Diabetics means no sugar, and lactose intolerant means no milk"

"Sort of. Diabetics means keep the sugar to a minimum. Lactose intolerant means no dairy, so not just milk, no cream or cheese or butter or owt like that."

"So just bring a fucking apple in then."

"Use any fruit you want, but be a bit creative with it. A fruit salad gets you a C. Make something more interesting, and that C becomes a B or maybe an A."

"You want an A in this too?"

"Nah, not so much."

"What are you making?"

"Shut up Joe. I'm not doing it all for you. Do some research yourself and I'll chat later."

"You know a good website I can look on?"

"Yeah. Google."

"Thanks for that." I throw back, sarcastically.

"If you manage to find google, type in, 'pudding', then type 'low-sugar', then 'lactose-free'. See what pops up. Skip page 1. Mrs Wilson looks stupid, but won't be with this."

"I'll do it later."

"Of course you will." Edward replies, knowing I'm full of shite right now.

----

38 DOGGY STYLE

Second day running, I reach registration to be told that Corey Hendricks will be waiting for me by the gates at 3.30. I neither rose to it nor ran away, but gave out a great big whatever. He'll not be alone. He never is. He can wait til I'm ready, and my preparation for this is taking low priority. I'd not planned to, in fact I'd rather avoid his lamenting a bruised ankle like it was an amputation, but Joe's been so totally headfucked by my wonderful presence, and I'm openly taking a guilty pleasure in observing his reactions, I went round for him. The deciding factor of this that made my mind up properly was the randomness of the question he texted me earlier.

"What swim trunx hav u got?"

I saw the chance for more headspinning. *"Are you trying to ask me on a date?"*

"They're not paedospeedos r they?"

I know where this is going. *"I'd send a sexy pic of me in them but, y'kno, my fone?"*

"Get sm shorts that don't look rapey and u can cm swimmin wi' us"

"Thanks for the very kind offer, I'm not gay tho. Will this matter to you?"

"Do u wanna go swimmin 4 free or not, nobhead?"

"Got peanut smugglers. Squeezes everything in nice n tight. You'll love them."

"Trunks. Primarni. £3. My house by 12. Or dress like Borat & piss off. Your call."

I totally engineered my way home. I deliberately sat next to Travis in English. He still has the sulks with me, so as I sat down I simply said, "Hello Travis, how are you?" Whereas on any other day I'd simply brush his infant-school reply off, today it was good enough to classify it as abusive enough to warrant me getting my coat. And possibly my mankini. Waited for the lesson to end though. After lecturing Joe on how important a subject English was, I'd be a hypocrite if I didn't stay for that. As soon as the bell went at the end, though, straight through the gates without looking back, onto the next bus home, through the front door, into the bathroom and grab the towel at the very bottom of the pile, a flowery-green one that's easily older than me that I've never seen get used. Then into my drawers, for my drawers. Damn I'd love to have had some paedotrunks. Imagine Joe trying to chat some lass up, just about to swap numbers, then I show up in a union jack thong. It'd crush him. I have shorts, old ones from my last school, more like PE shorts than trunks. I pack them, and some boxers too, just in case the mouse pops out of the house when I wear them.

Popped my whole human self out of the house, and over to Joe's. His Mum's already there.

"You all ready then Edward love?" his Mum asks, with a slight touch of dizziness she's a bit old for.

"Yeah thanks, are you OK?"

"Penny's sure you've grown out of your trunks, so I popped to't shops. Have these."

I don't even look at them. "It's OK, Mrs Barker, I found my speedos in my drawer. Fake leopardskin. I'm sorted."

I glance over at Joe. I was hoping to wind him up, but he's actually laughing. Not buying it.

"Edward, you'd be best off wi' these, love. Navy blue. Much nicer than leopardskin."

How would she know what I'd look good in half-naked? I won't describe too much what my bare legs and chest look like, but I have accepted over the course of time that I'll be dating Bollywood princesses based on my banter as opposed to any exterior attractiveness. I take the shorts with a thank you, and jump in the back of the car. I've only ever seen the friendly, motherly, altogether convivial side of Mrs Barker, but behind the wheel of a car she transforms, thug life all the way. We cross from one side of town to the other via places I don't really know, but will now forever identify as "that turn-off where Mrs Barker called a 4x4 driver a fat sweaty wanker who needs a car to match his dick" and "those traffic lights next to the KFC where Mrs Barker flipped the middle finger at the taxi driver who pulled out on her". I bet she's unbeatable at GTA. I seriously thought there was going to be violence, but Joe wasn't responding, like this kinda shit happened every day. If Princess Diana or Tupac were being driven by Joe's Mum on those fateful tragic nights back in the day, I'm sure they'd both still be with us. I've heard some rumour that nowadays Tupac lives in a shed on a beach in Cuba. Apparently the internet pictures of him in the morgue with half his head missing are fake as the tattoos don't match. Some kids said it in I.T a bit back, so they may know something, they may know nothing. They had similar controversial opinions, backed up by the undeniable evidence of whatever website they'd all vegged on, on Bob Marley, Michael Jackson, and that Diana lady. Unlike Tupac, they were all definitely dead, though, murdered. They insisted.

Anyway, we got to the pool. Changed in the special cubicle just in case Joe decided to check my bare arse out, then tiptoed through that footbath thing that's meant to make your feet hygienic even though there's a used plaster and a flotilla of fluff, pubes and snot floating about on top. I couldn't tell which was the shallow end or the deep so I sat on the side. A couple of old people slowly plowed from end to end with the slowest strokes ever, like turtles on valium. I sat dipping my big toe, then the rest of my toes, then my other big toe, followed by the rest of my toes, then the bottom of my foot, up to the ankle, then gradually my leg until both knees were immersed in a mixture of freezing cold water, chlorine and various body fluids, then Joe shouted over "Are you bloody getting in or what?".

I lowered myself in gently, like an old person would, then, as my feet turned blue and the rest of me turned purple, I realised that staying in the same spot was no longer an option. I've not been swimming since I was 9, when me and Lara were forced to go so we could get our badass 10 metre badges, which as a survival skill is pretty useless. Imagine falling into a big river or getting swept out to sea by a riptide and trying to use all the skills you picked up on your badass 10 metre to keep yourself from drowning. Still, that 10 metre award was a rite of passage, and to everyone else in the class it was legit proof that you definitely could swim. Armbands in the bin. Safe in the reassurance that I could definitely swim a width of the pool unaided, I tried to swim twice as long over to Joe at the other end with my finest doggy paddle.

I swallowed water within seconds, so stood up again, only managed to get half of it out, so I've now got ebola probably. Then I remembered my thermo-retentive powers weren't the greatest so I went back into the doggy paddle again, puffing and blowing for 33 paddles and kicks, and once I reached the other end, I was absolutely knackered. I got to my feet, then realised I was in the deep end, so I frantically paddled again, not getting far with any stroke, but after enough desperate flailing I made it to the total fucking life saver of a handrail that some considerate person had installed there decades ago and, though a bit wobbly, hadn't totally fallen off yet.

"You don't do this much do you?" Joe shouts over, stating the obvious.

"Nah I just go for the waterslides, and we've travelled across the whole city just to find the only pool in England without any."

I look around for anything remotely entertaining in here. No chance. This is one of those sensible pools where pensioners can get in for 50p, where fat old ladies come to flap their bingo wings about at one of those aquarobics classes, where learning disabilities groups do all that sensory stuff or infant school kids do swimming lessons desperately trying to get that totally badass "10 metres" badge of honour. I'm sure we drove past Ponds Forge on the way, and I'm sure Donny Dome's not at the other end of the universe either. There's a jacuzzi in the corner, which is about the nearest I'm going to get to any entertainment this afternoon. It's probably also full of pubes and toenails and ebola swirling about amidst the bubbles, but at least it's warm and I won't have to do anything.

"Sod this Joe, this is torture. Jacuzzi in 10 seconds."

"Not yet."

"What do you mean why not? You actually want to stay here and freeze your knackers off?"

"I'm doing 20 minimum."

"I've just done my personal record of 1. I'm very satisfied with that."

"You're doing 20 too."

"As if."

"Yep. Proper lengths too, none of that doggy paddle comedy shit you just did."

"This is for your ankle, right? How's about sod the lengths and let the bubble cauldron over there sort your ankle instead?"

"It will."

"Sound, let's go!"

"Once I've done me lengths."

"Are you mad?"

"I wish. My life's one of total sanity."

"Sanity as in cannot imagine any kind of life fulfilment aside from winning a football match?"

"Aye, the very one. I'm doing lengths. I have to."

"Off you go then. See you in a bit."

"Nah, you're coming too."

"20 lengths of doggy paddle?"

"Tek a look round. Old people. Minus the bifocals. You're just a hazy blur to them. Even if they could see you properly, they wun't give a shit."

"You'd see it."

"And I'd film you with what exactly?"

"Your words better than mine."

"Not from what I've worked out."

"Eh?"

"You've said nowt about the City match to anyone. You're safe."

"How do you know?"

"Because Snapchat would have exploded by now."

"I'm still considering the blackmail opportunities."

"Don't bother. I'll pay you back."

"How?"

"Properly. Get on these lengths wi' us and I'll show you to do a proper stroke. One day, when you're by the pool at that mansion party surrounded by Bollywood princesses and one of 'em tumbles in, you'll not be trying to rescue her and win her eternal love by doggy-paddling and nearly drowning. You can use these 20 to try them out."

"10, then jacuzzi."

"20, or St Kevin's buzzes wi't news that Edward Pendlebury wears armbands and a swimming cap so he dun't get his hair wet."

"15."

"18, and if Mum offers out take-away on't way home, I pick."

"18, nothing with onions in it."

Joe talks me through how to do crawl. He goes into motivational sports coach mode, teacher mode, talking and demonstrating at the same time, then I follow his movements, and his words are a procession of "yes!", "good!", "keep going!", "excellent". When I grab the rail at the other end for dear life, he's ready to hi-five me. I, meanwhile, spot a talent this lad actually possesses that might not be totally useless to him and might validate his existence. When the glorious revolution comes, he might actually not be amongst the first people I line up against the wall.

"Reyt, how u feeling?"

"As if you're bothered?"

I catch the enthusiasm on his face, his obsessive focus on something I can't understand, but I weirdly respect it. I immediately regret, only slightly though, my backchat of 5 seconds ago.

"Reyt, this time we proper master it. Don't kick so hard wi't legs, cos you don't need to, 'n keep yer head straight and yer fingers closed."

He even spotted what I was doing with my fingers?

"Yeah, close 'em." He puts his hand up, fingers spread, then closes them. "That way you pull more water past you and you get down't pool quicker wi' less bother."

"OK boss."

"Reyt, lets go!"

Same again. As suggested, I kick less, keep my head straight, shut my fingers, hoping that I'd get to the other end in the worst way possible so I could tell him he's full of shit. Disappointingly he's not. And I breezed it. He's all smiles and friendliness and it's like the sunshine's beaming naturally out of his eyes and mouth and nostrils. I see this from nobody, ever, and I'd especially not expect it from a dick like him.

"Nailed it. Reyt, couple more, then we can get that Michael Phelps officially shittin' his sen."

Off we go. 2 lengths non-stop, not even a wonky handrail break in between. He'll always be an arse of a man, but I have this warm glowy feeling that I've actually achieved something.

"Right, go on your todd now, I'll watch 'n catch up with you at t'other end."

I breeze it to the other side. He joins me in half the time. "How you feeling fella?"

"Like I've just found a natural teacher."

"Nah it's just coach patter. I hear loads of this at football. It works."

"It's just patter to you, but its motivational shit to me. You're good at it."

"So are you, but there's no way I'm telling anyone."

"I don't even do any exercise. I couldn't even coach dodgeball. You're full of shite."

"You know that Mockingbird book? I read it all."

"All of it?"

"Last night, reyt to't end, no stopping, not even when't Man United match came on. You were reyt. I just needed to get a couple o' chapters done, then it all kicked in."

"So what happened?"

"Right, you're OK for keeping yer mouth shut?"

"Have been so far."

"I got reading it and I got goosebumps in some bits, and got emotional, well nearly."

"So you found out you're human. What the fucks that got to do with me?"

"Well I could've just ripped off what you wrote, squeaked a half-arsed C- out as usual and not given a shit, but because you were a proper tosspot about it all, I ended up having to read it. Reyt to't end."

"So you're buzzing over classic literature, and I'm not swimming like a distressed giraffe."

Joe goes back into his coach mode. "Aye summat like that. Reyt, couple more crawl then I'm off into breast stroke. Up to you what you do, just stick wi't crawl if you want to master it."

I spot him looking ahead, weirdly focused like he's in an Olympic final or something, so I just push myself off the wall and go again. I stick with crawl. I've achieved something. I end up doing 20, because I've forgotten to count. It might even be 19 or 21 as I finish in the shallow end. I get into the jacuzzi feeling like I've actually earned a spell in there, as opposed to half an hour ago where I was treating it as an easy way of avoiding something I was appalling at. I perch on the side, immerse my feet, then calves, then knees, and keep going until only my spotty shoulders and wet head are visible above the bubbles. Joe follows a couple of minutes after, gets to the side of the jacuzzi, has a look at his ankle, well, the bruising, smiles to himself and then does the same manoeuvre as me.

"Joe, I honestly thought you'd be a proper arse with me when you saw me swim."

"Nah, I owe you for't book and for keeping schtum about stuff. Plus I listened to that tramp story and all that Mum stuff from back in't day, and I decided I've been kicking off about the wrong person. It's the least I can do. Plus if you think your world's shite you get to see what mine's like. It's not as awesome as you reckon it is."

"Your world. I've seen it. It's got football in it, and not much else."

"That's just what I'm passionate about. I had this dream when I were a kid, same as most kids had, but while theirs died, mine's still alive so I keep going. But there's sacrifices."

"You make it sound like you're getting tortured."

"Nah I just miss out on all't everyday stuff. You know on Friday nights when everyone's up til 5am? I'm in bed by 10. I'm not allowed to eat after 7, unless I've trained. Drugs, alcohol, fags and all that aren't a problem, but innocent stuff's gone too. No skateboarding, no roller skating, nowt that puts pressure on me ankles or knees. I went to't ice rink a few weeks back and guess what I did once I got there? Fuck all. Just sat at't side wi me jacket on scrolling down me phone."

"Seriously, is that it?"

"Fancy a bike ride? I'd fucking love one. I'm allowed 4 miles max. No scrambles, no stunts, not even a sneaky bunnyhop. Maccy D's, KFC? Not this year. Even a fizzy drinks off the menu. See that old snack machine over there? Guess what I'm having out of it? Unless it drops bananas or water out o't bottom, then fuck all. I saw one o'me team get bollocked for having cheesy Wotsits on't bus on't way to a match. One bad report from school and I'm off the team. I don't even need to say what'll happen if I ever get into any bother wi't coppers. Mates? If you had a mate who turned up at parties, drank nowt, smoked nowt, and went home at 9.30, would you hang around wi' em?"

"So, you're so boring that none of the girls in year 9 ever check you out each time you walk past?"

"Oh yeah, girls. I'm advised not to date anyone I've not known as a friend for at least 2 years. Throw in the fact that your social networks are looked at at any time, one dodgy status can get you released. Any more?"

"Yes, tell me about your terrible suffering". I ask, convinced he's clueless what it means.

"OK. Thanks to being injured, I lay in on Sunday. The last time I did that were back in't 6 week holidays. You're up at 7 for school for 5 days, I'm up at 7 every day. When you stretch your legs out on a Saturday morning wondering whether to get up or not, I'm sat on some motorway not knowing what time I'll be home again. At least 2 school nights, straight from school, I'm getting in after 9, so 2 less days to get homework done. If I actually had mates, it'd be a problem."

"Oh, so you're a billy now are you?" I'm ready to lay my arm across the back of this hot tub so he can get a good look at the scars, but let him continue.

"You saw that the other day. My team mates are only my mates while I'm playing in the same team as 'em. They can be released at any time, just like I can, so I never get too close. Wi' some kids its easy. There's a couple of kids in't team that I can't stand being anywhere near, but I play football wi' 'em well, but if I never saw them again, though, I'd be cool wi' it. There's others that live miles away so that'd be it wi' them. Then you get to school kids. The ones that like football talk so much shit all the time, I'd choose to spend time wi' them that don't do football at all if I could. It's less hassle, but then again if I palled up with them I'd have nowt in common wi' any of 'em. So, yeah, I'm a proper billy."

I've had enough. His sob story's as convincing to me as when one of some Hollywood celeb's private jet breaks down and they have to use Easyjet instead.

I open my lower arm out.

Joe spots the battle wounds, looks briefly at me and says, "I don't get it."

"What's not to get?"

"Well I know you've been cutting yersen, that bit's easy. I just don't get what it's all about?"

"My way of coping with my shit life."

"You've no other way?"

"Not always."

"Like you can't just go and get wasted instead?"

"Why'd I want to do that on my own?"

"I dunno. I've never thought about it."

"Have you ever met anyone who's truly unhappy? Not just salty about getting dropped from some football team, but going to bed not overly caring if they woke up next morning?"

"Like who?"
"I dunno, anyone."
"So you're like this every day?"

"No, not all the time. These scars here, these are the newest, but they're not that new."

"So when did you do them?"

"Remember the day that Cory Hendricks's crew jumped me at the gates, and no-one helped?"

"Couldn't you bide your time til he were on his own then injure him instead of yersen?"
"What if I don't want to live a life of violence?"

"Well he's still wanting to have a pop at you. It won't stop til you've put him on't floor."

"So how many people have you sorted out with violence?"

"I've never had to. It's a bit different wi' me, innit?"

"So you've never had enemies, not even with all that football drama you bang on about."

"It all gets dealt with on't pitch, you just wait til the refs not looking then u ge..."

"No, I mean in real life, not in some game."

"I dunno. Louis's got beef with me. Has done for years."

"But he's never tried to whack you?"

"He offered me outside o't gates in year 7, told everyone he were going to waste me but forgot that Shelly were in year 11 so everyone laughed at him. He kept his head down after, but I know if he had't chance, and't circumstances fell right for him he'd love another go."

"And if he did?"

"Can't see it just yet. Shelly's gone, but he sees me wi' Sam Blake so he knows the odds."

"And this is over a kiddie's football team? That's it? You're luckier than you realise."

"So what's the buzz wi' that stuff anyway?"

"You probably won't get it."
"I don't anyway, but that's why I'm asking. I'm curious about it."

"Well my Mum doesn't get it. My sister gets even less. My Dads a waste, so, in the absence of anyone I can talk to face to face, that leaves either my Granny or CAMHS. Don't even go there with either of those. So...I get a problem, I'm alone with it, full stop. Even if I'm in a bad mood, just a normal one like one of those Monday morning ones, no-one notices. But, once people see these scars they do."

"So your life's proper grim and it'll never get better? You've never watched one o' them TV shows where you see all them African kids starving and that?"

"Course I have. But when I do this it's not like I'm thinking straight. If somethings gone out of control, and I'm out of control, I get to this. When I've done it, I'm chilled again, like all the pain or unhappiness or whatever's just bled out."

"So you don't try telling anyone you're unhappy then? Like someone at school maybe?"

"Like who? They're worse than useless. Every time I get bullied they try to tell me I've initiated it all. I'm dealing with school though."

"Like why you're here now, or sat in Waterstones reading all their comics?"

"Yep."

"Aye that'll work, wanting to go to posh uni and shitting C's out cos you were never in't lesson?"

"It'll work as well as pinning all your hopes of future happiness on being able to make a football do unnatural bendy movements."

"The real world looks shit so I'll stay focused on that for now thanks."

"Depends where you're viewing it from. I walk out of school into it, and its way better than any classroom. You're looking at it from the centre circle, hoping you'll not have to step off the pitch and into it. But you will one day."

"Yeah, when I'm 40 hopefully."

"Dream on, sooner than that. Quick survival tip though. Teach or coach."

"I hate school."

"You're good. Can you imagine me trying to teach you to swim? I'd fail. You'd also drown."

I lift my hand from the bubbles. I'll have webbed hands and feet if I remain here any longer, the shrivelled pattern on my fingers looking like the beginning of that particular mutation.

"So are you going into school tomorrow?"

"I'll turn up in the morning and see how it goes. You?"

"Monday."

"Why not tomorrow? You're fit again."

"I'll get asked questions I don't want to answer. If I wait til Monday it's guaranteed everyone will be asking about some other batshit drama and not give a shit about owt concerning me."

"But they probably don't anyway."

"I know that. I've been learning this week. You know when I said I were a billy, and you didn't buy it? I meant school too."

"Yeah, I don't buy it."

"Who are my mates then?"

"Sam Blake."

"Until I have no more cheap footy tickets to sell him. From that moment, thin air."

"That lad on the bus with the beanie."

"We catch the same bus every morning. When we stop doing that, we'll be strangers."

"Ok, all those kids you kick a ball about with."

"I kick a ball about wi' em and nowt more. I could walk into any school, join in a kickabout and make identical friendships in 5 minutes and end them just as quick."

"OK. The girls then."

"Nowt that you're probably thinking."
"I've spotted it already. It's all friendzoned, I know, but there's still friendships there."

"Like who?"

"I dunno, Shironda? Her mate with the resting bitchface?"

"Shironda talks to everyone. Banter queen of St Kevin's. If anything, I'd rather chat to Sophia. She'll never talk footy with me, hates it with a vengeance, and I actually find that a bit attractive, no idea why, though I know she doesn't think the same. I know everything about Shironda, and nowt about Sophia. I prefer mystery."

"Ok, I've spotted who the keen sexual pervert is."
"You're gonna say Welshy aren't you?"

"Nope. You."
"As if!"

"I know where the jets in this thing are."

"Which means?"

"I sat where you did earlier. One of the jets sends its bubbles right where the sun won't shine. I thought to myself that if I was keen on anal stimulation, I'd sit right where you are for half an hour, but I was kind enough to move along, knowing you'd enjoy it much more. Comfy?"

Joe laughs, hasn't the words, so he sends the closest thing to a tsunami that he can produce with his hands, my way.

"Take care getting out of here too. Them trunks won't hide your happiness much either."

Another big splash, another big splash back. Within seconds we're grappling and ducking each other into the bubbles, calling each other dickheads. A few pensioners look on, concerned about us calling each other dickheads, forgetting that it's a term of endearment at 14. The lifeguard soon walks over to tell us to calm it, which we both meekly do without protest. We look at each other, briefly, before Joe bursts into giggles, and, for the first time in my life, I giggle with the exact immaturity that maybe I should have done a long time ago.

----

39. FRESH AS A DAISY

Back to life as I know it. Less than 5 minutes after entering Doctor Konstantin's consultation room, I were sat outside the gym waiting for the first teamers to leave. Some came out looking like they'd not even broken sweat, others just looked like they'd broken. Jamie Morales swagged his way out, Jimmy Mooney the old veteran centre forward benchwarmer hobbled out with both knees bandaged, looking less ready for a scrap with some equally ugly bastard of a centre back at the weekend than he was for a cuppa tea, a digestive and a comfy chair from Shackletons to rest in. He looked knackered, as did Adam Vukovic texting with one hand and supporting himself down a stair-rail on the other, blatantly trying to get himself a few weeks back home in Croatia by falling down the stairs and knackering himself. Tyler Oates said hello to us. I doubt he even knew who I was, just being polite at a guess, as he's the one who got media trained as it's always him that gets sent to talk to journalists and TV people after each game. I got in. The trainer put me on a treadmill for 20, dropping over every few minutes to change the speed or change the profile, did a similar routine with the bike for 20, then some calf raises and leg presses, then said "Right, you're good. Go down to reception and we'll get the coach over. Under-15s isn't it?"

Benny's already there, beaming, like he got up this morning and found the female residents of the Playboy Mansion had broken into his kitchen and made him a bacon butty.

"Ay up Joey lad, back wi' us then, eh?"

"Aye, good as new!" I smile.

"I thought you'd be out ages, but Doctor Kon says you've recovered proper quick. Gaz upstairs says everything's good too."

"I did all the stuff he said. Rested, swam, even did me homework properly and read me English book all o't way through." I say, hoping to pointscore. He probably thinks I'm lying.

"Reyt, there's no rush. It's just another grassroots side here this Saturday. Sit it out. We've got Notts Forest next week. A game wi' them should be right up your street. We'll need all our little magicians for that one, so we'd rather have you fresh as a daisy for that."

It was a grassroots team that messed my ankle up originally, so I've no complaints. Forest, on the other hand, play like us, well, most of us. It'll be a good game. Good test. Actually, change that, it'll be a belter. I know their players. They've got that Mason Ashcroft lad that looks and plays just like De Bruyne does for Man City and we have to stick an extra defensive mid in cos Brodie can't cope with him on his todd. Then there's that skinny dark haired lad who declared for the Republic and plays internationals, who can play left back, left wingback and left wing all at the same time. Dan has bad history with some of their players too, so either winds them up if we're winning or proper loses his shit if we're not. Either way it's entertaining.

"No worries, when do you want me in for training?"

"Reyt, train wi't shadow squad tomorrow. Don't wear no club gear or they'll kick lumps out of you if they suss you're already signed. Wear your own gear so it looks like you just got spotted. Do their drills, then I've said to Stevie just to do a 2-touch game at the end, so play that but put yersen deep. If you want a run out the 14s are at home on Sunday, Port Vale I think it is. Play that if you want, just from the bench though. You'll not get long, just a bit of a leg stretch to get you back into it."

It's a game, isn't it? If it was away, I'd say no. 5 hours on a bus just to play 20 minutes. Home's a different matter. And no pressure at all.

"Ok. Stevie will see you after that and if you come through that easy enough, have Monday to rest and we'll get you back in normal training on Tuesday."

I can cope with that. If I was to sit anything else out I might've been tempted to do something drastic and read another book right to the end. Anyway, Saturday morning came and went. The Shadow Squad were all strangers to me. Most of them don't stay long. They've a month or so to show what they can do and if they don't step up to our level then goodbye. I stuck my school team shorts and socks on and my Barca shirt on top. I had no waterproof or warm top that didn't have SCFC splattered all over it, so I ended up taking my best hoodie, the Adidas one, big logo, 3 stripes, which I wanted to avoid sweating in, so I stuck 2 skins on underneath and left the top in my bag until after. The drills were easy enough, receive a long ball, run towards some cones, turn through them and play wide with the outside of the left or right foot, sprint 10 metres then receive from the other wing and shoot into a tiny box shaped goal. Breezed it. Then they played a 4 x 6 game. I sussed they'd to be a bit desperate with their tackles, so I sat in defensive mid, put no tackles in, just blocks, sprayed the ball around, and fired shots from distance if the chance was there. Not my ideal position, but I don't get to choose.

Sunday went well enough. Some from the 14s knew me already. There's one, the keeper, that's taller than most of the 15s already, and has played a couple of games with us. In fact there's two or three of them that look old enough to get served beer afterwards, so I didn't stand out too much. Sat the first half out. The first time I've been sat on the bench and not been anxious and temperamental, but I got on for the last half and stayed on til around 5 minutes from the end. It was a very close 3-2 by that time, so the game got a bit frantic and the defending got desperate. The coach used his game management strategy of getting his big ugly lads on the pitch to muscle their way through the last 5 and leave the magicians on the sidelines. It's happened to me before in tight games, so I know the drill. I'd spent the game fitting in where I could, playing where I was told, which, for most of the time, was left-back. I was cool with that. Had Forest next week on my mind, so every time the Vale right winger came at me, I just held him off and held him off and held him off until I could get a block on something, or anything that didn't involve making a daft tackle or risking another whack on the ankle. I'm sure the coaches could see I was playing purely not to get injured, but I got forward a couple of times and got a couple of crosses in, high to the back post, and a couple of shots from distance that weren't far off. Stevie collared me after, no big in-depth analysis of my play, no criticisms, not even "How's your ankle feeling?" just "See you Tuesday. 6.30". Still music to my tender ears though.

Got in. Sunday dinner waiting. I don't like them that much, but I know they take ages to do so I didn't kick off. Started on that essay. My concentrations not great, as there's always something better to do than homework. I stuck Snapchat on and started scrolling. There was some kind of party in some woods last night, loads of people have posted stuff, drunk selfies mainly, but a bit of detective work says whatever went off got broken up by the coppers by 9.30. Keep scrolling. Oh dear, Sam Blake. Went to Grimsby away. Never made it into the ground. Can't work out how he landed himself in a police van but it looks like the coppers got to him before Grimsby's thug support did. Didn't take his phone off him though. He's shared selfies of himsen inside the van, couped up in some cage, him and some bald bloke who must easily be Dads age. I showed the pic to Dad to see if he knew him. He did, vaguely. Couldn't name him, but knew enough about him to give out a negative character reference. I'm off back to school tomorrow. All the banter will be about some rave in the woods or Sam Blake getting arrested. Mission accomplished.

I've decided already. As soon as Sam Blake leaves school in June, I immediately live the rest of my life without him in it. If I get offered pro-terms, the last thing I need around me is a grunting Stone Island liability. Besides, I can't get the logic of fully grown men trying to kill other grown men because of some entirely separate grown men kicking a ball about. Even if my team loses to Wednesday, Leeds, whoever, we still shake hands at the end then get on with the rest of our lives in peace, the exact same as rugby players and basketballers do. Even boxers and cage fighters act like gents after they've twatted the shit out of each other. Footy though. It really brings out the fucking worst in people, like as soon as idiots like Sam pull a replica jersey over their heads, they just get lobotomised at the same time. There's a reason my Dad never offers him along to the dome to watch me play. It's easy.

So, homework. There's only one man for the job. He's not on Facebook. He's not on Snapchat. He's too fucking cool for any of that. Whip my phone out. Messages to send. Actually, just one.
"*Edward, u bored?*"

It takes a minute

"*I'm never bored.*"

"*W U U 2?*"

"*Pornhub.*"

"*Behave!*"

"*Nah, not that much.*"

Mums in "You chatting to Edward, love?"

I should deny it so she doesn't get the satisfaction and go "Ah bless ya" and pat me on the head or whatever. But my life's returning to normal, so I'm chilled. I still sense her total glee at this news. All that scheming that her and her mate Penny have done. I'm not giving her the luxury. If Archie or Sam call over, her and Dad keep them standing outside, even if it's raining a proper monsoon down, but whenever old Eddie Pen turns up, the cakes and biscuits are all out, the full box, even with the Oreos and the Jammy Dodgers still present. I could twist this in my favour. I mean, essentially I've just been to Man City thanks to their scheming. I should hold out for Real Madrid or Barcelona next.

I continue "I can't stick him, but it gets me homework sorted dun't it?"

----

40. HAPPY BIRTHDAY

Me and Daisy Johnson from Marvel's Agents Of Shield were sat near a remote clifftop, having arm-wrestling contests for cake slices. I lost every single contest in seconds, but didn't mind, as I was happy to be distracted by watching the sea breeze ruffle through her hair, which, though she's one of the world's most beautiful badasses, made her look even more amazing than she ever did in the comics. Just as she was about to tell me something, something that would, no doubt, be infinitely more interesting to my ears than anything else I'd heard in my entire life, along came the bastard alarm at 6.30am to destroy the single most magical moment of my sub-conscious other life, a life way cooler than my conscious life will be for years, maybe decades yet, if at all.

Few things annoy me more than being interrupted during a very important conversation, and I wasn't tolerating it. I hit snooze, buried my head back into my pillow and tried to return to that remote clifftop, if only for 10 more minutes before the buzzer and it's disgusting lack of manners destroyed my fantasies once more. It didn't happen, dream over, crushed mercilessly if I must be honest about it. I stuck one leg out, then the other, then hauled my back up, and limb by limb manoeuvred to the bathroom, another place that's usually unkind to me. I avoid the mirror nowadays, it's equally as obnoxious a household implement as the alarm clock, one that I should throw in the bin and make my life altogether more pleasant. Though its honesty is as brutally accurate as I try to be with people, it's never good news. It probably never will be. I do, whilst pushing a big dump out, wonder how many lives have been ruined, how much worldwide mental anguish has been caused by the presence of mirrors. This weekend, I'll visit the comic shop in town where all the uni students buy crap to decorate their rooms with, buy 2 posters, one to fit over each side of the mirror. To the left, Dick Grayson from Batman, and to the right, seeing as there's females sharing this bathroom, Star Sapphire from Justice League.

I get down to the kitchen and I catch texts on my phone, which throws me as I've no plans for anyone to text me or even make contact with me. I had heard my Mum shouting up the stairs at me that my phone had been ringing, doing so excitedly in the same way she did years ago on Christmas Day morning when she'd call up that Santa had been.

I don't have any urgency to see who it is. I once behaved like that on the Skyrim forums when I got into slanging matches with dumb American kids and would refresh, refresh, refresh until I got a new insult from them and would fire one back, then refresh, refresh, refresh again til I got bored or tired. In the real world, though, it's different. I stick bread in the toaster and pull juice out of the fridge, pour it, and only when I have a spare moment waiting for the toast to pop up do I have a look.

"Wait for me at the bus stop, and I'll walk into school with you. 15 mins!"

Joe.

Barely 10 minutes ago, I had to prematurely end the most important conversation ever with an action comic fantasy superheroine, the overriding sense of disappointment and disillusionment throwing a very dark cloud over my outlook. I fail to see how any conversation in the real world can be as important as the subconscious one I just lost. I reply in accordance with my feelings.

"K"

Mum's been chatting to me for the last couple of minutes. I've not noticed, and she's not noticed I've not been listening, so I try to join her conversation halfway through. Apparently I've got food tech practical today. The ingredients are in the bag, in tupperware boxes, sellotaped. She knows there's every chance some prat could launch it all across the playground at any given time, so it's her way to keep my schoolbooks clean. I've no conversation to offer back, so I respond to her well-meaning but partially-heard dialogue with banter as unriveting as I just sent Joe.

"Thanks."

I look over to Lara. "Joe's on his way round. You're not going to be a dipshit when he knocks on the door are you?"

"As if. I went off him as soon as he palled up with you. If he has no credibility, I have."

Of course you did. "Has Libby gone off him yet?"

The truth here is she went off him as soon as she boasted to her mates that she was going to his house and once there he barely acknowledged her existence, plus blocked her on Instagram at least. I caught Joe at the front gate. The walk to the bus stop was as mundane as you'd expect from a Monday morning. The temperatures dropped a bit, autumns underway, winter clearly in the post. That Archie lad joined us outside the Co-Op, with a lass from our year, Alicia I think she's called, alongside him. I was unsure why they were in a rush to get to the bus stop, but once we were on the bus, Alicia unzipped her coat partly to pull a Galaxy Caramel from her art folder, Archie pulled a full-size Marvellous Creations from his inner coat lining, broke them into pieces, and handed out 4 ways.

"There's drama coming your way today so be careful." he looks at me, actually looking worried for my welfare.

"Like what?"

"Cory Hendricks has been calling you out on his pages. You've not seen them?"

As I said, keep life stress-free and all that.

"I won't have seen it."

"You know't other week when you shoved him in't back on't way to't headmasters?" Alicia asks.

"Vaguely." I offer back.

"Well Bronson Pearce got wind of it so he then shoved him over on't way out o't gates last week, same as you did, sent him flying and Bronson's mates all fell about laughing at him. It got filmed and went viral too. Corey's not exactly going to have a go back at Bronson, so he wants even wi you."

"He's just the willing idiot who does whatever his sidemen tell him. He doesn't worry me."

"He's been trying to collar you outside school for most of last week. Except you keep tekkin' off early, so he's trying to tell people you're running from him. No-one believes him, so he wants your blood." Archie adds, trying not to dribble liquid Galaxy Caramel down his chin.

"I know where you go." Alicia exclaims as if its big news, "My mate saw you in Starbucks wi' some tramps."

"I've got a very wide cross-section of friends, me. I just choose carefully."
"That's what Joe here says, except no-one ever invites him to parties." Archie says, offering Joe a single outstretched middle finger.

"As if I'm going to sack football off to sniff coffee whitener in't park wi' wastemen like you on a Friday night?"

"You've been injured. There's been parties. Still din't get an invite."

"And I missed so much, obviously."

"Nah, you didn't, really."

"So are you going to meet up wi' Cory Hendricks or not, Edward?"

"Like, he's offering me a date, is he?"

"For fucks sake!" Joe looks at me, gives a big breath out, and looks away.

"Check this." Archie pulls his phone out, scrolls down something and plays this video with Cory Hendricks in front of a camera, probably his phone, talking, animated. The volume's proper poor quality and whatever he's saying, the bus engine's drowning it all out.
"No idea what he's on about, CBA replying neither."

"Summat about he's got you a birthday present. What's that about?"

"He doesn't even know when my birthday is. He's batshit."

"You're not gonna tek off on your travels today are you?"

"Well, not straight away, but if anyone pisses me off, it'd be daft not to, wouldn't it?"

Archie turns to me "It's not Bronson or Sam calling you out. It's Cory Hendricks. If you faced him, you'd not just win, but you'd end all his bullshit too."

"And everyone would think you were Connor fucking McGregor."

"I don't want to be Connor McGregor. Or Bronson. I'm happy being me. Even though most of you lot can't handle it," I look at Joe, then Archie, then Alicia, "I'm cool with myself."

"So you're not feyting him then?"

"Not unless I really can't avoid it."

"Even though he's calling you out?"

"I've seen all that before. When Irish gypsies do it on YouTube, it's entertaining. When Cory Hendricks does it, that's entertaining too, just not how he thinks it is."

"Even though you could get it all done wi'."

"If I don't have to, I won't."

"I've even saved the video and screenshotted the comments for fuck sake."

"Why would you do that?

"Erm, for when school start asking for witness reports, Homer?"

"Ok thanks."

"Right, Ed, I'm not getting involved, but I'll walk into school with you. Do it my way though. Hang about outside a bit and only go in when you see't teacher on his way. It works, so tek me advice."

"But no-one wants to whack you, Joe?"

"Erm...you might not have noticed but me and Louis have beef. He's just waiting for his moment. It'll come one day."

"Yeah right. Half the school staff would side wi' you, cos they'll know you'd not have started it because City would drop you. Don't know why you're worrying?"

The bus pulls up outside school. As usual, some year 7 tries to go down the stairs too early and lands in the lap of some shopper. Joe playfully slaps him on the side of the head and says "What have I told you about that?" then tells the lady "I'm very sorry. I'll mek sure his Dad thrashes him and meks him kip in't shed 'til he learns to get off a bus properly" The old lady tries to reply but Joe's out of his seat and down the gangway already. He waits for me, and says. "Reyt, walk in wi' me and Archie. If you get through registration you can at least do a couple of lessons before you go for coffee wi' Donovan or whatever you're gonna do."

We cross the road, Archie says to me "You see them lasses down there?" I spot 4 year 11s in the distance, smoke rising above them. "When they stub out, we walk in. We'll be 2 minutes ahead of them, so we'll not be late."

So, 2 minutes pass. We stand outside the gates, aimlessly. As other schoolkids file in, a couple of them ask me, as they pass, if it's my birthday. It's not til March. This doesn't sound good. I'm not sure how, but somewhere in this institution, some stupid shit's about to go off somewhere. I really wish Ofsted would visit.

"And, if Corey's lot are round here?" I look over at Joe, still wondering why he's so anxious.

"They're not. I watched 'em in a bit back. If they were about, I'da kept us on't bus an extra stop."

"OK. I'd rather just go in. If there's drama, I don't see the point of hiding from it, do you?"
"Well, somehow, I'm trying to fucking protect you."

"Yeah, and somehow I'm involved too" Archie adds, looking over at Joe.

"This is daft." I state. "I'm going in."

"Aye, so am I." Archie adds

Joe clearly looks worried that something's going to happen, like we're going to get jumped or whatever, "OK, I'm coming. Fucks sake. Tek the long way though, at least."

"Nah, stuff that. I come here to get educated. This means I walk in this building, find a chair, they give me stuff to learn, and I learn it. I keep doing this until one day, if I've done well enough or badly enough, I go somewhere that suits me better. I quite like this concept, so when something stops me getting educated, that's when I decide I'm wasting my time here and I walk straight out. None of this hiding or walking the long way nonsense."

"For fucks sake, if you get battered, my folks will ask why I din't step in, which I can't bastard well do. I've only just got fit again. This time last week I were grateful just to be able to walk to't bog on me todd, never mind step in on a bunch of grunters who've beef wi' you over summat daft that I don't know jack about. I'm back to full training tonight. I'm risking fuck all. I'll help you, but for fuck's sake do it my way!"

"You don't need to do anything. I've not asked you to. Any nonsense and I walk straight back through the gates, just like I have for the last 2 months."

"That's your solution then?" Archie asks "Soon as someone gives you bother, you go home?"

"Well spotted."

Archie removes his beanie. "Hello? Ginger kid speaking. Strawberry blonde actually, but on that discrepancy, no-one cares. If I did what you do I'd have missed the whole of year 7. And year 8 too."

"Right, nice chatting to you. I'm going in. See you in there."

Joe runs his palms up his face then glances each way. I know why. No teacher on the horizon. He shuffles 20 paces behind me, muttering "can do wi'out this", "fuck's sake", etc.

I up my pace down the corridor. I open the door to registration, finding most people in the exact same places I'd expect to see them. I can see Shironda looking worried at me, Beth placing a sly pointed finger to her left, as if to tip me off to watch out for Corey, plus a couple of other girls looking at me and eyebrow-gesturing towards the back of the class, as if to give me a friendly warning. Whatever's kicking off, let it. I have my strategy and it works, plus doing something about it is schools responsibility, not mine. The more it happens, the more they responsibility they have.

Joe shuffles through the door after me, looks at me in disgust and takes his usual seat. As Joe sits down, I feel my personal space invaded by a foreign body, a foreign body that hasn't brushed his teeth and washed his jacket in the last month or so.

As I turn to look round, I feel a full shove on my right shoulder knocking me off balance though not flooring me. I get my balance back, and look square on at Corey Hendricks, his mates sat on the tables at the back, looking on, smirking, the contents of some poor kids food tech practical laid out on their desk.

I go straight back at him, pushing him then watching him stumble a few steps back, then I notice his pals getting out of their desks. Then I spot their ingredients. Corey grabs the first of these and attempts to smash them squarely onto my forehead, right where Gerald lives, but catching me on the top side of my head, I feel something shattering into pieces followed by lukewarm slime dripping down the left side of my head and my face, some of it in my eye.

Eggs for fucks sake. I clear my eyes, but the pictures still blurry.

"Happy birthday, ya fucking arsegremlin, I've made you a cake specially."

Right now, my walking out of school strategy won't work. I have two options. Fight or flight. If I run, it'll be Groundhog Day each time I walk in here. It'll never end. I've no way out. I'm resigned to it. It could be worse. I could get in bother for having my shirt untucked. Fight or flight.

Like it's even a choice.

I launch myself at him. He falls back quickly, and as he falls I pin him on the floor. I plant punches on him, though not with much strength, and can feel him lashing out at me. He's connecting too, but my tempers too far gone, and I'm in full rage mode. If he's punching me, I feel nothing. It could be a brick, it could be a cushion, it doesn't register either way. The adrenalines kicked in and I'm swinging arms and legs everywhere. Out of the eggy haze in front of my eyes, however, I spy his grunty sidemen moving towards me, all of them, Louis, Jordan, the other lad who never talks. Within seconds, there's flour and milk mixing in with the eggs.

----

41. POINT OF NO RETURN

I've done my best, but I really don't know why I'm fucking bothering. Here I am, good samaritan, actually giving a shit about someone, wondering the fuck why, and he's being a proper flange ferret and making it such fucking hard work. Even when Archie were taking the piss, catching the bus with him was no bother, not to me anyways. Everyone who rides that bus knows I sit wherever I want, with who I want. I could've easily watched him off from a distance then waited for the next one to pull in and jumped on that. There's a big part of me right now that wishes I fucking did.

So, there's me, Archie, Alicia, giving him life advice and survival tips all the way into town, and he maintains his, "I'm going straight into school as normal, and if anyone disrespects me I'll walk straight out and sit in the library reading manga's again". I could slap his spotty forehead so hard right now, but I slap my own forehead instead.

We get off the bus, and again, I make plans in his best interest. I tell him to hang about outside for a bit, watch everyone else in through the gates then we stroll in behind everyone. I even keep Archie and Alicia with me so I can try the "bus was late" excuse, even though no teacher's soft enough to buy that shitty fairytale. Any school staff seeing me and Archie walking into school with Edward Pendlebury would know something wasn't legit, so I manage to keep him with me for maybe 2 minutes, even with other kids walking past and blatantly glancing over at him more than he should be comfortable with, then he just pipes up with "This is bullshit. I'm going in. If Cory Hendricks wants to whack me I don't care."

Unfortunately, I care. I'm going to be involved, one way or another. I've done that witness stuff before. I'm cool with it. In return for my childlike honesty, some deputy head will promise me anonymity, and no-one will need to know any more. Its deffo my preferred outcome but it also means I can't let this fool out of my sight. He walks across the road and through the gates. Archie follows. Only now do I realise that Archie gets the same sanctuary from walking to school with me that I get from being Shelly Barker's brother, Sam Blake's mate, and all that emperor shit that goes with it. How else would a ginger who wears a beanie even in the middle of July never get savaged? It also means he'll not be too keen to attach himself to a lad so anxious to walk into school ignorant of the fact that some idiot wants his blood. He follows for a bit, but when I say "Let's go the long way!" he doesn't hear me, and goes his own way.

So, I walk slow, zimmer-frame pace, purposely to not be too far in front of the form tutor, but at the same time try to keep Edward Pendlebury in my sights in case he comes to the harm that's been promised online to him. I stop once or twice so as not to look a twat when other random people pass me, and also because I spot the form tutor, way behind me, stood still, chatting to some other teacher. Get a shift on for fucks sake.

Edward's out of my sight for 30 seconds tops. I stop at the corner of the corridor. I can see the door. I can see the form tutor, still talking shit about whatever irrelevant wanky golf handicap he's on. I stare down to the end of the corridor, willing the form tutor to just save it for fucking break time, staring in the hope that at least one of them spots me. Then I catch an uncomfortable silence from the form room, newly instilled by the boy that just walked in. There's a time and a place for silence. It's not when the adult world thinks it is, and it's not now either. I've no choice. I push the door open, look over at Edward, then over at Corey, then Sophia, grab my chair, turn my back on Sophia and position myself so that I can witness every single move Corey makes, and Edward too.

The storm breaks within seconds. Corey, after a nudge from Louis, gets out of his chair, does his wannabee gangster swagwalk down all of three desk rows to Edward, and pushes him hard in the back, sending him flying forward towards the floor, just like Ramos does to Messi in the Classico whenever the ref's attention's elsewhere. Edward doesn't quite land on the floor, but I catch Edward's facial expression. I've changed my mind. I really want to yell at him to get his bag and walk back through the gates again. I'll still have his back, anonymously. It'd be a waste of time though. The look on his face is like I've never seen it before, but maybe if I had, I'd have covered his back before. I predict imminent payback on its way for a decade's worth of phlegm, insults, slam-dunked school bags, unprovoked violence, coats in the urinals. I've got this so wrong. The moment for picking up his bag and walking out has gone, a plane that's well and truly risen off the runway and soared out of sight into the distant clouds. I spot it instantly, as does everyone else. Except one.

"Happy birthday ya fucking arsegremlin"

Make that 4. I spot groceries on Louis's desk. Food tech practical. None of these goons even do food tech.

"It's not even my birthday you idiot", Edward shoves his palms into Corey's chest, returning him stumbling all the way back to where he was sat 2 minutes ago. For a kid who's last-picked at PE, he's packing some strength there. Shit's getting real. Too real. This is going way past detentions or isolations. This is going all the way to the governors, maybe the police or whoever else after them. Where is that useless fucking form tutor, whatever his name is? If he can get here before McDonalds shuts, it'd be helpful.

Corey lands next to his sidemen, who put arms out to stop him crashing into wall and pass him eggs immediately. I catch Louis saying 'bake a fucking cake, fam'. I'm not feeling comfortable with this. I hope Edward keeps the upper hand. If this gets out of control I'll end up involved. First night back at bloody training. I should've had another day off. I'd have got away with it, too.

I can see not just Edward's hands shaking, but both of his arms. Corey throws himself towards him, pushing him backwards, then in the same movement smashes eggs into his head, 2 I think, but there's so much raw egg trickling down Edward's head it could be more. Edward's not having that, he's gone full radge. Point of no return. Arms and legs everywhere. Goosebumps all over them, probably. If either of them had pissed their trousers a little, I'd not be surprised. Within seconds Corey's on the floor, and Edward's above him jabbing fists into him, piston-like.

WHERE THE FUCK IS THAT FORM TUTOR?!?

My heart's drumming so fast I can hear it way louder than any of the shouting in the room. Corey tries to kick out at Edward, but Edward has his knee across his waist so he's nowt but flappy legs. For all the punches Edward's pistoning into Corey, he's not connecting with many. Other kids are off their chairs, out of the way before they get punched and kicked themselves. I walk to the door, open it, look down the corridor, in full faith that no-one's going to overpower Edward right now, not even Sam Blake or Bronson Pearce. Edward's going as wildly as Sam Blake did back in the day. I still can't leave the room though.

STILL NO FUCKING FORM TUTOR!

This will be the opening sentence in my witness statement. "The form tutor was absent from the classroom, and, having noticed the time, at least 7 minutes late arriving for registration. Had he carried out his responsibilities promptly and punctually, this incident may have been controlled or even avoided."

USELESS TWAT!!

In my anxiety I've not even noticed Edward being pulled away from Corey. For a split second I had this faint hope that Corey's crew were going to break the fight up, say "he's had enough pal", and do whatever's needed to avoid a chat with the governors. That split-second was bullshit. A cloud of flour, aimed at Edward, rises into the air and crosses the entire room, coating not just those brawling, but everyone watching too. Full bake-off mode. Louis grabs Edward's shoulder and tries to grab his arm. Always the sly one in that lot. I know what he's planning.

WHERE THE FUCK IS THAT TUTOR?!

I push my way to the front of the crowd. I need to witness everything.

Witnessing isn't enough. I'm gonna have to step in the middle of this aren't I?

Erm. Hello? Back to training tonight. Forest this weekend. Liverpool in 3 weeks.

Edward manages to get Louis off from his shoulder. He's absolutely coated in flour, as is Corey, and to an extent everyone else. Jordan smashes a punch to the side of Edward's head. If he'd not felt any pain so far, he definitely felt that. I spot him put his hand onto the side of his head to register it. He still keeps fighting.

I can't just stand here uselessly. It's 1 against 4. Not even Maldini or Beckenbauer could defend against that many on their todd.

FUCKING WASTE OF SPACE OF A FORM TUTOR!!!!

I shout out "WHERE'S THE TEACHER?"

A couple of people, Shabana, Joel, look over at me.

I yell at them "FETCH THE FUCKING TEACHER. THIS NEEDS TO STOP!!"

I can't spectate any more. Jordan's back with milk. Edward takes nearly the full carton over his head, down his neck, through his shirt.

I've been off school for 2 weeks. I sat out playing Man City at their place. I can't risk this.

Oh, for fucks sake, what kind of person am I?

I should be better than this.

Life's not just all about me.

I need to break this up.

One last try.

"FETCH THE FUCKING TEACHER NOW!!!!!!!!" Top of my voice, into Joel Clarke's face, pushing him towards the door. He looks at me like I'm docile. I'm not in the mood. A deathglare, a prod in the ribs and one more in-the-face yell, "MOVE! NOW!" If he can fetch the teacher, I can step in and hold out for 30 seconds. I'll have done my bit. There'll be witnesses. They'll all back me up.

Mind made up. One last big deep breath.

I brush past Shironda and Shabana, knocking their shoulders and themselves slightly forwards. "Outa my way!"

Both of them grab my lower arms, briefly.

"Joe. Don't risk it!"

"Do something Joe!"

Yeah, thanks for the advice. Come back when you fucking agree with each other. I dive into the middle of the scrum, shove Corey towards the wall, covering myself in whatever splodge he's covered in, and try to put myself in front of Edward, hoping that they'll see me and put their fists down. Bad idea. Jordan shoves me in the front, onto Edward, and I get up. "ENOUGH!"

Jordan pushes me again. I push back. He swings at me but I see it first and dodge it. I don't see a punch catching the side of my face from one of the others, but I feel it soon enough. What am I even doing here? I've never been a brawler, me. I'm proper useless at this.

LIKE THAT FUCKING ARSEHOLE OF A FORM TUTOR!!!!!!! FUCKS SAKE!!!!!!!! WHERE IS HE?!?

I move towards Jordan again, to try and push him out of the way, but, fucks sake, milk all over the floor and I don't even spot it. First there was John Terry's penalty, then there was Stevie G against Demba Ba. Now it's me. As my balance goes, I feel a shove on me way down to the floor. There's no referee. AND NO TWATBASTARD FORM TUTOR EITHER! Jordan lands on me and I try to go into foetal mode, head into hands, knees up, feet under my arse. I might make it to training tonight. I feel punches, aimed for my head, landing on my right hand instead. Out of the corner of my eye, I notice the door opening, the multiple feet of bystanders shuffling to one side to let the uselessly late teacher through. I feel the slightest of draughts.

And the sharpest of crushing pains.

Has someone just shot me?

Louis stands directly over me, beaming a grin that I know to never be good news. There's never anything good about the full force of 70 kilos of vindictive spiteful nobhead contained in a two-footed challenge landing on my newly-recovered ankle with maximum destruction in mind.

I no longer feel it. Not where I got hit anyway. I do feel pain, right enough, but in my stomach. I retch immediately. Now accompanying cake ingredients are bits of what's left of yesterday's Sunday dinner, mashed potato, carrots, all of it, splatted across the laminate. I retch immediately again. I look up again and still see Louis standing over me, his Roy Keane to my Alf-Inge Haaland. Suddenly he gets moved away, and someone else, I don't know who, some adult, kneels next to me, raises my head a little and cradles it. I hear a voice.

"DON'T MOVE HIM!"

Is that me? Why can't anyone move me?

I don't think I can move. I feel like sicking up again. And fainting too. I'm sweating. Like a cold sweat, the type I always thought junkies had when they're out of class A's. Why am I sweating? Why's my head so dizzy?

I try to wiggle my ankle. I can't feel pain. But then again I can't feel anything. Nothing feels right.

The rooms full of multiple adult voices shouting, but nothing they're saying makes any sense. I'm not sure I'm actually fully conscious at all. Next to me, some voice, that I should recognise, but don't, is holding my head back, and saying, calmly "Don't try to move anything yet chap, or you'll do more damage."

More damage?

What do they mean, more damage?

I don't get it?

WHAT THE FUCK'S HAPPENING?

I'm back in training tonight.

Nottingham Forest at the weekend, Liverpool after that.

I retch again. Nothing comes out though. A weird swirling, fizzing, takes over my head. This time, I close my eyes. The only way I know to escape it. Maybe I'll wake up later and this is all bullshit.

Whatever planet my swirling head takes me to, I've no idea how long I'm on it for. When I land back on earth again, I feel floury slop across my clothes, and smell the harsh stench of cleaning fluid on the floor next to me that's been wiped down. The cushion from someone's office chair supports my head, a cushion that's been host to a thousand different arseholes in its long life, and I've no idea what this blanket is, curtains at a guess.

I still don't feel right. I try to sit up.

"No, Joe. Try not to move. You need to stay still for now."

Adult voice. Probably a teacher. I try to look up. In doing so, I notice the door open, and two pairs of heavy-duty green trousers and very durable boots enter. I know the uniform too. There's always one on top of the ironing pile at home. The person that liked to joke about parking her van up outside the training pitch so that she could have the honour of blue-lighting me off to the hospital if I ever shattered my leg.

"Have I bust me leg?"

The voice that responds to me. It's familiar. It's one I've known a long time.

"No Joey love, not your leg. It needs looking at tho. Din't I say I'd be first in if owt happened?"

OK, it's not my leg. I try to shift it, but a hand I can't see grabs my shin, holding it still.

"Don't struggle, mate. Just keep it still for now."

A familiar, comforting hand places itself on my cheek. I now remember taking a punch there. I remember the whole morning, crystal clear. Every last bit.

"Is Edward all right?"

----

42. The Steamer

The steamer. A mobile classroom at the outer limits of the car park aside from the rest of the school, grey outside, grey inside. 1 week sentence. Day 3. I could argue passionately that I was the victim, but Mum advised to do my time, get it over with, and move on.

Sharing my sensory deprivation are a lass from year 11, a lad from year 8, strangers to me, and Cory Hendricks. Just him. He's never been alone, but hey-ho, he is now, and totally out of his zone. When he has to communicate, he's reluctantly civil. Something's happened with him, no idea what, but if anyone goes in and out of the engagement unit, across the car park, he peers through the closed plastic blinds before moving his head behind the curtain as if to hide himself, even though no-one can see in from outside anyway. He's spending this week completing year 5 maths quizzes, handing them to the supervisor, a grim old woman who sits either reading or doing puzzle books all day, says barely anything but her facial expression, where she looks at everyone as though they're dogshit, means she doesn't have to say anything anyway. Once she checks that he's answered everything, she screws it in a ball, plonks it in the bin then hands him a fresh sheet that, once completed, she'll do exactly the same with. We're in at 8.15, half an hour before anyone else, having lunch at our desks whenever someone can be arsed to bring four cold cheese paninis from the lunch hall, and remaining at the same desk til 4, half an hour after everyone else has escaped.

Within an hour of me being pulled away from Corey and his monkeys last week, Mum was sat in reception waiting for the meeting with the head she'd wanted since my first week. Fixed term exclusion til the end of last week, to give school the time to gather witness statements, then, though the head acknowledged my numerous mitigating circumstances, a week in here to give the issue time to go away and also to catch up on work I've missed, this deal conditional on me spending the full time in here as ordered. Just one attempt to go on my travels will result in an extra week and the same year 5 sums as Corey. I've doggedly adhered to my original decision to attend until someone disrespects me, then go walkies. However, there's 4 of us locked-down in a barren grey room in silence all day, so no-one's around to disrespect me. If even Corey Hendricks is being civil to me, I can't really see an escape. Corey's sidemen were also excluded, but only Corey's here with me. He's like a scared little year 3 now he has no back-up. I've heard Jordan's been moved to the engagement class, and Louis, due to what he did to Joe's ankle, is sweating over a meeting with the governors. He might be expelled.

Joe's ankle's a mess, plastered, and he's marooned on his sofa for ages yet. I was advised to talk to him about anything except football, but he doesn't really have an eclecticity of alternative conversation in his repertoire, and he keeps bringing it up. Everyone's told him to rest, hoping that his bone will recover properly and he can get back to where he was. The word to bear in mind in that lot though, is "hoping". I've worked out he's spent his entire childhood 'hoping', like playing all these fancy football matches 'hoping' to not get dropped, ending each season 'hoping' not to be one of the kids who gets replaced when some wonder-kid appears from elsewhere, 'hoping' that when he leaves school next year, he'll be the lucky one or two that gets kept for a couple more years when he could be doing an apprenticeship or a college course that could get him a career to last a lifetime and not just a decade. I can tell that everyone around him knows there's no 'hoping' to be done any more, just like it always ends up for 99.999% of kids that can juggle a football well, but they're staying positive with him and not breaking any tragic news to him, preferring to see if he can gradually, quietly, work it out for himself. Even Shelly, who has nothing good to say to him ever, is telling him to rest, and that he'll be ready to go again in no time. She's not lying. "In no time" as in "There isn't going to be a time". It's gone.

Shelly did tell me how proud she was of him, putting others first, stepping in, doing the right thing even when things were hopeless, backing up, being true, being real. I've told her that she should tell him that herself and not me. She reckons he'll just yell at her to piss off. Of course he will, but he'll think about it later, and reflect differently I think.

Anyway, some lass that I'd never seen before but I could tell she's one of those pupils that school loves - well-behaved, well-presented, essays always handed in on time, immaculate handwriting, no make-up, no big hair, no eyebrow weirdness - knocked on the door of the steamer at 3.20, straight after the bell, as all the other kids were going home. She was the first and only person any of us had seen all day, so all eyes in the room focused on her while she focused purely on the teacher. "I'm really sorry to intrude, but I've got a birthday card here for Edward. I know I won't see him while he's in here, but I don't want it to be late either. Is there any chance I can leave it with you please?"

My birthday's not til March. This sounds very suspect, but there's a red envelope, with girly love-hearts and emojis and little cupcake stickers on the cover, and my names written with a cloud drawn round it and a sunshine poking out of the top corner. So I'm curious.

"OK, thanks, I'll give it to him at the end of the day". The teacher shows a courteousy to this lass that she's shown to nobody else this week.

As soon as the perfect stranger and perfect student disappears, the supervisor instantly switches expression, like she's visibly offended to have eye contact with me. "You can have it at 4". She then returns to her book. The cover resembles 50 Shades or a sequel. Its deffo depraved porno filth, but calling her out on it isn't in my best interest. Not just yet. The final 45 minutes resemble 45 hours. I should be doing proofs, but my concentration went home at a reasonable time even if I haven't managed to. The supervisor eventually calls time without even looking up from her porno novel. I take long enough packing away to spot which way Corey Hendricks exits school, and I go the opposite way.

I leave the envelope unopened all the way out of school, off the bus, along the avenues and past the crescents, through the door, shoes off, coat off, bag down, up the stairs and into the privacy of my room. I know I'll either be slightly uplifted, or I'll be slashing my arms, no in betweens. Whichever it is, I don't want anyone to see me. So here goes.

A card. "I'm sorry". A bear wearing a dufflecoat, holding a balloon, whilst a tear falls from its left eye. Inside, signatures all over. Whoever wrote the letter inside it has the girliest bubble writing ever and a very abstract awareness of the English Language. Other stuff too. A couple of essays on lined paper. Pizza tokens? Whatever.

OK. It doesn't look like hate mail, so time to read.......

Edward!! xx

No fckin way wil skool let sm1 like me nr the steamer wen ur in ther, so whoeva givz u this is just sum 1 I got in there instedda me. The cards nowt 2 do with em.

I kno, cheeeezzy card, but the bear on it wears a coat like urs. I usd 2 rip piss out of it, but its not like n e of us r fckin perfect so Im so sory 4 B-in a cunt wi u. U dint desrv n e of that + I saw it all + did nowt. Its tru Im a fckin dsgrace :@-(

But I'l try not 2 b n e more!! :-)

Afta last wk I thght u mite get Xpelld so I med sur evry1 sed the same ont witnss statemnts but wi remixd lyrix. I got a few 2 say dey cldnt c much but I wernt sur that wer enuff so I foned my Mum. Her boyf (he'z propa <-->) went strait 2 de hedz offis widout evn nockin on his door, told him how u stepd in wen Cory sexuly harassd me, + he & his many bizness asociatz wer hopefl dat skool wud reach a decisn that wer "mutuly positiv". @;-) He dint kno bout that day I got harassd, heda gon mentl + got himsen lockd up if I told him, but he knoz about it now, so pls find 2 pizza tokns. He owns Chickn City :-). Do NOT orda fried chickn or Kbabs, srsly, trust me wi this, but the'rz b 2 XXL pizzas redy wen u r, n e toppngs. ++chilli frm wot I'v heard pmsl!!!

Sam also tipt off his Clty Casual Crew mates hu da lad is that wreckd their playaz ankl. They kno Louiss > 16 so 0's gna hapn but they all kno wen his b'day is.

Dis wld b easia if u had pages!!!! I admit it, I tried 2 stalk u (:-)) + ur so fckin invisibl its annoyin! I found Shelly C tho, nrly pissd mesen outa fear wen she ansad me, but I told her wot I wantd 2 do n she wer strait in helpin out :-#0 So.....We opnd u pages up. Snapchat Insta Facebook 1 x 1. If u dn't want em then bin em...Ur names "Eddie Pen", ur foto is a manga dude that I ??? but Shelly knoz it, + ur passwrd on each 1 is "a1a2a3a4". Only me + Shelly kno this so change it soon as. U gotta mad Q of ppl 1tin 2 ++ u :-) X. Im there so if u dont ++ me I'l 4get all this n hav u mrdrd insted!! :-). Shelly alredy ++ a grl calld Naomi O'Donnell who she chats 2. Shes in Lndn but Shelly sez her Dads mates wi u n ur Mum?

N E ways, its not just me puttin hands up, we'r all sory. Ur hmwrx in this card. Beths Frnch Qs n Shabanas EngLit S A. Jst redo the lyrix on the S A n miss the dashythings off Q9 on the Frnch so no1 gets dn! :-)

My hands redy 4 zzzzzzz, C u nxt wk! Preach on, brotha!!!

Shironda!X   **Beth (.(.** *Ami xx* Shabana   Ben

Kylie!! *Joel :-)* *Archie! :-)*   *Welshy :-):-)* SHOLA XX

:-) X :-) X :-) X

ps My m8 Jodi Ramsden ++ed u 2. Accpt her. She propa fanciz Joe, n last time he saw her he cldn't tek his (..)'s off her 2. If he cn't play footy 4 a bit he mite as wel get the best GF he can, + she the fittest lass at Firth Green!!! :-)

:-) XX

Yadayadayadayada. Whatever. Fucking pizza tokens. I'll give them to Donovan.

----

43 - The Retained List

"Here we are in April again, Stevie. The Head of Player Recruitment's favourite time of year. How busy are we going to be, pal?"

"Well Nev, it's no secret that we're ready for some new blood."

"Well the budget's not looking bad, but it's safe to say we'll not be competing wi' Real Madrid this year. Usual limits. One-in, one-out as usual. Does that mek things simpler?"

"I'll start wi't simplest. Keepers. No change. Outfielders that we released years ago showed up to't trials wi big Mickey Mouse gloves on. Sent 'em all home after 2 weeks."

"Shame, that. How many keepers have we got?"

"Just Oscar Joshua. In light of all that nonsense, I've not much choice but to keep him for now."

"OK, so that's the first name on't list. Anyone else we need to keep hold of?"

"Not many. You've got some letters to get typing. Shall we go through who I'm bringing in first?"

"OK, Stevie. There's financial considerations wi't overseas lads, but justify the cost to me."

"Right. The Bermudan lad, Charlie. Best defensive mid I've seen for ages. I want to get him in first and build the whole team round him. Then I want Luca, the Italian lad, through't door straight after him. Spotted him at a tournament last year. Perugia's scout did too, so he went there first. Thought we'd never see him again, but he rang me a few weeks later. Flew in with his Dad in for a week. English game suits him better than Italian."

"His English is up to speed, right?"

"Better than yours, Nev. I looked round the development centres. Nice money earner, but a waste of time, talent-wise. I got on't phone to London instead."

"We don't have anyone in London??"

"You don't, but I do. Remember Tommy Howard? Played for us 10 years back? He's a copper in London now. Does street football wi' some lads who he thought were worth a look, so he's been minibussing 'em up here every week. Two new centre-backs, a striker and an attacking mid, each of them two-footed, strong, fast. Their mates are all in trouble. Thanks to football, they're not. One of 'ems Dad's inside for drugs wi' people waiting to see him when he gets out. Tommy's chatted to all their families. They're all up for signing."

"And Tommy's happy to bus all these lot up together twice a week is he Steve??"

"Better than that, Nev. Tommy thinks if we get these signed, he's got younger kids just as good that'll want to follow. Tek the profits from the development centres and bank it all in this, Nev. It's a fucking gold mine."

"Gi' us his contacts. I'll see it I can chuck some funding his way, or get a link-up sorted."

"We're up to 6. 7 wi't keeper. Still not a full team yet."

"Nathan McCarthy got released by Man United 3 months ago so we had him in. Twisted every single one of his opponents inside out. Lives 20 miles away. Then there's another two lads, both local, one's just left Hull City, the other's been training at Leeds. Fed up of travelling."

"I'll date the forms for them two for 12 weeks time or I'll have the FA on my case. Any more?"

"Lee Barratt. Plays grassroots, been on trial at Derby, but lives round the corner and wanted to have a try here before deciding where to go. Full back. Left-footer. Will walk into Derby's team, but I can get in first. I'm keeping two more behind a bit longer. A midfielder and a winger. Want to give it a bit before I mek me mind up."

"OK Stevie, so the retained list."

"OK, Nev. Oscar the keeper, and Danny Flanagan. That's all."

"Ha ha!! Biggles. Bit of a character, in't he?"

"Massive character, Nev. Never beaten. Not physically, not mentally, never. Proper wind-up master. Played right back this year, but I could play him anywhere and he'd excel. This is the kid wi't best chance of hittin't first team. There's more to come from him, no doubt."

"And the rest, Stevie. Thank you letters?"

"I might need to keep a couple to fill spaces up, but we're talking fringe players at best. There's two I'll lose sleep over. First off, Brad. I hoped he'd step his game up after Joey Barker got injured. It din't happen, sadly. Other one's Kyle. Nice lad, but for a centre back, too nice. Might do OK lower down't pyramid if anyone's offering trials out?"

"Halifax are looking at some o't older lads we've let go. I'll give 'em a call."

"Cheers Nev. Of the others, I'll sleep soundly. Sam's like Beckenbauer against grassroots teams, freezes against anyone quality. Parents are a nightmare too. Mo and Jamal? Better athletes than footballers. Ben Witham's put weight on and got skinned near enough every game. Then there's Naz. The new strikers all have way more than him. Sonny and Otis have gone as far as I can tek 'em too."

"So that's 9. The others?"

"Gonna be fun this. Brodie."

"I must say I'm amazed you kept him here so long. It goes without saying I also know about his Mum."

"Yeah, so I've heard. One-footed, slow, and picking up strains that have took ages to go. Dr Kon's had a look. Classic case of overuse. Needs to rest it out like Joey Barker's had to, but try telling him or his Mum that. I can't be arsed wi' any of that Travelodge nonsense. Time up as far as I'm concerned."

"A relief I must say. I'll hand the letter out in person at the end of Tuesday's session, and keep security around in case there's nonsense. This leaves a squad of 12. Bit thin, that."

"We can borrow from the 14s. Its quality we need to go for, not quantity."

"OK Stevie, you've not mentioned Tyler Dolan, Tyrell Jones or Joe Barker. Letters?"

"If this winger steps up, Tyler's gone. The ability's there, the mental strength isn't. Keeping Tyrell a bit longer won't cost owt and it'll justify any spending on the better players maybe. Mek sure't small print's in there so I can release 'em in a few weeks if I need to."

"That brings us to Joe."

"Doesn't it just?"

"He's done everything the physio and Doctor Kon have told him to, but it's risky retaining a lad who might not be the same again. His ankle might never recover, be forever weak. The way he loves playing, Spanish, Dutch, whatever, he'll not get much of that in Division 1."

"OK, the clincher. Imagining Joe hadn't got injured, would he mek the new line up?"

"Like everyone else, Nev, it'd depend if we got anyone better in, so possibly not."

"So that's your decision?"

"Well, erm, no. Summat else nags at me a bit."

"Such as?"

"Did you hear how he got himself injured?"

Printed in Great Britain
by Amazon